CW01642886

# BURIED LIES

A gripping detective mystery full of twists and turns

CHRIS COLLETT

JOFFE BOOKS

**Revised edition 2018 by Joffe Books, London.**

First published by Severn House in 2013 as "Blood and Stone."

www.joffebooks.com



This book is a work of fiction. Names, characters, businesses, organizations, places and events are either the product of the author's imagination or are used fictitiously. Any resemblance to actual persons, living or dead, events or locales is entirely coincidental. The spelling is British English.



ISBN-13: 978-1-78931-034-4

To former DI Alan Crouch for the many years of invaluable expert advice, and to his wife Linda for her immeasurable patience. Thank you both.

# Chapter One

Day One

Every now and again, there comes an exquisite moment in one's interactions with other human beings that hits the sweet spot dead centre. Capturing a split-second of pure, unadulterated surprise on the face of a loved one is such a moment; like the joy of a young child on the Christmas morning when his parents, against the odds, have succeeded in providing a desperately wanted toy. Too fleeting and transient for any lasting pleasure, the next best thing is the anticipation, which can, in its way, be more of a thrill than the moment itself. Glenn McGinley had that feeling now. It electrified every fibre in his body, making his nerves tingle the way they did immediately after a hit of cocaine, and temporarily anaesthetized his pain. McGinley was a firm believer in heaven and hell. The idea had been sold to him early on and its simplicity had always made perfect sense. Logic therefore dictated that in the not-too-distant future he was going to burn in the fiery furnace. He'd done enough bad things in his life to make it a certainty. But thanks to a chance conversation, he had seen the light. Not the kind of light strong enough to redeem his corrupted soul, but the kind of light that made him want some company when he got there. There was no harm in that, was there?

He had the minicab driver drop him and his bin bag off a couple of streets away: no sense in announcing his arrival when his sole purpose was to surprise her. Night and day, for weeks now, he'd lain on that iron-framed cot picturing the expression on her face when she saw him again, and the prospect evoked an intensity of feeling close to euphoria. But, like Christmas morning, everything had to be orchestrated perfectly; he couldn't afford to screw anything up, so the important thing right now was to remain focused. Concentration had never been one of his strong points. Right back in nursery school, that much had been obvious. But if he could just keep it together for a bit longer, he knew that it would be worth the effort.

Dusk had turned to night hours ago, leaving the cold and windy streets deserted, which suited him fine. He approached number twenty-two from the narrow alley running between the gardens of the back-to-back rows of post-war social housing. Good old Kirkby. True, the place had moved on from being the grim sink estate it had been in the 1970s. Since then, tower blocks had been ripped down to make way for more respectable mixed-economy housing. In a defiant gesture, Liverpool FC had even relocated their training academy out here. But it was still a shit hole. McGinley was headed to the old part; the place they'd moved to thirty years ago, away from the back-to-back slums and into a spanking new slum, the widow and her sons. It was all part of the fresh start that didn't turn out to be quite what any of them expected. Even now, in the three-bedroom house, there was a room set aside for him, in case he ever chose to 'return to the fold' (her words). But she'd laid down too many conditions for that ever to happen. He'd been back plenty of times since he'd left for good, but always under cover of night and always without her knowledge. She would never have suspected a thing. Sometimes it was useful having an old girl who'd become a trusting and naïve religious nut.

McGinley's senses were heightened as they always were on re-entry; the feel of the cool evening air on his skin, the sharp smell of a recent rain shower that accentuated the sour notes of rotting refuse each time he passed a cluster of wheelie bins. As expected, there were no lights on at the house. She'd followed the same strict routine for years and he had no reason to believe anything about that would have changed. Whilst other middle-aged women might have been at the bingo or in the pub, most of her evenings were spent at the mission, helping those less fortunate than herself while making every effort to educate them about where, in their miserable lives, they were going wrong. She'd been doing it for years, ploughing doggedly on as her own family slowly disintegrated in the background.

The back gate was locked as usual, but McGinley had always been spare and lithe, and now, with the additional weight loss, he was practically skeletal. It took him a matter of seconds to scramble over — his traditional mode of entry — swinging the plastic bag ahead of him and dropping lightly onto the path on the other side beside the garden shed. No longer in use, it had been erected when they'd first moved here to accommodate Dad's old tools and belongings, and she couldn't bear to part with it. Fumbling for the padlock, he stuck in his key. Ice-cold in his hand, it was stiff from lack of use and took some effort to turn but then, as far as he knew, he was the only one to have come in here in twenty years.

The air inside the shed was undisturbed, thick with the pungent smell of dust and creosote. This was, in truth, the only space on this earth McGinley could call his own and the territory was so familiar that the faint light streaming in from the street lamps allowed him to locate exactly what he needed almost straight away. As he retrieved the camouflage rucksack from the far corner, something scuttled lightly over his hand and he had to stifle a cry. *Shit*! His heart pounded for a few seconds, then he shook his head in disgust. After everything he'd endured, to still be scared of spiders. It took him a matter of minutes to transfer his stuff from the bin bag to the dusty canvas sack, and after that he reached up on to a high shelf, behind a row of cobweb-strewn paint tins, and took down a steel toolbox. This too had an ancient padlock, for which McGinley was the sole key holder. The contents of the box were functional enough, but unlike most things in this shed, they were designed not for *con*struction but *de*struction.

Removing a couple of items from the top tray, he pushed them deep into the pack. They might prove useful later on. But what he lifted out last, and with reverential care, would come into its own very soon. He wondered what his mum's pals would think if they knew what she had been harbouring for years in her own back yard. Resting it in his palm for a moment, he savoured the comforting weight of it and felt his heart begin to pump a little harder. He checked the mechanism, which operated as smoothly as, well — he allowed himself a smile — a well-oiled gun. *Tonight Matthew, I'm going to be . . . Charles Bronson in* Death Wish II. From his inside jacket pocket, McGinley took the gift his cellmate had given him two nights previously and screwed it on to the barrel. It was a perfect fit. Astonishing what could be obtained in a Category C if you knew who to ask.

Finally, pulling on the latex gloves acquired at his last medical appointment, McGinley emerged from the shed, closing the door quietly behind him. He waited for a moment in the shadows, reassessing the houses on either side. He'd already noted a presence in each property, but as long as he was careful there would be no need for anyone to register what was going on next door. The illuminated kitchen to the left was still empty; and the lights in the house to the right were upstairs, behind curtains drawn shut. He walked softly up the footpath and tested his key in the back door. This one turned easily and he stepped into the hallway and back into the 1960s, an atmosphere made up of furniture polish and abstinence. Locking the door behind him, McGinley groped his way in the darkness along the hall, past the open kitchen door, where the light glinted back at him from various old-fashioned appliances, and into the lounge. She'd had a shift-round since he was last here, and amazingly the room now contained new furniture. He dragged one of the heavy armchairs in a half circle so that it faced the door and settled into it. It was quite comfy actually; one of those reclining ones. To amuse himself for a few minutes he played with the mechanism, firing off an imaginary bullet each time he slammed up the foot rest, until he got bored. By now he was desperate for a drink or a fag or both, but he needed to keep a clear head and the smell of smoke would immediately announce his presence, so the only thing left for him to do was to wait. Tucking the gun down out of sight between his outer thigh and the armrest, he leaned back and closed his eyes.

## Chapter Two

Tom Mariner paced the confines of his canal-side home, polishing his left shoe with a kind of restless fervour as if, somehow, the effort could hold in abeyance the cloud of grief that was approaching like a vast unstoppable weather front. Shoe-cleaning had been his first responsibility as a small boy. 'A man's job,' his mother had called it and since he had been, even at the age of four, the man of the house, the task had fallen to him. Ever since, he had found a comforting familiarity in the evocative smell of the wax polish and the simple, repetitive task, and it had become his last desperate hiding place. Mariner knew all about the cycle of grief; the unplanned voyage through shock, denial, anger and sadness, and he knew too that it was inevitable. Until now work had been his salvation. The last weeks had been chaotic, with several major cases hitting the courts at the same time, commanding his full attention and demanding that he be attentive and objective. There was no place for raw emotion. But tomorrow reality would come crashing in and already he could feel the edges beginning to fray.

His mobile rang; it was Tony Knox.

'Boss. How's it hanging?'

'Oh, you know, down and slightly to the right as usual,' Mariner said, irritated by the expression.

'You okay for tomorrow?'

Mariner could hear the diffidence in his sergeant's voice, everyone treating him like a fragile piece of porcelain. 'I'm fine,' he said, feeling anything but. His charcoal-grey suit hung on the door in its plastic dry-cleaning cover and the tie he'd chosen, one that she'd bought for him, was looped around the hanger like a careless noose. Everything ready, except for him.

'I'm picking up Millie at quarter to; we'll be at yours at about ten,' Knox said. 'See you then.'

'All right,' Mariner confirmed. Somehow, while he wasn't looking, Knox had conspired with DC Millie Khatoon that she would drive Mariner down to Herefordshire, not quite trusting the old man to do it himself, and taking yet another surreptitious opportunity for the close surveillance that he was failing to convince everyone he didn't need. Underneath it all though, Mariner knew that their intentions were sound, so he didn't complain. And this time tomorrow it would all be over, and both Millie and Knox would need to rethink their boundaries. Mariner glanced down at his shoe, which was by now polished to a varnish-like gloss. Placing it carefully down next to its partner he picked up the remote, switched on the TV, and dropped on to the sofa in another futile attempt at distraction.

## Chapter Three

McGinley had been far from disappointed. In fact, the long-awaited moment had exceeded all his expectations. There must have been a lot of souls to save tonight and it was coming up to eleven when he finally heard the key turning in the lock. He braced himself for what was to come. A light flicked on in the hall. There was shuffling and voices; she wasn't alone. He heard them go into the kitchen, a kettle being filled. His heart began to pick up speed. Finally her slight form, trussed up in that vile travesty of a uniform, appeared in the doorway and a sixty-watt bulb illuminated him in all his glory.

'Hello, Mum.' Despite the burning hatred that filled his chest, McGinley forced a smile and watched the domino effect of her facial muscles as they reacted in sequence. What was especially satisfying was the noticeable brief and transient hope that after all these years the prodigal son had returned; that he had finally come to his senses. In a way he had.

'Glenn. What are you doing . . .?' she managed to splutter. But in an instant she saw what he held in his hand and realized too late that he was not here for forgiveness but for retribution, and like snow thawing and sliding off a roof, he saw optimism mutate into disbelief, and then finally the recognition of what was to come.

Another face appeared beside hers, peering almost comically around the door frame. 'What's going on, Brenda?' A man stepped into the frame alongside her, tall but stooping, his hair straggly and grey. He was frailer than the last time McGinley had seen him, swamped by the overcoat he wore over his identical uniform. *Fuck me*, thought McGinley, *the Major, forgot about him, dirty old bugger*. Well, he was going to get more than he bargained for too.

'I've got something for you, Mum,' McGinley said, ignoring him, 'from me and Spence.' And, his heart pumping with elation, he raised the gun, aimed it at his mother's chest and fired twice; once to kill and once for luck. She crumpled to the floor with a dull thud, and the old man moaned in terror. 'Your lucky night too,' smiled McGinley, and before the Major could react, he shot him twice in the stomach. The old geezer toppled like a statue, writhed for a moment while something crackled unpleasantly in his throat and then he lay still, his eyes staring into some far-off place.

McGinley exhaled as with shaking hands he took out his cigarettes and lit one up, drawing on it deeply and taking great pleasure in blowing out the smoke into the uncontaminated atmosphere. In the light, the place looked stark and bare, with its basic furnishings and the marked absence of the decorative indulgences that were commonplace in most homes. There were no family photographs, especially not of the two sons who had each in their way brought such shame on the family. Without turning on any more lights McGinley went up the stairs and looked out of the darkened front and back bedroom windows. Everything was as quiet as it had been when he'd arrived, and there was no indication that anything he'd done had drawn special attention to number twenty-two. He would make his escape while it was still dark, but until then he had a few hours to find the rest of what he'd come for and to help himself to anything that he thought might come in useful to him over the days that followed.

The kitchen was stocked with the same stuff he'd been raised on, but McGinley's appetite was for bland food these days so it suited him. He scavenged a few slices of dry bread, a small hunk of cheese and half a packet of biscuits that would sustain him in the short term.

Next he turned his attention to the sideboard in the living room. The keys to the car and lockup were easy enough to locate, thrown carelessly into an old ashtray, and easily identifiable by the fob. Going through the sideboard drawers, McGinley found a tin containing a bit of loose change and a couple of fivers, but the familiar old brown envelope was more elusive. He nailed it eventually, caught behind a pile of papers in the drawer, the faded number still written in biro in the corner. He gave it a shake to check that the keys were inside and stuffed it in his pocket. Lastly, there were facts to be checked. Sliding back the doors of the main cupboard, he sorted quickly through the pile of old magazines and papers, including endless copies of the *War Cry*. One carried the headline, 'There is no peace, saith the Lord, unto the wicked.' Unoriginal, of course, but apt under the circumstances and impossible to resist. Tearing it carefully around the edges he placed the slogan beside the two bodies and it pleased him. But none of the rest of this stuff was any good, it was all too recent. What McGinley was looking for, the box files of old cuttings and mementoes she had preserved since they were kids, was gone. Maybe she had finally given up on him and thrown it all away. A tinny carriage clock on the mantelpiece struck eleven. He'd have to watch it. His mother had never been a party girl and the neighbours knew it. It wasn't ideal, but to maintain the charade of normality he was going to have to continue the search by the light of his torch.

Switching off the downstairs lights as he went, McGinley climbed the stairs and searched the bedrooms, but the wardrobes and cabinets were small, and contained only clothing and day-to-day items. He was surprised to find a computer in the tiny box room that had been made over into a sort of office, but again his torch picked out nothing of what he was looking for. It was as he was crossing the landing to descend the stairs again that he thought of the one last place they might be.

Fetching a stool from the bedroom, he climbed up and pulled down the loft hatch, sliding down the integral aluminium ladder. When the beam of light first swooped over the stack of cardboard boxes, he was dismayed by the scale of the task — he would be here all night sorting through this lot. But then it struck him that the arrangement was too neat. The boxes were proper archive boxes that were all precisely labelled in the same careful handwriting. They must belong to the Major. He would have brought them with him when he moved in; yet another way of completely dominating his ma's life. Towards the back of the loft space he eventually spotted a smaller stack, an odd assortment of cardboard grocery boxes and battered suitcases. That was her stuff. Heaving himself up through the hatch, McGinley picked his way carefully across, using the joists as stepping stones. In the second suitcase he opened he found what he was looking for, an envelope of yellowing press cuttings, old tickets and letters, along with one short newspaper report of a death in custody, and the subsequent internal police investigation that exonerated the officers involved. A second cutting, barely two column inches wide, described a tragic suicide. As a teenager McGinley had once overheard an indiscreet neighbour talking about the 'bad luck' that seemed to follow the McGinley family around. The Major had no doubt described it as God's will. But McGinley knew they were both wrong. Everything happened for a reason. This time, the reason was him.

Folding away the loft ladder and closing the hatch, McGinley was overcome by sudden exhaustion. Having found everything he wanted, he lay down on the bed in the spare room for a couple of hours' sleep. As he drifted off he thought about how weird it was, that he could be so relaxed with two dead bodies lying in the hall downstairs. These days he was a light sleeper and had no doubt that he would wake before dawn. But just in case, he set the alarm of his cheap digital watch for three a.m.

* * *

Mariner lay flat on his back waiting for the sky beyond the curtains to lighten. It had been after midnight when he'd climbed the stairs to bed but, as on so many nights of late, his brain had refused to log off. His body felt heavy and lethargic, weighed down by the prospect of the day ahead. But, as soon as he could more or less see without the aid of electricity, he forced himself to get out of bed, and pull on jeans and an old sweatshirt. There were preparations to be made.

Downstairs in the kitchen he brewed a mug of tea, but abandoned it on the worktop, too queasy to drink it. He'd been prevaricating but could do so no longer. Along the hallway by the front door, Mariner unlocked the hatch-like door that opened on the cellar. Cool, stale air that was horribly redolent wafted out, and he had to suppress an automatic, though fleeting, frisson of terror. Switching on the light, he was presented with nothing more threatening than what looked like a subterranean Oxfam shop; the discarded but 'might come in useful' stuff he'd accumulated since he'd moved in here nearly twenty years ago. An old vacuum cleaner, boxes of books and old vinyl LPs, pictures and picture frames brought from his mother's house. But the biggest pile by far was of walking gear; several previous generations of boots, rucksacks and camping stoves, some of it obsolete, along with the equipment he used now. And that was what he'd come down for this morning. On the rare occasions when he was compelled to retrieve anything from the cellar,

Mariner's strategy was always the same: identify what's needed from the vantage point at the top of the steps, go down to grab it and return as quickly as possible to the hall, with one eye on the open door at all times, in case it should suddenly and inexplicably slam shut. He was well aware that his fears right now were irrational. But they were grounded in real and terrifying experiences, so recognizing that fact did nothing to diminish their power. Today two forays were enough, and stacking everything in the hall, Mariner closed and locked the cellar door again, before opening his front door on the chill morning air. It took several journeys then to load everything into the back of his car, arranging his kit carefully as he always did, like a neat jigsaw puzzle, everything in its rightful place. For the first time he allowed himself to think beyond this day. He'd tried to make his escape once before but had been thwarted. This time was going to be different.

* * *

McGinley woke at the bleeping of his alarm, feeling groggy and sluggish. The sky was turning from cobalt blue to grey. Gathering his things and locking the door behind him, he exited the house the way he had come, emerging cautiously, just in case his presence had aroused attention. By the time he walked away he felt heady with what he imagined to be the satisfying feeling of revenge. This was how the old geezer at Long Lartin had said it would be. McGinley hadn't known whether to believe him at the time, but it was true, like a cleansing of the soul. 'Don't go out with a fizz, go out with a bang,' he'd told McGinley. 'Make people sit up and take notice of you. It's the last chance you'll get.' And this was just the start. If the rest of it worked out as planned, it was going to turn into something monumental.

Although he'd started young and had built up an impressive record, McGinley had always been small time, a tiny cog in someone else's machine. He'd snatched at opportunities as they were presented, but had relied on other people to create them for him. With the exception of the occasional petty offence, he'd never felt secure enough to go it alone, or to engage in any long-term preparation. Now, he couldn't get over how well this was playing out — better than he had a right to expect. It made him wonder if, with a bit of effort, he could have been more ambitious with other enterprises. Some of this new-found confidence, of course, came from knowing that now he had absolutely nothing to lose. Ironically the onset of physical weakness was exactly what made him feel strong. No one could touch him and that feeling of power was extraordinarily potent; he felt invincible.

His only tiny regret from last night's episode was that the moment of execution had been so short-lived. It made him wish that he'd filmed it, if only on a mobile, so that he could replay it and enjoy those few seconds all over again when he had time. But common sense told him that success depended on keeping things simple. In many ways, the anger had gone out of him by now, too. Ma wasn't a bad person — not in the way that some people are — but she had let them down. If she had done her job properly, things would have turned out differently, and for that she'd had to be punished. No, it had to be enough for him that she would be denied a peaceful old age. And he'd have to content himself with the images that lived on in his head.

There was more to do and right now, he had to focus and make sure his getaway was as clean as the operation. Once the bodies were discovered it wouldn't take long for the police to work out what had happened or who was responsible. But by the time they'd joined the dots they wouldn't stand a hope in hell of catching up with him. Duck and cover. He'd been learning about that for most of his miserable life. Retracing his steps along the streets, keeping to the shadows, he came to the row of lockup garages. The up-and-over door seemed to roar and clang in the quiet dawn as he opened it on the old generation puke-green Astra. It was perfect, average enough not to draw attention, and before setting off he carefully checked the tax disc, plates and all the lights, reassured that she'd kept it all in good order. With luck it would be a while before there was any police interest around here, but he had form, and the last thing he needed was to get caught out and be pulled over for a minor traffic offence. The adrenalin spike was starting to flatten now and the pain in his side was coming up to meet it, but he had to keep his wits about him for just a few more hours until he could relax.

## Chapter Four

Day Two

It was still early when Mariner finished his packing so he made another mug of tea in the hope that it might settle his stomach, then forced himself under the shower. Glancing down he saw a crimson spot drip on to the pristine white floor of the shower cubicle, a pinkish rim spreading out from it and making it look like a small fiery planet. It was joined by another, then another to form a whole miniature solar system. In reality it was a nose bleed. He'd been plagued with them lately, though luckily so far they'd been mostly first thing in the morning. Stress-related, the doctor told him when he'd casually mentioned it at his last medical. *Stress from what?* Mariner had almost asked, before realizing what a stupid question that was. Stepping out of the shower, it took him several minutes to stem the flow enough to be able to shave properly, but he left his white shirt on its hanger a while longer.

He was knotting his tie when he heard the sound of a car engine and glanced outside to see Millie Khatoon and

Tony Knox, arriving exactly on time. This was it. The discomfort grumbling away in his belly suddenly bubbled up into his throat in a bitter surge and, with the repeated and insistent chiming of his doorbell ringing in his ears, he ran for the bathroom and consigned the mug of tea to the toilet bowl. When the retching subsided, he swilled his mouth out and splashed cold water on his face. It was a gaunt visage that stared back at him from the mirror. He'd never had much colour but the strain of the last few weeks was showing in the pallor of his skin. The white flecks in his hair were on the increase too and even the blue seemed to have drained from his eyes, leaving them hollowed, with dark shadows underneath. Not for the first time he considered feigning an illness, thinking that perhaps if he refused to acknowledge today it might seem less real, less final. But common sense told him that in time it would be something he'd live to regret. The doorbell rang again, more insistently. Resolute, Mariner dried his face, jogged down the stairs and, grabbing his overcoat from the hook he strode out of the house, slamming the door shut behind him. 'Come on then,' he said, tossing his car keys to Millie. 'Let's get this over with.'

'And good morning to you too,' said Knox, throwing his colleague a glance. 'I'll see you down there.'

* * *

McGinley had driven carefully out of Liverpool via the Mersey Tunnel and on to the Wirral under cover of the breaking dawn, acutely aware that once he got beyond the large conurbations he'd be increasingly conspicuous. He was making excellent time through the Cheshire country lanes though, and what he'd thought might be a tricky piece of navigation was turning out to be surprisingly easy. Although he'd ceased to believe in 'the big man' many years ago, suddenly McGinley had the sense that this time some greater power really was on his side, helping him along.

He'd learned about computers while he was crashing at Froggie's place in between stays at Her Majesty's Pleasure. Apart from the porn on tap (Froggie's mouse was always suspiciously sticky) his mate had banged on about Friends Reunited. McGinley didn't have the faintest desire to be reacquainted with anyone he'd been at school with, not to begin with, anyway, and within a few short minutes he'd decided that the whole concept was total bullshit. Just an excuse for the successful wankers of the world to show off to everyone else about how wonderfully their lives had turned out, while, at the same time, rubbing the noses of people like McGinley into the shit that was their wretched lot. But when McGinley stumbled across the name 'Lindsey Appleby' he couldn't resist a peek.

He hadn't thought about her for years, but once he did, it became obvious to him that, like his mother, Lindsey Appleby (or Daker as she was now called) had also let him down. Badly. She'd done all right for herself, of course, he could see that from the profile — *married to Tim, a property developer* — with an address in the footballer territory of Cheshire. It was all so disappointingly conventional. *Would love to hear from anyone who knows me!!* screamed the blurb. McGinley took that as a challenge and got Froggie to show him how to send an email, typing it out painstakingly with his two index fingers. He was fully prepared for it to be ignored, but Lindsey had confounded his expectation and responded almost straight away as if they really were old chums. McGinley was immediately sceptical. Doubtless, she just replied in the same vein to everyone who contacted her, which simply confirmed for him what total bollocks it all was. So he emailed a question to try and catch her out: *remember the sparrow?* He never got the response because days later he was arrested for breaking and entering (well, if people will leave their bathroom windows open when they go out) and social networking isn't exactly encouraged in Strangeways. But that encounter across the *interweb* had stayed with him and it was when he was planning his escape route that McGinley had happened to notice how close he would be passing to where Lindsey Daker had made her perfect life.

It made complete sense that he was going to cross this area, of course, and time was on his side. There was going to be a lengthy wait at his destination anyway, so why not make a short detour? What did he have to lose? He quite literally had time to kill. That had made him chuckle, and it was disappointing that he couldn't share his new-found wit with anyone. It was altogether possible, of course, that Lindsey no longer lived at the address posted on the website, but on balance McGinley thought it more likely that she would be there, and he saw it as an opportunity. Some might even see it as an intervention of fate. He had no idea about the minutiae of Lindsey's life, though he could take an educated guess. He'd assess the situation, and if it looked as if it would be too complicated, then he would just drive on. Lindsey was only a bit-player, an optional extra. He had bigger fish to fry.

The detour had brought McGinley, as expected, into a very affluent neighbourhood. These were the homes every tart on Merseyside aspired to. The houses, if that was what you could call these palatial structures, were built with privacy in mind, and often could barely be glimpsed behind the tall trees, thick shrubs and long driveways. But privacy cut both ways, with a handy flip side called concealment, and the further he drove into these privileged country lanes the more McGinley warmed to this part of his adventure. Finally he came to the address scrawled on the torn-out notebook page. Jesus, it was a big bugger; modern and angular from what he could see behind the screen of conifers. Must be six or seven bedrooms. What the fuck did they do with them all? It was a little after five in the morning now and McGinley was banking on Tim the property developer being a workaholic. A couple of hundred yards back he'd passed the entrance to a water processing plant. He drove back there and parked up behind the cover of some dense bushes to wait until a more civilized hour.

By secondary school McGinley had already been marked out as a weirdo. Everybody seemed to know about what had happened to his dad, but far from being sympathetic they treated him with suspicion. Probably the old git's fault in the first place. Had to be some truth in it. That family's trouble. Stay away from them. Then, soon after they moved to Kirkby, Ma got into religion. Not any old religion but the sort that comes with maximum potential for humiliation, the Salvation Army. It spread like wild fire that he was in 'the army' and taking the piss out of a McGinley became a new curriculum subject, especially if he and Spence were seen up at the shopping centre in uniform at the weekend. It was something else to add to the growing catalogue of shame, from his old-fashioned clothes and haircut, to his crap school bag, to his family history. When he wasn't being taunted, he was mostly ignored — until Lindsey Appleby came along. Lindsey was on the outside too and went her own way, but for very different reasons. She was well-off and lived in a big house that wasn't technically even in Kirkby, but her mum and dad were social workers or something and thought it was character building for her to go to school with council estate scum. They were opposite ends of the same spectrum. While McGinley was really desperate to blend in, Lindsey went out of her way to be different. It was the start of punk and she dyed her hair and put safety pins through her ears. She chose not to hang out with the cool kids, which in itself made her cool. But maybe because of her mum and dad, she was also nice to everyone.

McGinley rode to school every day on an old second-hand pushbike with a torn saddle and no mud guards. One day, as frequently happened, the chain came off. Usually he could put it back on, no problem, but on this day it was so tangled it got jammed and he was forced to walk. He saw Lindsey up ahead some distance away, crouching over something. As he got up close he saw it was a sparrow flopping around on the pavement unable to fly. She enlisted him to help carry it the rest of the way to school. For the remaining time that his broken bike forced him to walk to school, he found her waiting for him by the same garden. The first time he nearly pissed himself with fear.

'Where's your bike?' she asked.

'I couldn't fix it.'

'All right, I'll walk with you.'

Terrified, McGinley wondered what the hell he would say to her. He didn't have to worry. Lindsey did all the talking — questions mostly — along with comments on their classmates and teachers that were savagely funny and observations of the world in general.

McGinley didn't know why she was interested in him. It would have been different had he been anything like his kid brother, Spencer. Spence was beautiful. People had been saying that since the day he was born. He didn't have McGinley's frizzy hair or crooked teeth (back in the days before braces were the norm). Spence had a happy disposition too, and that, ironically, had been his undoing.

Lindsey's interest had lasted for one wonderful term, when finally it seemed that McGinley might emerge from his lonely, friendless existence. Desperate to keep Lindsey's attentions, he started to bring her things — mostly sweets stolen from the local corner shop. He was deft and he was fast and it was the one thing that he could do well. To start with Lindsey encouraged him. Payback for your dad, she called it. Two fingers up to the filth. And by the time she started to go all self-righteous on him, McGinley was in too deep. He'd come to the attention of a talent scout. Not for Liverpool or Everton, but for Lee Brodie and his gang of about-to-turn-professional thieves, who recognized a house-breaking asset when they saw one. The late seventies were a boom time for portable electronic equipment and McGinley became an expert in acquiring it. Lindsey, though, had long ceased to be impressed and when two boys in school uniform were seen leaving the scene of a newsagent burglary, she shopped him. It was for his own good, she said, and it didn't seem to matter to her that it wasn't even him. The escapade got McGinley expelled from school; he never really went back and he never saw Lindsey again. In fairness, he couldn't blame Lindsey entirely; his life would probably have turned to crap anyway, but she hadn't exactly helped. And now he had a chance to redress the balance.

At seven-forty, a top of the range Mercedes slid smoothly past McGinley, the only occupant a male driver, and as it disappeared around the leafy corner McGinley caught sight of the rear personalized plate: DAK 4. Perfect. Taking what he needed from his rucksack, McGinley proceeded back to the house on foot. He was ready to scale the walls if necessary, but there was no need. Hubby had obligingly left the electronic gates open. *Tosser*. The 'hers' Merc, a little SUV crossover, was on the drive, in preparation for the school run.

McGinley strolled past it and around to the back of the house. He sank back as the kitchen door suddenly opened and an exuberant spaniel ran out. *Game over*, McGinley thought, but the stupid mutt bounded right past him and on to the end of the garden, racing around the shrubs and sniffing after animal trails. McGinley sidled along to the kitchen window and, peering in, his eyes fell on the kind of domestic scene that was being replicated the length of the country. McGinley had seen the photos online, so was prepared for how much Lindsey had changed, but even so, it was hard to reconcile the girl he'd known with the woman before him now. Gone were the panda eye make-up, pale skin and purple lipstick. She looked good for forty-six; slim and gym-toned in tight-fitting jeans and some kind of flowery shirt, her hair was lightened to a fake blonde, and fell to her shoulders. The hair, black and glossy as it was back then, was what

McGinley remembered most: that and her tits. They all used to queue up to watch her playing netball in her slightly too tight aertex shirt to see if they could get a glimpse of her nipples.

Lindsey was talking to a boy of about ten or eleven — *one son, James* — who sat at the breakfast bar, one hand lethargically taking a spoon from a cereal bowl to his mouth, the other cupped around some kind of hand-held gaming toy. In response to her words, but without taking his eyes off the game, the boy got up from the table and slouched out of the room. McGinley chose that moment to make his entrance. Lindsey looked up in astonishment: strike two. McGinley liked the symmetry of repetition. 'Hello Lindsey,' he said.

But then she floored him. 'My God, Glenn McGinley,' she replied, without missing a beat. Confused, she screwed up her face. 'What the hell are you doing here?'

*Fuck*. She really had remembered him. For a moment it nearly threw him off course, until he thought back to the humiliation of her casual abandonment. And now, of course, he'd put her in a position to spoil his plans. Having come this far there was no alternative but to finish it. He raised the gun and watched her eyes widen. 'Sorry, Lindsey,' he said, actually meaning it, and he fired twice.

Lowering the weapon, McGinley caught a movement on the edge of his field of vision. The boy had reappeared in the doorway and stood silently terror-struck, staring at him, his eyes spookily similar to his mother's. McGinley stared back. It was tempting to leave the boy be. The kid would suffer, but he still had his dad; he'd get over it. No matter that he could describe McGinley in detail to the police. Then McGinley noticed the dark stain spreading down the boy's trouser leg. He'd pissed himself, the little wimp. Suddenly McGinley saw Spencer standing there, shame written across his features, and anger rose up in him. This kid didn't know he was born. McGinley squeezed the trigger twice more.

Before leaving he walked over and looked down dispassionately at Lindsey's twisted body, still beautiful if you ignored the dark hole in her chest. And those tits; in other circumstances he'd have been tempted to slide a hand inside her blouse, but the medication had put paid to any inclinations of that nature, and besides, he didn't know how much time he had. A woman like Lindsey was bound to have some kind of domestic help. He was just rifling through his pockets for his cigarettes when he heard the door open and a voice behind him said, 'Morning, Mrs . . .'

McGinley turned to see a young man dressed in outdoor work clothes. He'd stopped abruptly, aghast as he took in the scene, and McGinley reckoned he had about three seconds before he dived for his phone. Raising the gun again, he shot the man in the chest, registering the wedding ring as he fell. *Shit.* This wasn't in the plan; two more victims he hadn't factored in. This could get out of hand. For a moment he was frozen to the spot, casting around him, half expecting someone else to appear. Then panic galvanized him and he ran back out through the kitchen door and to the car. Getting his breath back he lit up a cigarette to steady his nerves. He couldn't afford to lose it now, before the job was finished. What he'd achieved so far was mostly for him, but now he was on a promise. If he didn't accomplish this last part of it, then it would have all been for nothing. With trembling hands he restarted the car and in minutes was back at the junction, picking up the road where he'd left off.

## Chapter Five

DC Millie Khatoon drove carefully through the back streets of West Heath and Longbridge, the only sound in the car was the radio chuntering on low volume in the background. 'Well, at least the rain's held off,' she said eventually, accelerating down the slip road and on to the motorway. 'Might not be too bad.'

'Mm,' Mariner concurred distractedly, noting the clouds above that grew increasingly grey and threatening. He understood that she was making conversation and was only talking about the weather, but he couldn't see how this could ever be anything but the most appalling day.

'It'll be all right, sir,' she soldiered on. 'This is the worst bit. After today you'll be able to, well, you know . . .' She tailed off and they lapsed into silence once again. Suddenly she said, 'You do know, boss, that if you ever want to talk . . .'

'Yes, thanks,' Mariner cut in, before the embarrassment got too much. He cleared his throat. 'Have you got a date yet?' he asked, in the only way he could see of changing the subject. Millie's promotion to detective sergeant was long overdue in his opinion, and he'd been encouraging her to put in for the necessary exams for months now.

'Actually I haven't quite got round to it.' She was apologetic.

'Well, you should have done,' Mariner retorted, a little more sharply than he'd intended. 'You're wasting your skills running round after me and Tony Knox. I've always said that you've got great potential, but you need to make a start.'

'I know. It's just — it's been so busy lately . . .'

'There's never an ideal time,' Mariner reminded her. 'You've just got to get on and do it.'

'Yes, boss.' She seemed about to say something else. *Mind your own bloody business* would have been fair enough. But she left it at that and since Mariner didn't have anything helpful to add, silence reclaimed the car. A song came on the radio and Millie turned up the volume. Perhaps it was a song she particularly liked or perhaps it was simply a way of removing the necessity for further interaction.

* * *

The A55 was a good fast road, and McGinley had to work hard to resist pushing too hard on the gas. Although anxious to put as much distance between himself and those bodies, the enormity of what he had done was beginning to hit home. Drawing attention to himself now would mean blowing everything completely. So he forced himself to keep a steady speed which enabled him to blend in with the mostly heavy goods traffic that was heading west in the early morning. Once the police had found the bodies and worked out who it was they were looking for, it wouldn't take them long to identify his car, and then to pick it out on the CCTV that lined his route, but he could live with that. They'd be so fucking delighted with their own brilliance that it would be some time before it occurred to them that that was exactly what he had intended, but he couldn't let them get to him too soon. He turned on the radio to catch the eight o'clock news, but there was nothing yet to indicate the discovery of his first two victims. All in all, what with the stops to have a piss, and another to get his medication down him, the journey took only just over an hour. Coming into the town he was reminded that Wales isn't always about male voice choirs and pretty scenery. He headed first for the rounded steel hangar of the ferry port, then, seeing a Lidl supermarket, left the car there while he went into the terminal to buy his one-way ticket to Dublin, making sure that he stopped to examine it right in front of a security camera before he ducked out of the building and back to his car.

The supermarket was just opening up, so McGinley took the opportunity to stock up on a few essentials. He broke out in a sweat beside the spirits, but he didn't have the capacity for carrying bottles yet and he couldn't succumb. His side was starting to hurt and, standing in the checkout queue, he felt a sudden wave of exhaustion from the night's activities, but things were starting to get busy around here. He knew it wouldn't be wise to hang around for too long. Back in the car he wolfed down the last of the bread and cheese, washing it down with some milk and a painkiller accompaniment. A light rain had started to fall so, putting on his waterproof jacket and a woolly hat, he retrieved his pack from the boot, locked the vehicle and set off towards the railway station, dropping the keys into an industrial waste bin along with his ferry ticket.

So far McGinley had been blasé about his visibility, but from now on, if this was going to work, he needed to keep a low profile. Buying his train ticket, he kept his head down under the rim of his hood. He was one of a handful of people at the train station. His fellow passengers were mainly labourers and commuters from the look of it, slaves to conventional working hours, but their presence made it easier. As far as was possible, without drawing attention to himself, he stayed close to other passengers to avoid looking like a man on his own. Now that the thrill of the night before and the early hours had worn off he felt wired and edgy; today was a day full of uncertainties. There was no way of knowing how long the police would take to work things out, or if they would be fooled by his misdirection. Meanwhile, he had to cover as much ground as possible at the mercy of public transport. This was the one day when everything had the potential to go right for him — or very wrong.

* * *

Mariner flinched as an icy drip tumbled from a gap in the wooden rafters high above, smacking the back of his neck and sending a shiver through him. He breathed in ancient wood and incense. Aside from the rain drumming on the roof of the little country church, the congregation was hushed, the customary pause allowing everyone his or her personal thoughts of the deceased. Mariner could have stood there for days and it wouldn't have been time enough to revisit the memories, or to conduct the necessary mental and emotional self-flagellation. Nine weeks on, and still his imagination could not stretch to fully comprehend the fact that Anna — bright, passionate and full of life — lay, at this moment, cold and motionless in that insubstantial box in front of the altar, and that he was never going to see her again. The muscles of his mouth trembled involuntarily and sucking in breath he clamped his lips together to avert the spasm. From the corner of his eye he saw Millie cast him a surreptitious glance. Silently he willed her not to reach out and touch him; a comforting arm on his right now and he'd completely fall apart. Then mercifully the two minutes were up, the vicar gave the blessing and, as k.d. lang's rendition of Leonard Cohen's 'Hallelujah' echoed around the chamber, the mourners began to stir, picking up belongings and working their way slowly out of the tiny chapel and into the rain. Mariner stuffed the order of service into his inside jacket pocket as he shuffled along the pew, noticing for no reason that Millie's was the only brown face here.

They stood then in the sodden grass while the burial was conducted, amid all the clichés about the gods crying down. Mariner wasn't one of those who went forward to cast earth onto the lowered coffin. If anyone had asked he would have said he didn't believe in the symbolism. 'That's crap,' Anna tormented him, inside his head. 'You just don't want to get your hands dirty.'

'It was a good service.' Tony Knox fell into step beside him as they made their way out beneath the canopy of trees that provided some shelter from the wet April afternoon. Mariner didn't know what could possibly constitute a 'good' funeral for a woman cut down so young, but he appreciated what his sergeant was trying to do, so he nodded in agreement anyway. 'Still can't believe it though, even now,' Knox went on.

'Me neither.' Millie grimaced and shook her head.

'Tom? Tom Mariner?' They turned as one to see a man in his forties coming towards them, blond and dark-eyed; he'd been among the chief mourners in the front row of the congregation. Dr Gareth. Mariner had always said it with sarcasm and realized now that he didn't even know the full name of the man who had effectively snatched Anna from him. Unfairly perhaps, Mariner thought 'Dr Gareth' suited him, implying as it did some kind of false and shallow familiarity. Looking towards him now, Mariner did a double take. At Gareth's shoulder was a young woman, petite with cropped brown hair, at first glance a ringer for Anna. Gareth's sister? Mariner didn't think so. He was carrying a small cardboard box. 'I thought you might want to have this,' he said, holding it out to Mariner. 'There was some stuff of yours. I thought you might like it back.'

Taking the box from him, Mariner lifted one of the flaps and peered inside. Anna's face appeared before his eyes. 'Ta da!' she cried, showing off the russet-coloured cashmere scarf he'd given her, their last Christmas together. His gift buying had never been very sophisticated, but this spontaneous effort had been an unqualified success and she'd worn it often.

Tony Knox must have seen his face and recognized the tactlessness of Gareth's gesture. He stepped forward to take the box. 'Here, boss, let me . . .'

'No, it's fine,' said Mariner, his voice husky with emotion. He forced himself to look at Gareth. 'Thanks.'

'No probs.' With a brief smile, Gareth turned away. The young woman tucked her hand into the crook of his arm and together they headed off across the churchyard.

'Christ,' said Knox. 'Is that his new bird? He doesn't hang about, does he?'

'Who knows,' Mariner said, distracted, closing up the box and tucking it clumsily under his arm. *And who cares?* he added mentally. They stood there for a moment, adding further awkwardness to the growing accumulation, until, with some relief, they all saw the two uniformed police officers emerging from the church to walk up the path and out on to the road. One of the men acknowledged Mariner with a brief nod, throwing them a lifeline of normal conversation.

'Have they made any progress?' Knox asked.

Mariner shook his head. 'They're pretty sure they know who was responsible but there's not enough evidence to even pull him in. They can triangulate a couple of mobile phone calls made to roughly that area, but there's no clear reading of the registration number of the van from motorway CCTV and one of the chief suspects has a pretty unassailable alibi.'

'What about Lottie?' asked Millie.

'Too traumatized to be a credible witness,' Mariner said. 'She can't remember any useful detail. The descriptions she came up with could be any of a number of men; there was nothing unique about them. I think they've even tried hypnotherapy.' The casual tone of his voice belied the hopelessness he felt inside; Anna dead and her killer still at liberty. Although grateful for the effort his two colleagues had made to support him, now that the formalities were over he was impatient to be away from here, away from the platitudes and the sympathetic noises, to go somewhere where he could lick his wounds.

After another silence that seemed to go on forever, Knox finally said, 'Right, we'd best be getting back then, d'you think, boss?' His glance sought and received agreement from Millie.

'Yes, but I'm not coming back with you,' Mariner said. Millie and Knox both stared at him. 'My walking stuff is all packed in the back of the car, and I've booked a couple of weeks' leave, so I'm going on into mid-Wales to do some walking.'

'On your own?' said Millie.

'That's the general idea, yes.' Mariner looked pointedly at Knox. 'I tried to do it once before.'

'It was a bad idea, the state you were in,' Knox defended himself.

'I know,' Mariner conceded. 'But I'm perfectly fine now. I just want some time to myself.'

'But I don't . . . will you be all right, sir?' Millie asked.

'Sure you don't want me along?' Knox checked again, his shoulders hunched against the cold, and his hands thrust deep into his coat pockets. 'The gaffer would clear it. You know she would.'

'There's no need,' Mariner said, though he shared Knox's certainty about DCI Sharp. That was exactly why this time he'd been forced to spring it on them. They were desperate to keep an eye on him, make sure he wasn't about to come off his hinges. They didn't get that it was the very reason he needed to be alone; to work through his grief in his own solitary way. 'And someone's got to keep the mean streets of Birmingham safe while I'm away,' he added, not without irony.

'Does Katarina know?' asked Knox. That was below the belt.

'Like I said, it's just for a couple of weeks,' Mariner reminded him.

This time Millie couldn't resist reaching out to squeeze his arm. 'Well, look after yourself, sir,' she said, doubtfully.

'I will,' Mariner assured her, forcing some brightness into his voice. He and Knox shook hands.

'See you in a couple of weeks then, boss.' He made to move away then changed his mind. 'You are coming back, aren't you?'

'Course I bloody am,' said Mariner. 'What else would I do? Watch how you go now,' he added. 'And thanks for . . . you know.'

## Chapter Six

While they were saying their goodbyes, Mariner had become increasingly aware of a man standing a few feet away, apart from everyone else, as if he didn't quite belong. In late middle age, his black umbrella kept the rain off a balding pate and wild white hair that grew down under the upturned collar of his long, dark overcoat. Mariner felt he might know him, a feeling confirmed by the glances cast in his direction as, not as bold as Gareth had been, he waited patiently for the opportune moment. But as soon as Mariner parted company with Millie and Knox, the man took his chance and came over, stepping carefully across the boggy ground, his right hand outstretched in greeting.

'Inspector Mariner? Paul Jenner,' he introduced himself. 'We met once before, several years ago. I am — was — Anna Barham's solicitor.'

*Of course.* It seemed like a whole lifetime ago when he and Jenner had met, during the course of the investigation into Anna's brother Eddie's death. Even back then the man had seemed close to retirement. Mariner was amazed he was still going, though the Barham family wouldn't be requiring his services any longer. With Anna's death, almost the whole family unit was gone; parents and two siblings all unnaturally killed, but in three entirely different sets of circumstances, years apart. What were the odds against that?

'How can I help?' Mariner asked, genuinely puzzled as to what Jenner might want with him.

'It concerns Jamie Barham.'

'Jamie?' Conspicuous by his absence, Anna's sole remaining close relative was her younger brother. But Mariner hadn't expected that he would be here. With severe autism and learning difficulties, Jamie would have found the whole ceremony incomprehensible and intolerable. He might perhaps have noticed that his sister had stopped visiting him at the residential facility where he now lived, but he would, in time, get used to her absence. Suddenly Mariner knew exactly why Jenner needed to speak to him and it hit him like a train. 'I'm still Jamie's guardian in the event of Anna's death,' he said.

'Yes,' Jenner confirmed. 'That's exactly it.'

So Anna hadn't passed that particular responsibility on to Gareth. *Christ.*

'There's no need for alarm,' Jenner said, quickly, perhaps sensing Mariner's reaction. 'Nor is any immediate action required. The staff at Towyn Farm have been informed of . . . events. I think they had hoped to send someone along today, but it seems they were unable to after all. Jamie's place at the facility is perfectly secure, and the trust fund set up for him will cover his costs for the foreseeable future, so everything is in hand. I suppose it's just a question of keeping in touch and perhaps when you have time I can talk you through the legalities. Let me give you this, and perhaps you'd like to give me a call when it's convenient.' He passed Mariner his business card and, digging in his inside pocket, Mariner proffered his in exchange.

'Thank you,' said Jenner. 'And I'm so very sorry. You must be feeling Anna's loss as keenly as anyone.'

Watching Jenner walk away, Mariner wondered how much he knew about what had happened between him and Anna. It didn't sound as if he was entirely ignorant.

Jamie, his responsibility? That was a bombshell. Mariner couldn't begin to grasp the enormity of it. He'd never in his life had to take responsibility for another human being — at least, not in the legal sense. He'd felt it sometimes, especially recently since Katarina had come into his life, but that was a role he had chosen and it had never been official. The Towyn Farm Community where Jamie lived was not far from here. It had been part of the rationale for Anna moving out from Birmingham. But the move had happened shortly before he and Anna had split, so Mariner had never been to visit Jamie there. He would need to go and make himself known, and the sooner the better. He had set off this morning with a plan, but meeting Paul Jenner had changed things. On his way back to Birmingham at the end of his leave, he would go to Towyn and at least introduce himself and find out if Jamie even remembered him.

Despite the atrocious weather people were hanging around the church yard, reluctant to go, reluctant to leave her. Mariner knew the feeling, but it couldn't go on forever. There was just one person he needed to speak to before he left. He found Anna's best friend Becky standing, temporarily alone, sheltering inadequately under a spreading conifer.

'I'll be making a move,' he told her.

'Aren't you coming to the house?' she asked, referring to the cottage Anna had latterly shared with her new lover.

Mariner shook his head. 'I've said goodbye. I don't want to make it awkward for anyone.' As he spoke his gaze drifted over to Gareth, his new girl clinging to him, in earnest conversation with Anna's friend Lottie. Poor Lottie. She and Charles were meant to have been marrying in this very church in just a few weeks. Instead the woman had buried her husband-to-be and a good friend here a matter of days apart.

'Well, it's up to you, of course,' Becky said. 'You're going back up the motorway?'

'No. I've got some leave due. I'm heading out to Wales, do some walking; clear my head.'

'Good luck with that.' Becky made a show of peering out from the shelter of the branches at the relentless downpour. 'Seriously though, mind how you go. The roads will be bad.' She seemed about to say something more, but instead stretched out her arms and, after an awkward hug, in the course of which Mariner nearly dropped the box he was carrying, he turned to go, stepping back out into the rain. He'd walked ten paces when he heard Becky's voice again.

'It was a mistake you know,' she called after him.

'What?' Mariner turned back, not sure of what she was saying.

'Leaving Birmingham; leaving you.' She cast an anxious look towards Gareth but he was too far away to hear. 'Anna had got it wrong. She realized that. She sent me a text that day, telling me she'd seen you. She was so excited. I think it made her think about what she'd been missing. She would have come back to you if she hadn't, you know . . .' She tailed off, reluctant to say the word. 'I'm sure of it.'

*Thanks, Becky,* Mariner thought bitterly, as he trudged back to his car. *Twist the knife, why don't you?* Now to all the other crap weighing him down, he could add the knowledge that if Anna hadn't been stabbed to death by a complete moron in a freak road-rage incident, he might have got her back again. *Thank you so much.* Accommodating the cardboard box upset his system in the boot, forcing him to redistribute his rucksack to the back seat of the car. By the time he opened the driver's door his vision was blurring and it took him several seconds before he could blink it back into focus again and get the tremor in his hand under enough control to get the key in the ignition to start the engine.

## Chapter Seven

In practice it had all been more straightforward than McGinley could ever have envisaged. For once the British rail network had operated with something approaching efficiency and, apart from the obligatory unexplained twenty-minute wait outside Shrewsbury station that had threatened to make him miss his connection, each leg of his journey had passed without incident. He'd kept a surreptitious eye on the newsstands and so far had seen nothing of relevance, though he knew the story might well have broken on the broadcast media by now. He wondered which of them had been found first. It didn't matter really; if he'd done the job properly (as he was confident he had) no one would be looking for him here. And as long as he remained inconspicuous, there would be nothing for him to worry about.

Being invisible had always come naturally to McGinley. If he had to sum up his existence in one word, it would be 'insignificant.' His attire meant that he could make a rough attempt to pass himself off as a walker — more Rambo than rambler — but the hiking community were an eclectic bunch and up to now he'd got away with it. Luckily throughout the day the weather had turned increasingly foul, so when he finally disembarked from the last train he could reasonably take cover again beneath his woolly hat and the hood of his cagoule. What was less satisfactory was that the age of his waterproof meant it let in the rain, especially now it was pissing down. He'd passed a couple of outdoor clothing shops, but he had no idea what a new jacket would cost, and his funds were limited, so he would have to manage. All this wasn't to say that he was home free just yet. His destination for tonight was one he'd frequented before on many occasions but not for years. He was banking on it being unchanged. There was a Plan B if that went tits-up, but it would be much less satisfactory. He was beginning to feel tired and badly needed to rest.

As he left the town walking out along the main coast road, things were looking promising. To the right, on the seaward side, began a tentative row of static caravans, set back behind a simple chain-link fence and presenting a barrier from the dunes and then the sea. The row expanded into two and then three as the caravan park grew, and by the time McGinley reached the main entrance the site was about six vans deep, with more than a dozen rows on either side. But despite its size, McGinley was heartened to see that, in terms of facilities and sophistication, any kind of modernization had passed the park by. It remained basic and workmanlike, with just a small office building beside the farm gate entrance, to house the manager and supplies of calor gas. There was no shop, swimming pool or social club. In fact McGinley was amazed the place had survived. What it did have going for it, of course, was its immediate proximity to the natural amenities of sea and coastline, and the lack of frills meant that it attracted a particular clientele: hardened surfers and birdwatchers, and like McGinley's dad, fishermen, all of whom would continue to provide him with useful cover. Even this early in the season there were, he noticed, just enough cars dotted around for his arrival to go unnoticed.

Whether late in the day or early in the season, or perhaps because of the rain, the office was all closed up, and McGinley walked on to the site unchallenged. Navigating a path between the trailers, hazy memories of the geography resurfaced and he headed in what he remembered as being the right general direction. Picking up the sequence of numbers, sure enough, he came to the unit he wanted. None of the vans looked in great condition but number seventy-one, if anything, looked relatively well kept. The pale green outer shell was clean, the wooden steps to the door freshly varnished and the nets up at the windows, which would give him the privacy he needed, looked clean and white. For an awful moment, McGinley suddenly thought that perhaps the old bag had sold up after all, even though she'd retained the keys, and that some other family was keeping it spick and span. But the Yale from the old brown envelope slipped easily enough into the lock and turned without resistance, and once inside McGinley was further reassured by the array of cheap trinkets that had sat on those shelves since he was a boy. A strong wind had got up and was cutting right through him so it was with some gratitude that he stepped into the stagnant interior and shut the door. With a clink, he set down the carrier bags of provisions he'd just bought and took out three bottles of cheap Russian vodka. When this was all over he was going to celebrate in style. But that would be on another day. The place was freezing and he had no way of knowing when it had last been inhabited, or when the utilities had last been paid. He didn't even know how all that worked, so decided it would be too much of a risk to turn on the gas or electric, which meant he was in for a chilly time, but at least he had a welcome shelter from the worst of the elements. He'd rest up until tomorrow and once he was satisfied that the smoke screen was firmly established he'd put phase three into action.

For now, he unpacked some of his few possessions from the rucksack, among them the old envelope he'd retrieved from the loft, and he tipped out its contents on to the small Formica table that delineated the dining area. On top of the pile was a plain white postcard with an address on the back, in an unfamiliar hand. The message was written in his own ten-year-old scrawl. *Dear Mum, we are having a nice time. We have been rock climing and we have been to a water fall. Today we had sausiges and beans and chips. Hope your well, love Glenn.* Underneath his name was the barely legible scrawl of his younger brother. Seeing the date on the postmark, a fist gripped McGinley's heart for a couple of seconds. It was the very year it had happened. Collecting up the rest of the papers he put them back in the envelope. Then washing down a handful of painkillers with more milk, he grabbed some blankets and lay down on the couch to try and get some sleep.

* * *

It was not yet four o'clock but it seemed almost dusk-like as Mariner drove carefully through the drenched village lanes and out towards the main road north-west, the water crackling and hissing under the wheels of his car. The strange half-light continued until eventually the sun, wherever it was, sank down completely, sucking the remaining light from the sky. He continued on, through countryside and small villages, each one seeming smaller and more remote, until all that lay beyond the windscreen wipers was a vast black emptiness, and the only way that he could differentiate the fall and rise of the gradient in the road was through the changing pressure in his ears. After a couple of miles Mariner became aware of a blaze of headlights in his rear-view mirror. They had gained on him quickly and were now right behind him, the glare fully illuminating the inside of his car. It was a high vehicle, some kind of SUV, and driving much too close for the wet conditions. The narrow winding road made it impossible for Mariner to pull over and let the other driver past. He increased his speed slightly in an attempt to open up a gap, but the driver behind simply matched his pace, closing in again. Mariner touched his brakes gently, thinking it might prompt the vehicle to back off, but if anything the driver seemed more determined. Mariner's irritation began to rise. He had nothing against people driving too fast and killing themselves, but he didn't see why he should be part of that equation. For several miles this cat and mouse continued until finally the road widened a little and, slowing right down, Mariner signalled left and pulled over. For a moment he thought the other car was doing the same and it flashed through his head that history was about to repeat itself, but then, at the last minute, the other vehicle accelerated past him and the dazzling headlights veered off into the distance.

* * *

'Christ, this is a nightmare.' Tony Knox was leaning forward, straining to see his way through the sheets of rain that fell from the sky, exacerbating the blanket of spray thrown up by the column of HGVs in the slow lane of the M5. He'd slowed to fifty, but inevitably there were idiots overtaking at much faster speeds, even in these treacherous conditions.

'Do you think the boss will be all right out there on his own?' Millie said, gazing out of the window.

'It's his way of dealing with everything,' Knox said. 'You know him, he likes a bit of space. And I offered to go with him, didn't I?'

'He's so vulnerable just now though . . .' Something on the radio caught Knox's attention and, breaking off suddenly, he leaned forward and turned up the radio for the news bulletin. The headlines concerned an elderly couple who had been discovered during the day, shot dead in their home in Kirkby, Merseyside. They listened to the details. Burglary was cited as the probable motive, though the random selection of the house — the home of an apparently ordinary working-class couple — was so far baffling police.

'Sorry,' Knox said, when the bulletin came to an end. 'I tend to tune into stuff up there.'

'Of course,' said Millie. 'Your old patch, wasn't it? What sort of place is Kirkby?'

'The kind of place where incidents like that aren't exactly unheard of,' said Knox. 'Think of Liverpool's answer to Chelmsley Wood. It'll be a domestic of some kind.'

The journey back to Birmingham took longer than usual and it was a relief when Knox had dropped Millie off at her house and a little later pulled into his own drive. He rolled his shoulders to ease the tension. He could feel a tickling at the back of his throat that surely signalled the start of a cold. It was dark, but the rain had almost stopped by the time he let himself into his house. Nelson, his adopted border terrier, greeted him in a state of high excitement and immediately bounded back into the kitchen hovering by the door to be let out into the garden. It could only mean one thing: that Michael, his young neighbour who usually walked the dog, had not been round. It was the third time this week that he'd reneged on their arrangement without warning or explanation, and on this occasion it would have to mean a financial penalty. The lad had to learn that he wouldn't get paid for what he didn't do. The last couple of times Michael had been round, Knox felt sure he'd smelt something vaguely herbal on his clothes, though he couldn't be absolutely sure. He wondered if Michael's mum Jean knew what was going on. He decided to let it rest for now. Up until now his relationship with the lad had been a reasonable one and he didn't want to spoil it by sticking his nose in unnecessarily.

Heating up a microwave cannelloni dinner for two, Knox took it into the living room where he settled down to watch the Channel Four news. Among the inevitable top stories of severe weather and flooding across the country, one of the lead items was of the double murder on Merseyside. Knox had departed that force under something of a cloud and, apart from the occasional visit to extended family, he hadn't been back there for some years. He'd lost touch with his former colleagues and didn't recognize the SIO for this enquiry. What was reported only served to reinforce his first impressions. It would be a domestic of sorts, as was so often the case. There had been an additional series of shootings in Cheshire, but Knox never found out if any link was being considered, because at that moment his phone rang. Automatically he cut the volume on the TV before picking up the handset. It was Jean.

'How are you?' she asked.

'Fine, thanks,' Knox said, wondering what had prompted this. A while back he and Jean had enjoyed a bit of a fling, but it hadn't lasted long. She was an attractive woman and Knox had since come to understand that he'd been her get-back-on-the-horse shag following the death of her husband a couple of years before. They'd parted amicably though, and since then Knox had sometimes wondered if, when she was ready, they might pick up again where they'd left off.

Tonight she was apologetic and harassed. 'I should have let you know sooner, I've told everyone else. Michael will be fifteen on Sunday, and I wanted to warn you that he's having a party tomorrow night. And since I can't afford to hire anywhere I'm stuck with having it here. It goes against my better judgement, and I'm dreading the social media effect, but apparently all his friends are having them, so it's pretty much expected.'

'Sounds like fun,' said Knox, drily.

'I can't say I'm looking forward to it.'

'You want me to steward?' Knox asked. 'I've got some experience in crowd control.'

'That's really kind, but I think I'm sorted,' she replied, a little too quickly. 'Pete Lennox, a colleague from work, has offered to help out.' Knox wondered if Pete Lennox was the driver of the flashy sports car that had lately been much in evidence on Jean's drive, often late at night. He had a tendency to notice these things. 'Besides,' Jean added. 'I'm not sure if having a policeman on site . . .'

'No, you're probably right,' Knox agreed. 'But if you change your mind, you know where I am.'

'Yes, thank you.' She hesitated. 'Has Michael been to walk Nelson today?' she wanted to know. There was something in her voice.

'It doesn't look like it,' Knox said. 'Is everything all right?'

'I don't know,' Jean sighed. 'I've hardly seen him in the last few days. No, that's not true. It's more like weeks, if I'm honest. When he gets in from school he just goes straight out again, then he doesn't come home again until late.'

'But he *is* coming home?'

'Yes, although I don't know why he bothers. He can barely bring himself to say two words to me.'

'He's a teenager,' Knox said, conscious that he was pointing out the obvious. 'That's how they are.' He spoke from personal experience. He'd seen his own two kids through their rebellious phases, although mostly from a distance. Theresa, his ex-wife, had handled much of the fallout.

'I know.'

'Is he turning up for school?' Knox asked.

'As far as I know,' said Jean. 'He leaves the house at the right time every morning. But I do think he's started smoking.' There was a pause at the other end of the line, the cue for Knox to disclose his suspicions. But something stopped him.

'You want me to come and have a word?' he asked instead.

'He's not here right now — of course.'

'I'm sure he'll be fine,' said Knox, with more certainty than he felt.

## Chapter Eight

Mariner restarted the car. The rain, mirroring his mood, seemed to beat down harder than ever, drumming on the roof of the car in a macabre tattoo. Rounding a bend, his headlights, on full beam, bounced back off the reflective band on a jacket sleeve; a man, head down in full waterproofs, pack on his back, was pounding along the side of the road. Slowing down, Mariner pulled over to the verge, and as the figure caught up with him, he flicked on the interior light and lowered the passenger window. A face appeared, bearded, raw and dripping.

'Where are you going?' Mariner asked. 'I can take you as far as Tregaron.'

The man raised his arms to waist level. 'I'm pretty soaked through,' he said, in case Mariner hadn't noticed.

'That's okay,' Mariner said, reaching behind him to shove his rucksack out of the way. 'Put your pack in the back there.'

Opening the rear door, the man wrestled his rucksack into the back seat then climbed in beside Mariner, pushing back his hood. 'This is most kind,' he said. 'I was hoping to get there sooner, but the visibility on the hill back there was bad and I got utterly lost.' Removing a sodden glove, he offered Mariner a cold, wet hand and they shook. 'Jeremy Bryce,' he said, catching his breath.

It was a firm grip and in the dim light Mariner made his usual quick inventory, getting the impression of a man in his late fifties or beyond, with grey wispy hair going in all directions, his lower face obscured by a substantial beard and cheeks reddened by the elements. Mariner was reminded of Raymond Briggs' Father Christmas.

'Tom Mariner,' he reciprocated and, putting the car into gear, he moved off.

'Well, if there's one thing that can always be relied on, it's rain in Wales,' Bryce observed cheerfully.

'This year more than most,' Mariner agreed. 'How's the Páramo working out?'

'Sorry?'

'Your jacket,' Mariner clarified. 'It looks like one of the new Páramos. I've just bought one myself but haven't tried it yet.'

'Oh, it's excellent,' Bryce said. 'I might look wet through, but underneath I'm dry as a badger.'

'A badger?'

Bryce laughed. 'Sorry, an expression I overheard once. It stuck in my mind.' He was English, but well-spoken and his voice was accent-free, making it impossible to guess where he was from.

'Where are you heading?' Mariner asked. He dabbed at the windscreen as the condensation from Bryce's damp clothing began to mist it.

'I'm walking the Black Mountain Way, with a few of my own variations, some intentional and some not. I'm having mixed success with accommodation so far, too. A couple of nights ago I got to a place only to find that the pub had closed down years before.'

'It's happened a lot recently in these remote areas,' Mariner said. 'You haven't booked anything?'

'Oh no.' Bryce shook his head and drips flew. 'At home my whole life is governed by timetables, meetings and deadlines. Now and again I feel the need to climb down from my ivory tower and get out on to the open road, as it were, with no schedule and no commitments. It's liberating.'

'I know what you mean,' said Mariner. It was exactly what he had planned for himself. 'Do you know this area well?'

'I wouldn't say well. But I've been here before, years ago. How about you; where are you aiming for?'

'I'm starting out from Tregaron and heading west in the first instance and then, who knows.' Mariner tried to sound vague. Although Bryce's intentions seemed to mirror his own, something prevented him from sharing that. However convivial this man might be, the last thing Mariner wanted to do was to attract a companion. A blaze of lights appeared on the road ahead: a petrol station. Mariner checked his fuel gauge. I could do with filling up,' he said. 'Do you mind?'

'Not at all,' said Bryce. 'I can enjoy the benefits of being warm and dry for a few more minutes.'

The filling station was an old-fashioned one, with no self-service nonsense and a proprietor who moved at a leisurely pace, so it turned out to be almost twenty minutes, but eventually they were back on the road. After a while the dark, confining hedgerows gave way to pavements and a string of street lights that marked the way; they were coming into a settlement.

Bryce peered through the misted windscreen. 'That looks like a pub up ahead,' he said suddenly. 'Do you know, I think I might try my luck there after all. I'd really like to bridge the gap that I've missed this afternoon. Does that sound eccentric?'

'Not at all,' said Mariner, feeling some relief that they would be parting company. 'It's probably what I'd want to do.'

In the village centre he drew up outside the Lamb and Flag Inn. It was small and unpretentious, no more than a stone cottage set a little way back off the road.

'Thank you very much for the ride,' Bryce said, beginning to assemble his things.

'I'll wait here for a few minutes,' said Mariner. 'Make sure that you can stay the night. If not, you can come on with me into Tregaron. It's a bigger town; there will be more options.'

'I appreciate that.' Bryce got out of the car and, heaving out his bulky rucksack, he disappeared into the pub. Moments later he returned, minus his backpack. 'It's fine,' he grinned, peering in the passenger window. 'They have rooms.' He tilted his head back towards the pub. 'Can I buy you a drink for your kindness?'

Mariner looked up at the rain still pattering steadily on the windscreen. 'Thanks, but I'll be on my way,' he said. 'I'd like to get to Tregaron in time for dinner.'

Bryce stuck his hand in through the window again. 'Of course. Well, thank you again for the lift, and have a good journey.'

'You too,' said Mariner. 'Let's hope the weather improves — for both of us.'

Mariner drove on, arriving in Tregaron twenty minutes later. The Star Hotel was in the centre of the town and little more than a glorified pub itself, but it had a decent-sized well-lit car park in which, with the landlord's consent, Mariner could leave his car for a few days. His room was typical British small-town hostelry: cool and slightly musty, with cheap furniture, thin curtains and a TV on a bracket attached to the wall.

Leaving his bags unpacked, Mariner went straight down to the bar, taking a couple of maps with him. There were few other customers: three young men in overalls enjoying a loud and laddish conversation, and a middle-aged couple at one of the tables. The place was inviting however, with a living-flame fire and the small TV screen deep enough into the corner to be largely ignored, though when the news came on the barmaid turned up the volume. The main story involved a couple of shootings on Merseyside and the Wirral, and speculation that the key suspect may have headed south and across into Wales. *Great*, thought Mariner, *I hope Millie doesn't hear that. She'll be out here with a rescue party*.

Glenn McGinley. From habit, Mariner pinged a mental sonar far into the depths of his memory, but it registered nothing. The couple at the adjacent table were also watching intently and Mariner nodded towards the screen. 'Good thing I didn't know that earlier,' Mariner quipped. 'I just picked up a hitchhiker. He wouldn't have been so lucky.'

They smiled politely in response, and Mariner returned to studying the menu. It was pretty standard fare; Mariner ordered lasagne and chips and settled down with his pint, reacquainting himself with his maps. He'd been to this area several times before, once for a whole summer, but that was years ago, and he needed to re-orientate himself a little before he set off tomorrow. 'Where do you want this, love?' He looked up into the smiling face of the barmaid, who stood beside him balancing a steaming plate expertly on her arm. Mariner hastily cleared a space for her to deposit his dinner. Around forty, she was blonde and brassy and as she leaned over him, Mariner got an eyeful of a deep cleavage exaggerated by her snug, low-cut T-shirt. The food was good and after he'd eaten Mariner ordered another beer and chaser, then another, and another. It had been a tiring day, but had opened up a wound, and the longer he stayed here the longer he could avert the unwelcome thoughts that would come crashing back into his head the moment he was alone.

'It's okay, Bob, I can lock up,' Mariner heard the barmaid call out and suddenly he realized that the towels were on the taps and he was the only customer left. She came round to his table to collect the empty glasses.

'So what are you selling?' she asked.

'Sorry?'

'The maps and the suit, I figure you must be in travelling sales. What is it — agricultural machinery or fertilizers?'

Mariner smiled indulgently. It wasn't the first time that the mistake had been made. 'Neither,' he said. 'I'm on holiday.'

'Crikey, you dress a bit formal for your holidays, don't you?'

Mariner shook his head. 'I was at a funeral this afternoon.'

'Oh God.' She made an apologetic face. 'Me and my big mouth.'

Mariner eyed his scotch glass, still with an inch or so remaining. He was already feeling pretty light headed. If he drank that all at once he'd probably pass out. 'Sorry,' he said. 'I'm keeping you up.'

'You're fine.' Her smile seemed genuine. Her face was carefully made-up, her skin a smooth and creamy layer of foundation and lips flawlessly rendered in scarlet lipstick. Mariner was mesmerized by her voluminous breasts, and the faint definition of her nipples against the taut cotton. In contrast her nails were long and elaborately painted and Mariner was suddenly aroused by the thought of them digging into his flesh. A perfect hybrid of soft and hard, she wasn't at all the kind of woman Mariner was ordinarily attracted to, but at this moment, mellowed by alcohol, he was so turned on he was sure she must be able to tell.

'Was it someone close?' she asked.

'What?'

'The funeral? Someone you knew well?'

'Girlfriend. Ex-girlfriend,' he corrected himself as a pain needled him in the chest.

She was studying him and the row of empty glasses on the table. 'Not that ex, by the look of you,' she said sitting down on the bench beside him. 'I'm sorry. She must have been quite young. Was she ill?'

'She was killed in a road-rage incident.'

'My God, that's awful.'

Mariner's hand was resting on his thigh, and tentatively she reached out and laid hers over it, curling her fingers around and under the palm. Mariner wanted to press it against his stiffening cock, but instead they sat there unmoving for several minutes, until at last she reached out and picked up his glass, swallowing the last mouthfuls for him. 'Come on,' she said. 'Let's get you upstairs.'

Unsteady on his feet, Mariner ascended the stairs feeling the gentle pressure of her hands on his back, and when they got to the landing she took the key from him and unlocked the door, stepping back to allow him inside. As he passed, Mariner couldn't resist slipping an arm round her waist and leaning in for a kiss but, the smile unwavering, she carefully disentangled herself, placing a palm flat on his chest. 'Oh, I don't think so. You seem like a nice man, but I'm not that sort of girl.'

'I know,' Mariner said, piling on the pathos. 'But the kind of day I've had . . .'

She appraised him for a couple of seconds, her eyes lingering on the place where by now his erection was making a tent of his trousers. Sensing his chance Mariner cautiously reached out and cupped a hand under her weighty breast, smoothing his thumb over the nipple and feeling it rise beneath his touch.

She caught her breath. 'Have you got condoms?'

'Yes,' Mariner said quickly, idly wondering if condoms were governed by sell-by dates. He didn't have long to think about it. One minute she was gazing at him, prevaricating, and the next thing Mariner knew they were tumbling backwards into the room, and as he pushed the door shut with his foot, she was dragging off his jacket and pulling open his shirt.

'Just not too much noise,' she hissed into his ear. 'I don't want to have to answer any awkward questions in the morning.'

In the event, noise was the last thing they had to worry about. Things were going fine until Mariner reached for the condom. In that instant of a pause he suddenly, for no reason, saw Anna's face looking straight at him, and immediately the key part of his anatomy changed its mind. For several moments he tried frantically to remedy the situation, but after a while it became obvious that it wasn't going to work, and the mood, if there was one, had evaporated. The room went horribly quiet. 'Sorry,' he said, breathlessly. He was about to add 'this has never happened before' but that wouldn't have been strictly accurate. It was just that it hadn't happened in a while. And what would she care about that anyway?

'It's all right,' she sighed, making it sound anything but. 'You don't have to explain. It happens, I know.' *To old codgers like you.* 'Too much booze I expect.'

Being patronized didn't make it any better. 'Is there anything I can . . .?'

'No, it's fine.' Somehow she wriggled out from beneath him. They hadn't turned on the light and now, frozen with shame, Mariner lay on the bed listening while she pulled her clothes back on, and without another word, let herself out of the room. Then he muttered one single, bitter expletive.

For the rest of the night, Mariner slept fitfully in the bed that was too soft and giving, reliving his humiliation. The rich food lay heavy in his stomach and his dreams were vivid and bizarre. At one point he watched while Anna, sitting up in her coffin, led the congregation in a chorus of 'Always Look on the Bright Side of Life' as a rampant gunman (who rather bizarrely assumed the physical appearance of a desk sergeant at Granville Lane police station) approached her, grinning maniacally, a twelve-bore shotgun poised.

## Chapter Nine

Day Three

McGinley woke after a restless night on a bed swaddled by cold and very possibly damp linen, with the all too familiar nagging pain in his side. Even fully clothed and with all the blankets he could find piled on top of him he'd shivered throughout the night, and for the first time he allowed himself the thought that the game might be up already and that he would fail to complete. Ironic that after all the effort he'd put into creating an elaborate decoy, his plans might be thwarted, not by the police, but by his own physical shortcomings. As he came round he found the place smelled weirdly of his dad — old cigarette smoke and cheap aftershave — and McGinley was disturbed by the strength of the recollections that came on him with force; each stage of his life worse than the one before, until events had finally spiralled out of control.

Taking his medication, the milk he washed it down with was out of his dad's old Everton mug. If the old man had lived longer perhaps eventually McGinley would have been old enough to go to matches with him and get to know him. As it was he had very few memories of his dad, and over the years they had been distorted by time and interpretation. William McGinley hadn't been much of a family man. Even when they'd come here on holiday he'd spent most of his time fishing alone on the beach, or down at the pub, coming back late at night, roaring drunk and sometimes abusive. He hadn't deserved to die the way he had, but there was a certain irony that his twin passions of football and booze had been what combined to finish him off. He followed Everton everywhere, although Ma always reckoned the football was only an excuse for the drink. It was after a scuffle in a pub, following an away match against Aston Villa and whilst resisting arrest, that he'd had his 'accident.' The police officers involved were subsequently exonerated by an internal enquiry, but McGinley knew enough about the police by now to understand how far they would go to protect their own and he was far from convinced. He hated the filth with a vengeance. Ma chose to blame the drink instead, and when they made their fresh start in Kirkby, that was when she had found God — and not any old god, but one who was a firm believer in abstinence. Since then she'd managed to keep the alcohol away from their family but not the hatred, not the prejudice and not death.

Along with the milk McGinley wolfed down one of the buns he'd bought and felt a little better. There was an ancient FM radio in the caravan and after some minutes of frustration attempting to tune it, he finally managed to get a local station. He then had to wait some time until the hourly news bulletin, but when it came it was strangely gratifying. Both sets of bodies had been discovered the previous day, the first by a neighbour and the second by the domestic help. Already the police had identified McGinley as a chief suspect for the first but they weren't committing themselves yet to the second, despite the similarities. They were however looking for the vehicle in which he was thought to have escaped.

'Well done, lads.' McGinley smiled quietly to himself, picturing some poor bugger hunched over hours and hours of CCTV footage.

* * *

Overnight, Tony Knox's cold had well and truly taken root. Having run out of tissues he'd now resorted to wiping his nose on toilet paper. In other circumstances he might have taken the day off, but with Mariner away they were already short, and it was Friday, so all he had to do was get through the next few hours, though it didn't help that it was raining again when he left the house. He was in his car, blowing his nose yet again, when he heard a door slam and in the rear-view mirror he saw Michael emerge from his front door across the road. Wearing only a blazer, the boy's head was bowed against the weather and Knox watched him pause at the end of his drive to light up a furtive cigarette, before hoisting his school bag and slouching off down the road, shoulders hunched in an effort to minimize his presence. Knox gave him time to reach the corner, then he moved off and caught up with the lad as he was about to cross the main road. Knox signalled and drew up alongside him. 'Want a lift to the Cartland?' he asked, identifying a landmark close to the school. Checking first that there was no one around to observe, Michael shrugged in that 'whatever' way that teenagers have, and mumbled, 'Yeah, all right.'

'You'll have to put that out.' Knox indicated the roll-up gripped between his fingers. For a moment Michael weighed the pleasure of his fag against the discomfort of the rain, before tossing the former down into the gutter and climbing into the car. Amid the smell of tobacco, Knox was instantly aware of the more subtle herbal note that he'd noticed before. 'I wanted to talk to you about

Nelson,' he said casually, pulling away from the kerb. 'You haven't been in for him much lately.'

From the corner of his eye Knox saw the indifferent lift of the shoulders. 'Been busy.'

'No problem,' Knox said, easily. 'I can't pay you though.' The shrug was becoming a tic. 'Let me know if you're up for it again,' Knox said. 'Is everything else all right?'

Shrug.

'Got your birthday to look forward to,' Knox pointed out. 'I hear you're having a party tonight.'

A huge sigh and a screwed-up face this time. 'What did she have to tell you for? God, she's blurting it to everyone.'

'Hey, stop giving your mum such a hard time and show her some respect,' Knox said, starting to lose patience. 'It's called being considerate to your neighbours. I'd do exactly the same in her position. Be grateful she's letting you have a party at all; plenty of parents don't.'

'Yeah, it'll be crap now though, with all the neighbours watching out for us.'

Knox slowed as they reached the drop-off point. 'You don't know how lucky you are,' he said, mildly. 'Have a good one.'

Finally the lad mustered the effort to make eye contact. 'Cheers for the lift,' he said in an attempt to redeem himself.

'Sure.'

* * *

Knox was sneezing so loudly and with such force that he didn't hear DCI Sharp come up behind him on the stairs at Granville Lane.

'That sounds like a potent dose of something nasty,' she said, making a show of holding back slightly from him as they fell into step. 'Keep it to yourself.' A little taller than Knox, she looked as stylish as ever, dressed in one of her trademark trouser suits that even Knox could appreciate made the most of her slender frame and complemented her dark olive skin. 'How did it go yesterday?' she asked.

'Pretty grim,' Knox confessed. 'And, as you can see, I've caught my death.'

'It was a funeral,' she said. 'Someone always does. How was Tom holding up?'

'Not too bad, but he couldn't wait to get away. He kept that bit quiet. You both did.' Knox shot her a look.

'I know,' she said apologetically. 'But he thought that if you got wind of it you'd insist on going with him, and the whole point is that he wants some time on his own; really on his own. Hopefully it'll do him good. He might even stop beating himself up about what happened.'

'With all due respect, ma'am, I don't think there's much chance of that any time soon.'

'Yeah, maybe that's a bit much to expect,' she conceded. 'Meanwhile, if there's anything you need additional support with, let me know.'

'Yes, ma'am.'

Knox had barely sat down and switched on his PC when he glanced up to see Millie come in. She came straight over to him. 'Have you heard the latest on that news story?' she said. 'The gunman on the rampage in Liverpool?'

'I don't think he's on the rampage exactly,' Knox answered, momentarily distracted by the daily bulletin that had appeared on the screen in front of him. 'It looks like he might have killed a couple of people and then made himself scarce, for obvious reasons. What about it?'

'They're saying this morning that he could have escaped into Wales.'

Knox looked expectantly up at her, waiting for the punch line.

'It's where the boss has gone,' Millie said, as if that proved something.

'Wales is a whole country,' Knox reminded her. 'The boss is heading to the middle, and this McGinley is most likely in the north. There's no reason to think they'll be anywhere near each other. And anyway, the Merseyside plods will pick McGinley up soon enough, especially somewhere as remote as north Wales. If that's where he's gone.'

She set her mouth. 'Right.'

She wasn't buying it, Knox could tell. 'Anything else?' he asked, when she didn't move.

'No.'

'Okay,' he said, uncertainly. As Millie finally returned to her desk, Charlie Glover caught his bemused expression and shrugged lightly. 'Pregnant,' he mouthed, as an explanation, drawing a hand around his imaginary swollen belly.

* * *

Knox didn't have time to dwell on Millie's preoccupations. With Mariner away there was plenty to be getting on with; a couple of cases to prepare for the CPS and the follow-up on some bad drugs reported to be circulating the city. First of all though, he put a call through to Terry Dukes, the police community support officer with responsibility for Kingsmead High School. In the last few years it had become increasingly commonplace to base PCSOs within certain secondary schools to monitor pupils' behaviour and to support staff as part of 'Operation Safer Schools.' It was an initiative that had initially horrified Knox and his contemporaries, mainly because of what it said about the changing culture in schools. But the success of the scheme since then couldn't be denied. The mere presence of a uniformed officer had done much to improve communication and even relationships between the police and communities, and had been effective in helping them to stay one step ahead of certain troublemakers.

‘How’s it going?’ Knox asked.

‘All quiet today,’ Dukes said. ‘Though the weather doesn’t help. They’ll be climbing the walls if they can’t get outside at break time.’

‘Is a lad called Michael Purcell on your radar? He’s fourteen, coming up to fifteen, so that would make him . . .’

‘Year ten,’ said Dukes, as Knox was working it out. ‘It’s not a name I know, why?’

‘He’s a neighbour of mine. I think there’s a possibility he might have started smoking weed. Looks harmless at the moment, but can you let me know if he comes to your attention for anything?’

‘Sure. Nothing to do with Jean Purcell, is he?’ asked Dukes.

‘Yes, he’s her boy.’ Knox had forgotten that Jean had supply taught at the high school for a short time, so she would be known to him. ‘Why do you ask?’

‘Just interested. She always seemed a bit . . . how can I put this? Highly strung?’

It was a fair comment. ‘This isn’t coming from her,’ Knox said. ‘I’ve smelt it on him. Just keep a look out for me, will you?’

‘Of course. I’ll let you know if there’s anything to report.’

* * *

Mariner ate breakfast alone in a dim and cheerless dining room, the barmaid in absentia, which at least saved both of them further embarrassment. He’d woken early with a thumping headache, his face wet and the black dog lying heavily on his chest. As always, it had taken him a few seconds to fast forward to the present, bringing everything flooding back to him anew, and now he had a grim church service and the humiliation of the night before to add to his misery.

Fruit, cereals, tea and coffee dispensers were set out buffet-style on the dark oak dresser, along with insulated silver tureens of scrambled eggs and bacon that looked surprisingly fresh and appetizing. To make up for the lack of any human presence the regional radio station gabbled in the background what seemed to be wall-to-wall adverts for local traders. If Mariner could have seen where it was he'd have turned it off. After breakfast he packed his few belongings and checked out, letting the landlord know that he'd be leaving his car in the car park for a few days.

Outside it was cool and fresh; the rain had stopped but gunmetal clouds swept low across the sky, threatening the resumption of the downpour at any time. It could go either way, but hopefully by the time he set off it might have cleared. At his car he began sorting out what he needed to take with him as a minimum. It was a long time since he'd travelled so light, and he had to think hard before stuffing only the essentials into his rucksack: a change of clothes, soap and toothbrush, warm and waterproof clothing, a water bottle and a torch. His hand lighted on the cardboard box Gareth had given him yesterday and, unable to resist, he opened it and took out the scarf, soft cashmere in a golden brown that had perfectly complemented Anna's eyes. He did now what he'd wanted to do yesterday: holding it to his face he breathed in her perfume, and felt his nerve endings burn with pain.

'You sentimental dick,' Anna said, suddenly appearing beside him, a wry smile on her face. 'What's the hell's the matter with you? Last night, and now this? So I'm gone, and yes, it's sad, but I'm not coming back and nothing's going to change that. You've got to get a grip; get over it and move on. For God's sake leave the skanky scarf in the car, or better still, take the whole lot straight to a charity shop.' Mariner couldn't bring himself to do that, but he tucked the scarf back inside the box and left it in the boot.

It was as he was retrieving his map-case from the glove compartment that Mariner spied something shiny lying on the floor in the passenger foot well. A coin, he thought at first, but when he picked it up, he found it was a gold locket, oval in shape and with a red stone set into the centre of it. He hadn't seen anything like it for years, though he remembered a trend for them amongst the girls back when he was in primary school, mostly containing pictures of their pets as he recalled. It wasn't his, and he'd never seen it before. He considered briefly whether it might belong to Millie, but he'd never seen her wear anything like it and anyway she'd been in the driver's seat yesterday. The only other explanation was that his passenger had dropped it last night. Prying it open with a fingernail, Mariner expected to see photographs, but instead found that this one had been used for its original purpose, a lock of white hair curled around the tiny, oval compartment behind wafer-thin glass. The gold had an orangey hue and the pattern was worn, and just beneath the eyelet that a chain would have threaded through, was a series of tiny hieroglyphics — hallmarking that signified the possible value of the piece. Regardless of that, the fact that he carried it with him seemed to signify that it was of considerable sentimental worth to Bryce too. Mariner went back into the hotel, where the manager looked up the number for the Lamb and Flag at Cwm Gwyrdd and invited him to use the phone.

'Is Mr Bryce still there?' Mariner asked when he was connected.

'Who?'

'Jeremy Bryce, a backpacker. He stayed with you last night. Has he left yet?'

'We had no one staying here last night,' the man said. 'We're a pub. We don't have any accommodation.'

'Maybe he just had a drink then,' Mariner said, puzzled. 'He's a big guy, white hair and beard, fifties, educated.'

The landlord sounded genuinely confused. 'We only had locals in here last night, and not many of them, it was such a foul night. You sure you've got the right place?'

'I dropped him off outside,' Mariner explained. 'Is there anywhere else in the village he might have stayed?' Perhaps that's what Bryce had meant. They have rooms *in the village.*

'A couple of people do B&B. You want their numbers?'

'Okay.' It wasn't what Mariner had intended, but he felt duty-bound to call them. However, none of them had put up a hitchhiker called Bryce last night, nor anyone matching his description. Mariner replaced the phone.

'Track him down?' asked the landlord, reappearing.

'No,' said Mariner. 'He must have moved on. Do you know the Lamb and Flag?'

'Of course, nice place,' the hotelier said. 'Owen keeps a good pint.'

'They don't do accommodation then,' Mariner checked.

'Nah. Owen usually sends people here, if he's in the mood to.'

It was odd, Mariner thought, returning to his car. Nothing more than that; just odd. There would be a simple explanation. But why had Bryce implied that he would be staying in the pub, and where had he gone instead, on such a hostile night? Zipping the locket into one of the many pockets on his rucksack, he put it to the back of his mind.

Meanwhile, if he was going to get in the eight miles he'd planned to walk today, he needed to make a start. His first overnight was at a bothy that would, at most, give him a roof over his head and a wooden bench to lie down on, so he needed to buy food to keep him going for the next two days, maybe more in case things didn't go to plan.

The nearest supermarket was a small Co-op that reminded Mariner of the way shopping used to be years ago. The middle-aged woman behind the counter took her time with each customer, enquiring about their health, commenting on the weather, and by the time he'd filled his basket a small queue had formed in front of the checkout counter: a mother with a toddler, an elderly woman in a wool coat and headscarf, a workman with a high-visibility tabard over his donkey jacket. The older woman lingered after completing her purchase and as Mariner stepped forward to be served he caught the tail end of the conversation.

'. . . who shot all those people,' the woman was saying.

'They're after the son, aren't they?'

'Shockin' that. How can someone do that to their own flesh and blood?'

'Well, not the first time, is it? They reckon he might have come down here on the run.'

So, not only had Mariner got his shopping, he'd also learned something. That had never yet happened in his local Tesco Express.

* * *

After he'd eaten, the medication began to kick in and McGinley started to feel a renewed vigour for what lay ahead of him. This last part of his mission would also be the most physically demanding and he had no way of knowing exactly what awaited him or if he was really up to it. He couldn't be so sure of his mark this time either and was relying on second-hand intelligence with no way of establishing how reliable it was. This last target had been much harder to locate, but he'd got there eventually by good luck and common sense. Sometimes it was simply a question of looking in the most obvious place. And now the bastard's chickens were coming home to roost.

Chemotherapy is unpleasant and tedious. It involves a lot of waiting around. And when you've been clearly identified as undeserving scum you can make it time and a half. Usually it was just McGinley and a couple of screws who made the fortnightly trip to the hospital; one to drive and one to escort. But one day he had company; another prisoner with a different type of cancer, but the same fortnightly trip to hospital, co-ordinated so as to 'maximize use of resources.' This was when McGinley's scheme had been conceived. It had started off as nothing more than bravado — each man listing the individuals who had wronged him over the years, and what he would do to them if he ever got out again. It was a way of passing the time. The discussion was borne mostly out of frustration and fear, but the more McGinley talked, the more his ideas began to shape themselves into a plan, taking on a life of their own. And the old git had egged him on. Clinically speaking it was obvious that they were both hopeless cases, but when McGinley suddenly got parole on the strength of it, he didn't know how to break it to the older man. Somehow it didn't seem fair. As it happened the old boy was quite accepting of the situation, smiled and congratulated him. But that was when he made McGinley promise to back up his big mouth. 'Do it for me,' he'd said. 'I'm past it now, but you can make it right.' And now McGinley was going to do just that if it killed him, as it probably would.

He'd done what he could to dry out his damp clothing and had stocked up on essentials, but this would be the real test of his mettle. After a while he got up, put together his things and set off, leaving the caravan park behind him and starting out along the path winding out of the town and heading east into the wilderness.

# Chapter Ten

By the time Mariner emerged again into the blustery breeze, it felt as if the day was half over, but finally he was able to leave the small town behind going west, winding up a rocky bridlc path through ancient woodland. Belonging to the network of drovers' roads that criss-crossed Wales, the track would once have been heavy with the traffic of livestock being herded across the borders for sale at market; a practice that continued well into the twentieth century. The rain had held off so far today, but he'd been careful to stow his waterproofs at the top of his pack, as he felt sure it was only a matter of time until he'd be needing them. The path quickly steepened and as Mariner's boots clumped and scraped over the rocks, his breath began to labour and, finding his rhythm, he waited for that first buzz of elation that always came with the prospect of a few hours' solitary walking. Whilst many people in crisis seek the comfort of others, that had never been Mariner's style and his instinct was for the exact opposite. He needed to be alone, and there were few better places to achieve that than the wilderness of mid-Wales.

He was warm and dry, the weight of his pack had settled comfortably on his shoulders and stretching out before him were miles of open country, green and rugged and straightaway calming. The sheep were back on the hills after wintering in the valleys near the farms, the adult creatures awaiting shearing, their coats dirty and matted alongside the pristine milky-white fleeces of their offspring. But the pain in Mariner's chest remained and however much he tried to divert his thoughts away from her, he couldn't shift the vision of Anna's face, even though this environment was about as alien to her as it could be. Hiking was not something she'd ever considered to be fun. He remembered when he'd first met her, the high-flying businesswoman with the luxury pad and designer clothes. She was about as far from any of his previous girlfriends as it was possible to be, but that quickly became irrelevant.

Becky's parting words were eating away at him, mostly because they confirmed the impression he'd had at the time, though he'd assumed then that it was just wishful thinking on his part. Certainly Anna had seemed delighted enough to see him when they'd met by chance that Saturday in town. He'd replayed every detail of the encounter over and over, in an attempt to cling to those last minutes he'd spent with her. When their relationship ended, Mariner had developed the habit of seeing her everywhere in the guise of other women: his mind playing tricks on him. So when, on this occasion, the woman he'd spotted actually turned out to be her, he felt such a lurch of joy he could hardly contain himself.

*'How are you?' she'd asked him, as if it wasn't written all over his face.*

*'I'm fine,' he'd said, fighting the urge to throw his arms round her. 'What are you doing here?'*

*Her response came as a shock. 'Got a meeting with the wedding planner,' she'd smiled, inclining her head towards the nearby Brackley's department store.*

*'Wow. Congratulations,' he'd managed to say.*

*'Oh God, not for us!' Anna had shrieked. 'That would be a bit premature. It's for Charles and Lottie, you remember them? Lottie wanted some support so I agreed to come, but this is clearly the season to arrange weddings because so far all we've done is to wait in a massive queue, so I've popped out to do a couple of things while Charles is being measured for his suit.'*

*And before he knew it they were sitting opposite each other in a café in the Bullring, overlooking the concourse that led down to St Martin's church and drinking cappuccinos. Mariner was heady from the sight and the smell of her, and had had to consciously restrain himself from touching her. 'I was gutted for a minute there, you know, when I thought it was you and Gareth,' he'd admitted.*

*She smiled. 'I could see that. You haven't got any better at disguising your feelings.'*

*'So how is he?' he'd asked, of Gareth, almost choking on the words. And instead of the enthusiastic response he'd anticipated, she was measured and deliberate with her reply, not wanting to give too much away.*

*'We're taking it slowly,' she'd said, struggling to meet his eye.*

*At the time Mariner's optimism soared, though he tried not to read too much into it. There was no need to press her. If the cracks were beginning to show between her and Gareth it would just be a matter of time.*

Never had ignorance been so blissful or complacent. Less than twelve hours later she would be dead. It had even crossed his mind at the time that they should get a room, so powerful was the attraction. If he'd done that maybe Anna would have stayed; maybe she would have sent a text to Lottie telling them to go ahead without her. But deep down, he knew that it wasn't Anna's style. She wouldn't have let down her friend, even for him. So instead she had made that fateful journey; the one that, thanks to her courage, had ended her life. Why couldn't you have stayed in the car, Anna? Charles was done for. Why couldn't you let it happen? He knew the answer to that one too, of course. It was one of the many reasons he'd loved her, because she could never in her whole life have stood by and let anything 'happen.'

The path ahead of him blurred and a salty taste caught in the corners of his mouth. 'Why the fuck, Anna?' he muttered out loud, as he mentally replayed the scene for the thousandth time.

Lost in these thoughts and weaving his way down a narrow gorge, the ground was slippery underfoot, and piles of soil and scree across the path indicated a recent rock fall. A sudden loud clattering close by startled him into looking up, and straight into the path of a boulder the size of a football, bowling down the cliff towards him. Mariner leapt back, and the rock bounced past him, inches from his head, before tumbling down the hill. As he struggled to keep his balance, the loose stones on the edge of the path gave way and for a moment he flailed on the edge of the thirty-foot drop. Throwing his weight forward, he somehow recovered his equilibrium, breathless and his heart thudding. Jesus. That would have done him some damage if it had hit him. A plaintive bleat came at him from the mist above, sounding almost like an apology. Gazing up there Mariner could see nothing. 'Just watch where you're walking, will you?' he shouted up at the clumsy sheep.

The way-marking on the track was straightforward enough, though at several junctions Mariner had to consult the compass to make his decisions, and as he gained height, up on the fells the wind became stronger and the ground grew increasingly soggy underfoot. For several miles his thoughts remained preoccupied with direction and the physical task of negotiating the terrain, these primal concerns eliminating all others, and finally his mind began to clear. As Mariner climbed higher the cloud pressed down to meet him, and in the middle of the afternoon the rain started again, a heavy downpour that slashed across the hillside. Dumping his pack down on the springy heather, Mariner retrieved his waterproofs as soon as he felt the first wet spots on his face. Pulling his new jacket out he was surprised anew at how flimsy and lightweight the modern fabric seemed compared with his trusty old Berghaus. But he'd been assured by the salesman in the shop that he'd get more warmth and protection from it than a more traditional jacket. There hadn't been much of a choice in colour either, so he'd finished up with dark purple, like Bryce, which wouldn't have been his first choice.

Mariner stopped, reminded of a conversation he'd had with Anna soon after they met, when she'd been disparaging of his customary grey shirts. *You should try fuchsia*, she'd told him. Hm. In the time they were together she changed him in many ways but she never got him into a fuchsia-coloured shirt.

There's a knack to the timing of putting on waterproofs. Too soon and you sweat unnecessarily. Too late and you're already wet and clammy. By the time Mariner had wriggled into his over-trousers and jacket the rain had become a deluge, but he'd made it just in time. Moving up into the cloud, the visibility dropped too, and soon he was walking in a thick mist across the open moorland — criss-crossed with dozens of sheep tracks — entirely reliant on his compass for directions. The landscape that stretched out immediately behind and before him was indistinguishable and Mariner knew it was vital for him not to make a wrong turn up here, or he could end up floundering about for hours in the way that Jeremy Bryce had done the previous day.

He was just beginning to wonder if perhaps he had made the same mistake when suddenly the path dropped away into a narrow gully, with a rocky path that led down to the bothy, a simple stone hut with a slate roof that would shelter Mariner for the night. It was, as he had expected at this time of year, deserted. This place would only be regularly used in the summer, but it was well maintained, probably by local volunteers. Lifting the latch he pushed open the wooden door. Inside it was remarkably dry and peaceful, the solid walls firm against the elements, and smelling comfortingly of wood smoke. It was about the size of an average living room, with a stove to one side and space to cook on the wooden floor, then, at the back, a raised wooden sleeping platform. Many bothies didn't have running water, but this one did at least have an outside tap connected to a water butt. There was a small skylight that would have let in some light, but Mariner had brought his torch for after dark, which wasn't far away.

Dinner that evening was a simple one: bread and cheese, fruit and chocolate biscuits, with a couple of mouthfuls from his hip flask to warm him inside before settling down for the night. Even with the padding of his camping mat the platform was initially hard and uncomfortable, and sleep was a long time coming.

* * *

Tony Knox felt like death warmed up. During the course of the day he'd rubbed several layers of skin off his continually blocked-up nose, whilst coils of barbed wire seemed to have been positioned in his throat and an invisible brace around his head was squeezing his skull tighter as the day wore on. He was sweating and shivering at intervals and in the middle of the afternoon DCI Sharp appeared in her office doorway. 'Go home, Tony,' she ordered. 'You've looked up at that clock ten times in as many minutes. You're not doing anyone any favours by being here spreading your germs around. Get some rest over the weekend and we'll see you on Monday.'

Knox wasn't in any condition to argue. A couple of whiskies and an early night beckoned irresistibly. In the end he couldn't even manage to eat anything and, dosing himself up on paracetamol instead, he went upstairs at just before eight. The relief of sinking into bed and closing his eyes was indescribable, but it didn't last long. He was jolted awake a couple of hours later by the slamming of car doors and yelling on the street just below his window. As he came round he became aware of the insistent *boom-boom* pounding of loud music: Michael's party. Knox groaned. One of the beds was made up in the back bedroom, on the off-chance that Gary or Siobhan should ever stop by, so gathering up his duvet he sought refuge in there, where it was blissfully quiet.

Eventually he fell asleep again only to be woken almost straight away by a louder and more insistent hammering, this time on his own front door. Someone was trying to get his attention. He waited to see if it would stop, which it did, for all of five seconds, before almost immediately starting up again. Crawling out of bed, Knox pulled on jeans and a sweater and descended the stairs, his anger growing with every step. If this was some kid who thought banging on people's doors was a joke . . . He opened the door to a man of around thirty, slim and fair-haired with a thin strap of a beard that signalled the battle against a disappearing jaw-line. He was wild-eyed, a sheen of perspiration covering his face, and he was bouncing on the balls of his feet like he needed a pee. 'You're Tony Knox?' he sounded breathless. 'Jean told me to come and get you. One of the kids has collapsed. I've called an ambulance but we don't know what else to do.'

Knox was instantly awake, the symptoms of his cold reduced to a mere irritation as he tried to get his brain into gear. Outside the blast of icy air revived him a little as he followed the man across the road to where the front door of Jean's house was wide open, kids spilling onto the driveway and out onto the street, one of them, a young lad, throwing up noisily into the hedge. Knox vaulted up the stairs, his senses bombarded by the deafening thud of bass and the heaving mass of shrieking teenagers, and inhaling an atmosphere that was a stuffy mixture of alcohol, perfume and body odour. On the landing a couple of young girls, no more than fourteen, were waiting anxiously, one quietly weeping. 'Is she going to be all right, sir?' she asked the messenger. *Sir?* Christ, if this was Lennox he looked barely out of school himself, thought Knox.

The bathroom was crowded with more young girls and Knox had to force his way through to where a skinny pale youngster with red hair was slumped lifelessly against the side of the bath, eyes closed and her head lolling to one side at an impossible angle. 'Tony, thank God.' Jean was kneeling beside the girl but moved back to let him through. Knox squatted down beside them. Cradling the girl's head, he gently eased her over so that she was lying on her side on the floor in the recovery position. She was out cold, but breathing, and her pulse was regular and felt strong. 'What's her name?' he asked.

'Kirsty,' said Jean.

'Kirsty!' Knox called, gently stroking the girl's cheek with his fingertips. 'Can you hear me, love?' He lifted an eyelid and saw the pupil widely dilated, indicating deep unconsciousness.

'How much has she had to drink?' Knox asked, but suddenly none of the kids would look at him. One of the girls murmured something inaudible.

'What?' Knox's patience was non-existent.

'Kirsty doesn't drink,' the girl eventually spoke up. 'It must be something else.'

'What kind of something else?' The possibilities raced through Knox's mind as he turned to the girl nearest to him, who was standing in the doorway gazing wide-eyed at her friend and sniffling into a tissue. 'What was it? Was it pills?'

'I don't know,' she wailed. 'I think so.'

'Where did she get them?'

Terrified, the kid transferred her gaze from one teacher to the other and back again, fearful of what they'd say. 'I don't know,' she blurted out. 'A guy . . .'

‘Which guy?’ Knox demanded. ‘Go and find him and get him up here!’ He nodded at one of the other girls, bleary-eyed with drink. ‘You go with her.’

Suddenly Knox realized what he should have done straight away and he swore at himself for being so slow. ‘Get the names and contact details of everyone here,’ he commanded Lennox. ‘It’s important. And don’t let anyone leave before they’ve given you an address and a phone number.’

‘But some are already . . .’

‘Do it now!’ Knox yelled. He should have expedited it as soon as he got to the house. Startled into action, Lennox disappeared down the stairs.

In Lennox’s place Knox was relieved to see the green uniforms of two paramedics appear at the top of the stairs. He sat back to let them through, updating them rapidly with what he knew. The girl was still alive, thank God, but they worked quickly to get her on to the stretcher-chair and insert a drip in her arm. As Knox followed them down the stairs, he found that the music had stopped and lights had come on. Kids in varying states of drunkenness were loitering in the hallway, and sitting and lying in the garden outside. They were stunned and frightened by degrees. As the paramedics made their way to the ambulance with their grim cargo, one by one they fell silent and some of the girls started crying again. The boy with the pills was nowhere to be found, nor did any of the girls seem to know who he was or where he had come from. Their descriptions were vague.

‘Anyone here you didn’t recognize?’ Knox asked Jean.

She gave him a helpless smile. ‘Ask me about those I did,’ she said.

‘You’ve contacted Kirsty’s parents?’

Jean nodded wordlessly as Lennox came and stood beside her, slipping his arm around her.

*Definitely more than just a colleague then*, Knox thought absently. ‘Where’s Michael?’ he asked, suddenly.

Jean frowned. 'I don't know.'

A horrible thought crossed Tony Knox's mind. A search of all the rooms turned up nothing, but then coming back past the kitchen he spotted the tell-tale glow of a cigarette at the end of the garden. He went out into the darkness.

'Is she going to be all right?' The tremor in Michael's voice made him sound much younger than his fifteen years, and Knox even wondered if he'd been crying.

'Hard to say,' Knox said, truthfully. He heard something that sounded like a sob. 'It's not your fault, Michael,' he said. 'Not unless it was you who gave her the pill.' He had to ask. 'Was it?'

He expected an outraged, defensive response, but when Michael spoke, his voice was barely audible. 'No.'

'Any idea who might have done?'

'I was downstairs. I hardly saw Kirsty all night.'

'Then you have nothing to blame yourself for. All you did was ask your friends to a party.'

'But if I hadn't . . .'

Aware that the boy was standing close to him, Knox put out a comforting hand to squeeze his shoulder, and was astonished when Michael collapsed into him, his breath coming in wrenching sobs.

## Chapter Eleven

After a day on the move, McGinley was getting into his stride, pack on his back. It had been a thrill getting out of the city — away from the crowded streets and the masses of people — and the memories that came with it were bittersweet. He could remember the first time he'd come out here from the cramped little terraced house, and despite what had happened since, he still looked back on that time as the most amazing adventure. Most of the other kids had been completely freaked by all the open space and had whined to go home again, back to their TVs and record players, but McGinley was enthralled by the drama of the landscape; the huge skies and the towering peaks.

The stuff they did out here was exhilarating and for once it didn't matter that you couldn't write your name, or that you stumbled over every other word in the reading book. He'd gone home and raved about it to Spencer: 'You've got to come too!' So the next year he had. But Spencer was different. Even then McGinley knew it was true, even if he didn't know why. And what had been the making of McGinley turned out to be the breaking of his kid brother. The price of that adventure had been paid in full years later, when life kicked him in the balls yet again, even harder than before. That was when he'd learned once and for all that those you thought you could trust were the most untrustworthy, and that those you thought were your friends could hurt you beyond measure. Right now though, McGinley felt as if he was back in his natural habitat. After years of confinement, crammed into overcrowded cells, the freedom was heady and invigorating and transcended any immediate physical discomfort.

* * *

At more than one point during the night, Mariner was disturbed by rain beating on the skylight of the bothy, but such is the fickle British weather that the next morning when he woke, his shoulder and hip bruised from lying on the hard surface, the sun was shining and a fresh breeze blew white fluffy clouds across the blue sky.

Mariner washed his face under the cold tap and packed up his things, not sure if he would be coming back this way again. His next planned stop was officially no longer listed as a hostel — it was possible that it may even lie derelict — but he was hoping one way or another to be able to stay there. If not, it would be another bothy tonight. As he set off, a skylark trilled high above him, the sun was warm on his back, and today it felt more like June than April. After a while he entered the dense shade of a pine forest, the trees set out in regimented rows in one of the forestry commission's efforts to reforest after the deciduous trees had been torn up. Finding a shady spot, Mariner stopped for lunch. From his vantage point he saw hawks circling high above him, riding the thermals. He dug out his binoculars; as he'd thought, a pair of red kites searching for prey. He watched them for a while until his attention was snagged by a movement down below, too big and too dark to be a sheep; a deer perhaps, but it was gone before he could train the binoculars on it.

From here, the path began to rise higher and opened out on to a rocky ridge that climbed and dipped like the spines on a dinosaur's back. After several miles of undulating footpath, Mariner recognized the shape of the mountain that headed the valley, crested the ridge and saw the land spread out beneath, strangely familiar and yet somehow different. Taking out his binoculars again he scanned the landscape. Immediately below him was the patchwork of meadows belonging to Abbey Farm, though for a while he struggled to make sense of the newly configured territory. Created from a monastery that had been abandoned shortly after the Reformation (Mariner knew this because when he had last stayed here he'd been reminded of its history every other day), parts of the original building lay in ruins, marked out by a series of crumbling walls and archways. The main farmhouse was distinctive; a plain red-brick building with Jacobean features, one of which had definitely not been the dozen or so shiny solar panels that now covered the roof like the protective shell of a tortoise.

The motley collection of rundown outhouses at the back of the main house had also been joined by a sleek prefabricated steel shed that had yet to tarnish in the elements. And alongside this were a couple of small and modest wind turbines. The absence of cows in the outlying fields was unsurprising; Mariner had seen enough evidence of the extent to which the foot and mouth epidemic of 2001 had decimated the dairy farming industry out here. But instead it looked as if the land immediately surrounding the farm was being cultivated; there were three or four fields covered with white poly tunnels that gave the illusion of a covering of snow. But the climate was so inhospitable here it was difficult to know what could possibly be growing beneath them.

Beyond the farm, running along the valley north-east to south-west, or as Mariner saw it, from left to right, the road and river ran in parallel, their course marked out by a wide band of dense deciduous woodland, broad at one end like the shape of a giant comma, the high branches in the trees dotted with crows' nests. Beyond that end of the woods, the land opened out again onto Gwennol Hall, the estate and country home of Lord Milford. Its rolling acres of parkland were dotted with mature trees — a clear indication of the wealthy land-owning classes — with the imposing grey edifice of the hall in the centre. Between those two properties, strung out along the road and hidden by the trees from this angle, was Mariner's destination: the village of Caranwy. He could just see the two tiny dormer windows of a hostel attic poking out between the high branches. From here it looked as if little had changed in terms of development. As he stood watching a shot rang out, echoing around the hills. Mariner started for a moment until remembering where he was; it would be either clay-pigeon shooting or automatic bird-scarers, both completely harmless. Context is everything, he thought wryly.

Mariner swept the scene with the binoculars once more and they came to rest on the farm. A movement attracted his attention and into his line of vision, behind the outbuildings, came two men in conversation. The powerful ten-by-forty-two lenses of the binoculars brought the figures close enough to seem within reach and two factors made the scene compelling. One was the contrast in their attire. Although both men looked young, one was casually dressed in jeans, and a blue-and-white checked shirt, but the other was more formal and strangely out of place in the environment, wearing a dark suit, tight across the shoulders, complete with tie. Mariner remembered the misapprehension of the barmaid in The Star and immediately thought *sales rep*, though he could see no BMW parked nearby. The other interesting factor was their body language. Both men were leaning in, shoulders back, like two young stags squaring up. Either one of them was hard of hearing, or Mariner was about to witness some kind of confrontation . . .

But in the few seconds that Mariner stood watching, the dispute — if that was even what it was — seemed to be amicably resolved, as the man in the suit visibly relaxed, clapping the other companionably on the shoulder. There followed an awkward handshake, of the kind Mariner had seen many times on the street corners of Birmingham. Then, in perfect synchronization, both men looked skyward, as Mariner too became aware of the low pulsating throb of rotor blades. Rising up from behind Gwennol Hall came a small, private helicopter that flew out over the estate and farm, roared over Mariner's head and disappeared over the mountain behind him, into the blackening sky. When he looked back at the farm, the two men had gone. At the same time he felt the first splattering of rain on his head.

Stowing his binoculars, Mariner set off down the mountain towards the Caranwy valley, picking up a footpath he'd trodden many times before, and he confidently followed its winding course down off the tops, over craggy outcrops and into the pastureland below. Where the land began to flatten out, the path became a muddy bridleway that ran between hedges, the fields of Abbey Farm on either side, sloping down towards the forest-covered ravine — at the bottom of which ran the river. This was an infrequently used trail and as he approached the woodland became increasingly overgrown.

At the edge of the woods he came to a dry-stone wall with an integral stile and a crudely painted way mark pointing both left and right. He climbed over it and under the cover of the trees just as the shower really took hold. The woodland covered several square acres with a network of footpaths, and Mariner had two options for getting to a river crossing. To the right would take him a mile or so along the trail to a rudimentary bridge that used to comprise just a couple of rotting old railway sleepers, then through more woodland and up on to the road. To the left would take him out into the parkland and on to the drive of the Milford estate, to cross the river by a wide stone bridge that supported Gwennol's grand entrance gates. He chose that as the more reliable option, taking care to assess his bearings regularly and avoid going round in circles. All went effortlessly at first, but after about twenty metres the grass grew longer and intermingled with brambles and ivy that got gradually thicker until Mariner was waist-high in them, the path indistinguishable and the ground beneath lumpy and uneven. The rain had penetrated the trees here, making it muddy underfoot and several times, despite his boots, Mariner rolled over on to his ankle. Cursing and swearing to himself, he persevered, ploughing his way through while thorns clawed at his clothing, until finally he came to a complete physical and metaphorical brick wall.

Mariner consulted his map. Bought specially for this trip, it was bang up to date and clearly indicated the public right of way through the grounds of the estate. He could just see the main hall, concealed behind clumps of trees way off to his left. This was definitely where the path went, crossing into the country park for about a hundred metres to meet the long driveway, which went over the bridge, with pedestrian access through the impressive gates, and out on to the road. But with a blatant disregard for the right of way, the dilapidated stile had been all but removed and the public footpath sign broken off and thrown to one side. The wire fence bordering the estate was topped with loops of lethal razor wire, with a particularly unfriendly sign stating that trespassers would be prosecuted.

A further notice advertised the name of the security company patrolling the grounds, along with a sketch of one of the vicious-looking dogs they employed. Row upon row of sapling conifers had also been planted, which in the not-too-distant future would provide a dense screen. Someone was apparently keen to protect their privacy, which must have been a sudden development. Lord

Milford, Mariner remembered, had been well liked by the community and there had never been any issue about access to his land. Clearly his successor had different ideas. It confirmed what Mariner had already guessed from the helicopter: that the old and highly traditional lord had been succeeded by a young and modern heir.

For a few moments Mariner weighed up the risks of being bloody-minded and following the official footpath. Legally he was in the right and would be able to prove it in court. But that was a long way from the immediate physical threat of tearing his hands to shreds on razor wire, followed by a savage attack from a Doberman or two. Such security signs were often there for deterrent purposes only, and not necessarily backed up by the real thing, but whilst he couldn't see any animals anywhere, he had been conscious since dropping into the valley of a persistent barking somewhere not far away, and as further proof there was a fresh and disturbingly large turd on the other side of the fence.

Irritating as it was, the most sensible course of action was for Mariner to retrace his steps back along the path and take the alternative route to the wooden bridge, in the hope that it had been upgraded since he was last here. He was in for a disappointment. The crossing remained as flimsy and insubstantial as he remembered it and, if anything, had deteriorated in the intervening years. Mariner didn't fully trust it to take his weight, on top of which, months of sustained rainfall had created the added hazard of a deep and fast-flowing river rushing along immediately beneath it. It was always a toss-up in this situation of whether to tread slowly and carefully or get it over with quickly: Mariner chose the latter. Running across the planks, he made a lunge for the opposite bank, where he backslid for several agonizing seconds before he was able to grab on to a thorny branch that tore into the palms of his hands. It enabled him to get his balance and he was able to push on into the brambles and climb up to the dry-stone wall bordering the road. A scramble over the stile and he was on the road, breathless and with a pounding heart. 'Christ, I'm getting too old for this,' he gasped to himself, though on the plus side, the rain had stopped.

## Chapter Twelve

Out on the lane Mariner followed the wall along and into the village. There was a straggling main street of grey stone buildings, in total no more than about two dozen houses, among them a row of tied cottages, a chapel and a pub but little else. The post office looked as if it had long ago closed and been converted into residential accommodation, though the sign for the White Hart looked freshly painted. Then on past the end of the street, as he rounded a corner, the hostel, a two-storey L-shaped stone farmhouse, set back behind a yard and an open five-bar gate, came into view. A murmur of nostalgia tickled Mariner's stomach. The absence of a sign, a pale triangle on the moss-covered wall marking out the place where it had once been, confirmed what he already knew: that the hostel had long been closed to the public. Scaffolding erected around one end of the barn-like structure indicated that work was being done on it, or even that it could be in danger of collapse, but curtains at the windows made what used to be the warden's wing appear inhabited, and there was saturated washing on the line in the garden; child-sized T-shirts and a dress, the significance of which was not wasted on him.

All along, once the idea for this trip had crystallized, Mariner had never been naïve enough to think that things wouldn't be different here. His purpose, he'd told himself, was to revisit the places that had been important to him as a young man. But at the back of his mind had lain the possibility that he might also encounter some old friends along the way. Now it all seemed like a big mistake. Never in his life had he allowed himself to wallow in nostalgia, so why was he breaking that rule now? He couldn't imagine for a minute why he'd thought that it would help him to deal with the pain of losing Anna.

In all probability the complex would have been bought up many years ago by a couple of ex-London stockbrokers living out their rural idyll, and he'd be about as welcome as Judas at a disciples' reunion.

For the second time that afternoon Mariner was forced to realistically consider his options, the most sensible of which was to cut his losses and continue on through the village to the next climber's hut. It was about five miles away, but he would just about make it before dark, and would be passing through a couple of villages along the way, where, if he felt like it, he could succumb to a cosy B&B instead. He'd half turned and was about to double back the way he'd come, when she appeared from behind the house and Mariner's heart bounced in his chest. Slender and willowy, dressed in a grey Fair Isle sweater, jeans and boots, she exuded the air of casual chic that he remembered so well. Hard to imagine that this vision of femininity could competently handle a twelve-bore and skin a rabbit without flinching. Her thick raven-black hair was cut to her shoulders now and threaded through with grey. But it was her all right. Sensing his presence she looked up suddenly, green eyes framed with dark lashes, and saw him watching her.

'Hello?' She looked wary.

'Hello,' Mariner croaked, his voice catching. He cleared his throat. 'I see that the hostel isn't open any more but I wondered if there would be any chance of staying the night. I'm prepared to rough it.'

Straightening, she frowned with suspicion. 'Why on earth would you want to do that?'

'Sentimental reasons,' he said, testing her out.

She was studying him curiously. 'Do I know you?'

'You did once. How good's your memory?'

For several moments she said nothing, and when she did at last speak, it was with amused incredulity. 'Tom? Tom Mariner?'

'Hey, I'm impressed.' Mariner tapped the side of his head. 'Not much wrong with your little grey cells.'

'My God,' she looked stunned. 'How long has it been?'

'Too long. Twenty-five years?'

'Nearer thirty,' she corrected him. 'You took your time coming back.'

Mariner laughed. 'I can't quite believe you're still here.'

And finally she broke into a wide smile and came towards him. After a brief, awkward hug, they stood for a moment, uncertain of what to do. Too much like strangers after all this time, the past intimacies a distant memory.

'You've hardly changed,' Mariner said, lamely.

She pushed her hair back off her face, suddenly self-conscious. 'Me? You're kidding aren't you? I'm falling apart at the seams — hair going white, reading glasses. But *you* look exactly the same,' she said. 'And still carrying your home on your back.'

'Yeah, although at my age I'm not sure that it's a positive thing.'

'I might have to agree with you about that. Well you'd better come in.' She tilted her head towards the house. 'We've got some catching up to do.'

Mariner hesitated. 'It won't be an intrusion?'

'Bit late for that, isn't it? What were you planning to do — show up after all these years, say hello and then bugger off again?'

'Not exactly, no.'

'Well then, get your backside in here.' She disappeared into the house, so Mariner followed.

'It looks different,' was his first comment, walking into the light, airy kitchen, with its limed oak cupboards and stainless-steel appliances, though the farmhouse table and the Aga were still there.

Elena went to the sink and filled the kettle. 'What? You think I wouldn't have altered anything in all this time? We don't live in a time warp out here, you know. We even have central heating now, though admittedly that was put in by the last owners.'

Mariner took off his rucksack, stowing it by the door, and pulled out a chair, scraping it over the stone flags. 'So you haven't always lived here?'

Elena leaned back on the counter, shaking her head. 'When I got married I moved to the town, and then Dad got to the point where he needed to go into a nursing home and this place was too isolated for him.'

'God, your dad.' Mariner remembered the hefty farm worker with his great bellow of a laugh. 'He was scary.'

'Not at the end he wasn't. He got dementia; had to be cared for like a toddler.'

'I'm sorry. Do you think he ever knew about us?'

'Of course he did,' she grinned. 'And he'd never have let you get away with it if he hadn't liked you. As a matter of fact he used to ask after you from time to time. I think he was disappointed you didn't stick around.' She fixed him with a pointed gaze.

Even after all this time Mariner felt bad about it and had to look away, feigning an interest in the rest of the room. 'I was too young,' he said eventually, aware of how inadequate that sounded. 'I'd have been no good to you. Hadn't a clue what I was going to do with myself.' It occurred to him that not much had changed on that front either.

'Don't worry.' Her voice was devoid of rancour. 'I got over it — you.'

Mariner took the proffered mug of tea from her and watched her pull out the chair opposite him and sit down, resting her elbows on the table, the mug balanced between her fingers. 'So you're married,' he said, at the same time observing the engagement ring on her right hand.

'*Was*,' she said, emphatically.

'Anyone I know?'

She shook her head. 'He was a waste of space, except I didn't realize it until after the kids were born.' A tabby had wandered into the kitchen and came over to rub itself against her chair; she reached down to stroke it. 'When he gave me a divorce I wasn't sure what to do, but this place was back on the market and at a decent price. Dad was gone and had left me some money, so I bought them out. I'm looking to run it as a B&B eventually, though as you can see, there's a bit of work to be done yet.'

'I was sure the place would have been bought up by townies,' Mariner said.

'Oh, it was to begin with. When the YHA sold it, back in the late eighties, it went to a couple who decided after about six months that they couldn't hack it in the country. But we still get our fair share of ex-bankers and city types; plenty of holiday properties round and about. The difference is that they tend to get on with the renovations a bit quicker. Rex and I are doing this place up bit by bit and we're pretty strapped most of the time, so we have to rely on local lads moonlighting and doing it as a favour. It's going to take forever.'

'Rex?'

'My partner.'

So there was someone. Mariner had always assumed it would be so, but nonetheless he felt an irrational pang of disappointment. He hoped it didn't show. 'And your kids?' he asked.

'My son Gethyn went away on a gap year and hasn't come back yet; he's in Australia at the moment, so it's just me and Cerys, my eleven-year-old.' She looked up at him. 'What about you? You must be married? Kids?'

'No on both counts, though I've come close.' It hurt to say it.

She studied him. 'Hmm, that doesn't really surprise me. You always were pretty self-contained. So what have you been doing with yourself? You had some mad idea about joining the police when you were here, though I could never quite see it.'

For the second time that day Mariner half wished he'd brought his warrant card. Instead he gave a mock salute. 'Detective Inspector Tom Mariner,' he said, 'at your service.'

'Wow. Well, that's put me in my place, hasn't it? Good thing I never went in for astrology.'

'No future in it,' Mariner said, unable to resist. 'And you?'

'Oh, I've never really settled to anything much. Aside from doing up this place I work part time doing a bit of counselling in the town; bereavement, that kind of thing. I got into it after Dad . . . you know. But whatever else my ex might have been, he's always had a good job and been pretty consistent with the child support, so I've no room for complaint there.'

Tyres rumbled over the cattle grid out in the yard, a car door slammed shut and moments later a young girl came in, with long black hair and wide green eyes. No mistaking her heritage. 'Hi, Mum . . .' Seeing Mariner, she broke off.

'Cerys, this is Tom, an old friend of mine.'

'Hello, Cerys.'

'Hello.' She barely gave him a glance before dropping her school bag and heading straight for the fridge.

'Not too much now,' warned Elena, in what seemed to be a comfortable routine. 'You'll be having your tea soon.' The response was a mere grunt and the girl took her snacks and left the kitchen, her departure swiftly followed by the unmistakable burbling of a TV set.

'So how would you feel about me staying here tonight, in the hostel, I mean, for old times' sake?' Mariner asked.

'Well, on principle I've no objection, but you should know that the place is as derelict as it looks. We haven't even got round to fixing all the holes in the roof yet, so some of the rooms are uninhabitable, but we can probably find you a bed somewhere that's more or less dry.'

'I'll pay you,' Mariner said. 'And of course you'll get your reward in heaven.'

'Yeah, if only I believed in all that crap.'

'What, you don't go to chapel anymore?' Mariner pretended to be shocked. Sunday attendance had, as he remembered, been imperative.

'Not since I found out the Reverend Aubrey had been making improper advances to several youngsters in the village, no,' said Elena.

'You're kidding.'

'Not the kind of thing I joke about,' she said. 'That said, I'm not sure how true it was; you know how rumours can spread.'

'Was he charged?'

'Nah, it never got that far. I think he claimed that there had been some misunderstandings and everyone believed him. I didn't know that much about it at the time. It was back in the days before the clergy had developed their reputation, so even if there was something in it, it would have been much harder to make a case.'

'Did he ever try anything with you?' Mariner asked.

She smiled. 'Luckily, I didn't have the right equipment. I think his preference was for little boys.'

'So what happened to him?'

'Nothing much. By the time all this emerged he was pretty close to retirement anyway and he still lives up the valley, away from the village though and pretty isolated. You'll have seen his cottage as you came down off the tops. He lives quietly and doesn't bother anyone.'

Mariner drained his mug and replaced it on the table.

'What have you done to your hand?' she asked, seeing the gash torn by the bramble.

'Argument with a thorny branch,' Mariner said. 'It's fine, though I wish I'd had my ID with me,' Mariner said, obliging her. 'I might have challenged that re-routing of the footpath next to the estate.'

'Ah, so you've found the battle line. That thin strand of razor wire is the only thing that's keeping the residents of Abbey Farm and Gwennol Hall from tearing each other to pieces.'

'And here was me thinking it was all peace and loveliness out here. So what's the difference of opinion?'

'Not so much a difference of opinion as an ideological gulf,' said Elena.

'The humble farmer taking on the landed gentry?'

'Not quite; capitalist baron versus liberal leftie is more like it.'

'Let me guess. The capitalist is the one with the guard dogs. That doesn't seem like batty Lord Milford's style.'

'Oh, Lord Milford's long gone. The old man passed on about ten years ago and since then the estate's fallen into Russian hands.'

'Isn't it the tradition normally to hand over to the son and heir?' Mariner queried.

'Unfortunately in this case the son and heir was a waster. Long before he died the old man tried to get him to take over the running of the estate, but it didn't really work out.'

'That sounds like a deliberate understatement.'

'You could say that. The young viscount was more concerned with enjoying himself than running the estate.

There was a half-hearted attempt to do it up and open it to the public for a while, and he even tried to promote it as a venue for weddings.'

'It had a certain shabby charm to it, as I remember,' Mariner said.

'Maybe, but out here there was never going to be enough passing trade to make it work. The next money-making venture was to sell off some of the tied cottages in the village to raise some cash.'

'I bet that went down well,' Mariner said, sardonically.

'Oh yes. They were sold as holiday lets, so the families living in them at the time had about six months' notice.'

'That smells of desperation.'

'I think while the old man was still alive Milford junior felt compelled to try and make a go of it for his father's sake, but it was all just for show. As soon as Lord Milford passed away the hall went up for sale. So now we have our very own Russian oligarch, known locally as *the Czar*, mainly because his name is pretty much unpronounceable.'

Mariner laughed. 'That's a bit rich coming from a bunch of people who don't believe in the use of vowels. So what dodgy dealings has he been involved in to make his money?'

'To be honest, I don't know. Cerys could probably tell you more than I can. Her best friend's mum works up there as a cleaner.'

'Well, at least he's supporting the local labour force,' Mariner remarked.

'By employing a couple of domestics?' Elena was determined to remain unimpressed. 'He's kept on the estate manager, Phil Bevan too, but that's the extent of it. All his other staff have come with him. Not that it's of any consequence. He has nothing to do with us locals, except when he's in residence to remind us of his presence with his wretched helicopter several times a day.'

'A chopper flew over on my way here,' Mariner recalled.

‘That’s nothing. Last weekend he had one of his regular house parties. He has some high-profile friends and guests at his soirées and the air traffic was pretty constant.’

‘That sounds annoying.’

‘Quite a few of us have petitioned the local council to see if anything can be done. The farmers complain about it upsetting the livestock, and the holiday cottage brigade who come out here for a weekend of peace and quiet don’t appreciate the disturbance either.’

‘Don’t tell me you’re on their side now? You used to resent the weekenders like mad.’

Gathering Mariner’s empty mug alongside hers, Elena got up to put them in the sink. ‘We don’t go around burning their cottages down any more, if that’s what you think. We’re quite civilized these days; all part of our acceptance of the evolving economy. Come on, let’s go and look at the accommodation while you’ve still got time to change your mind and book a room at the pub.’

## Chapter Thirteen

Stepping back into the youth hostel, that unique smell of cooked food, musty blankets — and, in this case, the pervasive smell of damp — took thirty years off Mariner's life in an instant, projecting him back to the successive summers he'd spent hitching around the country staying in accommodation just like it, one or two nights at a time, sometimes more. It had been a liberating existence, during the course of which Mariner had met some fascinating characters. Most of the places he'd stayed in back then no longer existed; few people these days would put up with such basic amenities, or the enforced separation of the sexes. Not that there weren't ways around that particular rule. Over those summers Mariner had enjoyed several liaisons. There had been no shortage of young women, mostly blonde and bronzed Australian girls, as he recalled, who for some inexplicable reason seemed to find him attractive.

Caranwy had been one of Mariner's longer sojourns, taking up five or six weeks, thanks to the dual attractions of some paid labouring work on the nearby Abbey Farm and his relationship with a certain local girl. Walking the creaking floorboards, he could almost hear the voices of the other hostellers he'd shared with during that time: the compulsory gaggle of foreign students, several middle-aged couples — usually teachers — with their belligerent kids and the occasional lone male of indeterminate age. These days the latter would be treated with some suspicion, and statistically he'd since realized it made sense that some of them must have been there for not entirely wholesome reasons.

He followed Elena along the short hallway past the boot room on the right and the kitchen to the left and climbed the steep stairs to the first landing with its communal shower and bathroom, two larger bunk rooms, for males and females respectively, plus a couple of smaller rooms set aside for couples and families — less of a priority back in the days before the YHA had become family friendly. Both of the larger dorms were in a state, a big damp patch and the ceiling wallpaper peeling off in chunks in the one, a badly cracked window letting in a draught in the other. Mariner was beginning to wonder if this had been such a good idea after all. Elena was clearly thinking the same. 'I'd have you to stay at my place,' she began. 'But with Cerys . . .'

'Of course,' said Mariner. 'That's fine.'

'It's just that she sees her dad a couple of times a week. He's got used to Rex being around but if he hears about someone else and gets the wrong idea . . . He can be a bit of a prick sometimes.'

'It's okay,' Mariner reassured her. 'I wasn't expecting anything. In fact if this is going to make life difficult for you . . .'

'No, you're all right. Let's see along here.' She led the way along the landing to one of the smaller rooms, which looked in much better condition. Facing south-west, a weak, late afternoon sun had broken tentatively through the cloud and was taking the chill off the air, and the windows and ceiling seemed to be intact. Mariner put his rucksack on one of the two sets of bunks.

'This will do fine,' Mariner said, testing the mattress. 'It's loads more comfortable than where I slept last night.'

'I can give you some aired blankets, and there's a portable heater knocking around somewhere,' said Elena. 'It'll get even colder during the night. The showers are on the electric, so they should be okay. And you can come and eat with us if you'd like to.'

'I really don't want to impose,' Mariner said, truthfully. 'That wasn't the idea.'

She smiled. 'So you said. It's fine. Rex is over tonight so you'll be able to meet him. Do you still play chess?'

Mariner pulled a face. 'God, probably not since your dad repeatedly annihilated me all those years ago, why?'

'Cerys is taking on the family tradition and she can already outplay me most of the time. She'd love a new opponent.'

Mariner grimaced. 'Sounds as if she'll destroy me too.'

'Better brush up on your Sicilian defence then,' Elena smiled. 'I'm sure there's an old set down in the games room somewhere you can practice with. We'll see you at six.'

Mariner flashed a humourless smile. 'Thanks.'

'Oh,' she called back, as an afterthought. 'Don't try locking the door behind you when you come over, it sticks solid anyway and you'll never get it open again.'

After Elena had gone, Mariner sat down on the lower bunk and for a few minutes simply savoured the environment. Much as he had anticipated this moment, he hadn't really expected it to become a reality, and so far he hadn't been disappointed on any count; not with the accommodation anyway. This was the room he remembered most vividly. Because he'd spent the whole summer here, there were times when he'd had the hostel to himself. It was on one such night that Elena had come to him. He'd woken with a start in the small hours, alerted by a movement in the room. Opening his eyes he saw a figure beside the bed, still and staring down at him. 'Are you awake?'

'Shit,' said Mariner. 'I thought I was seeing a ghost.'

Elena giggled. 'How many ghosts do you know that wear winceyette pyjamas?' she whispered. 'Not very sexy, I know, but it gets cold up here.'

'I'd noticed,' said Mariner. He didn't know quite what to do. He'd never had a girl present herself to him like this. She sat beside him on the edge of the bed and slid a hand under the bedclothes. 'Well, are you going to let me in before I freeze my tits off?'

Mariner lifted up the edge of the sheets and blankets and, pulling off the pyjamas, she slid into the narrow bed alongside him, as simultaneously her lips fastened on to his. Her flesh was soft, warm and giving, and in seconds he was hard, burrowing into her and making her moan. It had been the start of his first proper relationship that had lasted the whole summer under the watchful eye of her overprotective father, which had given their encounter a special frisson, even though it turned out now that he'd known about it all along.

The room overlooked the yard and beyond, along the lane towards the farm, but afforded enough privacy, so he walked naked along to the bathroom. The showers were communal, modesty protected only by flimsy nylon curtains. The sinks in the shower room were too low to be practical, still at the height they would have been when this place was some kind of outward-bound centre for city kids back in the sixties and seventies. Mariner turned on one of the showers. It spluttered and for a few seconds the water ran brown, but the flow soon ran smooth and clean and, as Elena promised, was hot within seconds.

After the shower he changed into a clean shirt but decided against shaving. His beard was starting to establish itself and would soon be beyond the itchy stage, so easier to just let it grow. With a few minutes to spare, he took time to explore the hostel, re-orientating himself, and wondering again how sensible this whole enterprise really was. Rationalizing his behaviour, after all the turmoil of the last few weeks, this was probably some pathetic attempt to find a safe haven, coming back to a place that represented one of the rare times in his life when he had felt genuinely secure and happy. But now he was here he couldn't clearly identify what it was he had expected to achieve. He'd been unbelievably lucky with the gamble that Elena would recognize him and make him welcome, but now what? All he was really doing was gate-crashing the life she had built for herself, and he had no right to do that. He'd stay here one night and then move on.

Shortly before six, Mariner left the hostel and walked back over to Elena's cottage. A mud-spattered Volvo estate was now parked in the yard, and Mariner had been in the kitchen just a few seconds when a man appeared from upstairs, stocky and with a ruddy outdoor complexion, his dark hair cut in an old-fashioned short back and sides that was greying at the temples. 'Hello, you must be Tom,' he said, crossing the kitchen in two strides and squeezing Mariner's hand in a firm grasp. 'Rex Monroe.' Mariner stood at six feet tall, but he felt dwarfed by this man, who was perhaps no taller, but seemed equally wide, muscular and strong, his physical presence dominating the whole room. It was an effect compounded by the loud checked shirt he wore tucked into jeans.

'Good to meet you,' said Mariner. 'I hope you don't mind my just showing up like this.'

'Not at all.' The sentiment seemed authentic although the eyes remained a little wary. 'I'd heard about you before, so it's good to put a name to the face.'

'Really?' Mariner was taken aback.

'Don't get too excited,' Elena chipped in cheekily. 'I forgot all about you years ago. It was Dad who used to mention you from time to time, especially when his mind started to go.' She walked over to the kitchen door and called into the lounge. 'Cerys, your tea's ready.'

'Beer?' Rex offered, gesturing Mariner to one of the chairs.

'Great, thanks.'

They sat round the kitchen table to eat, with the TV on low in the background. When the men had finished their beer they moved on to wine.

'It's a decent bottle,' Rex said, pouring Mariner a generous glass of something French and red.

'Can't compete with any of the stuff Bob Sewell used to produce though,' Elena said, lifting her glass. 'Cheers.'

'Cheers.' Mariner smiled at the memory of the farmer. 'His cellar was a revelation. He was the last person on earth you'd have expected to be an expert on that sort of thing. Not that I was old enough to appreciate any of it.'

'Oh, he knew his stuff all right,' Rex agreed. 'He's put it to good use now, too. That's where he's gone, retired to the Loire valley where he owns half a vineyard.'

'Wow.' Mariner was genuinely surprised. 'Who'd have thought?'

'He was helped on his way by circumstances,' Elena said. 'The cellar at the farm is a natural cave that links up to a whole network of limestone tunnels round here, so when we had a particularly bad rainfall in 1998 his whole collection got flooded out. It ruined thousands of pounds worth of vintage stuff. Then a couple of years later, when foot and mouth struck, he decided that it would be sensible to up sticks and go to where the weather was warmer and where he could make his own wine instead of just collecting other people's. He's doing well at it by all accounts. We get a card from him every Christmas, along with a couple of bottles.'

'You're from round here then, Rex,' Mariner said.

'Llangybi,' Rex said, naming one of the numerous outlying villages, 'though I spent a few years in

Aberystwyth. Came back — ooh, must be going on twelve years now.'

'We ran into each other in Tregaron,' Elena said. 'Rex's firm handled the power of attorney application for Dad.'

'You're a solicitor,' Mariner deduced. So much for the rugged outdoors look.

Rex grinned. 'Yeah, don't quite look the part, do I?' He knew he'd had Mariner fooled.

'So how do *you* know my mum?' Cerys piped up, suddenly, fixing Mariner with a gaze.

'I stayed here once, a long time ago,' Mariner said. 'We were friends.'

She absorbed that. 'Were you her boyfriend?'

For some unaccountable reason, Mariner felt his colour heightening, and he glanced across at Elena and Rex, who both seemed to be enjoying this turn of conversation rather too much. 'Yes, I suppose I was.'

'Why did you stop being her boyfriend?'

'Oh, I'm sure your mum could explain . . .'

'No, you're doing fine; carry on,' said Elena, far too entertained for Mariner's liking.

'Well, I went back home to Birmingham, but your mum stayed here, so that was that.'

'This was in the days before we had texting or Facebook,' Elena reminded her daughter. 'We had to rely on real letters delivered by the postman.'

'We didn't even have mobile phones,' Mariner added. 'If I wanted to talk to your mum without my mum overhearing I had to walk down the road to the phone box.'

Cerys was regarding them both with fascination, as if they were weaving fairy stories. 'But didn't you visit?' she asked Elena.

'I did once, but it wasn't really the same.'

Mariner remembered that weekend. It was pretty bloody awkward as he recalled, his mother insisting that Elena sleep in the guest bedroom.

'Mum said you're a policeman.' Cerys had moved on.

'That's right.'

'Like Ryan.' She looked enquiringly at her mum, who shrugged.

'I suppose so.' Elena glanced at Mariner. 'A friend of ours,' she said, dismissively. 'Anyway,' she said to Cerys. 'Tom was asking about the Czar. And as you're the local expert . . .'

Cerys wrinkled her nose. 'What do you want to know?'

'Where he made his money,' said Mariner. 'I could do with some tips.'

'It was timber originally as I understand it,' said Rex. 'Though I think he owns a few media companies and that kind of thing.'

'How do you know all that?' asked Elena.

'He's doing a bit of business with the firm,' Rex said.

'Is he?' She seemed a bit put out. 'What kind of business?'

'Well, it might turn out to be something or nothing,' Rex said. 'He's asked us to look at some of the land demarcations. That historian who's working for him has uncovered documents that suggest some kind of anomaly on the boundary of the estate; there seems to be some question about the ownership of several acres that border it.'

'Which several acres?' asked Elena.

'I can't tell you that, love. Until we've established that there's a case to answer we haven't even told the current owners of that land; there's no point. My feeling is that an explanation will be found and it will just fizzle out. Meanwhile, if Mr Shapasnikov is happy to send some of his considerable fortune our way, we're just as happy to take it.'

'Making hay while the sun shines,' Mariner said.

Rex grinned. 'Something like that.' He cast each of them in turn a meaningful look. 'Needless to say, this must all stay within these four walls.'

'Of course,' said Mariner.

'Well, there you go,' said Elena, gathering up their empty plates. 'I've learned something tonight.'

'Can we play chess now?' Cerys asked Mariner eagerly. Barely waiting for a response, she produced a traditional rubberwood set and laid it out on the table.

Mariner felt ludicrously apprehensive facing the eleven-year-old. 'Sure you don't want to play dominoes?' he asked, blatantly buying time. 'I'm much better at dominoes.'

Cerys rolled her eyes and held out closed fists containing white and black pawns. Mariner indicated the one nearest him and was rewarded with the black. She would go first. She started confidently and, as Elena had said, had clearly inherited the family gene.

After a couple of moves though, bits of strategy started to come back and Mariner felt confident enough to continue the conversation. 'The new owners have made a few improvements up at Abbey Farm,' he observed, making his move.

'Yes, that's changed a bit since Bob went,' Elena said. 'Not everyone thinks it's for the better, but we get on with them okay.'

Cerys made her move and Mariner studied the board. 'Who's them?'

'It's owned by a guy called Willow,' Elena said. Mariner looked up at her and she rolled her eyes in response. 'I know. His real name is Nigel Weller, but Willow is his "new age" name. The place was pretty rundown when he bought it, let me see, must have been about 2001. He's from out your way actually — Birmingham or Solihull?'

'Don't let anyone from Solihull hear you say that,' Mariner warned. 'There's a big difference, you know. Though neither is particularly known for its agriculture.' He moved his rook across to block an attack from Cerys.

'I don't think his background is farming exactly, but it started off as experimental,' Rex said. 'He runs it as a sort of eco project; a farm that runs more or less self-sufficiently to produce organic vegetables and other stuff.' He raised his eyebrows at Mariner. 'You want to watch your queen there,' he murmured.

'Rex!' Cerys protested. She moved her bishop decisively to threaten Mariner's king and distract him.

'That's no easy task in this climate,' said Mariner, frowning. He blocked with his knight.

'From what I understand, Weller was a chemist by profession and has developed some kind of new soil treatment,' Rex went on. 'A fertilizer, I suppose, that raises the temperature of the soil and allows things to grow in less hospitable climates for a greater part of the year and gives good crop yields.'

'That sounds ambitious. Does it work?'

'He's been there going on for ten years now. It's taken a while to get it all up and running and to begin with he relied on volunteers to help him out. The farm was operated along communal lines with people who used to come out here to work on it just for short periods, students and the like, although inevitably some of them ended up staying. Now he seems to manage with a small core who have been there a while.'

'And it's enough to turn a profit?' Mariner asked.

'Hm, that bit's rather murky,' said Rex. 'I heard rumours when it first started up that he was pretty wealthy and was able to invest a lot in it, but nevertheless it seems to be thriving. They produce enough to sell at the farmers' markets locally and I think they have some kind of mail order arrangement too.'

‘We get most of our veg from there,’ Elena said. ‘It’s good stuff.’

‘Check mate,’ said Cerys, with a quietly smug smile.

‘What?’ Mariner looked down at the board. She’d beaten him, in just a few short moves. How the hell did that happen? ‘Your granddad’s got a lot to answer for,’ he told Cerys with a wry smile as they shook hands over the board.

‘Right now, bed,’ said Elena. ‘You can have your rematch tomorrow.’

Cerys started to protest but it sounded pretty half-hearted and she did as she was told nonetheless.

‘Remind me, how old is she?’ Mariner asked when she’d gone.

‘Eleven.’

He shook his head in disbelief.

‘Don’t worry, man.’ Getting up to fetch another bottle of wine, Rex put a sympathetic hand on Mariner’s shoulder. ‘We’ve all been through it.’

‘So whose side would you be on?’ Mariner asked, replacing the chess pieces in their box. ‘The capitalist or the liberal leftie?’

Elena shrugged. ‘I like Willow,’ she said. ‘He’s eccentric all right and can be a bit up himself, but we’ve kind of got used to him. There was some resistance when he first took over the farm — he started with the disadvantage of being English, after all. But as soon as it became clear he wasn’t going to ruin anything around here people changed their tune. Soon after he turned up, Ron and Josie took over the Hart and between them all they’ve put some life back into the village, so we’re not complaining.’

‘We’ve all had to adapt,’ Rex added. ‘Foot and mouth was a disaster. Hospitality and tourism are about the only things we’re good for round here now, so a bit of successful farming is a bonus.’

The conversation continued, along with the drinking, until nearly midnight. Mariner was exhausted, but the couple were such good company, it was easy to put off being left alone with his thoughts again. But finally he could delay it no longer. The sky was clear and a half moon shone, making it a cold night as he lurched across the yard. He was a little woozy and realized that he'd been drinking steadily all evening, consuming far more than he would ordinarily. He had to concentrate on finding his footing, which meant that he almost didn't notice the glossy black bulk of a Range Rover skulking on the opposite side of the road. Despite the lateness of the hour, as his gaze swept across it, Mariner thought he could make out a figure sitting in the driver's seat, even though the lights were turned off. Mariner had done his share of surveillance, so, resisting the urge to look directly at it, he kept on walking. As he opened the hostel door and stepped into the shadows, he took the opportunity to turn back and observe the vehicle more carefully from the cover of the doorway. It was more difficult to tell from this angle, however, whether what he was seeing was simply the outline of the headrests, or if there was an occupant.

Going into the hostel Mariner felt uneasy about that vehicle, but upstairs his view of the street was obscured by the branches of the beech tree in the yard. He knew, though, where there was a much better vantage point. He'd only been up to the attic room once before, when he and Elena had been seeking privacy one afternoon. It was accessible via a narrow flight of steps at the end of the landing and, taking his torch, he ventured up there now. It was a little tower room no more than eight feet square, with windows on all four sides. Despite this, what little heat there was in the building had risen, and it felt marginally warmer than the other rooms. It seemed in better condition too, with more snug-fitting windows and for a minute Mariner wondered if he might be better off sleeping up here, though that would require the effort of moving all his things, and creating some suitable space. There wasn't much room to spread out, thanks to the clutter of old furniture and pictures, and a couple of spare mattresses propped against one wall, but Mariner managed to pick his way over to the window.

As he did so, he heard the low murmur of a high-performance engine igniting into life and peering down, he watched as the Range Rover glided away, lights still extinguished. Mariner thought back to the SUV that had tailed him out here on Thursday afternoon, before realizing that connecting them didn't really make any sense. Anyone passing through the village could have just parked up for a few minutes here for a break, or maybe to make a phone call. It was most likely to be one of those ubiquitous sales reps returning home after a long evening of schmoozing a customer. Mariner undressed and got into his arctic sleeping bag. He fell asleep quickly, strangely reassured by the familiar smell of the hostel.

## Chapter Fourteen

Day Five

When Mariner awoke on Saturday morning in a creaking bunk it was to the sound of a woman's voice echoing up the stairs. 'If you're quick you can join us for breakfast,' Elena called. It was just after seven-thirty.

'It's an ungodly hour, I know.' She was apologetic when he arrived in the kitchen, having hastily pulled on his clothes. 'But you know us country folk. How did you sleep?'

'Fine thanks, though I might try the attic room at some point. It seemed a bit warmer.' Mariner considered telling Elena about the car hanging around outside last night, but something stopped him. Instead he remarked on the absence of the Volvo from the yard.

'Rex often puts in a half day at the office on Saturdays,' Elena told him. 'He's always worked long hours.' She put down a plate of bacon and eggs in front of Mariner.

'I could get used to this,' he said.

Cerys, chewing lethargically on a piece of toast, pulled a face. 'Ugh, how can you eat that at this time of day?'

'Oh, I'll manage.' He looked across at her. 'Want a game before I go?'

He didn't need to ask twice and an hour later Mariner had evened the score.

'Best of three?' Cerys said hopefully, quickly returning the pieces to their rightful squares.

'No,' said Elena. 'Tom isn't just here to entertain you. He's here on holiday. Leave him alone.'

'That's right,' Mariner agreed. 'Much as I'd *love* to while away the day locked in conflict, I have other plans.'

'Like what?' Cerys wanted to know.

'I'm going up to Devil's Mouth. I thought I'd do the proper tourist bit.'

'Only if it's not raining,' said Elena. 'And you haven't got a dicky heart, have you? Health and Safety have gone to town up there; you can only visit the falls if the sun's shining and you're glowing with health.'

'Can I come with you?' Cerys asked.

'No again,' said Elena straight away. 'You don't even like walking. You'll get bored after five minutes and the last thing Tom needs is a whining eleven-year-old trailing after him. Anyway I thought you had plans.'

'Oh yes, what are they?' Mariner asked.

Cerys gave an indifferent shrug. 'Me and Emily are going down to the stables to muck out the horses and maybe get a ride if we can.'

'Sounds like much more fun,' said Mariner.

'Here, you can take these; they're past their best.' Elena passed her a couple of apples.

'They're all wrinkled,' Cerys grumbled.

'But still in their prime,' shot back Elena. 'Just like me.'

Cerys brightened. 'Can we do some baking later?' she asked. 'There's a cake sale at school next week.'

'If I can get some more eggs. I've just cooked the last ones for Tom.'

'I'll pick some up for you while I'm out,' Mariner offered. 'It'll give me an excuse to go and have a nose round the farm. I'm curious to see what it's like now at close quarters.'

'Okay. They don't usually sell direct, but if you tell them they're for me I'm sure they will. And if you go first thing you'll catch them before they go off to the markets. Look out for Theo; he's a nice lad.'

Since they were initially heading in the same direction, Mariner set off along the road with Cerys but before getting to the centre of the village he wished her a good day and, remembering his undertaking to pick up some eggs, branched off along the gravel track up to Abbey Farm.

The three-storey farmhouse that dominated the yard had always been impressive alongside the odd collection of ramshackle barns, though everything was neater and in much better condition than back when he'd worked here. In Mariner's time it had largely been a dairy farm with a few sheep that were put out to graze on the hillsides. One of Mariner's main tasks that summer was to help make the hay that would sustain the animals for the winter. Now the only form of livestock seemed to be the chickens and ducks that clucked and waddled about the yard. A brand-new van parked next to one of the sheds announced the farm's current line of business: *Abbey Farm Organic Vegetables; all produce locally grown.* That in itself was an impressive declaration, and measures had been taken to make that happen. The new shed was a pre-fabricated aluminium structure, with a generator at one end that emitted a faint, slightly eerie humming noise. Just behind that was a huge pile of what looked like manure, but from the innocuous smell and in the absence of any animals to produce it, Mariner guessed must be some kind of compost.

'Can I help you?'

Mariner's snooping was cut short by a voice from behind him, cultured and polite, yet with a definite edge. He turned to face a man who looked to be in his mid-sixties, tall and rangy with lank grey hair, too long for a man of his years, and the ravaged face of someone who'd seen the wrong end of a few chemical substances. He was incongruously dressed in country attire: jeans, waxed jacket and Wellingtons, and nestling in the crook of his arm was a twelve-bore shotgun. This must be Willow.

'I came to buy some eggs,' Mariner said, pleasantly.

'We don't sell here.' It was a statement of fact, pure and simple, the pleasant tone echoed back. 'We have a stall at the market over in Llanerch. We'll be there later on in the day.'

'Yes, I know, but I'm staying with Elena Hughes,' Mariner countered. 'She said you might let me have some. She told me to look out for Theo.'

'I'm afraid Theo's not around. You'll have to make do with me.' Willow broke into an unexpected smile, revealing stained, uneven teeth, and offered Mariner his hand. 'I'm Willow. Elena perhaps mentioned me too?'

'Tom Mariner.' Mariner shook the hand, firm in its grip. 'Yes, she did.'

'Ah, well, Elena will have been kind to us at least.' Willow turned and began walking across the yard. 'The hen houses are over here.'

'Yes, of course,' said Mariner, falling into step beside him. 'Actually I was glad of the excuse to come down here. I worked here one summer, about thirty years ago.'

Willow turned to look at him. 'Thirty years? That's going back a bit. I hope you see a difference in the place.' They went across to the small wooden hen house, where Willow picked up a carton the size of a shoebox, lined with straw. While Mariner watched from the doorway he walked around the coop retrieving a dozen eggs, placing each gently in the box.

'Just a bit,' said Mariner. 'But it's good to see that it's still a working farm.' Mariner nodded towards the humming barn.

Willow shrugged. 'We do all right.'

'You must have to work hard to make it successful,' Mariner said. 'I can't imagine the climate can be that conducive out here.'

Willow smiled. 'It's not the Vale of Evesham, that's for sure. But my background is chemistry. I had an idea a while back for a kind of fertilizer that could help maximize, or even raise, the temperature of the soil. I've been experimenting and we're still in the early stages, but we are starting to see some success with it.'

'That sounds rather modest,' said Mariner. 'I heard it's been doing well.'

'In some respects, but we haven't perfected the formula enough to get entirely consistent results yet. We're still trying to work out what are the most successful products and the optimum conditions. It doesn't work for everything.'

Closing the egg box, Willow walked Mariner out of the hen house and across to one of the giant pig bins, where he lifted the lid. Mariner reeled back as the stench of rotten vegetation rose up to hit them. When he took a breath and peered inside he saw a sweating tangle of stunted and twisted brown roots.

'Parsnips,' Willow said. 'At least that's what they were meant to have been. It's back to the drawing board with those.'

'All the same,' Mariner said, trying not to inhale. 'This fertilizer you're developing must have huge potential. You're surely attracting some big investors.'

Willow gave a wry smile. 'I guess there will be people who'll be interested in it eventually, but at the moment we're still making too many mistakes for them to make any kind of firm commitment.' Willow smiled. 'Besides, I'm not really a fan of big business.'

'Your motives are more altruistic,' Mariner guessed.

'If you want to put it that way.'

'Well, whatever your intentions, I wish you luck with it.' Mariner took the box of eggs from him and carefully stowed them at the bottom of his day sack. 'Thanks. How much do I owe you?'

Willow shook his head. 'Tell Elena we'll settle up next time I see her.'

But Mariner had already retrieved a handful of loose change from his pocket. 'I need to pay my way,' he said.

'Call it one-fifty then.'

As Mariner passed the coins to the reluctant Willow, a couple of them slipped from his grasp and went clattering to the ground. As he bent to retrieve a twenty-pence piece, something else caught his eye, a few inches away, trampled into the ground. He smiled to himself; why did that come as no surprise? Straightening he passed Willow the money.

As he left the yard, turning to close the gate behind him, Mariner saw looking back that Willow was standing watching him go, and had been joined by a young woman. Slight and frail with a cascade of gold-blonde hair backlit by the sun and framing her pale face, she looked as if she'd just stepped out of a pre-Raphaelite painting and reminded Mariner of a fragile china doll his grandmother used to have sitting on the mantelpiece. She came to stand beside Willow, who slipped a protective arm around her, reminding Mariner of what Elena had said about his waifs and strays.

* * *

That was the convenient thing about hillsides, McGinley thought to himself, lowering his binoculars. They provided excellent vantage points. And wooded hillsides were even more advantageous as they came with the benefits of cover that protected the hunter from the worst of the elements and enabled him to stalk his prey without being seen. After a gruelling two days of heavy climbing and descents, he was finally here. At times the pain in his abdomen had got so bad he thought he wouldn't make it and in the last stages he'd had to stop at intervals to vomit, but it was amazing what reserves the human body could find. And just when he'd thought it was all going to be too much, he'd stumbled across a completely uninhabited cottage; a holiday home he guessed, locked up for the winter but with some pretty crap security. It did, however, have running water and a comfortable bed. There was even a supply of tinned food in the cupboard and after heating up two cans of beans, he'd caught up on a few hours' sleep in the dry and relative warmth and felt revitalized. A collection of assorted waterproof clothing in the porch meant that he was also able to upgrade his jacket to one that actually kept out the rain. Poor old Goldilocks would be in for a shock when she turned up for her summer holiday. Now he was back to sleeping rough, but his target was in sight.

He'd brought with him the radio from the caravan and when he could, he took the opportunity to catch up on where he featured in the news cycle. They had made up their minds now that he was their suspect and were linking him to Lindsey. They must also have found the car. The news reader, quoting a 'police source,' described him as '*recently released from prison where he had been serving a ten-year sentence for aggravated assault, and thought to be heading for the Irish Republic. Police have warned the public not to approach as he is believed to be armed and dangerous.*'

McGinley couldn't decide which bit of that last sentence he liked the best: 'armed and dangerous' or 'heading for the Irish Republic.' They had fallen for his ruse. His delight was cut short by a sudden wave of crippling pain. Now he lifted the binoculars to observe once more. His target was in sight and going about his business. Those first couple of killings he'd been lucky; he'd remained cool and detached, which meant that things had gone smoothly, but this time it was going to be more of a challenge because he'd be confronting the man who had wreaked the most damage on his life. This was the man who made Glenn McGinley angry, and what fuelled his rage most was the certain knowledge that this individual was oblivious to, and had remained unaccountable for, the havoc and suffering he had caused. Until now he'd managed to just about keep his feelings in check, but now, feeling the powerful surge of hatred, he realized that this time he would be at the mercy of his emotions. He couldn't decide if that really mattered. So what if it did turn out to be a disaster? He had nothing to lose any more; it would be like walking into the hail of bullets.

## Chapter Fifteen

What with the activity of the previous night and the effects of his cold, Tony Knox didn't surface until late on Saturday morning. Immediately he phoned Jean. 'Any news?' he asked. From where he was standing in his lounge he could see the marked police car parked outside her house.

'I've been in touch with the hospital but there's no change. Those poor parents, I can't imagine how they're feeling.' There was a catch in her voice.

'I hope you're not blaming yourself,' Knox said, though he knew that she would be.

'I was responsible,' Jean pointed out. 'Their daughter was in my care.'

'Strictly speaking she wasn't. You didn't have to be there. It's the kind of thing that could have happened anywhere.' He was just trying to make her feel better but he knew it would be unlikely to have any effect.

'If you say so.' He could hear from her voice that she wasn't persuaded.

'I do,' Knox insisted. 'You didn't offer Kirsty the pill, and you didn't force her to swallow it. The only person at fault here is the little bastard who gave it to her.'

'The police are going round interviewing all the kids,' Jean said. 'They're here right now talking to Michael.'

'I can see,' said Knox, watching from the window. 'Have any of his mates identified anyone they didn't know at the party, an older kid perhaps?'

'I don't think so.'

'Okay. I'll come and see you later,' Knox said.

'Thanks, I'd like that.'

'Can you tell the officers with you to call in on me before they leave?'

'Yes, of course.'

Knox was the middle of his breakfast when two uniforms rang the doorbell; officers he knew by sight from Granville Lane, though he'd never had direct dealings with them. He took them through to the kitchen and got out his notebook. As soon as he'd returned home in the early hours Knox had made detailed notes about his involvement in the night's events and now, as a key witness, he talked the officers through what he'd recorded. 'Who's SIO for this?' he asked.

'DC Glover.'

Knox was glad to hear it. Charlie Glover would do a thorough job. When the uniforms had gone, he immediately put through a call to him.

'Of course,' said Glover. 'I knew that address rang a bell. Is there anything else you can tell me?'

'Only what I've given to the two plods who were just here, and it's not much. How's it going?'

'Slowly,' Glover told him. 'Can't get anything out of the kids we've talked to so far. They either genuinely don't know anything or there's some kind of conspiracy of silence going on.'

'They may not know,' Knox said. 'Thanks to Twitter and Facebook, dealers can just show up at gatherings they hear about, blend in for a while and then disappear. I'll keep an eye on how things are across the road,' Knox said. 'Let me know if there's anything else I can do.'

Ending the call Knox went through and picked up his overcoat from the peg in the hall. 'Come on,' he said to Nelson who was hovering expectantly. 'Let's go get some exercise, clear our heads and fulfil our other obligations.'

* * *

Mariner had planned his route to Devil's Mouth, over the mountain and along the next gorge, but it was early and there was somewhere else he wanted to visit before he went to the waterfall, so he struck out instead around the side of the mountain. After about ten minutes he came to it; an unexpected dip in the landscape that led into a small tree-lined dell, sprinkled with boulders. It looked different now, of course. The gorse had grown thicker, leaving barely any exposed grass, but it was unmistakably the spot where he and Elena had liked to bring a rug on the long summer evenings, to get some privacy away from the hostel. A number of birch trees remained dotted around, though the landscape had changed, and Mariner spent some time scrambling from one to the other inspecting the bark. He was about to give up when finally he spotted what he was looking for, almost obscured by the frills of pale green lichen that coated the bark: *TM and EH* over a crudely carved heart. Love didn't come more clichéd than that. She'd disapproved when he'd taken out his pen knife, afraid that the tree might be mortally damaged. Mariner looked up into the branches of the solid tree. 'Didn't do you any harm though, did it?' he murmured to himself. He felt a ridiculous sense of relief at finding the initials still intact; a kind of portent, he supposed — or would have done had he believed in that kind of thing. He didn't have to think too hard about what Tony Knox's observations would be if he could see Mariner standing there grinning like an idiot. Confirmation that the boss was losing it after all. Kicking away the clods of sheep shit, Mariner cleared a patch so that he could sit with his back against the tree for a few minutes.

After a drink and a breather, Mariner resumed his ascent of the mountain. The path rose almost vertically ahead of him and Mariner tackled it slowly, his laboured breathing a sign of how unfit he'd really become. Cresting the hill and coming into the next valley, Mariner picked up the footpath that ran along the sides of the ravine towards the gushing spout known as the Devil's Mouth. Elena was right about the changes. The route was peppered with directional signs, stating the obvious, and any number of warnings about steep drops and the treachery of wet rocks, just in case anyone was too stupid to work out either of those things for themselves. Mariner was soon caught up in a steady trickle of tourists who were walking from the main car park, but even so, he hadn't expected to have to buy a ticket at the booth that had been set up before the last half-mile or so. From this point, the path wound along a narrow shelf high above the river and was quite awkward in places, where erosion by the weather had taken its toll. What had begun as a background murmur, increased to a roar, as the path opened out beside the rushing waterfall. After all the recent rain, it was in full spate, tumbling over the rocks and plunging down into the deep pool, forty feet below. Mariner stood for a while feeling the fine mist on his face and watching as, now and again, the sun broke through the clouds to create rainbow arcs from the spray. Beyond the falls, many of the tourists were heading for the entrance to the limestone caves. Much was made of the fact that pot-holers were very close to connecting a huge network of caves to the east of Devil's Mouth with an equally extensive network to the west of Caranwy, which would make it one of the largest underground routes in Europe, adding a whole new attraction to the area. Mariner studied one of the new information boards that had appeared to explain the development in more detail. The diagram looked like a cross-section of the inner ear. The last passageway joining the two systems was a two-mile long, impossibly narrow tunnel that must have been painstakingly cleared, rock by rock. Apparently by lighting incense sticks at each end, the cavers could tell that there were only, at most, a few metres to go. Members of the public were being invited to go into the cave at this end to view progress and today there were a handful of people queuing up to don hard hats and do just that. As the attraction was still new, there was a young man, a student Mariner guessed, trying to encourage people to go in.

'Would you like to explore the caves?' he asked Mariner.

'Not today,' said Mariner, inwardly shuddering. He could think of little worse than being enclosed by tons of solid rock; the mere thought of it made him break out in a sweat. Disconcerted too, at suddenly being among so many people again while he was walking, Mariner didn't linger at the falls for long, preferring to get back on to the quieter footpaths. He made his way back around the mountain and as he began the descent towards the pastureland of Caranwy, the cloud began to thicken again, the breeze strengthened and he heard the first rumble of thunder. By the time Mariner had climbed the wall and dropped into the woods on the other side, the rain was pelting down and the storm was moving directly overhead, with thunder booming periodically. Nearing the village, and peering through the trees Mariner saw the wind buffeting the sides of Willow's poly tunnels, and wondered if it had been a profitable day at market. It occurred to Mariner that the farm must really be thriving if it generated enough produce to sell locally and to distribute more widely. He was pondering the logistics of this, and trying to calculate tonnage and turnover, when a howl, like a human cry of anguish, ripped through the air and made the hairs rise on the back of his neck.

Mariner stopped walking and stood stock still, straining his ears for the slightest sound. He could hear nothing now, except the rain pattering on the leaves and the last clap of thunder dying slowly away. Maybe he'd been mistaken or had imagined it. Somewhere up in the trees a crow cawed loudly and Mariner shook his head with relief. He ploughed on through the dense undergrowth, the footpath eventually opening out again close to the wall, and he had just started to make good progress along it when, out of nowhere, Mariner caught a brief flash of fluorescent green before something hurtled into him, sending him flying sideways into the scrub, where he landed on a bed of brambles and nettles. Scrambling to his feet Mariner lunged for his assailant, before he or she could escape, and received a heavy clout to the side of the head in return. Despite Mariner's efforts to restrain him, the figure kicked and fought like an animal, though Mariner had an impression of a man, small and wiry, dressed in black Lycra and a high-visibility waterproof jacket.

'Get the fuck off me!' he was shouting. 'I didn't see anything, I'll swear to it. Let me go!' But Mariner was bigger and more experienced at this kind of tussle and after sustaining several further blows, he had the man pinned to the ground, face down, with his arms high behind his back, both of them gasping for breath. 'Please,' the man said, pleading now. 'I can forget it. I swear I won't tell a soul. I didn't see your face and I'll walk away without turning round . . .'

'Relax,' Mariner said, gulping in air. 'I'm not going to hurt you. I don't know who you think I am but my name is Tom Mariner. I'm a police officer. I'm staying in Caranwy and I'm walking back there after a day out. That's all. What's your name?'

He tried in vain to wriggle out from Mariner's grasp. 'Why the fuck should I tell you that?'

He had a touch of the Irish brogue, Mariner noticed. 'All right, that doesn't matter. Just tell me what it is you're running from.'

At that the man seemed to suddenly accept defeat and relax in Mariner's grip. 'My name is Hennessey,' he wheezed. 'Joe Hennessey.'

'Right, Joe, I'm going to let you stand up,' Mariner said. 'Then I want you to tell me exactly what's going on. Understood?'

Hennessey nodded. 'Deal,' he said.

Bit by bit Mariner released his hold and Hennessey got to his feet, stretching out an arm to lean on a nearby tree trunk for support, but keeping a distance between them. Somewhere in his early thirties, he was slim and pale with mouse-brown hair that was either fashionably, or as a result of the rain and the wrestling, untidily mussed. He was wearing what Mariner could identify now as running gear, complete with trainers, the twin earpieces of an mp3 player dangling around his neck. It was now that Mariner also saw blood mixed with the mud on Hennessey's high-vis jacket. 'So?' he asked.

Hennessey drew a breath. 'There's a man, back there. He's been . . . he's dead . . . oh fuck.' The horror of it seemed to strike him anew. 'I was just out running and I slipped and fell down the bank and landed on top of him, on the ground. Someone's killed him. I thought you must be . . .'

'Show me,' said Mariner.

Hennessey's eyes cast wildly about. 'Ah fuck it; can't we just go get someone?'

'We will, but first I want you to show me.' Mariner put a hand on Hennessey's shoulder. 'Take some deep breaths. I told you; I'm a police officer, although I can't exactly prove it right now. All I'm asking is that you take me to where he is.'

Finally, Hennessey seemed to pull himself together. 'Sure, okay, okay.' He took a deep breath. 'It's back this way.'

He led Mariner back along the footpath towards the rickety bridge. After they'd been walking for about three minutes they came to the edge of a small gully, with the river running along at the bottom, and Hennessey slowed his pace. Then he stopped at a point where the side of the footpath had broken away, and there were deep gouges in the mud that disappeared down the steep embankment. 'It's at the bottom there,' Hennessey said in a hoarse whisper, looking anywhere but into the gully.

'All right, Joe,' Mariner said, firmly. 'I'm going to take a quick look and then we're going to report it. But you must wait. You're an important witness so I need you to stay right here with me.' Hoping that Hennessey wasn't about to scarper, Mariner scrambled down the bank and as he reached the riverside, a wave of nausea swept over him. He'd witnessed unnatural death in many different forms but could never get used to the initial shock. A man, or more accurately the remains of one, was lying on the ground face up, his chest a mass of blood and raw flesh where he had been repeatedly hacked in what looked like a frenzied knife attack. His face, or what was left of it, and clothing were covered in mud, intermingled with the blood, as if he'd been rolled in it. A split-second image of Anna, lying covered in blood on the roadside, careered into Mariner's head and he rapidly deflected it.

Bracing himself, he knelt by the body and checked the pulse points knowing that it was futile. The skin was cool to the touch and he could feel the beginnings of the onset of rigor mortis. He also went through the pockets to check for any identification, but there was nothing. Remaining where he was, to avoid the risk of disturbing forensic evidence, Mariner cast a look around the immediate area but could not, on the face of it, see any sign of a murder weapon, though he could determine what appeared to be blood smears on the foliage to his right and there were some signs that a half-hearted attempt had been made to conceal the body with leaves and brush. Careful to retrace his exact steps, Mariner clambered back up the steep side of the ravine. The top was slick and greasy and he was grateful when Hennessey reached out a hand to help him up the last couple of feet. He noticed again the blood on Hennessey's clothes.

'He really is . . .?' Hennessey tailed off, reluctant to say the word again.

Mariner just nodded his head. He'd already taken his phone out, but it was useless. 'There's no signal,' he said to Hennessey. 'Where's the nearest place you can get one around here?'

'I don't know,' Hennessey said defensively. 'I'm just staying at the pub for a couple of days. I mean, I've tried, but it's never consistent, one day to the next.'

'There must be somewhere.'

Mariner cast around him; in the confusion he'd completely lost his bearings, and the trees here were so impenetrable as to block any landmark from sight. As eager as he was to raise the alarm and to preserve the scene, he didn't want to lose sight of Hennessey — he was in a dilemma.

'We're nearer to the Hall,' Hennessey said, eventually seeing Mariner's uncertainty. 'The edge of the estate is just a couple of hundred yards up that way.' He pointed up to the left.

Mariner considered. Gwennol would at least have the benefit of landlines and would provide a useful reference point for the police when they came. 'Shit,' he said, thinking aloud, 'it might be nearer, but there's all that bloody barbed wire to negotiate.'

Hennessey swallowed. 'There is a way through that,' he said. 'But if anyone finds out . . .'

Mariner glared. 'A man's been killed,' he reminded him. 'We're not pissing about here. Show me.'

'I don't know.' Hennessey was suddenly uncertain. 'It might look as if . . .'

'Never mind that,' said Mariner impatiently. 'We're losing valuable time. Now move.' Mariner gestured towards the path, making sure that Hennessey went ahead of him. From the state of the man, he was pretty certain that he was telling the truth about his discovery of the body, but one could never be sure. Again they had to battle their way through deep brambles that ripped at their clothing, emerging at the end of the path alongside the tantalizingly close estate park, the tarmac road clearly visible a few yards ahead of them, in parallel with the barbed-wire fencing. 'Christ,' Mariner murmured under his breath. 'What is it about people round here?'

'Come up this way,' Hennessey said, leading Mariner about ten metres along the fence. Suddenly, he crouched down beside it. After a few seconds' manipulation, he pulled open a panel large enough to crawl through, where the wire had been cut.

Mariner gave him a sideways look. 'I can see why you'd want to keep this a secret,' he said.

'I'm not doing any harm,' Hennessey grumbled. 'I take photographs. There's some unbelievable wildlife here, especially around dawn, and with the trees in the background you can get some great shots across the parkland and through the mist. Sometimes even the odd stray deer. I'm not hurting anyone.'

Mariner hesitated before crawling through. 'What about the dogs?'

'They're only part-time,' Hennessey said. 'They work Mondays, Wednesdays and Fridays.' He had done his homework.

They scrambled under the wire, picking up the darkened line of the footpath across the grass, then following it until it emerged part way along the tarmacked drive of the manor, from where they could see the solid

Palladian building towering up ahead. Mariner led the way up to the main entrance.

'I'm not sure that they'll appreciate me being here,' Hennessey said, hanging back.

'I can't imagine they'll be overjoyed to see either of us, particularly the state we're in,' Mariner said brusquely. 'But there are more important things to consider, so get over it.'

Broad, shallow steps ascended between twin statues and up to the huge double doors. Mariner sprinted up them and pressed on the bell. They waited and waited some more. Mariner had little idea of how such grand houses were run and had the sudden thought that they might have made a serious mistake in coming here first. There may not even be anyone at home. The storm itself had passed, but the rain was still coming down — and for as long as that was happening, the crime scene was being disturbed, not to mention any wildlife that might be interested.

'Have you seen the helicopter this afternoon?' he asked Hennessey.

The Irishman shook his head. 'Can't say that I have,' he said. He'd gone deathly white and his teeth were starting to chatter, the enormity of the last hour starting to impact on him. Delayed shock was setting in and he looked close to passing out.

Cursing inwardly, Mariner was just trying to calculate how far they were from the village itself, when the heavy oak door swung open. The woman who stood behind it was dwarfed by the oversized doorway. She was petite to the point of childlike, with black hair tucked back behind her ears, and olive-skinned oriental features. She wore a business-like white blouse and dark skirt, making Mariner think he must be looking at the housekeeper. As she took in the walking and running gear, the mud and the blood, Mariner watched her half-formed smile falter. 'Can I help you?' she asked.

Mariner had expected some kind of exotic Eastern European accent, but if those were her origins she'd worked hard to disguise them. 'I'm Detective Inspector Mariner,' he said, feeing oddly ineffective without his warrant card. 'I need to use your phone to call the local police. A serious incident has occurred in the woodland bordering this property to which we are both unfortunate witnesses. We need to get the police here as soon as possible, and this man needs to go somewhere warm and get a hot drink inside him.' He became suddenly aware of Hennessey swaying on his feet and put out an arm to steady him.

Whether due to the unexpectedness, the uncompromising tone of Mariner's voice, or simple common sense, the woman set aside any objections she might have been considering and opened the door to let them inside. They walked into a cavernous reception hall with wide staircases sweeping up from each side, and handsome portraits looking down from the walls.

'Christ,' Mariner heard Hennessey breathe beside him.

'You can use the phone in here,' the woman said, taking them into a room to the right, which appeared to be some kind of study, traditionally and somehow appropriately furnished straight out of an Agatha Christie novel, complete with leather Chesterfields and dark mahogany furniture, the walls lined with bookshelves. A huge walnut desk was incongruously topped with a state-of-the-art computer, printer and phone.

'Thank you,' said Mariner. 'We could use some blankets, and if you could organize some hot drinks, please?' he ordered, nodding towards Hennessey, who had slumped on to one of the sofas. He picked up the receiver. Clearly reluctant to leave them, the housekeeper nonetheless did as Mariner had asked and, as he punched in three nines, he heard her speaking urgently to someone just outside the door. In seconds the dispatch centre cut in and Mariner described what they had found and the location, keeping his voice low so as to minimize any alarm. As he was doing so the housekeeper reappeared moments later with an armful of fleecy rugs, which she took over to Hennessey. Ending the call, Mariner nodded his thanks. 'The police will be in here in whatever time it takes them to get from where they're coming.'

She hovered uncertainly, wringing her hands, clearly uncomfortable with these developments. 'We ought to let Mr Shapasnikov know what is happening,' she said. 'I'm not sure how he'd feel about the police coming here . . . it's not really my place to give permission . . .'

'It's not a question of permission.' Mariner was pragmatic. 'This has happened adjacent to his property.' He could see her trying to work out exactly what was going on but didn't want to give away anymore until the police had the full story.

'Yes, but all the same, he should be contacted.' With an apologetic nod, she left the room. As she did so, another younger woman appeared carrying a tray of tea and biscuits that she placed on a table in front of Hennessey. 'Thank you,' said Mariner. Loading sugar into the mugs, he passed one to Hennessey before taking the other himself. Then, unable to sit still, he got up and paced the room, noting from the photographs that covered any blank areas of wall that Mr Shapasnikov appeared to be a man with influential contacts.

## Chapter Sixteen

Hunched over the stream, Glenn McGinley was retching his guts up in ugly rasps, and watching the water that flowed away from him turn a pale reddish green. His throat burned and his ribs and stomach ached, but it didn't matter; the job was done. He had found 'closure' as they say. Again the surprise factor had worked in his favour, but if he was honest he would have to admit that on this occasion his temper had got the better of him and rather spoiled the experience. It was messy. All the years of misdirected anger and resentment had come bubbling to the surface and this time he had lost control. But he didn't care. The outcome was the same, and every bit as satisfying as his previous efforts, giving him a sense of achievement he'd rarely felt before. In different circumstances he could imagine this kind of buzz developing into an addiction of sorts.

And now he had fulfilled his commitment. 'I did it for you!' he bellowed at the sky.

* * *

Tom Mariner's house was a former lock keeper's cottage on the edge of the Grand Union Canal, between the back of a small cul-de-sac and the wide, green expanse of Kingsmead Park, a popular public space. Despite being in the city suburbs, its position was relatively isolated behind the cover of trees, and although secured as well as any policeman's house was likely to be, it was always vulnerable on the rare occasions when Mariner was away for extended periods. Knox drove to the far side of the park and he and Nelson did almost a full circuit of the playing fields, before branching off down the narrow footpath to the canal. When Knox's marriage had broken up a few years earlier, leaving him temporarily homeless, he had lodged with Mariner for a while and had appreciated the seclusion as much as he knew the boss did. But being so remote also had its drawbacks. This morning everything about the property seemed outwardly fine. To make sure, Knox opened the gate and went into the garden to look in through the window. That was when his day took a downturn.

Where Mariner's TV usually stood there was a conspicuous space. Knox wasn't aware that Mariner had ditched his TV; in fact only a few days ago they'd been discussing the European Cup game they'd both watched the night before. Taking out the key he'd retained since his stay there, Knox let himself into the house and Nelson skittered in behind him. A swift glance around told him that the stereo was missing too, and after a tour of the other rooms he'd added a computer, microwave and a couple of radios to the list. He considered checking the cellar to see if Mariner had just been security conscious enough to lock all the valuable stuff all away out of sight, but when he got to the kitchen and found the mess of beer bottles and spilled beer and opened food packaging, he knew that the boss hadn't left things like this. The curiosity was that, though he checked thoroughly, Knox could find no indication anywhere of a forced entry. The sturdy locks and window fastenings were all intact, meaning that this was the work of someone with a key. The only other obvious candidate, besides Knox himself, was Katarina, and while it was not impossible to think that she might have borrowed some of the appliances, it didn't explain the mess in the kitchen. She would never have been so inconsiderate as to leave it like that. Knox spent a fruitless few minutes hunting around for her contact details but found nothing and had to conclude that they were stored on Mariner's missing computer. Reluctantly he called Mariner's mobile. It went straight to voicemail, so he left a message.

* * *

Mariner had just stood up to get himself another hot drink when he saw, through the window, that the local police were drawing up quietly outside. It was encouraging to see they hadn't been gung-ho enough to herald their arrival with a blare of sirens and squealing brakes. Hearing the subsequent activity and voices beyond the door, he went out into the vestibule to meet them. The plain-clothes officer leading the pack was not tall but was solidly built, with a shaved head and a thick neck that didn't sit comfortably in his pristine-white shirt collar. His scrubbed complexion was high, with a network of broken veins on his upper cheeks.

'Mr Mariner?' he asked briskly, taking a foil pack from his pocket and popping a tablet Mariner recognized as nicotine gum into his mouth. 'I'm DCI Bullman and these are my colleagues DI Ryan Griffith and DC Debra Farthing.'

'Tom,' said Mariner and the two men shook hands.

Griffith was blond and good-looking in a rough-hewn sort of way. The woman standing a little behind him came up to his shoulder and was slim, with dark hair pulled back in a severe ponytail. 'Actually I'm a DI,' Mariner added carefully. 'With West Midlands. I haven't got my warrant card, of course but . . .'

Bullman regarded him levelly. 'Well, I'm sure we can verify it, should we need to,' he said. The handshake was firm but Mariner's confession had introduced an almost undetectable wariness into his eyes. 'What have we got?' he asked.

Mariner briefly recounted the events of the last hour or so, describing the location of the body and how he had come across Hennessey. At the mention of Hennessey contempt spread across Griffith's features. 'Do you think he's involved?'

'I can't say for sure, of course, but I don't think so,' Mariner said. 'He was panicked when he ran into me. I think he thought I might be the killer. He claims he was out running, fell down the ravine and on to the body.'

'You believe him?'

'The footpath where he fell is badly eroded, and the body felt cool. Rigor was starting to set in. I'd say that it happened a number of hours ago. Also Hennessey's got some blood on him, but the attacker must have been covered in it. I checked the body for ID but there doesn't appear to be anything.'

'Right.' Bullman turned to Farthing. 'Take a statement from Mr Hennessey, Deb.' He nodded towards where the man sat, dazed, on the sofa. 'And bag up his clothes. Then as long as we keep track of where he is, after that he can go.' He turned back to Mariner. 'And if you could take us back to the scene. SOCO are on their way but they have to come from all over, so I'd like to go and take a preliminary look.'

Dusk was beginning to draw down as Mariner and his police escort set out again towards the woods armed with torches and the wire cutters Mariner had suggested. He couldn't be confident of finding Hennessey's way through in the dark, and he was also hoping that he'd be able to negotiate the path back to the body. The temperature had dropped and rain was still coming down steadily, and the last thing they needed was a whole team of people floundering about all over the woods lost and destroying important evidence.

'Joe Hennessey seemed a bit reticent about coming up here to the Hall,' Mariner observed to Griffith as they crossed the grass.

Griffith turned to Mariner as if trying to ascertain if Mariner was winding him up. 'I don't think Mr Hennessey has done much to make himself popular around here. He spends a lot of time hanging around these woods, poking around with his long lens. A couple of times he's strayed on to the property and our lads have had to escort him off again.'

'He told me he was photographing the wildlife,' Mariner said.

'Did he now?' said Griffith, in a tone that implied disbelief.

The cutters made short work of the barbed wire and, with powerful torch beams lighting the way, Mariner led the group slowly down the path and into the woods, careful to retrace his and Hennessey's steps exactly. After about five minutes he came to the deep skid marks gouged in the mud and started down into the gully. Under the glare of the torches the site looked more gruesome than ever and Mariner even wondered if animals had been at the body since he was last here.

Bullman and Griffith seemed to pretty much agree with Mariner's assessment of the situation, and Mariner took them through the sequence of events again in relation to the location. 'I did a quick recce for a murder weapon,' he said. 'But if it's been discarded here, it won't be easy to find.'

'Too dark now to conduct a search,' Bullman agreed. 'We'll get this covered up, cordon off the woods and start a search at first light.' He looked up at Mariner. 'You can leave us to it now, thank you, Tom. If you wouldn't mind going back up to the Hall to give DC Farthing your formal statement, then you can go. You're staying somewhere nearby?'

'Yes,' said Mariner, hoping to leave it there, but Griffith's questioning look wanted more. 'I'm staying at the old hostel,' he added. 'Elena Hughes' place. In fact, I should let her know where I am.'

Griffith held his gaze for a moment, his eyes gleaming in the artificial light, clearly intrigued, but aware that now wasn't the time for that discussion.

'Well, thank you for your help, Tom,' said Bullman, breaking the tension. 'We'll keep in touch.' He turned back to the scene.

Within the short time that Mariner had been away, the activity back at the Hall had stepped up apace. Close to the perimeter fence, mud was being churned up by the tyres of a low loader delivering a mobile incident unit, and drums of heavy-duty cable with which to service it. Although there were plenty of uniformed police milling about, Mariner went back into the Hall to find that Hennessey had already gone. Mariner stood in the entrance hall and took off his now dripping wet forensic suit. Seeing him come in, DC Farthing looked up from where she was sitting at the desk in the study, scribbling notes, and came out to meet him. She brought with her a brown paper evidence bag, and a bundle of navy blue clothing. 'Sorry, sir, I'll need you to leave your clothes with us.' From the deference in her tone Mariner guessed that they had, by now, checked up on him and established his identity. He was glad. She handed him a police-issue tracksuit and trainers. 'There's a cloakroom through there.' She indicated a door towards the back of the hall.

Stripping to his underwear Mariner put on the sweatshirt and joggers which were, in turn, too big and too small for him, though the trainers were not a bad fit. He couldn't imagine what he looked like, but the clothes were at least dry and began to warm him a little. He folded his own things and placed them in the evidence bags, sealing them carefully. Should it come to that, any fibres found at the crime scene would be matched with both Mariner's and Hennessey's clothing, for elimination purposes. Taking the bags he went back to the study.

'Are you ready to give your statement, sir?' Farthing asked.

'Could I just call the friend I'm staying with, to let her know where I am? She'll be expecting me back at any time.'

'Of course. And you'll be discreet?' Farthing said tactfully.

'Don't worry, I'll keep it brief,' Mariner reassured her.

'Thank you, sir.'

Mariner could feel Elena's curiosity burning down the phone line as he explained to her that he'd been 'detained' at Gwennol Hall, but she accepted his vagueness nonetheless. 'I'll be able to tell you more when I get back,' he said.

Replacing the phone he took a seat alongside Farthing. She reached over and pulled a map to the centre of the desk. 'Can you show me exactly where you were walking today, sir?'

Locating the hostel, Mariner traced a finger across the field, through the woodland and up the hillside towards the Devil's Mouth gorge, passing close to where Hennessey had made his gruesome discovery.

'What time did you set off this morning?' Farthing asked.

'I can't say exactly, but it would have been between nine-thirty and ten. I'm fairly sure the chapel clock was just coming up to half past when I came through the village. I walked along the lane, leaving it at the entrance to Abbey Farm, just here,' he indicated on the map. 'I went and bought some eggs at the farm, then afterwards I picked up this footpath through the fields.'

It was way too early to have had a time of death confirmed yet, but Mariner felt sure the murder had occurred many hours before the discovery of the body; possibly even before he'd set off that morning. If Farthing had any thoughts about that she didn't allude to them.

'Did anyone see you go?' she asked.

'No. But Elena was at the hostel when we left; she can confirm the time. I started out with Cerys, her daughter.'

Farthing's nod said that she'd already noted that. 'Did you notice anything unusual in the village — anyone around who you wouldn't have expected to see?'

'I'm not local, so I don't really know anyone. But if you're asking did I see Joe Hennessey at that time, the answer is no, I didn't.'

'How about when you were going along the footpath past the woods?'

'There was nothing out of the ordinary,' said Mariner. 'It was a peaceful day; the only sound I remember hearing was birdsong.'

'And you walked to Devil's Mouth?'

'Yes, up here.' Mariner pointed again on the map.

'And you got there at what time?'

Mariner fished in his pocket and produced the ticket he'd been issued with. The number stamped in the top right-hand corner indicated the time that he'd been admitted to the site.

Farthing looked at the ticket, then back up at Mariner. 'So you didn't get there until one thirty-four? You look pretty fit, but it took you a long time to get there.'

Despite himself, Mariner coloured slightly. For some reason he was pleased not to be talking to Griffith. 'I didn't go straight there. I took a longer route to extend the walk.' No need to tell her that he was revisiting a former shag-site for old times' sake.

'Is there anyone who can corroborate any of your route?'

'Not until I picked up the main footpath to the falls,' Mariner said. 'I passed other people walking along there, but whether they'd remember me is a different matter.

And I suppose the guy in the ticket office might have noticed which direction I approached from and where I went. It wasn't that busy.'

'And can you tell me what happened when you bumped into Joe Hennessey?'

Mariner had already been over this twice now with Griffith, but Farthing was only doing her job. She and her boss would be checking for consistency, so he painstakingly repeated it once more.

'And what are your plans for the next few days, sir?' Farthing asked, when he got to the end.

'I hadn't really got anything specific in mind, though I was hoping to stay on here for a couple more days and walk locally before heading off towards the coast,' Mariner told her.

'Well, we would appreciate it if you could keep us informed of your whereabouts, should you decide to move on.'

'Of course. The people I'm staying with, they're bound to ask questions. Once the incident is made public we're — sorry, *you're* — going to need the help of local people . . .'

Farthing was quick on the uptake. 'I'm sure it will be fine for you to give them the bare facts, sir, without giving away any of the important detail, of course.' She meant anything that might help them identify the killer.

'You can rely on my discretion,' said Mariner.

Farthing had been scribbling down all that he said, but now she looked up and into his eyes. Hers was an intelligent face, with big grey eyes and a smooth, youthful complexion. 'Thank you, sir,' she said politely. 'That's been very helpful. I'll arrange for someone to drive you back into the village. And if you should think of anything else . . .' And in line with routine procedure she gave Mariner the card with her contact details on it.

## Chapter Seventeen

Crossing the lobby on his way out of the building, Mariner caught sight of the housekeeper through the open door of the room opposite. She was leaning over something on the table before her, her head and shoulders illuminated by a halo of lamp-light. Knocking lightly on the door, Mariner hovered on the threshold of what appeared to be a dining room, with a long, highly polished table and enough dining chairs arranged round it to seat more than twenty people. A sideboard at the far end was loaded with silver serving dishes. The table was not, however, set for dinner but was covered with papers, some stacked in neat piles and others spread randomly across its glossy surface. The housekeeper looked up with a smile of recognition, and in this light Mariner noticed that she had the most extraordinarily dark brown eyes.

'I'm sorry to disturb you,' he said. 'But before I go, I just wanted to say thanks.'

She seemed genuinely puzzled. 'For what?'

'For not making a scene when we first arrived, and for not asking too many difficult questions. It wasn't a particularly conventional entrance.'

Waving away his gratitude, she straightened up from her work and came round the table to him, eyeing up his rather eccentric clothing. 'It was obvious that something very serious had happened,' she said. 'I can't believe it really. It's a terrible thing. That poor man.'

Mariner wasn't sure if she meant the victim or Joe Hennessey but acquiesced anyway. 'Did you manage to get hold of Mr Shapasnikov?' he asked.

'One of his staff has been in touch I think. His English is pretty good, but I thought it better that he should hear it in his native language,' she smiled.

'Oh.'

Another smile; this time broader and with a hint of mischief that formed a dimple in each cheek. 'You thought I was on his staff too,' she guessed, accurately. 'No, I'm not permanent. I just happen to be here doing some work for Mr Shapasnikov.'

'What kind of work?' Mariner was intrigued.

She indicated the table. 'The library is full of historic documents relating to the house. Mr Shapasnikov has employed me to archive them, and at the same time I'm putting together a sort of rudimentary history of the place.'

'Ah, you're the historian,' Mariner realized.

She gave him a questioning look. 'You make it sound as if I have a reputation.'

'Not at all. Someone I spoke to happened to mention that you were working here. For some reason I imagined a middle-aged man, all side whiskers and tweed jacket.'

'Hm, I think you might be confusing me with an old-fashioned stereotype.'

'That's very likely, I'm sorry.'

But she didn't appear to have been offended and held out a hand for Mariner to shake. It was cool to the touch, with long, delicate fingers, plainly manicured. 'Suzy Yin,' she said.

'Tom Mariner,' Mariner said, in case she had forgotten.

'Yes.' She hadn't.

'It looks like a challenge,' Mariner said, taking in the extent of the paperwork.

She lifted her eyebrows. 'You can say that again.'

One item, an old ink-drawn map, caught Mariner's eye. 'That's Plackett's Wood, isn't it?'

'Yes.' Going back over to the table, she separated it out from the other documents. 'It's the one the river runs through, on the edge of the estate. Amongst other things, I've been going over all the original land registry papers for the area. They make fascinating reading; the land round here has been carved up frequently by different land owners over the centuries, according to who was in and out of favour with the monarch of the time. The Tudors were devils for it. And though the physical boundary encloses Plackett's Wood as part of the Abbey Farm land, I've found some documents that would seem to indicate that the monks who were there in the mid-sixteenth century did some kind of deal with the incumbent Earl of Wroxburgh and handed it over to him.'

So this must be the land dispute Rex had mentioned. 'Why would they have done that?' Mariner asked.

She shrugged. 'Could be any reason really. This was around the time when Henry VIII was giving the monasteries a hard time, so perhaps they gave over a bit of profitable salmon fishing in return for being left in peace, or even in exchange for protection.' As her enthusiasm for her subject shone through, she became more animated and, not for the first time, Mariner wished he'd paid more attention to this stuff when he was at school, so that he could make sense of how these communities had existed.

'But as you said, land changed hands frequently,' he reminded her. 'Couldn't it just have reverted back at some later point?'

'It's the obvious explanation, though the evidence so far seems to suggest that when the abbey was finally closed down as a religious order, the man who acquired the land just grabbed the opportunity to seize it back. Or it may just have been that the physical boundaries at that time weren't clear and an assumption was made. That's what I'm continuing to research, and I think Mr Shapasnikov has hired a local firm of solicitors to look into it too.'

'It's where the body was found,' Mariner told her.

'Oh God.' She recoiled slightly. 'I didn't know. You don't think . . .?'

Mariner shook his head. 'It's probably just an unfortunate coincidence. Who knows about the dispute?'

'*Possible* dispute,' she corrected him. 'I don't know. I haven't told anyone about it but I can't speak for Mr Shapasnikov. As I said, he was talking about taking on a local law firm, though I don't know if he's done anything about it yet. I can't imagine it would be something he'd want people to know until we're certain about it.' She clasped her arms around her. 'It makes me wish I hadn't found it now. Mr Shapasnikov pounced on it, but I mean, it's not as if he hasn't already got lots of land.'

'Have you mentioned anything to the police?'

She understood his implication. 'Are you suggesting that Mr Shapasnikov would . . .? I'm sure he wouldn't go that far. In any case he hasn't even been here in the last few days.'

Mariner didn't like to point out that a man as powerful as Shapasnikov wouldn't need to soil his own hands. 'It probably isn't anything to do with anything,' Mariner admitted. 'But it would be better to let the police make that decision. They need to have as much information as possible. You should tell Superintendent Bullman or one of his team about it as soon as you get the chance, so that they have the full picture. It's the sort of information I'd want to have.'

She looked at him strangely, before understanding dawned. 'Of course, you're a policeman too, aren't you? Well, if you really think I should say something, then of course, I will. It's a horrible thing to have happened, and in such a beautiful spot too . . .' She tailed off.

'And the member of staff,' Mariner asked. 'Did they manage to get hold of Mr Shapasnikov?'

'I think he's on his way back here now.'

Mariner cast his eye over the table again, then back over the neat and rather attractive form of Suzy Yin. 'Well, I'll leave you to your work.'

'Yes, thank you, I should get on, though I'm not sure I'll be able to concentrate very well after this. It somehow makes it all seem quite frivolous.'

'It might be more important than ever,' Mariner said.

## Chapter Eighteen

The area car driven by a police constable dropped Mariner off just outside Caranwy hostel, by which time the rain had finally stopped, but the wind was gusty and strong. Passing by the White Hart, Mariner caught a faint whiff of cooking food and suddenly realized how ravenous he was. The number of cars in the tiny car park indicated a brisk trade, and Mariner thought he might add his contribution tonight after he'd got cleaned up. Thanking the constable, he got out of the car and walked up the slight incline, his footsteps echoing around the deserted yard, and knocked on the door of Elena's cottage. He found Rex in the kitchen, coffee and something clear and brown in a tumbler in front of him. 'I thought I should just let you know that I'm back,' Mariner said.

'Come in, man.' Rex was instantly on his feet. 'Elena's upstairs trying to persuade Cerys to go to bed. She'll be down in a minute. Have you eaten? You must be starving.'

'Thanks,' said Mariner. He shook his head. 'I'm fine. I'll get changed and go back to the pub. It looks pretty lively down there tonight.'

'I'll bet it is. Word is out already that the police are up at the Hall. Everyone's speculating about what's going on. I'd have thought the last place you'd want to be is down there; particularly if they find out that you're involved. They won't leave you alone.'

He was right and Mariner knew it.

'We've got a bit of chilli left over. Why don't you go and clean up and I'll get it heated up for you?'

'You really don't have to . . .'

'Ah, come on, man. It's what friends do, isn't it? Besides, I have to admit, we're pretty curious to know what's going on too.' He was honest; Mariner had to give him that.

Mariner went across to the hostel, had a hot shower and changed into his remaining clean clothes, realizing that he was going to have to find a launderette before long, or talk very nicely to Elena. By the time he returned, she too was in the kitchen and as he pulled out a chair, she put a piping-hot plate of chilli and rice in front of him. Both she and Rex had the courtesy to let him eat a few mouthfuls before bombarding him with questions.

Mariner kept his account of what had happened short. Returning through the woods Joe Hennessey had run into him (literally) having found the body of a man who had almost certainly died of unnatural causes. No, Mariner didn't know who it was, and in any case, that wasn't the sort of thing Mariner could disclose ahead of the police making it public.

'Oh God,' was Elena's response.

'Unbelievable,' said Rex, looking bewildered.

'What about Hennessey?' Elena asked suddenly. 'Why was he hanging about in the woods?'

'He's a photographer,' Rex said. 'He was probably photographing the wildlife.'

'The sort of weather we've had today?'

'He was out running,' Mariner said. 'He was wearing all the right gear and he'd got an mp3 player plugged into his ears. You know him?' he asked Rex.

'He was propping up the bar of the Hart at the weekend,' said Rex. 'We just got chatting, like you do. He's particularly interested in the peregrine falcons that have been seen over Gwyn Mynydd. At least, that's what he said.'

'As long as he's not after the eggs,' said Elena. 'We've had enough trouble with that in the past.'

'I don't think so,' Rex said. 'He seemed to have all the right equipment. Looked as if that's what our Megan thought too. She was mooning all over him.'

'Megan moons over anything in trousers,' said Elena. 'Ron and Josie's daughter,' she added, for Mariner's benefit. 'She serves behind the bar.'

'She's a mousey little thing though,' said Rex. 'I should think Hennessey's way out of her league.'

Elena shuddered. 'I'm still trying to work out how something so brutal could happen out here for no reason.'

'Oh, there'll be a reason,' Mariner said. 'There always is. It's just that we can't yet see it.'

Rex reached out and put a comforting hand over Elena's. 'Sorry, love, but I'm going to have to get going,' he said, getting to his feet. He glanced apologetically at Mariner. 'I help coach the under-16s rugby squad. We've got an important match tomorrow up at Harlech, so an early start.' He and Elena went to the door. 'You'll be all right here tonight?' Mariner heard him ask.

'We'll be fine,' Elena replied, 'especially with Tom just across the yard.' By the time she returned to the table Mariner had finished eating. 'That was delicious, thank you.'

Taking his plate, Elena flashed a wry smile.

'What?'

'You must have thought you'd come out here to get away from this kind of excitement.'

It had crossed Mariner's mind too. 'DI Griffith wanted to know where I'm staying, of course,' he said. 'I could have made something up but it wouldn't have been very sensible, so I'm afraid I told him. I hope that's not going to make things awkward for you.'

Elena shrugged, as if it wasn't important.

'So what's the story with you and DI Griffith?' Mariner asked, carefully.

'What makes you think there is one?'

'Oh, I don't know — copper's intuition?'

She gave a weary sigh. 'We went out for a few months; about eight years ago, before I met Rex.'

'Who ended it?'

'I did. I couldn't take any more. He could be very intense. In bed, he was ferocious, brutal even.'

Mariner balked. 'He abused you?'

'No, nothing like that. It was just . . . There was a lot of anger inside him, and that seemed to be where it all poured out. At first I found it exciting, exhilarating, but then I realized it was the only way he could operate. He used to have nightmares too, about the things he'd seen in Bosnia.'

'He was out there?'

'He's ex-SAS.'

Somehow Mariner wasn't surprised. It explained why Griffith had taken in the murder scene so serenely. 'If it will help, I can move out,' Mariner said. 'I might attract a bit of attention over the next few days.'

'No, it's fine,' Elena said straight away. 'Besides, until they find out who did this it will be quite nice to have the security of a man around all the time.'

'I don't think you need worry. The police will be all over everything for a while.'

'Including the farm, I suppose, given how near it is. Willow won't be very happy about that,' said Elena. 'It'll be like the last time.'

'This has happened before?'

'Oh, not a killing, of course, but the police interest. When Willow first moved out here, before we really knew what he was up to, he was enlisting volunteers to help him. It led to ridiculous rumours that he was starting up some kind of religious cult, and that young people were being recruited via the internet.'

'Not true?'

Elena laughed. 'No, not even a bit. I think it was down to pragmatism; he couldn't afford the labour so he advertised for young people to come and work there, like a kind of gap-year experience. That part's true, but none of the rest of it is. The raid happened years ago and there was no evidence of anyone being held there against their will, or being indoctrinated in any way, so the furore soon died down again. But at the time it was tough on Willow; there were even calls to close him down.'

'On what grounds?'

'On the grounds that he was different and people didn't understand him. Then once the business side of it started to become clear and people could make sense of what he was trying to do, and especially when it began to look as if he might make a go of it, people became more accepting.'

Mariner wondered how long that would continue, if his own suspicions about Abbey Farm were confirmed.

Although it was close to midnight when Mariner retraced his steps across the yard, his mind was still buzzing and he felt fully awake; a phenomenon that often occurred when he was involved in a case. Even though this one wasn't his, he couldn't help mulling over what might have happened in Plackett's Wood, and when. The identity of the victim would be central, of course, and Mariner had no way of knowing who it was. If he was local then at least one credible motive had already surfaced, in the form of that potential land dispute between Shapasnikov and Willow, but after his visit to the farm today, there was one other possibility lurking at the back of Mariner's mind.

The sky in the direction of the Hall was pale from the glow of crime-scene floodlights. Knowing sleep would be a long time coming, and interested to see exactly what was going on, Mariner retrieved his binoculars from his rucksack and climbed the stairs to the attic room. The area beyond the woods and just inside the park's perimeter was as brightly illuminated as an evening-fixture football pitch, and he could see the swollen hulk of the incident unit to one side, though the lights were out. He became aware of a movement in front of it and with the naked eye he could just about make out a string of figures, tiny and insect-like, moving slowly around. His Dyfed colleagues going about their business even in the dead of night, responding to the pressure on them to get a result, even though realistically Griffith and his team could hardly expect to pick up anything meaningful at this hour.

As he lowered the glasses some further night-time activity caught Mariner's attention. This wasn't around the murder scene, but much closer, at Abbey Farm itself. Through the tops of the trees Mariner could just distinguish the main farmhouse and surrounding buildings, and scanning down from that he saw a transit van parked in the yard, with its rear doors open. Two figures were moving back and forth between the back of the van and that shiny new barn, each staggering under the weight of several crates stacked on top of one another, delivering the contents of the barn to the van. One was making heavy weather of the work, while the other moved with ease. A third man seemed to be directing the proceedings, occasionally lifting his arms and pointing, apparently supervising. There wasn't enough light to make a precise identification, but from the height and build of this person, Mariner surmised it to be Willow. As he watched, the last of the crates were loaded into the van and the doors were closed. A conversation ensued between two of the men, one of whom then walked round to the front of the van and climbed into the driver's seat.

Moments later the vehicle moved off, and through the foliage Mariner saw the twin headlights bumping along the track towards the lane. It must have turned left out of the farm entrance because, though Mariner waited and watched, it didn't come past the hostel. Since the internet had taken off Mariner was well aware that many haulage and delivery companies worked around the clock and, behind the dense screen of woodland, the goings-on were unlikely to disturb anyone in the village. All the same it did seem like an unusual time to be doing business. Given today's discovery and the proximity of the farm to Plackett's Wood, it might have been reasonable for Griffith to have sealed off the farm and had his officers monitor any comings and goings. This didn't appear to have happened, perhaps because of limited manpower, or maybe even to avoid conflict with the locals.

The legitimate explanation for the night-time activity was that Willow had orders to fulfil and didn't want to let down his customers. But he must also have worked out that amongst the tasks for Griffith and his team the next day would be a thorough search of the area surrounding the murder scene, and that would include the farm. Mariner couldn't help but wonder if there was a reason why Willow particularly wanted his new shed emptied tonight.

Mariner had been watching out for the van, but now, as he looked back at the farm, he saw that the yard lights had gone off, the work finished for the night. Right from the start his curiosity had been piqued about the place. Try as he might, he couldn't reconcile the area of land with the business it was apparently doing, and now there was an added layer of mystery. What really interested Mariner was that new shed — exactly what it was being used for and whether what he had seen on the ground earlier in the day provided a clue. If he was right about that, it meant serious business, the kind of business Willow wouldn't want Ryan Griffith to find out about, and the kind of business that could easily get a man killed. Mariner had been on the verge of sharing his thoughts with Griffith, or even Farthing, this afternoon, but without anything tangible to present them with, all he had was empty speculation, and few coppers, himself included, would be interested in that. The very least that he needed was, at this moment, lying on the ground in the farm's compound. Mariner was still fully awake. He had a good torch. What better opportunity would there be for sneaking down to the farm than now, while all was quiet, to see if he could retrieve it?

Outside again, the half-moon cast a blue light over everything and Mariner's eyes quickly adjusted to the dark. Plackett's Wood itself had been cordoned off as the crime scene, which meant approaching the farm from across the fields, so he walked down the lane and clambered over the gate. As he neared the farm he could see the kind of standard security lights illuminating the compound that most farmers had these days. The van had long gone, but Mariner was surprised to see two people, standing by the farmhouse door, one of them smoking, and engaged in a murmured conversation. Mariner found a spot and waited in the cold.

After a while the moon disappeared behind a cloud and a light drizzle started to fall. Eventually he heard the men saying goodnight, the door opened and slammed shut, and the yard went quiet. Mariner waited another few minutes to be sure, then climbed the fence and dropped into the compound. Keeping close to the buildings he skirted round to the barn. Using the buildings as reference points he tried to ascertain the exact spot where he'd conducted the conversation with Willow and positioned himself as carefully as he could, before crouching down and sweeping his torch back and forth methodically across the ground around him. After a while it seemed hopeless; all he could see in the compressed earth were assorted stones and the occasional glint of broken glass. Several times he mistook bark chippings and other innocent plant matter for the evidence he was seeking. And he was beginning to think that the day's rainfall might have washed it away or even that he might have been mistaken, when suddenly, on the periphery of the spotlight cast by the torch, something registered fleetingly in his visual field. Slowly, he tracked back the path of the beam, and there it was, flattened into the ground, but unmistakable; a single leaf, quite distinctive in shape. Curbing the impulse for a triumphant cry, Mariner eased the leaf out of the compressed soil without tearing it and slipped it carefully into the back pocket of his jeans.

Standing upright again, Mariner began to make his way slowly back across the yard to the field, but now he was here and so close it was impossible to resist taking a look in that new shed. Even though he was pretty sure that its contents had just been removed, the generator at the far end continued to hum and he was certain he could see a faint glow emanating from around an air vent. Rounding the end of the building he noted the heavy padlock on the doors. In mild frustration he gave it a tug and was so surprised when it fell away in his hand, that he fumbled and almost dropped it. Recovering, he unhooked the padlock, and placed it carefully on the ground before releasing the flap and easing open the sliding door. Instantaneously a floodlight snapped on, dazzling him, and seconds later he heard the bang of slamming doors close by, followed by shouting and heavy running footfalls. *Shit*! He must have triggered some kind of alarm within the farmhouse.

Behind the shed Mariner had the advantage of darkness and, leaping back into the shadows, he crept back along the length of the shed and round to the back where, out of sight, he could hurl himself over the fence and, staggering back to his feet, run down the edge of the field, trying to ignore the mud that caked his boots and weighed him down. Arriving breathless at the far gate Mariner risked a look back, but even with the backlight of the yard he couldn't see if anyone was following him, so he kept on going. Back at the hostel he stripped off his outdoor clothes, leaving them in the boot room, before creeping back into the dorm and into bed. The temperature had dropped, inside as well as outside, and it took Mariner a long time to get warmed up, and when he woke in the early hours he had to put on his thick walking socks to warm his feet.

## Chapter Nineteen

Day Six

Mariner was woken early the next morning by the sound of a vehicle arriving at speed, and when he looked out into the yard he saw a couple of uniforms going into Elena's kitchen. He'd stay out of the way until they had finished doing their job. Breakfast was in the hostel kitchen and made up of his bothy leftovers, and he sat to eat it at the old wooden table in the main dining room, a draught blowing under the door and his breath misting in the cool air.

The kitchen was exactly as it had been back in the early eighties, when it was already old-fashioned, with a large stone sink and wooden drainer, an antiquated fridge, a geyser on the wall to heat the water, and a simple four-ring electric cooker that everyone fought over to cook their evening meal on, before going to sit and eat at one of the two long refectory tables with benches either side. It all smelled fusty and unused, and there were mouse droppings on the floor in a corner. The only attempts at interior decoration were on the wall at one end: a couple of framed black and white photos and a pale outline where a crucifix had once hung.

Mariner had rarely known a Welsh Sunday when it didn't rain, and today was holding to that tradition, with low cloud and a light but persistent drizzle that looked to have set in for the day. The hostel was too cold to stay in all day and he had no wish to hang around getting under Elena's feet, so Mariner decided to do a low-level walk along the valley to the next village where he knew there used to be a decent pub. He could buy a Sunday paper and catch up with what was happening in the rest of the world. He also wanted to talk to Griffith, now that he had some hard evidence to support his suspicions. Before leaving the hostel he went across to Elena's to check that all was well.

Elena was peeling potatoes and Mariner stood and watched her for a second. He wondered if she and Rex had any idea about what else might be being produced on Abbey Farm, and if they would enjoy the relaxed relationship they seemed to have with Willow if they found out. At that moment Elena looked up and saw him and beckoned him into the kitchen. She looked pale and distracted. 'Would you like some breakfast?'

'No, I'm fine, I've already eaten. I'm not going to disturb you today.'

'Oh, we've already been disturbed,' she said. 'The police were here.'

'Yes, I saw.'

'The man you found . . . It was Theo Ashton.'

'The boy from the farm?' said Mariner.

'Well, hardly a boy any more, but much too young to die, and in such horrible circumstances. Apparently when one of Ryan's officers went to tell them at the farm about what had happened in the woods, they realized Theo hadn't been seen all day.' Elena looked up at Mariner, her eyes gleaming. 'What's going on? Why would something like that happen here of all places? I've just told Cerys. It's freaked her out, of course.'

'How well did you know him?'

Elena shook her head. 'Not well at all really, but he's been around for a while. He seemed such a nice lad, sort of shy. I can't begin to imagine who might have done such a thing. Do they have any idea?'

'It's hard to say,' said Mariner. 'It's the very early stages and the police will be trying to gather as much information together as they can. If they had any thoughts about it last night, they weren't sharing them with me. It wouldn't have been appropriate to.'

'Oh God, I keep thinking about poor Amber.' Elena saw Mariner's quizzical look. 'Theo's girlfriend. And after losing the baby too.'

'They had a baby?'

'When she and Theo first fetched up here Amber was pregnant, about six months gone. They were both just kids, about fifteen or so. The consensus was that they'd run away from home because of her condition. Then just before the baby was due Amber had a miscarriage and lost the child. I know it was a few years ago now, but she's always been so fragile. And now, losing Theo, this might just be enough to kill her too.'

'Just as I was leaving the farm the other day, a young woman came over to Willow; a thin waif of a thing, with long blonde hair.'

Elena nodded distractedly. 'She's got beautiful hair.' So that was Amber.

* * *

After what he had witnessed during the night, Mariner's intention was to walk first of all up to the MIU, but he had no need to; on his way out of the village he came across DI Griffith, lurking by the entrance to Gwennol Hall, drawing on a cigarette. His suit was creased and the curve of his shoulders made him look shifty.

Mariner raised a hand to acknowledge him and was encouraged when Griffith waved him over.

'How's it going?' Mariner asked, expecting no more than a vague reply about 'ongoing enquiries.'

Griffith shrugged. 'We've no murder weapon yet, and thanks to the weather, bugger all useful material evidence and a time of death that's little more than a shot in the dark,' he said, confounding Mariner. 'Other than that, it's goin' great.'

'One of those,' Mariner sympathized. He'd been up against enough dead-end investigations himself.

'One of those,' Griffith agreed, taking the final drag on his cigarette before tossing it on to the road and grinding it flat with his shoe. 'About the only thing we're sure of now is the victim's identity.'

'Theo Ashton,' Mariner said. 'Elena told me.'

'Did you know him?' Griffith was understandably surprised.

'No. I'd heard the name though. Elena mentioned him, and there can't be too many Theos around here. When I went up to the farm to get some eggs yesterday, she told me to watch out for him. That was before we knew . . .' Suddenly Mariner remembered the two men he'd seen, and their heated discussion. If Theo had been one of those then there might be a sniff of something, however vague. 'Actually, I might have seen him.' He recounted what he had witnessed through his binoculars two days before. 'The man who was casually dressed was probably about six-foot, slim, fair haired. Does that sound like him? It was hard to tell anything from what I saw in the woods.'

'It sounds about right,' Griffith said. 'Do you have any idea who he was talking to?'

'No. It was another man, a little older perhaps. Strange thing though, he looked out of place. He had a sharp haircut and was wearing a suit and tie, like a sales rep or something, though I couldn't see a car anywhere.'

'I'll check with Willow if they've had anyone call. You didn't catch the gist of this conversation?'

'No, they were much too far away, and it was more the tension between them that was evident initially; the way they were standing. But they seemed to part on good terms. I couldn't swear to it, but I thought something might have been handed over too, something small, in the guise of a handshake. Do you have any sign of a motive yet?' Mariner asked, since it seemed he was being invited to engage.

'Nothing that specifically points to the victim,' Griffith said. 'Theo Ashton appears to have been a popular lad; polite, considerate. Most people have described him as being quite shy.'

As did Elena, Mariner remembered. 'Was he from round here?'

'No, he's one of those that Nigel Weller — Willow — has picked up along the way. The family's from Bristol. Nice, normal middle-class family. A bit shocked when their only son ran away with his girl five years ago, but tolerant enough to have let him stay on here.'

'And the others who live there?'

'There's just Willow and Amber now.'

'I wonder how they'll manage the farm between them.'

'It's made the corroboration of alibis straightforward enough though. The time of death is estimated as early in the morning. Amber is fully out of the picture, having got the early bus into Llanerch, and Willow was about on the farm before going off to the market. Talked to you, didn't he?'

'Yes, he gave me the eggs.'

'So nothing there to worry me. Seems to be all happy families; no quarrels, no fallings-out, though we'll keep probing of course.'

'If it's not personal then, the killing could have something to do with the business of the farm,' Mariner said, that leaf in his pocket beginning to take on a whole new significance.

'Possibly.' Griffith dipped his head. 'I understand from a woman working up at the Hall there's some kind of potential land dispute, so we're looking into that too.'

So Suzy Yin had told him. Mariner was glad that he wouldn't be required to break Rex's confidence. 'But what about the farm's production?' he pressed.

'What, you mean Willow's magic formula?' Misunderstanding, Griffith didn't appear to take the suggestion very seriously. 'I suppose we can't rule it out, though Willow insists that Theo didn't know enough about that side of the business to get him into trouble.'

'If that's what the main business really is,' Mariner said.

'What do you mean?'

Mariner took the leaf out of his pocket. It had dried a little and was squashed, but to his eyes there was still no doubting what it was, and from the expression on Griffith's face, he instantly recognized it too.

The DI stared. 'Where did that come from?'

'I found it on the ground in the main compound of the farm, not far from that shiny new barn,' Mariner said.

'Shame you didn't show me this yesterday.'

'I didn't have it yesterday. I thought I'd seen it on the ground, when I was talking to Willow, but I couldn't be a hundred per cent certain. There was no opportunity to pick it up then, not without arousing suspicion, so last night I went back for it. Abbey Farm is quite a busy place in the dead of night.'

'Weller told me that he needed to get his mail order deliveries out last night. I agreed that he could.'

'If that's really what he was doing.'

'You think there's another sideline . . .' Griffith looked down, considering the leaf he was holding between finger and thumb. A hint of defensiveness had crept into his voice. It might have been a resistance to being told how to do his job. Mariner would probably have felt the same way. But it had also crossed his mind in the course of their conversation that Griffith might have already guessed what was in that shed and was choosing, for whatever reason, to turn a blind eye to it. Corruption was too strong a word, but it was not unheard of in these remote areas for the local police to put their loyalty to the local community above other more professional considerations. There was even a chance that Griffith may have been profiting from the enterprise himself. The difference now was that someone could have been killed for it. Mariner would need to tread very carefully. 'Having your permission to load up a transit and send it on its way would have been a great opportunity to dispose of any incriminating evidence,' he said.

'Christ.' Griffith scratched the back of his head. 'He told me he would lose money if he didn't get the order out, and I believed him. We didn't know until this morning that the victim was directly related to the farm, so I couldn't see what harm it would do.'

'And maybe it hasn't,' said Mariner, generously. 'But there are some things about Abbey Farm that don't quite add up,' he went on.

'Like what?' Griffith frowned at him.

'It's obvious that the property has had enormous amounts of money spent on it in the last few years,' said Mariner. 'And even with Willow's "magic formula," which he admits is still in the development phase, I can't see how growing organic veg is that profitable.'

'It ought to be,' remarked Griffith drily. 'Bloody stuff's expensive enough.'

'But if you look at the acreage of those fields, and consider that they're regularly selling in markets, and apparently also by mail order, I can't see how it's even sustainable, let alone as profitable as it appears to be.'

'I've always been impressed with how they keep it all going on such a small staff,' Griffith admitted. 'There's a lot of hard work to be done there and Amber looks as if she'd blow away at the first puff of wind.'

'And that new barn's a conundrum,' Mariner continued. 'If its function is to store vegetables, why does it need that level of insulation and a generator powered by two wind turbines? I think whatever is stored in there has to be kept very warm. I tried to take a look last night while I was there and triggered an alarm system. All hell broke loose, which begs a further question: why does a barn used for storing vegetables need to be alarmed?'

Griffith held up the cannabis leaf. 'This would certainly help to square that particular equation.'

'And might offer an explanation for Theo Ashton's murder,' Mariner said.

Griffith seemed to consider for a moment. 'We've had a preliminary look at the farm house, but the team is up there finishing off,' Griffith said. 'Now might be a good time to go and assess their progress. Want to join me?'

Mariner was surprised; he'd expected Griffith to be more guarded. Perhaps he'd read the man wrong after all. As they approached the farm it looked as if the search was coming to an end and the boiler-suited forensic scene-of-crime team was starting to pack up.

'If what you say is true, let's just hope they've been careless,' Griffith murmured to Mariner. He called out to his team leader, a stocky man with cropped hair. 'How's it going, Steve?'

Steve wandered over. 'Nothing we could find specifically relating to the murder. We've taken some notebooks and bits and pieces along with a couple of computers, which your man Willow has been relaxed enough about. We've done a pretty thorough search in and around the house for a murder weapon, but even if it originated here, it would seem pretty foolish to bring it back again. There is one thing we'll need to include in the report though; you might want to come and take a look.'

Mariner and Griffith followed the officer through the farmhouse to a conservatory where there were, in plain sight for anyone to see, about a dozen cannabis plants lined up on a windowsill. 'I'm assured that they are for personal use only and given the number it would seem plausible.'

'And who can argue with that?' said Griffith, throwing Mariner a meaningful look.

'It doesn't rule out . . .' Mariner began.

'I know,' said Griffith. They'd emerged from the house and were crossing the farmyard when Griffith indicated the new barn, seemingly as an afterthought. 'Have we looked in there?' he asked one of his officers.

'No, sir.'

Griffith turned to Willow, who had followed them outside. 'Do you mind?'

Willow raised his arms in a *be-my-guest* gesture.

Mariner walked, with Griffith, over to the shed. It was unlocked, Mariner noticed, with no sign of the padlock anywhere. Griffith slid back the door and, as they walked in, the temperature dropped considerably. The barn wasn't, as Mariner had thought, being heated, but was being refrigerated.

Willow seemed to guess what he was thinking. 'One of the issues we wrestle with is that the vegetables we produce are, for various reasons, not as hardy as one would hope,' he said, from just behind them. 'Even with our own turbines it's an expense, but it reduces the wastage for us.'

The interior of the shed was lined with heavy-duty steel shelves. Most were empty, but a complete row of them on one side held about a dozen insulated plastic crates, similar to those Mariner had seen being loaded into the van last night. He slid one out and peered at the contents, a jumble of soil-encrusted carrots. Pushing it back, he studied the slogan on the end of the crate, which was in a foreign language. He walked the length of the barn, casting his eye over the empty shelves, though no longer sure what he was looking for. Unless he really was a miracle worker, not even Willow could grow cannabis in these sub-arctic conditions.

'Actually, I do have one confession,' said Willow, rather sheepishly, as they were leaving the barn. Both men turned to him expectantly. 'These crates.' He placed his hand on one of the empty ones stacked just inside the door. 'We "acquired" them from a Dutch producer, and not entirely legitimately.'

Griffith walked back down part of the farm track towards the road with Mariner.

'Sorry,' said Mariner. 'A false trail you could have done without.'

Griffith dismissed the apology. 'You weren't to know. It might have been the breakthrough we needed.' There seemed no hint of satisfaction in his voice and Mariner sensed that his disappointment was genuinely shared.

'So, aside from that possible motive, it could be that Theo Ashton was simply in the wrong place at the wrong time?' he speculated, following the same thought processes as he would have been going through in Griffith's shoes.

'That's about all we're left with,' Griffith said. 'The possibility that he heard or saw something he shouldn't have, either at the time he was killed or prior to it. The lad was a keen artist. He liked to draw the birds and had set up some nesting boxes in the woods that he spent time observing. It was common knowledge amongst anyone who knew him that he was often in the woods in the early hours.'

'And you're happy about Hennessey?' Mariner asked.

'I'm not sure if happy is the right word, but we can't place him at the scene when Theo Ashton was killed. Around that time I understand he was being provided with comprehensive room service by Megan, the bar maid at the White Hart.'

The two men parted company at the entrance to the Hall, and Griffith, hands shoved deep in his pockets, headed up towards the MIU.

'I hope you get your break soon,' Mariner called after him, and got a nod in response. He didn't envy Griffith the task ahead. The way the weather had been yesterday it was unlikely that there would be much evidence remaining in the immediate vicinity, and the murder weapon, if discarded, could be concealed anywhere around here. Griffith would be relying on the accuracy of the time of death, piecing together Theo Ashton's last known movements and hoping that somewhere an eye-witness had seen something of significance. It wasn't possible to consider suspects without knowing more about Theo Ashton, but surely a kid of that age couldn't have had many enemies.

As he was walking away Mariner remembered the vehicle from Friday night. 'Oh, by the way,' he called out, 'do you know anyone around here who drives a black Range Rover?'

Puzzled by the question, Griffith shook his head, 'No, why?'

'There was one hanging about in the village late the night before last, trying not to be noticed.'

'Did you get a registration?'

Mariner shook his head. 'Too dark,' he said.

'I'll look into it.'

'Thanks.' Mariner walked on.

Mariner felt uneasy and slightly guilty. Elena had been right. He had come out here to get away from criminal activity, but in actual fact it was proving to be a welcome distraction. Last night, he realized, was the first time since her death that he hadn't dreamed about Anna in one way or another.

## Chapter Twenty

While Mariner was ambling through a neighbouring village, his mobile suddenly bleeped into life. He'd forgotten to switch it off again after the discovery of Theo Ashton and must have walked into an area with coverage. He'd decided before this holiday that he would only use his phone for emergencies and was tempted to switch it off again without checking for messages. But in the end he couldn't resist. There were a couple from his network that he deleted straight away, but there was also a voicemail from Tony Knox, typically short and to the point: *Hi, it's Tony Knox. Give us a call if you get the chance, boss. There's some information I could do with.* The message had been left only the day before. It didn't sound urgent, but amid his grief for Anna, Mariner knew that his head had been all over the place in the last few weeks and that there was every possibility he'd overlooked something at work. Among other things he'd been putting together a couple of cases that Knox might have to present to the CPS while he was away and could easily imagine that he could have neglected to include some piece of vital paperwork. The active area must have been a small one because when he tried to call

Knox back all he got was the 'no service' alert, but when he got to the next village he was greeted by a rare sight — a public phone box and, incredibly, one that apparently still functioned, so he used his credit card to call through to Knox's home number on the off-chance of catching him there.

'Boss! How are you?' Knox sounded his usual ebullient self, and Mariner could picture the Sunday afternoon scene, Knox slumped on the sofa in front of the TV amid a landscape of scattered beer cans.

'I'm fine,' Mariner said. 'This is just what I needed — in some respects. I picked up your message.'

'Ah.' Knox's voice dropped. This was not good news. 'I stopped by your place,' he said. 'I'm afraid you've had visitors.'

*Shit.* 'Much damage?' Mariner asked, fearing the response.

'Not damage as such,' Knox said. 'Just a few missing items and a puzzle.'

'What kinds of items?'

'Oh the usual: TV, stereo, microwave . . .'

'All the stuff that's easy to flog,' said Mariner. 'So what's the puzzle?'

'The weird thing is that there's no sign of forced entry,' Knox said.

'Are you sure?'

'Absolutely certain, I've been over the whole house thoroughly.'

Mariner knew that would be true.

'Does Katarina still have a key?' Knox asked.

'Yes, but she wouldn't steal from me.'

'I'm not saying that, but . . .'

Mariner second-guessed him. 'She might know someone who would,' he acknowledged.

'I'd at least like to go and talk to her, if only to rule it out,' said Knox.

'Have you got a number for her?'

'Not yet but it'll be on record from her interpreting duties.'

'I'll give it to you anyway.' Mariner recited Kat's mobile number and her address.

'And is she still with that Giles fella?' Knox asked.

'Yes, as far as I know.' Mariner added Kat's boyfriend's details.

'Anyway,' Knox said. 'I thought you'd want to know, rather than coming back to the surprise.'

'Sure, thanks.' Mariner felt depressed by it. 'Everything else okay at that end?'

After a beat of hesitation Knox said, 'Yeah, just getting on with it. How's the walking going?'

'Good,' Mariner said, 'though not completely uneventful. Have you picked up the news about a murder out here, Caranwy?'

'That little place? You're near there?'

'It's the village I'm staying in.'

'Christ. You haven't got involved, I hope?'

'No choice,' Mariner said. 'It's complicated, but I was there when the body was found. And it's a pretty small place so you can't help but be aware of the investigation going on.'

'It doesn't mean you have to join in,' Knox pointed out. 'You're meant to be on your holidays, remember?'

'Yeah, I know,' said Mariner, unwilling to admit how much he welcomed the diversion.

'So what do you need?' Knox asked, reading him perfectly.

'Funny you should ask that,' Mariner said. 'I wouldn't mind knowing a bit more about a guy called Nigel Weller. He's in his sixties, I'd say. He used to live in the West Midlands area, so I'm told, possibly Solihull. Can you see if we've got anything on him, might be drugs related? Also, I'd be interested in anything you can dig up about a Russian businessman, Nikolai Shapasnikov.' Mariner spelt it out. 'He's bought a country pile out here, Gwennol Hall.'

'That I can do,' Knox said. 'I'll give you a call back when I know something. Anything else, boss?'

'Yes, can you look up the number and address of the Towyn Farm Community, where Jamie Barham's living now? It's a long story, but I could do with having that too.'

'Sure.'

'Great. Leave a message if you can't get hold of me. Getting a signal's hopeless around here. I'll pick it up when I can.'

At the village shop Mariner bought a Sunday paper and took it along to the pub. However the experience fell some way short of the relaxing lunchtime drink he'd envisaged. The place was newly upgraded to a gastropub, so consequently most of the seating had been given over to a formal restaurant that would have looked at home in Brindley Place and lacked any decent beer. Many of the customers seemed to have driven some distance to enjoy their outrageously priced Sunday lunch and were dressed for the occasion. In his walking gear, Mariner hardly fitted in and was treated by the staff with an air of mild resentment for occupying a table for four to order only soup and a freshly oven-baked (he was tempted to ask how else it could have been baked) roll. He stubbornly stood his ground until the arrival of a noisy sixteen-strong party, at which point he decided it was time to leave. He'd just about had the opportunity to catch up on the details of Theo Ashton's murder, and the latest on the Merseyside killings, before he was forced to abandon the pub. The 'Kirkby massacre,' as it was now being dubbed, had been fully attributed to the recently paroled Glenn McGinley, who was now thought to have escaped in a stolen car, via Holyhead across to Dublin. A link, mostly based on the MO, was being sought with a triple murder in Cheshire on the following morning.

It was late afternoon when Mariner got back to Caranwy, and despite the increased number of cars in the pub car park, he decided to drop in for a decent pint of proper beer, to make up for his lunchtime disappointment, before returning to the hostel. The Welsh had come a long way since 'dry' Sundays, and it took him several minutes to push his way through the crowded and rowdy bar, by which time the idea wasn't looking nearly as appealing but having made the commitment he decided to stick it out.

Perched on a bar stool, Joe Hennessey was digging into a bag of salted peanuts and pushing them into his mouth. Seeing Mariner he nodded a brief acknowledgement, but any further conversation was made impossible by the noise and the distance between them. And in any case Hennessey was being monopolised by the girl behind the counter. Megan, Mariner surmised. He could see now what Elena and Rex had meant and couldn't help but remark on the contrast between her and the barmaid from the Star in Tregaron. Megan hardly looked old enough to be drinking, let alone serving behind a bar. Although attending to a steady stream of customers, her eyes rarely left Hennessey and at one point he seemed to be making a joke of it, at her expense. Megan turned away, blushing fiercely.

Eventually Mariner caught the attention of the older barman working the till nearest to him and while he waited for his pint to be pulled, he surveyed the room looking for a free seat, preferably one tucked away in a quiet corner. On the face of it he was going to be unlucky, as all the tables seemed to be taken, but amongst the mass of strangers he spotted one familiar face. Suzy Yin, the archivist he'd met up at the Hall, sitting with a modest half pint in front of her on the table and her head down studying some papers, even though she looked off-duty today, dressed in jeans and a chunky sweater. A roar of laughter from a group around the fireplace made her raise her head momentarily and, as her eyes locked with Mariner's, that wide smile lit up her face in greeting. He was just picking up his pint, and recognizing the lack of seating, she gestured that he should join her. Mariner battled his way through the crush to where she was sitting. 'Are you sure you don't mind?' he said. 'I can easily stand, and you look as if you're in the middle of something.'

She shook her head. 'Not really,' she said, gathering up the papers. 'This is my single woman's defence against unwanted company. I'll be happy to take a break from it. I'm at risk of becoming one of those dreadful people who doesn't know when to switch off from work.'

As he sat down, Mariner turned away so that she wouldn't see the wry smile cross his face. He wasn't quick enough.

'Oh God,' she said. 'You're one of those people, aren't you?'

'I think I probably am,' Mariner admitted.

'Well, given what you do for a living, I suppose I find that rather reassuring,' she said. 'How's that for blatant hypocrisy?'

'Shameful,' said Mariner. 'What are you working on?'

'Oh, this and that,' she said, tucking the paperwork into a folder. She lifted her glass. 'Anyway, cheers.'

'Cheers,' Mariner reciprocated. 'So why a historian?' he asked, after a moment. 'Isn't that a bit . . .' he searched for the right word.

'Dry? Dusty? Lonely? It's all right. You can say it.' She laughed easily, soft and gentle like a wind-chime, and Mariner had the feeling that she never took herself too seriously. 'Believe me, it wasn't what my parents wanted for me. They would have rather preferred a doctor or lawyer. But history is my passion so they didn't have much choice. And in the end I think it was enough for them that I went to university.'

'It's more than I did,' said Mariner. 'Where are they from, your parents?'

'Canton. They did what thousands of other Chinese did and came here in the sixties to open a restaurant and have their family. A couple of years later I showed up.'

So she was a little older than she looked, Mariner thought. 'And they named you Suzy,' he said. 'It doesn't sound very Chinese.'

'Oh, it isn't. All part of their assimilation, I suppose. And yes, mine can be a solitary profession, but that doesn't bother me. I'm an only child so I'm happy with my own company — up to a point.'

Mariner nodded. 'Me too,' he said. 'I can understand the appeal.'

'And you're a police officer,' she smiled. 'Like me, an investigator of mysteries.' As she finished speaking she had to raise her voice above the roar of laughter from a group beside the fireplace.

'And what do you think of your boss?' Mariner asked.

'He's very charming and well mannered,' said Suzy. 'Though there's something underneath that I wouldn't quite trust; a bit of a ladies' man from what I gather from the other staff, and I suppose some would say he's good-looking in a rough and ready kind of way.'

'But not you?'

'He's not really my type, a little too macho. I'm more drawn towards quiet intellectuals, I suppose.'

'So that rules me out,' said Mariner lightly, regretting it instantly. He was saved by a burst of raucous laughter from the group around the bar that distracted them both momentarily.

'Journalists,' Mariner said. 'I'd bet big money on it.'

Either their presence or Mariner's remark prompted Suzy to start gathering up her things. 'I think it's time to go,' she said apologetically. 'This beer is going down a bit too well. I try not to do too much drinking alone, but I did need to get out for a while this afternoon. The four walls were driving me mad.' By now it was getting dark beyond the windows.

'How are you getting back to the Hall?' Mariner asked.

'I'll walk,' she said, sliding into her coat. 'Calling a carriage is so nineteenth century. Besides, I'm not really used to drinking at this time of day — the fresh air will revive me a little.'

'There must be a local taxi firm who could take you up there,' said Mariner.

'What, to drive me all of three quarters of a mile? That would make me incredibly popular.'

'Will you let me come with you then?' Mariner said, picking up his jacket. 'You shouldn't walk up there after dark, not with everything that's happened.'

'Why? Do you think I could be in danger?'

'I don't suppose so, except perhaps from opportunistic journalists,' Mariner admitted, 'but I'd feel happier if you'd let me walk you.'

'That's very chivalrous,' she smiled. 'How could I possibly refuse?'

'I do have an ulterior motive, of course,' Mariner admitted. 'I'm interested to see what progress is being made.'

'Honest at least,' she laughed.

Outside though, as they crossed the road, Mariner missed his footing, tripped heavily on the kerb and stumbled.

'Are you sure I shouldn't be walking *you* home?' Suzy observed. When he was beside her again she slipped her arm into his. 'I'd better hold on to you. You clearly can't be trusted out on your own.'

'You sound too much like my sergeant,' Mariner said, drawing her in closer to him, noticing how easily they seemed to fall into step. For a while they walked in comfortable silence, their breath clouding the night air and Mariner wondering if she was as acutely aware of his physical presence as he was of hers; the scent of her hair and the occasional pressure of her hip as it rolled against his outer thigh.

As they walked up the drive they could see the light flooding from the windows of the mobile incident unit, though the Hall itself appeared to be in almost total darkness. 'Mr Shapasnikov lives mostly at the back of the house,' Suzy explained. Instead of approaching the main entrance, she turned off before they got there, leading Mariner round to the side of the building. 'As do I. I have rooms above the stables,' she explained. 'I know my place.' Mariner saw for the first time that the Hall was built in a square shape around a wide central courtyard. They entered this by walking underneath a narrow archway. Three sides of the square were made up of the main house, and the furthest a block of two-storey buildings and outhouses. It was well lit by floodlights and to one side was a double garage. One of the up-and-over doors was open and inside, like beasts peering out from their lair, were two identical, sleek black SUVs. Two young men in dark trousers and white shirts loitered in the doorway of the garage, murmuring in low voices. One of them was smoking and, seeing Suzy, raised his cigarette in acknowledgement.

'Who's that?' Mariner asked.

'Reggie and Ronnie,' Suzy said softly, waving back.

'You're joking,' said Mariner.

'Sorry,' she chuckled. 'It's what I call them, though not to their faces, I'm ashamed to say. Mr Shapasnikov's got several drivers-cum-gofers. I can never remember their names, though I do know that most of them would sound perfectly at home in a Tolstoy novel: Andrei, Vasili, Arkady — you get the idea. And to say so is probably racist or sexist, or perhaps both, but they all look the same to me with their cropped hair and sharp suits. When Mr Shapasnikov has his weekend events there are about a dozen of them scurrying about tending to his guests, but I've no idea what they do the rest of the time.'

Short hair and sharp suits? Mariner didn't recognize either of the men by the garage, but that profile would nicely fit the man he'd seen talking to Theo Ashton at the farm. It might also explain the absence of a car. He made a mental note to mention it to Ryan Griffith.

Stopping alongside a wooden flight of steps, which led to the upper floor of one of the stone outbuildings, Suzy hunted in her bag for keys, before producing them with a flourish. 'Well, thank you again for walking me home,' she said. 'Now I shall have to worry about *you* getting back safely.'

'Oh, despite appearances, I can more or less take care of myself,' Mariner said. 'I might even manage to not fall over.'

She seemed doubtful. 'Well, if you say so.'

After the slightest hesitation, Mariner leaned in to kiss her on the cheek, but at that precise moment she must have had the same idea, so that their mouths collided, taking them both by surprise.

'Sorry, that didn't go well,' Mariner said.

'It was a start,' she said, and stood on tiptoe to peck him lightly on the cheek.

'I'll just wait until you're safely inside,' Mariner said, the cold suddenly feeling less penetrating. He watched her climb the staircase and close the door as a light inside came on before turning on his heel.

## Chapter Twenty-One

Making his way back through the village, past the lights of the pub, Mariner became suddenly aware of a recognizable figure up ahead, bowed under the weight of a heavy pack, coming towards him into the village from the opposite direction. He was about to call out a greeting when abruptly the man turned off into the only lane that left the main road just here. As he got to the junction Mariner was convinced he'd recognized the man and called out to him. At his call Jeremy Bryce turned.

'Hello again,' Mariner called out. 'Tom Mariner. I gave you a lift the other night.'

Bryce peered at him through the darkness as gradually recognition dawned. 'Well, well, my good Samaritan,' he said, walking back towards Mariner. 'You had quite a head start on me. I didn't expect to catch you up.' His voice was hoarse and nasal.

'I'm staying here for a few days,' Mariner said. 'Visiting . . . someone I know. Where have you walked from today?'

'Oh, I came up and over the tops.' Bryce waved a hand vaguely in the direction of Devil's Mouth, though given the man's record Mariner wasn't sure how meaningful that was. He was grinning broadly. 'Well, this is a coincidence!'

Mariner wanted to point out that it wasn't really, given that they were both walking the same footpath in the same direction, but he didn't like to quash Bryce's enthusiasm. In truth he was surprised that he hadn't appeared sooner, but then it was likely that there would have been a couple of unscheduled detours along the way. The man was quite literally a walking liability. 'I tried to track you down after I gave you that lift,' Mariner said. 'But you didn't stay at the Lamb and Flag then.'

'Ah, no.' Bryce managed a sheepish grin. 'I must have misunderstood. I couldn't stay there after all. I pride myself in speaking a bit of Welsh, name like mine and all that, but clearly I'm not as competent as I'd like to think.' Averting his face from Mariner, he let rip an explosive sneeze, before blowing his nose loudly. 'It was pretty chilly in the climbing hut last night. After getting so wet, I think I might have caught a cold.'

'Really?' said Mariner, but the irony was lost on Bryce. A steady drizzle was beginning to fall again; Mariner could see it in the lamp light. 'Where are you planning to stay tonight?' he asked Bryce, noting that the lane he was on would take him out of the village.

'I had considered the pub here, but it's heaving.' Bryce lifted his map case, running a finger over it. 'There's a climber's hut up on the hillside here I think. It's just a couple of miles away over in the next valley.'

Mariner knew that route; he'd covered part of it two days before. It wasn't easy even in daylight, and it was rather more than a couple of miles. 'It's a long way to go after dark and that'll be freezing too,' Mariner said. 'Don't you think the warmth of a B&B might be better tonight?' he suggested.

'Well, I fear I might have left it a little late,' Bryce said. 'I don't seem to be very good at planning.'

Mariner made an impulsive and somewhat risky decision. 'Look, I'm staying at an old youth hostel just up there. I know the owner. It's basic but there's a hot shower and some heating, and you could at least get some food at the pub. Why don't I see if you can come and stay there until you're feeling better?'

'Do you think that would be acceptable?' Bryce jumped at it.

'I'm sure it would,' said Mariner. 'You can get a good night's sleep and tomorrow you can pick up the trail again. No sense in being a martyr, is there?'

'Well it does sound rather attractive,' Bryce conceded, by now visibly shaking with cold.

'Don't happen to play chess, do you?' Mariner asked as they walked back along the main street.

'Well, yes, I do.'

Even better. 'This is a fortunate meeting anyway,' Mariner said. 'I think I have something that belongs to you.'

'Oh?'

'A locket.'

'The locket. Heavens, I hadn't even noticed that it was missing. If I lose that I will be in the dog house,' he said. 'My wife despairs of me; head in the clouds most of the time.'

That Mariner could well believe. Back at the hostel he knocked and somewhat cautiously put his head around the kitchen door, where Elena was standing stirring something savoury and delicious-smelling in a saucepan. 'I was wondering where you'd got to,' she said. Mariner saw her gaze shift slightly as she noticed Bryce out in the yard. 'Ah, that's sweet, have you found a friend?'

'Sort of,' Mariner said. 'His name is Jeremy Bryce. I picked him up as a hitchhiker a few nights ago, on my way out to Tregaron, and we've just run into each other again. He's walking the Black Mountain Way, doing what I am really, but he's caught a cold and is in quite a state. How would you feel about him staying in the hostel too? It'll just be for a night or so, until he moves on. He seems like a nice guy, but I think he's some kind of academic and orienteering is definitely not one of his strengths. I think it would be irresponsible to send him out into the night again.' Mariner left a dramatic pause before adding, artfully: 'He's a chess player.'

'Is that meant to impress me?'

'Well, he's another opponent for Cerys, and if he's a college professor, I bet he's good,' Mariner pressed his case home.

Elena rolled her eyes. 'And what will he eat?'

'That's no problem; we'll go down to the pub.'

She broke into a pained smile. 'It's all right. I've made enough of this to feed a couple of battalions of the Welsh Guards. I was going to freeze it but you may as well have it.'

'You could look upon it as training for when you've got the B&B up and running,' Mariner said, helpfully.

Elena made a show of grimacing. 'Go and get yourselves cleaned up. It'll be on the table in half an hour.'

* * *

After a brief introduction to Elena, Mariner took Bryce up into the hostel. Knowing already that the room he was sleeping in was the only one habitable, they tested the bunks and found that the one directly over Mariner's would be the only one strong enough to take the big man's weight.

'I'll go up there,' Mariner offered. 'You take mine.'

But Bryce wouldn't have it. 'No, you've found me a warm bed for the night.' He tested the mattress. 'And a soft one. This is more comfort than I've had in days. I can manage perfectly well up there.'

Mariner let Bryce go first in the shower. He'd unpacked some of his things and his wallet lay on the table in the dorm. Mariner couldn't help himself. Flicking it open he saw a faded and creased snapshot of a very pretty woman with her arms draped around two smiling little girls, one blonde and one dark. Lucky Bryce.

While the two men ate, Elena had the TV on low in the kitchen and after a bit, the local news bulletin came on. Elena turned up the volume so that they could hear. News about Glenn McGinley's progress, not surprisingly, had been displaced by the murder of Theo Ashton.

'I don't understand,' said Bryce. 'Is that what all the police activity is about? I saw several police cars when I came into the village, but I thought that perhaps it was part of the manhunt for this fugitive. I saw the headlines on a newsagent's board a couple of days ago indicating that he might have headed into Wales.'

'Nothing to do with him,' Mariner said. 'A local lad was stabbed to death in the woodland down the road yesterday.' Mariner decided not to reveal his part in it yet.

'Good God,' Bryce said, grimly. 'This is the last place you'd expect it.'

Theo Ashton was described on the news as a young man in his late twenties who had lived at the eco-project for several years. His distraught parents were filmed arriving at a hotel in nearby Llanerch. There followed some picturesque footage of the village, and a piece to camera by a reporter standing outside the pub saying that police were continuing their enquiries.

Suddenly Elena leapt up and switched off the TV, under the pretence of clearing away some of the dishes. 'All right, sweetheart?' she said, as Cerys appeared in the kitchen doorway, and clearly signalling a change in the conversation.

'Hi Cerys, this is Jeremy, a friend of mine,' Mariner said immediately, hoping that Bryce would have understood the signals and would respond appropriately. 'Jeremy, this is Cerys.'

'Pleased to meet you, Cerys,' said Bryce, apparently unfazed. 'You must be the chess player I've heard so much about. How about a game?'

'Okay,' Cerys said. She looked tired, Mariner thought, dark circles under her eyes, but perhaps this would take her mind off things. She fetched the chess board and offered up the pawns. Bryce drew white and opened the play, and it was obvious straightaway that he would be more of a challenge to her than Mariner had been. He was also far more patient, talking Cerys through her options on several of the moves, to help her think her strategy through and almost, in essence, playing against himself. 'Are you a teacher?' Mariner had to ask after a while, watching from the sideline.

'Of a sort,' Bryce said, concentrating on the move ahead. 'Except my students are university undergraduates.' Cerys made her move. 'Are you sure about that?' Bryce asked her mildly. 'I can see quite a tasty *prawn* exposed there if you do.' Cerys giggled and hastily withdrew the move, making another seconds later. 'Much better,' Bryce encouraged, with a conspiratorial twinkle. 'That's given me more to think about.'

Mariner watched as the game became ever longer and more complex.

'Checkmate!' said Cerys suddenly and with almost as much surprise as triumph.

'Ah, you have me!' exclaimed Bryce dramatically, sitting back and slowly shaking his head, as if he hadn't just engineered his own defeat.

'Bed now, young lady,' said Elena. 'I'll be up to tuck you in.'

Elena followed on soon after and now that they were alone, Mariner felt able to tell Bryce more about his involvement in the events of the previous day. Keeping his voice low, he described to Bryce what had happened. 'Goodness, what a dreadful experience,' Bryce said, as

Mariner recounted the discovery. 'I'm sure I wouldn't have a clue what to do in those circumstances.'

Mariner could believe it. Commonly when meeting anyone new, he tended to be vague about his profession, citing something like 'security consultant,' but Bryce would find out the truth soon enough so there was no sense in his being coy. 'Actually I've had a bit of practice,' he said. 'I'm a police officer with the West Midlands service.'

Individual reactions could often be interesting, but Bryce took it in his stride. 'Oh, I see,' he said. 'What a stroke of luck that you were there and knew exactly what to do.'

'In the practical sense, yes.' Mariner looked up as Elena came back into the kitchen.

'What an extraordinary life you must lead,' Bryce said to Mariner. 'It makes my existence seem very dull by comparison.'

'I'm sure your job must come with its own pressures,' Mariner said.

'Of course, but all this makes what I do for a living seem rather pathetic. I couldn't even hack it as a teacher; those who can, teach, those who can't . . . You know the rest. It was the discipline I struggled with, that and the increasing numbers of children who really didn't have any interest whatsoever in learning.'

'But you're in a unique position now to help young people achieve their goals,' Elena said. 'There must be some satisfaction in that.'

'Well, yes, though I'm not sure that we're preparing them for anything useful these days, nor am I convinced that many of them appreciate the education for its own sake.'

'You sound rather disillusioned,' Mariner said.

'Really, do I? Oh well, perhaps I am a little, but that isn't to say that I don't enjoy my job. It allows me a wonderful opportunity to indulge my passion for reading, even if the fruits of my research are wasted on many of my students.'

'Which institution are you at?'

'Oh, not a particularly academic one; it's one of those that started out as a polytechnic.' He seemed preoccupied. 'So this killing; they're sure it couldn't possibly be him, this man McGinley, I mean?' he persisted, changing the subject abruptly.

'There's no indication that it's his handiwork,' Mariner said. 'What makes you say that?'

'Nothing, I mean . . . goodness.' Something was bothering him.

'What is it?' said Mariner.

'This morning I was coming down off the top of Troel Maen when it started to pelt down with rain. There was a derelict hut, a byre or something I suppose. Anyway, I ducked inside out of the rain to get my waterproofs on, which I did, but then my eyes adjusted to the dark and I noticed that there were signs that someone was living there; some empty cans, a bit of what looked like firewood and some firelighters, a couple of recent newspapers. And I thought I heard something.'

'What kind of something?'

'Well, like a movement, a rustling sound, and I had a definite feeling that I wasn't alone. I just finished getting my jacket on and got out of there as quickly as I could. Afterwards I just thought I could have been imagining it, or that perhaps it was simply a scavenging rat or something. After all, I didn't actually see anything; only what someone might have left behind.'

For the first time Mariner felt a vague unease about Glenn McGinley. There didn't seem to be any question that he'd headed west, rather than south. But Mariner, more than anyone here, knew that police deduction wasn't entirely infallible. Once again he heard himself saying, 'Given what's happened I think it's worth reporting. It may be nothing, but equally it could be important. I'll give the local police a call. I'm sure they'll want to come and talk to you.' Mariner took out Farthing's card from his wallet. 'Do you mind?' he asked Elena.

'No, of course not.'

'If you just show me roughly the whereabouts of the hut, I can give them co-ordinates,' he said to Bryce.

'Yes, I think I can do that.'

Locating the byre was no easy task, as Bryce's map-reading skills were limited to say the least. When Mariner put through the call a few minutes later, neither Griffith nor Farthing were available, which didn't surprise him at this hour. Speaking to the civilian operator, Mariner simply reported what Bryce had seen, giving the map co-ordinates, leaving his Welsh colleagues to draw their own conclusions.

Bryce's eyelids were starting to droop and soon after the call he announced that he would like to turn in. Elena stopped him as he was going out of the door. 'Don't know if this might be useful,' she handed Bryce a bottle of Night Nurse. 'Might help you sleep.'

'Thank you, that's very kind,' Bryce said. 'I must say, I'm ready for my bed now.'

'I'll catch you up,' Mariner said to Bryce. 'Let you get settled.' And seeing Bryce across the yard, he followed Elena back into her kitchen. 'Sorry to drop Bryce on you as well,' he said. 'I felt sorry for him. You're sure you're okay with it?'

'Doesn't make much difference,' she said, lightly. 'In fact it might be better. If my ex turns up now, I can just tell him you're a gay couple.'

'Thanks,' said Mariner sardonically. 'Well, I'd best make tracks too.' Getting up, he put his mug in the sink. 'Thanks for the dinner, and for taking pity on us both.'

'We do seem to have a thing about waifs and strays round here,' said Elena. She got up too and came to the door to lock up behind him.

'Make sure you lock it securely.'

She made a mock salute. 'Yes, Officer. I don't know how I'd manage without you here.'

'Sorry.' Mariner's smile acknowledged his mistake. 'Force of habit.'

'I forgive you,' she said and stepped back, gently closing the door.

Bryce was in the kitchen making a hot drink when Mariner got to the hostel. 'I'm terribly grateful to you for arranging this,' he said, waving his arms around vaguely. 'I don't know what I'd have done.'

'No problem,' said Mariner. 'You look done in.'

'Yes, I think I'll sleep quite soundly tonight. Although I can't stop thinking about what happened to that young man. I don't know,' said Bryce. 'You do what you can to keep your children safe, but sometimes you're utterly powerless.' There was catch in his voice as he said it.

'You sound as if you're speaking from experience,' Mariner said, carefully.

'The locket,' Bryce said. 'Did you open it?'

'Yes.'

'The lock of hair was my daughter's,' he said, his voice trembling with emotion. 'It's all we have left of her.' He looked up at Mariner, his eyes glistening. 'But that's a story for another day,' he said before Mariner could ask.

'I'm sorry,' Mariner said.

Getting to his feet Bryce gripped Mariner's shoulder before shuffling past him and up the stairs, suddenly looking like a very old man.

As he ascended the stairs some time later Mariner became aware of a growing rumbling sound. Bryce was asleep and snoring so loudly through his blocked nose that the room itself seemed to vibrate; something Mariner had failed to anticipate. It was going to be like trying to sleep on the runway at Elmdon. After a moment of indecision, he gathered up his sleeping bag and retreated up to the attic room where he cleared a space, threw a mattress on the floor, bedded down on that and fell instantly into a deep sleep.

## Chapter Twenty-Two

Day Seven

First thing on Monday morning Tony Knox arrived in the office to find Charlie Glover leaning against his desk, arms folded and his naturally cheerful face grim. He looked in need of a shave and a change of clothes and was instantly recognizable as an officer in the middle of a tough investigation. With Mariner out of the picture, this would be Glover's first big one. 'Kirsty Fullerton died in the early hours of this morning,' he told Knox, without drama.

'Jesus.' Knox slumped down into the chair behind his desk, suddenly exhausted although the day had only just begun. 'Do they know what it was?'

'Mephedrone probably.'

'Meow-meow,' said Knox, using its street name.

'It's consistent with what the post-mortem tells us and one of the kids got a look at it too — said that it was a bright green pill.'

'Did she know where Kirsty got it?'

'No such luck,' said Glover.

'You think she had a bad reaction?'

'That's what it looks like. If we can establish who gave it to her, we could be looking at manslaughter.'

'Any progress with that?'

'We're continuing to gather witness statements from all the kids. With the help of her parents I've been monitoring her Facebook page too, in case any of them lets anything slip. But to be honest they're still all over the place, and most of them don't know anything. You know what it was like there.'

'Yeah, dark, chaotic and noisy,' said Knox.

Glover nodded. 'A lot of them don't even seem to remember seeing Kirsty, let alone who she was hanging out with. We're getting the picture that it all happened upstairs in one of the bedrooms. I'm pretty sure a couple of the girls who arrived with her know more than they're letting on, but we can't get them to open up, even though we've made it quite clear that they won't be in any trouble if they do. I get the impression that it's not us they're worried about.'

'So who or what are they afraid of?' Knox speculated. 'Their parents?'

'Gut feeling?' said Glover. 'The parents are as anxious for answers as we are. There but for the grace of God, and all that. If this was a different group of kids in a different part of the city I'd say they were terrified of grassing up the wrong people, but this is not that kind of neighbourhood. These are nice kids from good homes.'

'Well, keep me posted,' Knox said. 'And if I think of anything . . .'

'Thanks, I appreciate it. Any news on the boss?' Glover asked.

'Yeah, I spoke to him yesterday,' said Knox. 'He's fine; enjoying himself.'

'He's not worried about this McGinley then.'

'The only one who's concerned about *him* is Millie, for no other reason than her overactive imagination,' Knox said. 'We've all got enough on our plates without going looking for more trouble.'

'That's what I thought,' said Glover, satisfied. 'Anyway, I'd best get on. I need to check in with the Fullertons again.'

'Sure,' said Knox. 'And Charlie?' he called as his colleague reached the door. 'Don't forget to eat and sleep, or you'll be no use to anyone.'

When Glover had gone, Knox sat for a few moments reflecting again on the events of the previous Saturday, racking his brains to think of anything he might have seen that would give a clue as to the identity of the supplier, but he could come up with nothing.

After a while he switched on his PC and spent the time he had before his main business of the day — a court appearance — surfing the web for the information Mariner had asked him to track down. In the short time he had, he managed to come up with some interesting findings, and by ten o'clock he was hanging around inside the city law courts, waiting to give evidence against two thugs he'd charged months previously with aggravated burglary.

It was one of the most frustrating aspects of the job — the hours spent waiting to be called as a witness. Though at least with the advent of mobile phones, that time need not be completely wasted. It was while the court was working its way through the forensic evidence with the help of several expert witnesses that Knox slipped out of the front entrance and put through a call to Katarina's place of work. He'd tried phoning her on the mobile number Mariner had given him, but without success. Eventually he gave in and tried the work number Mariner had given him for the Brasshouse language centre, where she was an Albanian translator. But he didn't get much joy there either. Despite the fact that Kat had not shown up for work for several days, her boss Luke Mayer seemed very relaxed about the situation. 'She works hard,' he told

Knox. 'She's called out at all hours, quite often for you guys, and has been working solidly for months. I wouldn't be surprised if she's taken a few days off.'

'She called in to let you know?'

'She doesn't have to,' said Mayer. 'Kat is one of our freelancers, so it works the other way around. She calls us to see if there's any work for the day; if there is she agrees to what she can do, if not, we're not committed to paying her. It's an arrangement that suits us both.'

'And does she often not call in for work?' Knox asked, as the door opened and an usher stuck his head out and caught his eye. Knox started back towards the building.

'I wouldn't say often,' Mayer said. 'But from time to time she has a break. Like I said, she works hard.'

'Okay, thanks,' said Knox, hurrying back into the court. 'I might need to call you again, okay?'

* * *

Mariner woke at first light in the attic room of the hostel and, gathering up his sleeping bag, crept back down to the dorm. Bryce's snoring had declined into heavy, raspy breathing, but Mariner didn't want him to feel awkward about it, so he left his sleeping bag arranged as if he'd slept there all night and went and had a shower. When he finally surfaced, Bryce didn't feel well enough to walk, so Mariner went off alone, leaving him at the hostel. He walked across the yard as Cerys and Elena emerged from the house, the girl looking pale and washed out.

'She didn't feel like going in on the bus today,' Elena said. 'So I'm giving her a lift to school. Quite a treat isn't it, my love?' Cerys managed a smile as she opened the car door.

Mariner's walk that day took him over towards the coast but he felt drained and tired and couldn't shake off the feeling of gloom that had descended on him again. He was back by the middle of the afternoon, deliberately passing by Gwennol Hall in the hope that he might see Suzy Yin, but there was no sign of her and he didn't feel he knew her well enough to intrude on her day. The village, as he walked through it, seemed unnaturally quiet, the focus of the police investigation having shifted now from the streets to the incident room. When he got back to the hostel, it too had the feel of the *Mary Celeste*. He knocked on Elena's door. 'Hello?'

There was no answer from within, but as his knuckles made contact with the wood panelling, the door swung open with a peculiar groan. Inside, the kitchen looked as if someone had left in a hurry. A pan of onions, half fried in oil, was on the stove, alongside garlic ready chopped on the board, and a mug of tea stood developing a scummy film on top of the counter. Mariner put his fingers around the mug; it was lukewarm.

The only sound was the slow dripping of a tap. Something filled him with foreboding and he did a quick check around the ground floor of the house. It was empty. He went across to the hostel and up to the dormitory. Bryce had vacated his sleeping bag and some of his things were gone. His mind racing with possibilities, Mariner ran back down the stairs, and as he did so Elena's car pulled into the yard, Cerys in the passenger seat.

Elena greeted him cheerfully. 'Hi, everything all right?'

'Fine,' Mariner gasped, his heart beating double time, although why, he didn't quite know. 'Just wondered . . . it seemed quiet around here.'

'That's the countryside for you.'

Cerys climbed out of the passenger seat and, with a weak passing smile, went into the house.

'She was invited to a friend's house after school,' Elena explained. 'It seemed like a good idea at the time, something to take her mind off things. But she rang me to come and fetch her.'

Elena eyed Mariner's muddy clothing. 'You look as if you've had a walk.' As she spoke, she went round to the boot to retrieve a couple of carrier bags of groceries.

Mariner automatically stepped forward to help. 'Yeah, I was just going in to shower.'

'If I hadn't got so much to do I'd come and scrub your back.'

'Don't let Rex hear you say that. God, what have you got in here?' he asked, picking up the last and heaviest of the bags. He carried them into the kitchen and was just emerging, when Bryce appeared at the gate.

'I felt much better this afternoon,' he told Mariner. 'Thought I could do with some fresh air, so I stopped in at the pub too for a glass of ginger wine. It's not a bad little hostelry, in fact I'd like to take you there for dinner tonight,' he went on. 'My treat, for the kindness you've shown me. Do you think your friend Elena would come along?'

'I'm sure she'd love to, but I'm not sure about Cerys, given it's a school night.'

'Oh, of course,' Bryce said. 'Silly me. Do you think she might like another game of chess though?'

'I wouldn't be at all surprised,' Mariner said. 'Why don't you use the shower first, then you can go across.'

* * *

Knox was on the stand until the court adjourned at the end of the day. No point in returning to Granville Lane, so instead, on his way out of the city, he stopped by at Katarina's flat on the off-chance that she might be there. The complex where she lived was a newly built development opposite the county cricket ground at Edgbaston, with limited parking for non-residents, except by expensive meter. Knox then had to wait around for someone to leave the building until he could gain access. The muffled sounds of music playing, children shouting and the occasional raised voice could be heard from behind the flimsy walls of the flats as Knox ascended three flights of stairs and walked along Kat's landing. But on the whole it looked well-kept and still smelled clean and newly decorated. He rang the bell to Kat's apartment three times, at intervals of several minutes, noting the absence of any sound coming from the other side of the solid wood door. Squatting down he lifted the letterbox flap but could see nothing beyond the wooden floor of the hall and a closed internal door.

'Hi, can I help you?'

The young Asian woman who came up behind him made him jump slightly and automatically Knox drew out his warrant card. 'I'm looking for the woman who lives here,' he said. 'Do you know her?'

'Katarina? Yes, I do,' the girl said. 'We moved in here at the same time and we used to work together. I'm Saira Mahmood. What's happened?' She looked suddenly worried and Knox realized his mistake.

'Nothing,' he assured her. 'Well, nothing to be concerned about. I just need to talk to her.'

'She might not be back for a while,' Saira said. 'She stays a lot with her boyfriend.'

'Giles Ridley-Coburn?'

'Yes. Are you a friend of Tom Mariner?' she asked.

'I work with him,' said Knox. 'He's gone away for a couple of weeks so I said I'd keep an eye on things. If Katarina contacts you, can you ask her to give me a call straight away?' He gave Saira one of his business cards.

'Yes, of course,' she said, though she seemed to be having sudden difficulty meeting Knox's gaze.

* * *

After he'd showered and changed, Mariner went back across the yard to wait for Bryce. 'They're upstairs,' Elena told him.

'Is that wise?'

'Don't be such a copper. He's a nice man. Cerys wanted to show him some chess game on her computer.' She crossed to the foot of the stairs. 'Your dinner date's here, Jeremy!' she called. 'And he's getting impatient.'

Moments later Bryce appeared shaking his head ruefully. 'She'll go far, that young woman,' he said. 'She had me on the ropes again. I need a drink.'

Mariner and Bryce walked down to the pub in companionable silence. It was early and a Monday evening, so the bar was a little less frenetic than it had been the night before. Mariner could smell the press a mile off though, and they were still well represented here. He and Bryce took a table in a secluded corner and Mariner tried to avoid eye contact with any of the other customers.

Bryce lifted his pint. 'Well, here's to you, Tom,' he said. 'And your kindness. As you so rightly predicted, after a day's rest I feel reinvigorated, and tomorrow I shall be on my way again.'

When they walked back again later that evening, Mariner let Bryce go on ahead into the hostel, while he called in to check on Elena and Cerys.

'There's no need,' Elena told him. 'We're fine.'

'I wanted to,' said Mariner. 'With any luck by the time I go up Bryce will already be asleep, then I can sneak up to the attic room again. I don't want to offend him by telling him he's keeping me awake.'

'You want a night cap before you go?'

'All right, go on then.'

Bryce, as Mariner had predicted, was rumbling away like a motorcycle with an exhaust problem by the time he followed on across the yard. He wondered how Mrs Bryce could stand it, although it might explain why she didn't holiday with her husband. On the few occasions when Anna had accused Mariner of snoring he'd also swiftly been relegated to the spare bedroom. Gathering up his sleeping bag again, he climbed the stairs to the attic room. He checked his phone briefly to see if Knox had been back in touch, even though he knew it was probably too soon, then quite suddenly weariness overtook him and he drifted into sleep.

Mariner woke with a jolt some hours later. Something had disturbed him, and as he came to, he became aware of voices, and the low thrumming of an engine somewhere down in the street below. Unlike the previous night, the temperature in the attic had dropped significantly and it was with reluctance that he crawled out of his sleeping bag and went to the window, half expecting to see the black Range Rover back again. But this time the vehicle was just a regular car, idling outside one of the tied cottages a little way back down the street. Its headlights on, the driver seemed unafraid of being seen. As Mariner watched, someone emerged from the end cottage and walked down to the car. The interior light briefly came on as he or she climbed into the passenger seat, and seconds later the car pulled away.

Mariner shivered. It was frigid up here now. Terrific. Now he had the choice of Bryce's snoring or frostbite. But now that the car had moved off he realized that the hostel was quiet. Bryce had stopped snoring. Triumphant, he crept downstairs to the dorm, where the air felt marginally warmer, got carefully into the lower bunk to avoid disturbing Bryce and setting him off again, and quickly fell into another deep sleep.

* * *

Day Eight

When Mariner next awoke, the first thing he noticed, aside from a nagging headache, was that his face was wet, even though he had no recollection of having dreamt about Anna. In fact, he'd slept so deeply he couldn't remember dreaming about anything at all. They should have opened a window. The room was stuffy and his head was muzzy from a lack of fresh air. Lifting his head from the pillow he saw, in the dim light afforded by the curtains, a dark stain. Not tears then, but another nose bleed; probably why his head felt stuffed with cotton wool. He hoped he wasn't about to contract Bryce's cold. His watch told him it was still early: only 6:20. Careful not to wake Bryce, Mariner slipped out of bed and, taking the soiled pillow with him, he padded along the corridor to the bathroom, the stone flags freezing under his bare feet.

He looked a sight in the pocked mirror, blood smearing his face, though it seemed now to have dried up. He rinsed his face in cold water, the shock of its iciness making him catch his breath. He couldn't do much with the pillow, so he left it on the bathroom floor and, taking a spare from another dormitory, went back to the bunk room, in the hope of grabbing another hour or so of sleep. His blood, he noticed, getting back into bed, had spread on to the flimsy mattress too. He'd need to try and get that off.

Bryce didn't seem to have stirred. Maybe not that surprising given the amount of booze he'd consumed last night. Hoping that his nose wouldn't start bleeding again, Mariner rolled on to his back, and that was when he felt the tingle of a drip on his cheek that trickled warmly down behind his ear. He felt it again. His eyes snapped open. The underside of the top bunk was in shadow, but now that it was getting light, Mariner could make out a dark patch immediately above his head, about the size of a grapefruit. His heart hammering, he turned over and swung his legs out of bed again. Standing up brought him level with Bryce's bunk and what he saw made him cry out in horror. Bryce lay supine, his eyes closed and his arms folded neatly across his chest, exactly as if he were sleeping, though Mariner knew with absolute certainty that he wasn't. His throat had been slit from ear to ear and Jeremy Bryce lay in a dark pool of crimson blood that matted his beard, the spray splattered in a scarlet arc across the wall behind him. In one reflexive movement, Mariner doubled over and vomited on the floor, retching uncontrollably over and over until his stomach was empty. *Christ, what a mess.*

Stepping round the revolting puddle he went over to the window and wrenched back the curtain. The sudden flood of light revealed the full extent of the bloodbath and for some time Mariner simply stood, staring at the obscenity, his mind racing. How the fuck had this happened? And Elena. Oh God, Elena. How the hell was he going to break this to her? But he would have to, and he would have to do it soon. Glancing down, Mariner noticed spots of blood on his T-shirt. Bryce's blood. It was on his face again, too, and he felt an overwhelming, desperate urge to cleanse himself of it. He wanted to tear off his clothes and get under a scalding hot shower to scrub at his skin until it was red and raw. But rationally he knew that it was the last thing he ought to do next. Even in these last few minutes, as his brain struggled to make sense of all this, it had become obvious that he himself would be the prime suspect for Bryce's murder. Any attempts to clean himself or his clothing would reflect very badly on him. As he stood shivering, considering what to do next, he heard the distant sound of the door scraping across the stone floor, followed by Elena's voice echoing up the stairs. 'I hope you're decent, you two. I've brought you tea.'

*Fuck, why had she chosen today of all days*? Snatching up his fleece, Mariner bolted out of the door and pounded down the stairs, meeting her at the bottom, relieving her of the tray and shepherding her out through the door, in one smooth action.

'What is it? What's going on? You two got women up th . . .?' She tailed off, staring at his face, and then down at the bloodstains on his T-shirt.

'We have to call the police.' Mariner was breathless. 'Jeremy Bryce is dead. He's been murdered in his bed.'

'*What*? Is this some kind of wind-up?' Elena started towards the hostel again and Mariner had to hold her back.

'You can't go up there, Elena. It's carnage. And it's also a crime scene. We have to call the police. Now.' Grabbing his boots from the drying room and pulling them on over his bare feet, Mariner steered her back across the yard towards the kitchen. 'Where's Cerys?' he asked, his voice low.

'Brushing her teeth, I think. She'll be off to school in a bit. She said she'd be all right to catch the bus today.'

'I've got to phone the police straight away. Can you keep her upstairs for a few minutes and try to behave normally. It's probably best that we don't tell her anything yet, just let her get off to school.'

She was staring at him. 'But if he's dead . . .'

'I didn't do it, Elena.' Mariner held her gaze for a moment. 'Someone must have got in during the night.' He had no way of knowing if she believed him or not, but that was too bad.

'But how come you didn't hear?'

'I don't know; I was out cold. The booze, I suppose.' Mariner shot her an agonized look. 'Please, Elena, we can talk about this later.'

Inside the house Elena disappeared upstairs, while Mariner dialled 999 and reported what he had found. Then he swilled his face under the kitchen tap to remove any traces of blood and zipped up the fleece to cover up what was on his T-shirt, before sitting at the kitchen table, shaking and feeling sick. He pulled himself together when Cerys appeared, coming down the stairs with her school bag in hand. 'And so, another exciting day at school, eh?' he said with excessive enthusiasm.

Cerys curled her lip. 'I'd rather stay here.' She brightened. 'Is Mr Bryce about? D'you think he'd like a game of chess? Mum could always take me in later.'

'I don't think so. Anyway Mr Bryce is having a lie-in.' Mariner cringed inwardly, a euphemism if ever there was one.

'Come on, love, off you go,' Elena breezed down the stairs, her recovery from the initial shock impressive. 'I'll walk you as far as the gate.'

'Have a good day,' Mariner called after them.

Elena returned no more than a couple of minutes later, the facade of forced cheerfulness collapsed. 'Now what do we do?' she said, dropping into the chair opposite Mariner.

'We wait,' said Mariner. 'Any chance of that cup of tea?'

## Chapter Twenty-Three

They had drained their mugs and were sitting at the kitchen table, listening to the washing machine finish its cycle, when the cattle grid rattled in the yard. An unmarked vehicle had pulled in followed by a squad car, its light flashing. Mariner and Elena went out to be greeted by Ryan Griffith and a uniformed officer, a young, gangly lad with dark red hair and a bad complexion, whom Griffith introduced as DC Blaine. The absence of Chief Superintendent Bullman told Mariner that he was content to steer this investigation from behind a desk, trusting Ryan Griffith to do a good job.

'Where is he?' Griffith asked.

Mariner gestured towards the hostel entrance. 'Top of the stairs, second room on the right.'

The two policemen followed Mariner's instructions and Mariner heard their footsteps echoing on the floorboards, followed by an exclamation. Seconds later the younger man reappeared, hand clamped to his mouth. He staggered out into the yard and, bent double, brought up whatever it was he'd eaten for breakfast. Griffith took his time and it was several minutes before he emerged again, calm and unruffled. 'Sorry,' he said, regarding his colleague, who had straightened now and was wiping his mouth on a handkerchief. 'I don't think he's ever seen anything like this before.'

*But you have*, thought Mariner, remembering what Elena had told him of the man's history with the SAS. Griffith tilted his head towards the stairs. 'Who is he?'

'His name is Jeremy Bryce.'

'And he's a friend of yours?'

'Not exactly. I met him just a few days ago.'

Griffith walked over to the two uniforms now standing by their car and spoke to them for a couple of minutes, before coming back to Mariner and Elena. 'I'll need you both to go with these officers to make statements.'

* * *

The journey to Llanerch was a seven-mile drive into what turned out to be little more than a large village. Mariner and Elena remained quiet in the car, confining themselves to the occasional exchanged glance. Elena seemed nervous, but then it was undoubtedly the first time she'd been through anything like this, and she would be worried about Cerys too. Mariner wanted to reach out and take her hand but he didn't want to do anything that could be misinterpreted by their two escorts and fed back to Griffith. In a local area like this the squad would be tight. The police station was a square Greystone block set back behind parking bays. It must have been there a while, and still had the old-fashioned blue lamp hanging outside.

Mariner was taken first to the medical examiner. Except for a brief sympathetic smile as he went in and the minimal necessary instructions, the FME worked in silence; taking a blood sample, swabbing and scraping, and then removing several hairs from different parts of his head. Mariner accepted it all without complaint. Although his hair was cropped short he had plenty to spare, and it was the evidence from those samples that would help to put him in the clear. If he'd cut Jeremy Bryce's throat, the blood spatter would have found its way into his ears and the fine spray could have penetrated as far as the roots of his hair. Its absence wouldn't in itself be enough to rule him out as the killer, but it would form part of the wider picture. Finally the FME handed Mariner a couple of brown paper evidence bags. 'And I'll need you to do the honours again, sir, please.' Another police-issue tracksuit was folded on the chair and she left the room to allow Mariner to change into it.

After processing, Mariner was shown to an interview room, where a uniformed officer came and took his written statement, and then he sat twiddling his thumbs for a further hour and a half. By now he had a blinding headache and it was actually a relief to be left in peace for a while. Elena would be going through the same process in a separate room. The waiting couldn't be helped; Mariner knew that and he hoped Elena realized it too. Griffith would be sealing off the scene and waiting for the SOCOs to get there. In a rural area like this it could potentially take hours. Aberystwyth was probably the nearest main base. And he had no reason to grumble. The custody officer was attentive and courteous, offering refreshment at intervals, including some painkillers, and apologizing for keeping him waiting. Even so, Mariner felt a certain apprehension, knowing that having clearly been the last man to see Bryce alive he would inevitably be the focus of the questioning. And the trouble was, he couldn't explain it, except that it must have happened while he was sleeping up in the attic room. He'd racked his brains to remember if, at any time during the night, he'd heard or even sensed anything out of the ordinary but could come up with nothing. There was no way of proving to Griffith that he hadn't been in the bunk below Bryce's all night. What would he be thinking if he were in Griffith's shoes? Eventually he was offered the opportunity to make a phone call.

* * *

Tony Knox was at his desk, going over some of the statements Charlie Glover's team had collected from the kids at Michael's party to see if he could spot something that had been overlooked. So far it had been a fruitless exercise, exactly as Glover had said. It was like coming up against a brick wall, and a pretty incomprehensible one at that. All those people in such a confined space and none of them had seen a thing . . . Knox was starting to share Charlie Glover's feeling that some of the kids knew much more than they were letting on. He focused his efforts on Emily and Georgia, Kirsty's two best friends, who surely would have been the ones around her all night, but both claimed that they had been dancing downstairs immediately before the incident. Something was nagging at Knox, and he was vainly trying to identify what, when his phone rang. That it was Mariner was unexpected. 'Hi, boss, how's things?' He saw Millie glance up from her desk.

'Not all that great, as it happens,' Mariner admitted. He sounded muffled, far away, on edge.

'What's going on?' Knox was instantly alert. The information Mariner had asked him to put together was under a pile of other papers and he tried to retrieve it with his free hand.

'You know that killing here in Caranwy?' Mariner said.

'Yeah, it made the national news. Some kid wasn't it that was killed?'

'Yes. There's going to be a further news item today. There's been another one; a tourist has been murdered in what used to be the youth hostel, less than half a mile away.'

'Christ, so you're near all that too?'

'Pretty near,' said Mariner.

'Have they got anyone for it?' Knox asked.

'That would be me,' said Mariner. 'The guy was sleeping in the bunk above mine when he was killed.'

There was the merest beat of a pause while Knox absorbed that. 'Christ,' he said again. 'Are you under arrest?' Knox immediately felt, rather than saw, half a dozen heads swivel in his direction as the noise in CID faded to nothing. Instinctively he turned his back to the room and covered the phone's mouthpiece.

'Not quite,' Mariner said. 'But I could use a friendly face. How soon can you get out here?'

'I'll talk to the gaffer.'

'With any luck she already knows. Round about now the Dyfed police will be contacting her to inform her that I've been taken in for questioning.'

'Who's running the show?'

'A Superintendent Bullman is in charge, though the man controlling things on the ground is DI Ryan Griffith.'

'What's he like, this Griffith?'

'To be truthful, I can't make up my mind. Outwardly he seems okay. We've had a couple of conversations about Theo Ashton — the first victim — and he seemed to genuinely welcome my input.'

'But?'

'I don't know how close he is to some of the locals.'

'Is that going to be a problem?' asked Knox.

'Not for me, but for the case? I guess we'll have to wait and see. Listen, I might be here a while,' Mariner went on. 'I could do with a change of clothes. And did you manage to do that research for me?'

'I'll bring it along.'

Knox didn't want the whole of CID to know yet — they'd get the details soon enough — so he took Millie to one side to explain, before going and talking to DCI Sharp.

'So two people have been killed out there and they haven't got a suspect,' she said.

'That's about it,' said Knox.

'And Glenn McGinley?'

'What about him?' Knox asked wearily. This obsession of Millie's was becoming tiresome, especially as it was pretty well established by now that McGinley had got away to Ireland.

'Don't you think it's just too easy that he left his car where everyone would find it and let himself be seen buying a ticket to Dublin?' Millie persevered.

'He hasn't been caught yet, has he?' Knox reminded her. 'So it wasn't that easy.'

'Exactly,' Millie retorted. 'Maybe that's because he's got everyone looking in the wrong place. What if he didn't get on the ferry at all?'

'The man's committed a double and a triple murder,' Knox reminded her. 'It would be in his interests to get as far away as possible.'

'Unless he isn't finished yet.'

Knox took a deep breath. 'Look, Millie, this isn't the time . . .'

'Why is nobody listening to me?' Millie was beside herself.

'Because all the evidence indicates that McGinley's well away,' said Knox, exasperated. 'His car was found in the ferry car park. And all his victims were shot, not stabbed, so these killings in Wales are not at all consistent with his MO.'

'Unless he was provoked. He's a career criminal. His path could easily have crossed with the boss's in the past.'

'Do me a favour, would you?' Knox said, rubbing a hand over his face. 'Forget Glenn McGinley and look up a DI Ryan Griffith, Dyfed Police and see what you can get on him.'

As anticipated, the Welsh police had already been in touch with DCI Sharp and she was fully prepared for Knox to travel down to Wales. 'There will be an explanation for this, Tony,' Sharp said, unnecessarily. 'Don't let him do anything stupid.'

'He sounded calm and rational over the phone,' Knox reassured her. 'He'll be okay.'

* * *

High on adrenalin, Glenn McGinley had scrambled his way back to the unoccupied bungalow and let himself in. This time he found the electric emersion heater and celebrated with a hot bath as well as something to eat, before subsiding on to one of the beds feeling weakened and drained, the lack of adequate nutrition over the last few days beginning to take its toll. From the radio he learned that his car had been found in Holyhead and the search had shifted to the Republic of Ireland. 'My work is done,' he congratulated himself, before falling into a deep and heavy sleep.

* * *

Before leaving the city Knox called in at Mariner's house to pick up some things for him, but this time he drove along the service road to park right outside the house. He could see at once that something was wrong; the front door was hanging off its hinges and it was immediately obvious that the place had been trashed. For the first time Knox thought about the murders in Wales and what was happening here. What if Millie was right and this was all part of something bigger? Squeezing in through the battered door, he was instantly aware of a presence, even before he heard the voices coming from the direction of the kitchen. Stepping around the broken glass on the floor, he crept along the hallway. No, not voices: one voice, male, moaning and chuntering to himself. Knox cursed that he had no baton with him, nor was there anything to hand that he could use to protect himself. He inched his way forward and as he did so, the open door behind him swung and creaked in the breeze. The talking stopped abruptly and a face appeared in the kitchen doorway, long enough for Knox to glimpse a young man, with long, untidy hair and several days' growth on his chin. Knox met his startled gaze momentarily, before the trespasser turned and bolted, clattering out through the back door and on to the canal towpath.

'Hey!' Knox yelled, taking off after him. Outside he saw the figure in jeans and a hooded top running off in the direction of the city. Knox gave chase, but his fitness levels weren't what they used to be and his breathing was congested by his cold. After about fifty yards it became clear that the fugitive was younger and fitter, and that the gap between them was rapidly widening. Heaving for breath Knox stopped and took out his phone. First of all he called the ops centre and had a car dispatched to the next main road junction with the canal, along with a description of the man, though he knew it was a long shot. Then he called Millie. 'See if you can swing it to get a couple of SOCOs down to the boss's place,' he gasped. 'I've just disturbed an intruder. I think he's been here before so it would be good to find out who he is. The place has been given a good going over.' He then gave Millie as detailed a description as he could manage, to add to any trace evidence that might turn up.

'While you're on,' she said. 'I made some enquiries about the Welsh copper, Griffith. He's ex-SAS so started out in Hereford. Has had a couple of commendations, but nothing else is flagged.'

'Okay, thanks, Millie. You know this idea you've got about Glenn McGinley?'

'Yes.' She sounded suspicious, as if she was expecting him to tear her off another strip.

'Keep on it, will you?'

'Okay.'

Returning to the cottage, Knox found that, in addition to the highly visible damage, the kitchen worktop was now also littered with the essential paraphernalia of the habitual heroin user. Of course, the guy he'd disturbed could simply be an opportunist, who had found the door off its hinges and decided to use the place as his personal drugs den, but Knox didn't think so. Either way he was going to miss his equipment, and with any luck he would have left behind a few decent latent prints that that could be matched with a set already on the national database. Leaving all that for the SOCOs to find when they arrived, Knox went upstairs and grabbed a few of Mariner's clothes, before rigging the front door as securely as he could, and setting off for mid-Wales.

## Chapter Twenty-Four

It was early afternoon when Griffith finally appeared along with Superintendent Bullman, the latter's jaw already working on his nicotine gum. Bullman presented a freshly laundered contrast to his subordinate and was as immaculately turned out as the first time they'd met. The strain on Griffith was beginning to show in ways that Mariner recognized only too well. His tie had slipped down another few notches and his shirt collar was slightly grimy and losing its shape. Mariner couldn't be certain if the slight unwashed smell in the interview room was coming from Griffith or himself.

Understandably, and perhaps for the benefit of Bullman, Griffith wasn't quite as friendly towards Mariner as on their last encounter, and Mariner wondered if he now regretted sharing as much as he had on the Ashton case. It felt very odd for Mariner to be on this side of the questioning, even though this wasn't the first time. A couple of years back he'd found himself, with the help of a third party, deliberately implicated in a serious crime. On that occasion he'd been rapidly exonerated. He hoped that the pattern would hold.

Mariner had declined the option of a solicitor or a Federation Rep. Although it was obvious how the events of the previous night might be construed, he had nothing to hide and, rightly or wrongly, he was depending on Griffith's ability to grasp that for himself. But, having set the scene for the benefit of the recording equipment, it was Bullman who took the lead in questioning. 'Perhaps you could start by telling us what happened last night, sir,' he began. He wasn't being overly polite; the 'sir' was a necessary means of putting some distance between them.

'I don't exactly know,' Mariner said, truthfully. 'I met Jeremy Bryce the evening before last on my way back to the hostel. It was after dark and he was in a bad way, but because the pub was crowded he was planning to walk on several more miles to find shelter for the night. I didn't think it was a good idea, so I took him back with me to the hostel. Elena Hughes agreed that he could stay there. Last night was the second night he stayed. He and I went down to the Hart for something to eat, then Bryce returned to the hostel and I followed him across a little later.'

'Why the delay?'

'I went to check on El— er, Mrs Hughes, to check that she was all right.' Mariner sensed Griffith's eyes on him.

'Did you have reason to think that she might not be?' Bullman asked.

'Not specifically, no, but after what had happened to Theo Ashton . . . Anyway, by the time I went over to the hostel Jeremy Bryce was already asleep in his bunk and was snoring loudly. He had a nasty cold. Believe me, as I'd learned the night before, he could snore. So I took my bedding and went up to the attic room to sleep. I'd done this on the previous night too. I slept for a while, but in the early hours I woke up again because it had got very cold, so I came back to the dormitory. Bryce had quietened down by then.'

'He'd stopped snoring?'

'So I thought.'

'And what time was this?

'I can't say for sure, but it was still completely dark, so could have been anytime between about one and five a.m.'

'That's a pretty big window,' Bullman observed. 'You can't be more specific?'

'There was a car.'

'A car?'

'Outside one of the tied cottages, picking someone up. That's what woke me; either the door slamming, or the voices, or it might have sounded its horn. I looked out and saw someone from the cottage get in, and then it drove off.'

'Can you describe this car?'

'It was a saloon, quite big, maybe the size of a Passat or something and light coloured: silver or grey. It's not much but it would prove what time I was in the attic. I could only have seen it from the window up there. The view from the dormitory is blocked by a tree.'

'And then you went down to the dormitory,' said Bullman. 'Did you notice anything out of the ordinary at that point?'

'Only that Bryce was no longer snoring. I fell asleep again. I was woken some time later — just as it was getting light — by his blood dripping on me, although I didn't realize straight away what it was.'

Bullman turned to Griffith, who placed one of the brown evidence bags on the table, the cellophane window displaying a brown and white garment: Mariner's blood-stained T-shirt. 'Do you recognize this?' he asked.

'Yes, it's my T-shirt,' Mariner said. 'And it has Jeremy Bryce's blood on it. As I said, it had dripped on me during the night and I was wearing it when I found him.'

'What did you do, when you realized what had happened?' asked Bullman.

'I threw up,' said Mariner. 'Then I went to tell Elena — Mrs Hughes.'

'You went to her house?'

'I didn't have to. She'd come over to the hostel to bring us tea. She called up the stairs. I didn't want her to see what had happened, so I ran down to stop her.'

'And if Elena hadn't come across, what would you have done then?' asked Bullman.

'I would have gone to the house.'

'Are you sure about that, sir?'

'Yes, of course I am. What else would I have done?' Realization dawned. 'You think I was going to run away, in my boxer shorts and boots?'

'The crime scene officers reported that most of your things were packed away,' said Bullman, consulting his notes. 'Are you usually so tidy?'

'As a matter of fact I am,' Mariner said, calmly. 'You can ask my sergeant. What could possibly have been my motive for killing Jeremy Bryce?'

'Until we've established exactly who he is and where he's come from, that's impossible to say.'

Mariner was surprised. 'There were no personal details in his wallet?'

'There was no wallet,' Griffith interjected with a frown.

'Then it's been taken,' Mariner said. 'He definitely had a wallet. I saw it on Sunday night when he unpacked some of his stuff. It's black leather, and it has some photographs in it.'

Griffith made a note on his pad. Bullman turned to Mariner. 'If you didn't kill Jeremy Bryce, then how can you explain it?'

'I can't,' Mariner admitted. 'Someone must have got into the hostel during the night.' He was stating the obvious but it was important to have it all recorded.

'There's no indication of a forced entry,' Bullman pointed out.

'There wouldn't need to be,' said Mariner. 'The hostel door sticks so I was advised not to lock it. Anyone could have got in, killed Jeremy Bryce and then left again.'

'Without disturbing you?'

'As I told you, I slept half the night upstairs in the attic room. And cutting a man's throat doesn't have to be noisy.'

'I think we'll let the pathologist decide that,' said Bullman. 'When you went up to the attic room, would there have been any indication to anyone outside that you were there?'

'I didn't switch on a light, if that's what you mean. I'm not even sure that there is one. I did check my phone for messages when I first went up there, though. There may have been a residual glow from my phone when I did that, but I don't know if that would be visible from outside the hostel.'

'We might have to try it out.' Bullman glanced at Griffith. 'And you were up in the attic until the early hours, when this car picked someone up from along the street.'

'That's right,' said Mariner. 'It would make sense that Bryce was killed while I was out of the dorm.'

'What makes you say that?'

'He was going like a chainsaw when I left the room but the snoring had stopped when I came back. I remember feeling relieved. I didn't do it,' said Mariner. 'Though I understand that for the moment I have to be your prime suspect.'

'That's very good of you,' Bullman replied evenly, but there was an edge of sarcasm to his voice. 'And Jeremy Bryce just "turned up" in Caranwy on Sunday evening?'

'Yes, I spotted him up ahead of me as I was walking back to the hostel. I called out to him.'

'Why?'

'We'd met before. While I was driving out here on Thursday I gave him a lift along the road to Tregaron.'

Bullman raised his bushy eyebrows. 'So you'd arranged to meet in Caranwy?'

'No, it was a coincidence, though perhaps not so strange. We were both walking the Black Mountain Way. I stayed in Caranwy longer than anticipated, so I suppose it was inevitable that Bryce would catch me up.'

'Do you know where he'd been, immediately prior to you meeting him again?'

'It's hard to say really. He wasn't the most skilled at map reading, so where he'd been before that is anyone's guess. That first time I picked him up was after he'd got lost, and it seemed to be par for the course. But he'd come over from the direction of Devil's Mouth the day before yesterday. That would have been when he came across the byre. Did that turn up anything?'

'What?'

'The derelict byre that Bryce mentioned.' Mariner looked from one man to the other. 'He told me there were indications that someone had been sleeping rough there. I phoned it in on Sunday night.'

'This is news to me,' Bullman said, turning to Griffith.

Taking his cue, the DI stood up. ''Scuse me.'

Bullman notified the tape of Griffith's departure, and he was gone for about ten minutes during which time Mariner guessed that someone was getting a bollocking.

Eventually Griffith returned, and he and Bullman spent a few moments conferring in low voices.

'This puts a slightly different complexion on things,' Bullman said, finally turning back to Mariner. 'That byre is only in the next valley and within easy walking distance. Anyone hiding out there could possibly be our killer. We need to consider that whoever it is didn't like being disturbed and thought that Bryce might have seen something he shouldn't have.'

'Bryce could easily have been followed and killed to prevent him from giving anything away,' added Griffith.

'But it was too late,' Mariner pointed out. 'Bryce had already talked.' He took it as an encouraging sign that Bullman was prepared to explore ideas with him. The Superintendent would hardly be so open if he was still considering Mariner a suspect.

'Could Bryce have seen something on the day Theo Ashton was murdered?'

'I don't see how,' Mariner said. 'According to him, he'd only walked into the area on Sunday.'

Griffith paused a moment. 'There is another explanation, of course.'

'Which is?'

'You were very much in the area on the day that Theo Ashton was killed. Perhaps whoever killed him thinks that *you* saw something. It would also have been known that you were staying at the hostel.'

'So he killed Bryce thinking he was me?' Mariner let that sink in.

'Who else knows that you've been staying at the hostel?' Bullman asked.

'Quite a few people,' said Mariner. 'I've met Elena's partner, Rex, and I told Nigel Weller at the farm when I met him. Some of the staff up at Gwennol Hall will know too, of course. I've spoken to Suzy Yin, the historian who's working up there.'

'Would any of these people be aware of Bryce?'

'Probably not, given that he only showed up a couple of nights ago. Elena and Cerys know about him, of course, and we might have been seen together walking through the village or in the pub last night, but more people will have seen me around.' For the killer to have mistaken Bryce for him made a certain kind of sense.

'Have you noticed anyone taking a particular interest in your presence here?' asked Griffith.

'Not especially, but the police and the media in attendance means there's a lot more activity in the village right now. There were certainly people about, and as we all know the press are curious about everything and anything.'

'Tell me a bit more about Jeremy Bryce,' Bullman said.

'I don't know very much,' Mariner said, truthfully. 'He was one of those people who listened more than he talked. He was a tourist, in Wales on a walking holiday, like me.'

'That's all?'

'He was a university lecturer of some kind. He didn't say at which institution; only that it was formerly a polytechnic. He seemed interested in historical sites.'

'Oh well, that narrows it down then,' said Bullman with irony. He sat back in his chair. 'Okay, let's take a break. You realize that we'll need to keep you here for the moment.'

Mariner nodded. 'Yes, I understand that.'

Terminating the interview, Bullman switched off the machine and left the room. Griffith made to follow him but stopped in the doorway. 'Humour me,' he said to Mariner. 'Why have you really been staying in the hostel? I mean, it's not even a going concern anymore.'

'Elena,' said Mariner. 'She and I go back a long way.'

Griffith stared at him, wanting to know more about that, but knowing equally that it was of limited relevance right now. 'So you've been to Caranwy before?' he said.

'Only for a short time; one summer in the eighties.'

'Does that mean you also know other people in the village?'

'I don't think so. Most other people have moved on.'

'It's a mess, isn't it?' Griffith concluded. 'We'll try not to keep you waiting too long.'

'How's Elena doing?' Mariner dared to ask.

'She's fine,' came the expected reply.

## Chapter Twenty-Five

Knox arrived at the police station in the middle of the afternoon. He was impatient to see Mariner, but protocol demanded that he report to the senior investigating officer. DCI Bullman was unavailable, so he met first of all with Ryan Griffith, for which Knox was glad. It wouldn't hurt to get an idea of who and what they were dealing with. His first impression was of a consummate professional. 'We're holding DI Mariner because he was the last person to see Jeremy Bryce alive, and he was sharing a room with him the night Mr Bryce died,' Griffith said.

'And what is he saying?'

'That he didn't do it, of course. He claims that he was out of the room until the early hours of the morning. It's not enough to get him off the hook, of course. We haven't got a time of death yet, and when we do it's unlikely to be that specific.'

'But he didn't do it,' Knox said, with absolute conviction.

'No, I don't think he did,' Griffith confessed. 'But until we've got anything more substantial . . .'

'Yeah, he gets that and so do I.'

'We're working on it,' Griffith said.

'Who was this Bryce?' Knox asked.

'A tourist. Your boss picked him up a few days ago, and then they met again on Sunday in Caranwy.'

'That's all you know?'

'He's apparently some kind of college professor, history possibly, but we've no address and no one has apparently reported him missing. His wallet seems to have disappeared. My chief is doing the press stuff now, including putting out a media appeal for anyone who might know him to come forward. We're having to tidy up one of the post-mortem photographs to use, which isn't ideal, but it's all we've got.'

'Are you linking it to this other murder?' asked Knox.

'It makes sense to,' Griffith said. 'This is a remote country village. Murder doesn't happen here, so when you get two this close together, chances are they're related. But although they're both knife attacks the MOs are pretty different. Theo Ashton's attack was frenzied, with multiple stab wounds. This one was clean and controlled.'

'And a murder weapon?'

'We haven't found anything for either yet, though we've had to send DI Mariner's pocket knife for analysis. He's been carrying it around in his backpack the last few days.' Griffith cast his eyes down to something suddenly important on his desk. 'What would you say about his mental state?'

'He's been through some personal difficulties recently,' Knox said, cautiously. 'An ex-partner died suddenly. He was still close to her. But we've been more concerned about him being a danger to himself than to anyone else. I'd like to see him now.'

* * *

Knox was shown down to the holding cells, which replicated those in any police station across the country, distinguishable mainly by the smell of disinfectant that barely masked the odour of human sweat and excrement. It was, Knox thought, the genuine smell of fear. The boss looked in reasonable shape, all things considered. He was pale and bearded, and the shapeless track suit looked incongruous on him, but Knox was relieved to note that there was no outward indication that he was losing his mind.

'Am I glad to see you,' said Mariner. The men shook hands.

'How are you?'

'I'm okay. How's it looking out there?'

'They're doing their job.'

'I'm glad to hear it.' Mariner's eyes locked on to his sergeant's. 'You know I didn't do this.'

'Yeah, and I'm pretty sure Griffith knows that too. I'll be honest with you. When you first told me, I did wonder if . . . you know . . . the grief and everything. But I can see that I was wrong. Want to give me your side of it?'

Mariner recounted his story, from the point at which he picked up Bryce for the second time. 'I feel terrible. He was a nice guy and now I'm wondering if I could somehow have been responsible for his death. If it is a case of mistaken identity, if he hadn't come with me and stayed at the hostel . . .'

'Not your fault, boss.'

'We don't know that. Are they getting anywhere with finding out who Bryce was?'

'Bullman's about to put out a media appeal.'

'So now we just wait,' said Mariner. 'Did you find out anything useful about our other local residents?' Mariner asked. 'How about Nigel Weller?'

'There was more about him on Wikipedia than on the PNC,' said Knox. 'He was something of a celebrity, back in the day; one of the founding members of some rock band called Easy Money?'

'*The* Easy Money?'

'You've heard of them?' Knox looked up in surprise.

'If it's who I'm thinking of, they had a couple of hits back in the seventies or eighties. They were pretty big in the Midlands. You remember "Lookin' for Love"?'

'That a question or a song title?' quipped Knox. 'Oh yeah, as it happens I do now, but I needed reminding. I don't think they were quite so popular in Merseyside. Anyway, that sort of makes sense then, because his other claim to fame was his part-ownership of the Mellow nightclub in Solihull into the 1990s. He sold up his share of it just before he moved out here.'

'So no criminal record for our friend Weller?'

'I didn't say that. He had a couple of possession of cannabis charges and one assault charge, but all years ago, probably about the time he was pretending to be a rock star. Since then it's been all peace and love, man.' Knox mockingly raised the two-finger palm salute.

'Hm. Just because any criminal activity hasn't been logged, doesn't mean he hasn't retained his interest.'

'In what? The drugs?'

'It's what I think.' Mariner told Knox about his experiences at the farm and the conclusions he'd reached.

'But a few plants for personal use aren't going to land him in too much trouble, are they?'

'I'm still convinced that there's more to it than that,' said Mariner.

'But based on what?'

Knox was right. It was nothing more than a gut feeling, and it wasn't enough. 'What does Griffith think?' he asked.

'I don't know,' said Mariner. 'He played along with me, but I think he was satisfied with the explanation Weller came up with.'

'You think he knows more than he's owning up to?'

'It's possible. This area was hard hit by foot and mouth. Elena said it herself; everything around here was getting pretty run down, but in the last few years the investments that Willow and now Shapasnikov are making in the local area are helping to turn things around. Griffith is from round here and would be aware of that transformation. I'm just saying that he'd have an interest in seeing that it continues.'

'Do you want me to go and poke around a bit more?' Knox asked.

'No, leave it for now,' Mariner said. 'There's enough activity going on now with the murder investigations. They're going to be on their guard. What about Shapasnikov?'

'Even less on him,' said Knox. 'Just a couple of paragraphs in the popular press, mainly relating to him buying the Hall, and one magazine mention as part of a feature about wealthy Eastern Europeans taking over the country. Unlike most of your Russian oligarchs, the man would appear to be, if not completely squeaky clean, at least largely legit. He was born in St Petersburg and made his fortune through timber. He has a worldwide export firm, though his business interests are many and varied. One of which is a chain of nightclubs across different cities in the UK, called RedZone.'

'Isn't there one of those on Broad Street?' queried Mariner.

'There is. Shapasnikov enjoys life too. There are plenty of paparazzi shots featuring him escorting glamorous young models to various high-profile social events, and he owns a couple of racehorses.'

'Well, he wouldn't be a proper oligarch if there weren't a few of those in the picture. I understand the weekend parties he holds out here are pretty big affairs.'

'Maybe we should find out who's on his guest lists,' said Knox.

'Not a bad idea,' Mariner agreed. 'Birmingham must seem a bit dead — forgive the expression — compared with all this.'

'Not exactly,' Knox said, grimly. 'We've had our own brand of excitement while you've been away.' He filled Mariner in on the dramatic events of Michael's party.

'Christ. So Charlie's got a potential murder investigation on his hands. How's he managing?'

'He's doing fine,' said Knox. 'There have been further developments at your place too, and not good ones.' Knox told him about the ransacking. 'Sorry. I've ID'd a suspect though; caught him in the act.' Knox described the man at the cottage. 'Does he sound like anyone you know?'

'Apart from all the dozens of scrotes I've dealt with over the years? Not especially,' said Mariner. 'Have you talked to Kat?'

'Not yet,' Knox said. 'I've been round to her flat but according to her neighbour she doesn't go back there much.'

'I think she spends most of her time with the "dog's bollocks,"' Mariner said gloomily.

'You mean the fragrant Giles? Not jealous, are we?'

'Of what — the youth, the looks or the money?' Mariner snorted. 'Why on earth would I be?'

'She hasn't been doing much work for Brasshouse lately either; they hadn't seen her for a while.'

Mariner felt the first murmur of unease. 'That I don't understand. Kat loves her job.'

'But maybe she doesn't need it if Giles is keeping her,' Knox suggested. 'Doesn't he earn big bucks?'

'That's not the point.' Mariner frowned. 'Kat wouldn't want to be kept. You know what she's like. After what she went through, her independence and freedom are sacrosanct to her. When's the last time anyone saw her?'

'A few days ago is what everyone's saying.'

'I don't like it,' said Mariner. 'Goran Zjalic may have been put away for fifteen years, but he has some powerful friends.' With Kat's help, Mariner and his colleagues had successfully had the man responsible for the trafficking convicted and sentenced, but as they both knew, that was never the end of the story.

'You think . . .?'

'I had an odd experience driving out here after the funeral,' said Mariner. 'I thought I was being followed. Someone was too close on my tail, headlights on full beam, some kind of dark-coloured SUV. The other night there was another one, a hulking great black thing, hanging around in the lane opposite where I'm staying. It looked out of place. I mean, there are plenty of off-road vehicles, but not many are that shiny. What if Zjalic's mates are after both me and Kat?'

Mariner's question didn't provoke the response he'd hoped for. He wanted Knox to dismiss the idea as far-fetched, but instead his sergeant was thoughtful. 'There's something else you should know about Nikolai Shapasnikov,' he said, frowning. 'He has business interests in Albania. I mean, they're distant, but they are there all the same.'

'Any names come up?'

'None that I recognized.'

'But if we're saying he's connected with what's happening out here, I've never even met the man. How would he know about me?' Mariner was struggling to piece it all together.

'If this is about Zjalic, he could have been monitoring you for months,' Knox pointed out. 'You've been to Shapasnikov's place, met his staff?'

'Not his staff as such,' Mariner said distractedly, thinking of Suzy Yin. Had she told Shapasnikov about him and where he was staying? 'Or all this could be about someone trying to frame me for murder. They failed with Ashton so tried again with Bryce.'

As they were considering this, a knock on the door preceded DI Griffith. 'The good news is that we're going to let you go,' he said. 'Even if I thought you did kill Jeremy Bryce — which, for the record, I don't — what we have so far is only circumstantial and not enough to bring charges. It will be best if you don't leave the area just yet, though, and if you'd check in from time to time I'd appreciate it. You need to be careful too. If someone did kill Bryce instead of you by mistake, they might be tempted to have another go.'

'There's a comforting thought,' said Mariner.

'I wouldn't go wandering off on your own just now,' Griffith advised, unnecessarily.

'This makes finding Kat a bit more urgent,' Mariner said to Knox. 'I'd feel happier if I knew where she was. I can't quite see how, but if this should happen to be anything to do with Goran Zjalic, someone could be after her too.'

## Chapter Twenty-Six

When Mariner was released, Tony Knox drove him back to Caranwy on his way back to Birmingham.

In the car Knox said, 'I don't know if you've been keeping up with the outside world, boss, but do you know about this McGinley story?'

'The murders in Liverpool?' said Mariner. 'That's more your territory than mine.'

'So the name McGinley doesn't mean anything to you?'

'Not that I can think of. Why?'

Knox emitted a derisive laugh. 'Millie's convinced that Glenn McGinley has come down here. She even started cooking up some tenuous link you might have had with him.'

'What kind of link?'

'An imaginary one probably,' said Knox, playing it down. '*Six degrees of Kevin Bacon,* probably. You know, someone shared a cell with someone who shared a cell with someone who was on remand with . . . I wouldn't get too worked up about it. Millie's being a bit weird, but that's about what you'd expect at the moment.'

'What do you mean?'

'What with her being pregnant and all that,' said Knox cheerfully. 'Theresa was off the planet half the time, when she was expecting our two.'

'Millie's pregnant?' said Mariner.

Knox shot him a look. 'Oh shit, she hasn't told you?'

'Clearly not.' Mariner thought back to that drive out to Upper Burwell. 'I think she might have been on the verge though. But why has she kept it from me? It's good news, isn't it?'

'For her, yes, but she wasn't sure how you'd take it, after what happened to you and Anna, then Anna . . . you know.'

'That's why she didn't tell me? Oh, come on, I haven't been so bad, have I?'

Knox's face said it all. 'It's called being sensitive,' he said. 'I think it's a girl thing.'

'So what will it mean?' Mariner said.

Knox looked at him askance. 'Well, it'll be about nine months of her belly getting gradually bigger, and then, at the end, a baby,' he said. 'Did no one ever tell you . . .?'

Mariner managed a weak smile. 'And what will it mean for her *career*, do you think?'

'I don't know. Maternity leave maybe, then pick up where she left off?' While they'd been driving they'd taken up position behind a slow-moving tractor pulling a trailer of mud-caked turnips. 'Come on!' muttered Knox, in frustration.

'And what does Suli think about that?' Mariner asked, remembering that Millie's husband was rather more of a traditionalist.

'I'm not sure that they've discussed it yet. Anyway, talking of Anna,' Knox said, carefully.

'Which we weren't,' Mariner reminded him.

'Well, whatever, you asked for this.' Reaching into the glove compartment, one hand on the wheel, Knox passed Mariner a computer print-out of the Towyn Community address. 'Are you planning on going to see Jamie Barham?'

'I feel somewhat obliged. Apparently now that Anna's . . . no longer around, I'm his legal guardian.'

'Christ almighty!'

'Frankly? I wish he'd got the gig.'

'Finally!' Knox slapped the steering wheel, as the tractor turned into a side road. 'Is there anything you want me to do?'

'Nothing to be done as I understand it,' said Mariner. 'I'll go and see him and we'll take it from there.'

* * *

The hostel yard, when they arrived, was cordoned off with police tape and there were vans and personnel milling about, so Knox dropped Mariner off at a discreet distance, a little way down the lane. Following that tractor had given Mariner an idea. 'Wait here a couple of minutes, will you?' he said to Knox. 'There is something else I'd like you to do for me.'

Walking up the lane and crossing into the hostel yard, Mariner knocked on the kitchen door. Elena opened it. She looked pale and harassed, and there were a couple of packed bags sitting on the floor by the door.

'Hi, they've let me out,' Mariner said.

'So I see.' She gave him a wan smile. She seemed to be in the middle of emptying the fridge and stopped for a moment, letting the door sway open. 'Nice outfit. Very "care in the community." You okay?'

'I think they more or less believe me,' said Mariner. 'How are you holding up?'

'I'm fine,' she said, looking far from it. 'Got dropped back here a couple of hours ago.'

'I hope they didn't give you too hard a time.'

'They did what they had to do.'

'I'm sorry to have put you though all this.'

'It's not your fault,' she pointed out. The second time today someone had told him that. 'You don't even know if it's anything to do with you.'

'But if it hadn't been for me, Bryce wouldn't have been staying here.'

She lifted her shoulders. 'Well, it's happened. Not much we can do about it now.'

'Listen, I know this is a weird question, but have you got any vegetables from Abbey Farm knocking around?' Mariner asked.

She stared at him. 'I've got a few potatoes and parsnips, why?'

'Could you spare me a couple? I can't really explain now, but . . .'

Closing the fridge door, Elena disappeared into the pantry and came out with a couple of soil-encrusted parsnips. 'Do you want me to wash them for you?'

'No, thanks, they'll do fine as they are,' he said. 'But have you got a couple of sandwich bags, and a spoon I can borrow?'

'This gets weirder by the second.' She got them for him. 'What are you up to?'

'Probably nothing,' Mariner said. 'I'll be back in a minute.' Out in the yard he put the parsnips in one of the bags and sealed it up before going over to Elena's vegetable patch, where he scooped a couple of spoonfuls of soil into the second bag, then walked back up the lane, to where Knox was patiently waiting in the car.

'See if you can persuade the forensic lab to analyse these,' Mariner said, handing him the two bags. 'Talk to Rick Fraser. He owes me one. I want to know if Willow's formula is kosher. The soil around the parsnips should contain his "magic potion" but the soil in this bag won't. I'd like to know what the difference is; if he really is on to something or if it's just the emperor's new clothes.'

'I'll give it a go, boss. Keep in touch, eh?' his sergeant added. 'And try not to get yourself caught up in anything else?'

'I'll do my best,' said Mariner.

* * *

When Knox had driven off Mariner went back to Elena's kitchen.

'They let you have your stuff back,' she said, seeing his bag.

'No, my sergeant's been across. He brought it for me. I knew they wouldn't let me back into the hostel any time soon.'

'It's screwed up our business before it's even started,' she said, wryly. 'Who's going to want to stay there now?'

'Oh, you never know. You might get the morbidly interested.'

'I've spoken to Ron and Josie Symonds at the pub,' Elena told him. 'They can put you up there for a few nights. On the down side you might have to put up with Joe Hennessey for company, but I'm sure you can manage to keep out of his way.'

'Thank you. And you?'

'We'll be fine.' She nodded towards the bags. 'Cerys and I are going to stay at Rex's place in town for a few days. He's been asking us to move in with him for ages, so he'll be delighted.'

Cerys appeared down the stairs. She looked in a bad way, her eyes red-rimmed.

'She knows what's happened,' Elena said.

'It's not fair,' said Cerys. 'I really liked him.'

'I know,' said Mariner inadequately.

## Chapter Twenty-Seven

Walking down to the pub, fatigue hit Mariner like a tidal wave and it was hard work to simply continue putting one foot in front of the other, so that when someone called out, he barely even registered it.

'Hey!' This time it was more insistent and Mariner looked round to see Suzy Yin, pushing a thin package into the village post box. With a little wave, she jogged to catch up with him, her hands shoved deep into the pockets of her parka.

'Sorry, I was miles away,' Mariner said.

'How are you?' she asked. 'Apart from completely shattered. I heard about what happened at the hostel.' Of course. It would be all over the news by now, not to mention the local grapevine.

'I've been helping the local police with their enquiries all day,' Mariner said. 'It's been strange to be on the other side for once, but I think they're satisfied that, despite my proximity, I had nothing to do with it.'

'Do you make a habit of stumbling across dead bodies wherever you go?' She grimaced. 'Sorry, that was an incredibly crass thing to say. I can't imagine how awful it must have been.'

'It wasn't the most welcome start to the day,' Mariner confessed.

'And now you're leaving?' She noted the holdall.

Mariner shook his head. 'For obvious reasons I can't stay at the hostel for the moment, so Elena's found me a room at the inn.' Mariner nodded towards the pub where there was a jam of vehicles in the car park.

'Well, that looks like it'll be fun.'

'Yes, I probably should get it over with. I haven't eaten much today either, so I'm hoping they'll be able to feed me.'

'Well, if you get stuck there's always a stir-fry on offer at my place,' she said, suddenly. 'It's what I'll be cooking tonight. Sorry to play to type, but you'd be very welcome to join me — if you'd like to, that is.'

'Wait, I wasn't hinting . . .' Mariner began.

'I know,' she said pragmatically. 'It would be nice to have someone sensible to talk to. I'm beginning to get rather bored with my own company. And I can guarantee it'll be a bit quieter than in there.' She nodded towards the pub.

'Well, thanks, that would be great,' Mariner said truthfully.

'You'll need some time to check in and all that. How about seven o'clock?'

'It sounds perfect,' Mariner said.

Feeling curiously revived, Mariner walked into the lounge of the White Hart and, as he did so, Megan the barmaid looked up hopefully. Despite how busy the pub was, Mariner noticed that the stools adjacent to the bar were empty and he realized she must be waiting for Hennessey. 'I'm Tom Mariner,' he told her. 'I understand there's a room booked for me here tonight.'

'Hang on, I'll get my dad,' she said. She disappeared, returning seconds later with Ron Symonds, flushed and perspiring, a tea towel slung over his shoulder. From a board behind the bar he handed Mariner a key on a large wooden fob. 'Room six, first floor,' he said.

'I can find my own way if you like,' Mariner said as he signed the booking card.

'Thanks,' said Symonds, gratefully. 'We are a bit rushed just now. It's up the stairs and along the landing to the left.'

'I suppose all this has been good for trade,' Mariner remarked.

'Not the kind of trade I'd want ideally, but I'd be stupid to resent it. Will you be eating with us?'

'Not this evening,' Mariner said.

'Probably just as well.' There was a shout from the kitchen and, with an apologetic nod, Symonds disappeared again.

Before going up to his room, Mariner bought a bottle of wine from Megan. It was a South African vintage, costing all of five pounds ninety-nine, and Mariner didn't know how good it would be, but at least he wouldn't be going up to the Hall empty handed.

He picked up his bag and climbed the narrow staircase to his room. Overlooking the main street, it was low-ceilinged and very feminine, all floral chintzes and frills, and the first thing Mariner did was to consign half a dozen lacy cushions to the top of the wardrobe. It had been a long day, and what he really wanted to do was flop down on the bed and close his eyes but standing under the hot shower enlivened him a bit. Mariner couldn't help wondering if food and conversation would be the only things on the menu with Suzy Yin tonight. He reminded himself to not get carried away. She was simply being friendly. From what he had seen of her, it was her way with everyone. He changed into the one set of clothes Knox had brought him, found he had enough of a signal to send his sergeant a brief text to let him know where he was staying, and an hour later he made the short walk up to the Hall.

When she came to the door Suzy looked effortlessly gorgeous in tight jeans and a soft grey sweater that left one shoulder bare. Aware that he might be gawping, Mariner presented her with the wine. 'It's probably terrible but there wasn't much choice,' he apologized.

'Good thing I'm not much of a connoisseur then,' she smiled, taking it from him. 'Thank you. Come through into the kitchen, and I'll start on dinner. You must be famished, and it won't take long.'

Inside, the flat was ultra-modern and Mariner sat at the breakfast bar and watched, captivated, as she moved around the kitchen expertly chopping, dicing and throwing vegetables, apparently at random, into a large skillet. Fifteen minutes later she delivered their plates, piled high, to the table and after a brief toast with the South African plonk, they tucked in. Perhaps because he was so hungry, for several minutes Mariner couldn't speak, so exquisite were the flavours. 'God, this is fantastic,' he managed to say eventually.

She smiled. 'Courgettes and onions courtesy of Abbey Farm.'

'You're wasted on those bloody documents.'

'Hey, that's my career you're belittling,' she protested mildly. 'Anyway, it's dead easy. Anyone could do it — even you.'

'Seriously, with those knives?' Mariner said. 'I'd be a danger to myself and everyone else.'

There was a beat of a pause as they both absorbed what he'd said.

'The man who died,' Suzy said carefully. 'He was just here on holiday?'

'Yes, the same as me, trying to get away from it all.'

'So I don't understand. Why . . .?'

'At the moment the strongest possibility seems to be that he either saw something connected to Theo Ashton's death, or . . .'

'What?'

'Someone thinks I did and they mistook Bryce for me.'

She shuddered. 'There's an unpleasant thought.'

'Bryce was a historian too,' Mariner said. 'At least he had an interest in history. He was a university lecturer. Maybe your paths have crossed?'

'It's unlikely. Teaching is quite a separate branch of academia; different worlds really. Which institution was he at?'

'He didn't say. The local police are trying to locate his family, his wife, anyway.'

'How awful,' Suzy said. 'That poor woman will be going about her business, not yet knowing that her husband is dead.'

'Yes, I can't imagine . . .' Mariner broke off, suddenly realizing that this was one thing he *could* imagine and that it was one of those trivial factors that had caused him almost as much distress as the loss itself. On dozens of occasions over the years he had broken the news of sudden death to a victim's relatives, and so many — mothers of daughters, husbands of wives — had reported some kind of premonition or portent. But on the day Anna had died Mariner had felt nothing unusual. It had been a perfectly ordinary day. There had been no ghost walking over his grave, no sudden, unexplained vision of her. If anything, he'd been in a buoyant mood and looking forward to seeing her again. Then DCI Sharp had walked into his office and his world had imploded.

'Hello,' said Suzy, placing a hand over his. 'Where did you go?'

Mariner dismissed her concern with a brief shake of the head. 'Some other time,' he said, and then, to break the tension: 'So tell me about your boss.'

'Mr Shapasnikov?' She shrugged lightly. 'There isn't much to tell. That is, I don't know very much about him. I've only met him twice; once when he interviewed me for the position and once when I met briefly with him to report on what I had learned about the Hall so far. That was about a fortnight ago.' She smiled. 'I tend not to get invited to any of the social gatherings; nowhere near as important or glamorous enough.'

'Well that's not true,' said Mariner, which rather touchingly made her blush. 'I understand they're big events.'

'They certainly generate a lot of fuss; helicopters coming and going, outside caterers and all that. And he has some big names — politicians, actors — but to be honest, once the events are underway I'm not even aware of them, tucked away up here.'

They sat for a moment in companionable silence, Mariner struggling to think of anything more to say. Suzy chuckled. 'Look at you, you're worn out. You need some sleep.'

Mariner pushed back his chair. 'Yes, I should get going.' They both looked up as the wind splattered a squall of rain at the window.

'Not in this you shouldn't. Why don't you stay here? There's plenty of space.' It was so casually said that Mariner didn't quite know what was on offer. Worse still was the fear that he may not be able to live up to whatever that might be. She saw his bewildered look and laughed. 'Come and see.' Taking his arm she led him through to the bedroom, almost entirely taken up by a low, king-sized bed covered by a voluminous duvet. 'All yours,' she said to Mariner. 'I'll tidy up in the kitchen and you can just crash here.'

'But what about you?'

She looked at him in surprise. 'It's a big bed,' she pointed out. 'And we're both sensible, mature adults so

I'm sure we could manage to share it without any . . . um . . . complications, couldn't we?'

*Could they*? 'Yes, right . . .' Mariner mumbled.

So exhausted was he that Mariner would have happily collapsed onto the bed there and then, but he managed to clean his teeth with a spare brush she found for him and strip off some of his clothes first. After the last few nights of roughing it, the soft mattress and fresh, clean sheets felt like the height of luxury. He was certain he'd be kept awake by the knowledge that Suzy would soon be joining him, but then someone, somewhere, must have flicked his off switch.

When he came to, it was in a thick, claustrophobic darkness and Mariner was unable to immediately orientate himself. This didn't feel like his bed at home, and it wasn't the musty, creaky-springed hostel bunk. Added to which, he couldn't see a thing and it was so quiet he could hear the blood roaring in his ears. As he flailed his arms to get some sense of space, something fluttered against his face and he yelled out in fear.

'Tom,' said a soothing, female voice nearby. 'It's all right. I think you were dreaming.'

Suzy. Exhaling with relief, Mariner sank back on to the pillow. 'Sorry. I forgot where I was. Did I wake you?'

'No, it's fine.' Her hand had fallen on to his bare chest. 'Shall I come a bit closer?'

Oh crap. 'Won't that . . . um, complicate things?' Mariner asked, with some apprehension.

Somehow he could hear that she was smiling. 'Oh, I'm not *averse* to complication,' she said. 'But you were so obviously worn out that it didn't seem the right time to be suggesting anything . . .' She wriggled across the bed and as she pressed her body against his, Mariner realized with a start how little she was wearing. He was of course instantly aroused, but all he could think about was that abortive encounter at the Star Hotel. He couldn't face a humiliation like that with Suzy. 'Actually,' he heard himself say, 'I'm still pretty shattered. And what with the alcohol . . . I wouldn't want to disappoint you.'

She was trailing her fingertips through the hairs on his chest. 'You wouldn't,' she said brightly, showing remarkable faith. 'But you've got a lot of catching up to do, so that's fine. I can wait. That's the thing with us historians. We can be very patient.'

*Thank Christ for that,* thought Mariner.

## Chapter Twenty-Eight

Tony Knox drove back to Birmingham feeling a weight of responsibility on his shoulders. He hadn't wanted to leave the boss but had recognized that there was nothing more he could usefully do in Caranwy. And meanwhile there was the small matter of Katarina.

Although it was mid-evening by the time he got back to the city, he took a detour in person via the forensic service labs, where he knew they would be working late, to persuade Rick Fraser to take the soil samples for analysis. Laying it on a bit thick that this might help get the boss out of a tricky situation elicited a promise to expedite the testing to take 'no more than a couple of days.'

Then Knox returned to Granville Lane to report to DCI Sharp what was going on. Knox passed through a busy front office and climbed the stairs to CID, which, at this time of night, was largely dark and deserted, except for the light coming from Sharp's office. She rarely left the building before seven in the evening, a fact that served as a deterrent for quite a few fellow officers considering a climb further up the slippery pole. He heard laughter as he approached and found her, typically, in conversation with the office cleaner. It was one of Sharp's strong points that she treated everyone who worked with her (never 'for' her) with equal respect. Perhaps being a mixed-heritage gay woman had shaped her outlook, but maybe not.

'Tony!' she greeted him and brought her chat with the other woman to a close. 'How did it go?'

Knox went into the office and, taking the chair opposite her, summarized the events of the day.

'And you think DI Griffith is happy that it wasn't Tom?' Sharp asked.

'The man's not an idiot,' said Knox. 'They've let him go but they want him to stick around for the moment.'

'That would make sense,' said Sharp. 'And he's not due back here for another week at least, so no reason why he shouldn't. If Griffith has anything about him he might even see Tom as an asset.'

'Actually, I think he does, ma'am.' Knox told her about Mariner's suspicion that he was being followed. 'Though it beats me why Zjalic, or anyone, would wait until the DI's in the middle of nowhere to take a pop at him. I'd have thought there would be a better case for picking him off while he's in the city. Could be dressed up as anything then and be more anonymous.'

'More chance of getting the right man out there, though?' Sharp hazarded. 'Less possibility of confusion?'

'Well, that didn't exactly work, did it?' said Knox.

'Have Dyfed had any response to the appeal to identify Jeremy Bryce?' Sharp asked.

'They hadn't when I left.'

'Well, whether or not it turns out to be Mr Zjalic behind all this, your priority for the moment has to be to track down Katarina,' said Sharp. 'If she's also in danger we'll need to think about some kind of protection.'

'That's assuming he hasn't already got to her,' said Knox. 'I've got her boyfriend's address now, so I'll go and see him first.'

Sharp frowned. 'Not forgetting to make time to go home to eat and rest,' she reminded him.

Knox gave her a pointed look. 'Isn't that the pot calling—' He stopped abruptly and Sharp laughed.

'The kettle black? It's all right, Tony, you can say it. It's an idiom, not a racial slur. And yes, I suppose you have a point.' She started gathering up the papers on her desk. 'About time I showed my face at home too.'

They walked out of the building together. 'Has Charlie Glover got any further today with Kirsty Fullerton?' Knox asked.

'Not that he's said,' Sharp replied. 'The kids have all just clammed up; a conspiracy of silence, Charlie calls it, and I think he's right. You know one of them, don't you?'

'Yes, my neighbour. It was his party.'

'A gentle word from someone he knows might help,' Sharp suggested mildly.

'Yes, ma'am. I'll look out for him.'

* * *

Giles Ridley-Coburn lived in exactly the kind of up-market place Knox would have expected; a luxury pad in one of the burgeoning developments around St Paul's Square in the Jewellery Quarter. Knox found a parking meter bay in the vicinity and walked past a couple of fashionable pubs and bars to the former Victorian factory that had been refurbished as loft apartments.

Knox had never met the man Mariner referred to as 'the upper-class tosser' face-to-face, but he recalled the boss's chagrin when Giles had come into Katarina's life. Having personally freed her from forced prostitution, Mariner had seen it as his singular mission to protect the girl against anyone and everything, so was not impressed when Giles had appeared on the scene. But unusually on this occasion the boss's instinct had let him down and he had eventually been forced to concede that Giles was 'an *all right* upper-class tosser.'

This evening, however, although his manners were plainly in evidence, Giles was distinctly cagey, hanging back behind the barely opened door.

'I'm looking for Katarina,' Knox said, after introducing himself. 'Can I come in?' Giles deliberated for a few seconds before reluctantly stepping back to allow Knox across the threshold. Once inside the flat, the reason for his reticence became obvious. Even by bachelor pad standards the place was a tip and while Knox stood taking it all in, Giles went hurriedly round picking up stuff at random and stowing it away. He wasn't quite quick enough to kick a stray syringe under the sofa and out of sight. Knox let it go for now; he didn't think Giles was diabetic, but neither was he certain of that, and he remembered that Mariner had been caught out by false assumptions before.

Having offered a drink, which Knox declined, Giles managed to create enough space for them to sit down awkwardly opposite each other on the sofa and arm chair respectively. Tall and healthy-looking with a mop of straw-coloured hair and perfect teeth, Giles was the kind of man for whom life had gone well. But tonight his composure seemed to be unravelling and he struggled to meet Knox's eye for more than a passing second. 'I haven't seen Kat for a couple of days,' he admitted. 'We had a bit of a . . . row the other night and she left my flat late at night and in a strop.' He scanned the room as if hoping she might suddenly appear. 'I haven't seen her since.'

'What was the row about?' Knox asked. 'It wasn't about the state of this place, by any chance?'

'Broadly speaking,' Giles admitted, picking at a nail. 'Kat's been spending quite a bit of time here. She had more or less moved in and it was going really well. Then a couple of weeks ago a friend of mine, Hugo, turned up. He was in a hole and needed help, so he's been crashing on my sofa. He and Kat haven't exactly hit it off.'

'Who is this Hugo, apart from being a complete slob?'

'Just a guy I know from way back. We went to the same school, though he's older than me. I thought he was a laugh, turns out he's rather a nightmare.' He tried a nervous smile.

'So ask him to leave,' Knox suggested.

'I can't,' Giles said awkwardly. 'It's . . . complicated. Our parents know one another and, well, you know . . .'

Knox didn't really. The Liverpool comprehensive he'd gone to wasn't big on brotherhood or loyalty, and your mum and dad's friends weren't in any way relevant. And that wasn't his concern. 'Has Kat been in touch with you at all since she left?' he asked.

'No. We don't live in each other's pockets,' Giles said. 'I'd quite like to, as it happens, but Kat isn't like that. She's more independent.'

*Mariner would be delighted to hear it*, thought Knox. 'There's a possibility that the man Kat helped to put in prison might have accomplices out looking for her,' he said.

'Oh shit.'

'Yeah, oh shit,' agreed Knox. 'Though I notice you don't sound that surprised.'

Giles licked his lips. 'Things haven't been easy with Hugo around, but even before he showed up I had a feeling that something was bothering Kat. She was always security conscious, but it was starting to border on the obsessive.'

'In what way?'

'Locking and re-locking the doors and windows, double and treble checking them, even during the day sometimes. I've even started wondering if she might have some OCD thing going on. And you can see the street from up here. She started spending ages just staring out the window at it.'

'As if she was watching for someone?' Knox asked, going cold inside.

'It could have been, yes,' Giles admitted. 'When I first met Kat she used to have this fear that the men who snatched her in Tirana would come back for her, to punish her for what she did, for escaping. On one level she knew that it was irrational — the likelihood of it happening again. I just thought she was succumbing to those fears again; being paranoid.'

'Wouldn't you be scared if you'd been through what she has?' Knox asked, perhaps a little harshly. Kat had effectively been snatched from her home city, trafficked from her native Albania and sold into prostitution, until Granville Lane officers, he and Mariner among them, had rescued her along with several others in a dawn raid on the property where she was being held. Prats like Giles couldn't begin to imagine what that might be like, or how deeply rooted its effects might be.

'Sorry, poor choice of word.' Giles was contrite. 'But logically Kat knows the chances of them picking her up again are slim. Apart from anything else she's wise to them now.'

'You make it sound like she'd have a choice,' Knox pointed out.

'But surely those men are now either dead or in prison,' said Giles.

'They don't operate in isolation,' Knox said. But all the speculation wasn't really helping. 'The point is, I need to find her,' said Knox. 'If she's not at her flat and she's not here, where else might she have gone?'

Giles shook his head. 'I don't know. I think she has friends, or even just contacts in London, but I don't know where exactly.'

'Do you have a key to her flat? I need to have a look round, see if she's left any indication of where she might have gone.'

'Yes, sure.' Giles got up and went over to a pot that stood on a wooden chest. Lifting the lid, he took out a handful of keys, separating out one from the others.

'Do you keep all your keys in there?' Knox asked, taking the proffered one from Giles.

'Normally, yes.'

'Does Kat put hers in there too, when she stays here?'

'I think so.'

'And would Hugo know that?' asked Knox.

The look told him enough.

'What does he look like, this friend of yours?' Knox persisted. 'Long hair, growing himself a beard, by any chance?'

'Why?' Giles was suspicious now.

'A couple of days ago I disturbed an intruder at DI Mariner's place,' he told Giles. 'He ran off and was too fast for me, but someone had been in there before and given it a good going over. The first time I went in stuff was missing and the kitchen was a mess, but there was no sign of a forced entry. Does Hugo know that Kat has a key to that house?'

'I suppose he might have worked it out.'

'Jesus Christ.' Knox glared at Giles. 'Well then, I'll want a word with him too.' Knox gave Giles a business card bearing all his contact details. 'If you don't want to end up in a bigger jam than you are, you'll let me know immediately either of them turns up. Do you understand?'

'Yes, of course.' Fumbling to remove Katarina's key from his own bunch, and handing it over in exchange, Giles looked as if he was about to cry.

* * *

On his way home Knox stopped off for a pint and to pick up a takeaway, so that by the time he drove into his cul-de-sac it was late. It wasn't bin collection day, so he was surprised to see Jean walking around her garden, gathering up what looked like rubbish. Getting out of his car, he went across to her. 'What's going on?'

'Can you believe this?' she said, clearly in some distress. She was clutching an assortment of cellophane-wrapped flowers and teddy bears. 'People keep leaving them, as if this is some kind of memorial! I feel as if I'm being accused of something.'

'Here, I'll get rid of them.' Knox took them from her, noting how tired and drawn she looked. 'How's Michael coping with it?' he asked.

She managed a brief smile. 'It's opened his eyes to the reality of drugs,' she said, 'at least for the moment. He's talking to me a bit too. I suppose that's one good thing that's come out of it. Did you know he was smoking weed?'

'I had an idea,' Knox said.

'I don't know if people have been having a go at him too. He's stopped going out so much and now I'm worried that he might be getting isolated. How ironic is that?'

'Are his mates okay with him?'

'I don't think anyone's blaming him, if that's what you mean.'

'Who *are* they blaming?'

'I don't know.' She glanced away down the street, and Knox wondered if she might know more than she was telling him. 'Like I told you, Kirsty had issues anyway. I think they're putting it partly down to that. The inquest is next week I understand.'

'Well, tell Michael that Nelson could still use some exercise, any time he feels like it,' said Knox.

'Thanks, I will.'

Jean disappeared into her house, and as Knox crossed back over the road an unfamiliar car drew up outside, driven by a middle-aged woman. He watched as she got out, along with a girl of about ten, and deposited a bunch of flowers and a candle on the grass verge. Taking his warrant card out of his jacket pocket, Knox stalked back over the road just as they were returning to their car, gathered up the flowers and thrust them back at the woman, making sure she got a good look at his ID. 'This is not a commemorative site,' he said. 'If you want to pay tribute to Kirsty Fullerton, go to her funeral or post a message on Facebook.' He was about to walk away, but stopped to ask, 'How did you know Kirsty?'

The woman looked mildly uncomfortable. 'Oh, we didn't know her personally. But we saw it in the paper and on the news.'

Knox walked away, shaking his head in disbelief.

## Chapter Twenty-Nine

Day Nine

Despite the electrifying proximity of the near-naked Suzy Yin, Mariner must have dozed off again, because when he next awoke it was light and he could hear rooks cawing outside the window. The bed was empty beside him and getting up to go to the bathroom he found a note on the kitchen table telling him to help himself to breakfast and stay as long as he wanted to. But without her presence the place was much less inviting and by the middle of the morning he was back at the pub.

Climbing the stairs to the landing Mariner came face to face with Megan. For a moment he wondered why she was lurking there, until he realized she was waiting for him.

'You're a policeman, aren't you?' she said timidly. 'I'm worried about Joe — Mr Hennessey. He hasn't been to breakfast for the last two days.'

'No law against having a lie-in,' Mariner pointed out, then seeing her distressed expression immediately regretted his flippancy. 'You mean you haven't seen him at all?'

‘No, and he’s not answering his phone. What do you think I should do? I mean, I know he’s a guest here and doesn’t have to answer to anyone . . .’

‘He is a witness though.’ Mariner frowned. ‘The police won’t want him going AWOL.’ She stared at him blankly. ‘They won’t want him to leave without letting them know. When did you last see him?’

‘Monday lunchtime. He had a drink and a sandwich in the bar. We were going to spend the afternoon together, but then he suddenly said he had to go out instead.’

‘Did he say why?’ asked Mariner.

‘No, but it’s happened before. Sometimes the weather conditions are just right for taking photographs, or mean that there’s more chance of seeing the falcons.’

‘You haven’t seen him at all for two days? What about his car?’

‘It’s gone from the car park.’

‘Are you sure he hasn’t just moved on?’ From what little Mariner had seen of Hennessey he could imagine that to be his style. It seemed to him that Megan’s was a heart just waiting to be broken.

‘If he has, Dad will be annoyed. He hasn’t paid his bill.’ Her eyes glistened. ‘He said he liked me. I’m sure he wouldn’t have gone without saying goodbye.’

‘No, I’m sure you’re right,’ Mariner said. In truth he was anything but sure. Hennessey was an attractive, red-blooded male. The most likely explanation Mariner could think of was that he had met another woman, someone who was a bit less needy than Megan, and had shared her bed for the last couple of nights (he would have bet a week’s wages that Hennessey wasn’t plagued with any difficulties in that department). But that wasn’t at all what Megan would want to hear.

‘Have you got a spare key to his room, and a pair of rubber gloves I could borrow?’ he asked her. She nodded to both. ‘Let’s have a quick look to see if he’s left anything behind, and if there’s any clue to where he might have gone.' All of which, strictly speaking, was ethically questionable, given that Mariner was on leave. But he was being pragmatic. Megan appeared to be quite a highly strung young woman and Griffith had enough on his plate already without worrying about a misper that might not be. This could save the overworked DI a wasted journey and time he didn't have.

Turning the key in the lock of Hennessey's room, Mariner had a sudden gruesome flashback to his discovery of Jeremy Bryce, but on pushing open the door he exhaled. Hennessey wasn't there in any shape or form, but he had left a lot of stuff behind, and it looked to Mariner at first glance as if the room had been turned over.

'He's not a very tidy man,' Megan said from over his shoulder, anticipating his thoughts. It was quite an understatement: stepping into the room Mariner had to pick his way over clothing, magazines and an impressive collection of empty beer bottles. It didn't appear to be work that was keeping Hennessey out; if he had gone off on a photography expedition, he had neglected to take the crucial equipment — his camera bag with the camera body and half a dozen different lenses was still sitting on the floor. Mariner thought about cameras and how easy it was for them to get someone into trouble, should they be pointing in the wrong direction. A notebook-style laptop on the desk was switched off, its lid closed, but Mariner knew better than to tamper with that at this stage. At first glance there seemed to be no sign of Hennessey's wallet or phone, so using only his gloved fingertips Mariner eased open the camera bag, but there was nothing in there either.

'I still don't think there's anything to worry about,' Mariner said to Megan. 'But I'm just going to let DI Griffith know. Can I leave you to lock up?'

Her eyes widened. 'You think this is bad too, don't you?'

'I'm sure there will be a simple and innocent explanation,' said Mariner, not entirely truthfully. 'But Mr

Hennessey is an important witness and DI Griffith does need to know where he can get hold of him.' She'd have to make of that what she liked. Mariner hadn't overlooked Joe Hennessey as a possible suspect. If not at the pub, then where was he on Monday night when Bryce was killed? And why had he disappeared? At the back of his mind Mariner had always acknowledged to himself that he could have misread the reason for Hennessey's panic in Plackett's Wood, when Theo Ashton's body was found. Fear and guilt could present in exactly the same way, regardless of the reasons behind them, and it didn't take too much imagination to see Megan lying, or perhaps stretching the truth to provide Hennessey with an alibi. In the privacy of his room, Mariner got on the phone to Griffith.

'Did Joe Hennessey let you know that he was moving on?' Mariner asked.

'Not that I'm aware of,' said Griffith.

'Well, this might be nothing, but he hasn't been seen for a couple of days,' Mariner went on.

'Oh, Christ.' Mariner could hear the weariness in Griffith's voice.

'There may be no need for concern,' Mariner said. 'His car has gone from the car park. I took the liberty of having a quick look around his room — don't worry, I didn't interfere with anything. He's left some of his stuff behind and I couldn't at first glance see a phone or wallet, so it could just be that he's gone away for a day or two and plans to come back.' He lowered his voice. 'Megan here is pretty intense. He may have just needed some time to himself.'

'Might he have gone on a longer expedition?' Griffith asked.

'Not to take photographs,' Mariner said. 'He's left the camera equipment behind.'

'And now he's disappeared,' said Griffith. 'This I could do without.' There was a momentary pause while

Griffith gathered his thoughts. 'Ordinarily it wouldn't matter, of course — Hennessey's life is his own — but I did specifically ask him to notify us of any movements. He didn't seem to have a problem with that.'

'He might have just forgotten,' Mariner pointed out. 'He seemed a relaxed sort of guy.'

'I'll send over a couple of lads,' said Griffith. 'Just to give his room the once over. They can talk to Megan as well. She might have some idea of what he's really up to.'

'You can try but she was the one who alerted me. Wherever he might be, it doesn't seem as if he's let her in on it.'

'Have you got the details on his car? I'll get my boys to keep a look out for it.'

Mariner passed on the make, colour and registration as Megan had given the details to him. It was unremarkable; the kind of car that would easily blend in. 'If he's taken his phone with him it might help you to locate him, as long as he's not in a dead area.'

'The way my luck's going? What are the chances of that?' Griffith said wryly.

'Like I said,' Mariner reassured Griffith, 'it's probably nothing at all; he may well show up again at any time. I just thought that given what else is happening around here and his proximity to it, you wouldn't want him to slip completely off the radar.'

'Thanks,' said Griffith. 'I appreciate it. And you'll let me know if he shows up again?'

Mariner assured Griffith that he would.

* * *

In the event Ryan Griffith himself came down to supervise the search of Hennessey's room. Mariner had returned to his own quarters along the landing by now, but he heard voices and the men's heavy footfalls on the stairs. Shortly afterwards there came a knock on Mariner's door. It was Griffith.

'Anything?' Mariner asked.

'Not much more than you already told me. But you might want to come and have a look at this.'

Mariner followed Griffith down the landing to Hennessey's room, where he nudged the wireless mouse that sat beside the laptop on the little wooden desk. 'It seems Mr Hennessey is interested in a little more than the wildlife.'

The screen revealed dozens of folders of photographs, many of which seemed to relate to the locality; they were simply labelled with dates, all of them in the last couple of weeks. Griffith double-clicked on one of the folders. It contained a few close-range shots, but none of them were of wildlife, nor any other particular subject that Mariner could see. If anything they just seemed to be random shots of the village and its inhabitants. 'From what I can determine so far, the early stuff seems to concern the village itself and then moves on to the farm. Later ones seem to centre on Gwennol Hall. I'd love to get into the hard drive to see what else is on here, but if we start poking around that and Hennessey shows up again, he'll probably sue.'

'Good old data protection,' said Mariner grimly.

'If he's trying to disguise his real intentions he's been pretty smart about it,' said Griffith. 'There's such a wide range of pictures on here that it would take an age to figure out what his actual target is.' Mariner could see long-range shots of a helicopter and some passengers getting off them. Further scenes had been captured of the farm, including, Mariner noticed, his conversation with Willow. Mariner suddenly wondered if Hennessey held the same suspicions about Abbey Farm that he did.

'So what the hell is he doing out here?' Griffith was thinking aloud.

'Based on this folder, I'd start with Shapasnikov,' said Mariner.

'Any particular reason?' asked Griffith.

Mariner indicated a couple of the pictures that had caught his eye. They were a sequence of shots recording the arrival of Shapasnikov's helicopter, with the Russian walking out to greet his guests. 'That might be one good reason,' he said, pointing to a man alighting from the chopper.

'I understand Shapasnikov made much of his fortune out of gas and oil. Is there a reason he's cosying up to the energy secretary, do you think?'

'Well, when Hennessey turns up again he'll be able to enlighten us himself,' said Griffith, optimistically. 'Anyway, aside from being desperate to get out of that MIU, one of the reasons I wanted to come down here is to run a couple of things by you.' He looked at Mariner. 'Have you eaten? I'm starving. Want to grab a sandwich?'

They went down to the bar where Ron Symonds found them a private corner and brought them some food including bowls of chips hand cut from Abbey Farm organic potatoes. Griffith waited until Symonds moved away before saying: 'We've been up to the byre Jeremy Bryce told you about. He was right, there's plenty of evidence that someone has been living there recently, probably for some days, and recently, judging from the sell-by dates on some of the food packaging. And we could have had a breakthrough. Screwed up and stuffed into a crevice we found a set of waterproofs covered in what looks like blood. They've gone to the lab. We're also looking at a burglary at a holiday home about twelve miles west of here. We're not sure yet if that's at all related, but if whoever was hiding out at the byre escaped on foot, they may have stopped off there too.'

'But going west? If it's someone who followed me out here from the Midlands, wouldn't we expect them to go back the way they came?'

'Like I said, the break-in is probably no more than coincidence. But we also found this at the byre.' Putting down his knife and fork, Griffith fished in his inside jacket pocket and produced an evidence bag, which he passed to Mariner. Mariner stared at it blankly for several seconds, trying to make sense of what it contained. It was a white pamphlet with a photograph on the front of a smiling young woman. Anna. 'That's the funeral I was at last week. She was my . . .'

'I know,' said Griffith. 'Tony Knox filled me in.'

'But I don't get it,' said Mariner, baffled. 'How the hell could that be there?'

'Who else knew that you were coming out to Wales after the funeral?' asked Griffith.

'No one,' said Mariner. 'I mean, my gaffer, DCI Sharp, but literally no one else. I didn't even tell Tony Knox or DC Khatoon until I was leaving.' Mariner thought back to the journey over to Tregaron. 'I might have been followed though.' He told Griffith about the SUV. 'At the time I thought I must be imagining things, but maybe I wasn't.'

'You said there was a Range Rover hanging around the village the other night too.'

'That may have belonged to Shapasnikov. He's got a couple of those in his garages.'

'Okay, so that might take care of that one,' Griffith said. 'But was there anyone at the funeral you didn't recognize?'

Mariner grunted. 'Loads of people. Anna had only recently moved out there from Birmingham, but she'd already picked up a whole new set of friends. In fact it was a perfect funeral for anyone who wanted to blend in; new friends would assume that any strangers were from her old life and vice versa.'

Griffith was studying the order of service. 'Anna Barham,' he said, as if testing out the name. 'She was in the force?' he asked. It was a reasonable assumption.

'No.' Mariner shook his head as if trying to shake off the memory. 'Though we met through a case I was working. We lived together for a while. I was still . . . very fond of her.'

Then it came to Griffith. 'My God. She was the girl involved in that incident off the M5, wasn't she?'

'Yes,' said Mariner, and the old familiar pain in his chest that had lain dormant for a couple of days chose that moment to cut through him with renewed intensity.

'Jesus, I'm sorry,' Griffith said. 'It was a high-profile murder, wasn't it? It would have been easy for anyone to get information about her funeral. Would it have been reasonable to expect you would be there?'

'Anyone who knows anything about me would have put it together. This isn't the first time I've wondered about Goran Zjalic's reach either. At the time I thought that he might have had something to do with Anna's murder; that perhaps it was more than just a random attack. I'd met Anna in the city that day and if I was being watched . . .'

'Didn't they have a couple of blokes in the frame for her killing?' asked Griffith.

'Yes, but there hasn't been enough evidence to make any arrests,' Mariner said.

'It was Hereford, wasn't it?'

'Very near there.'

'My old stamping ground.'

Mariner nodded. 'Elena told me you were SAS.'

'I still have a few mates out that way. If you think there's anything I can do . . .' He let the sentence hang.

'Thanks,' said Mariner, briefly, not at all sure what Griffith had in mind. 'Anyway,' he said, pulling himself together. 'This isn't helping you.'

'This man Zjalic, he's into organized crime?'

'Everything you can imagine,' Mariner said. 'Has anyone come forward to claim Jeremy Bryce?' he asked suddenly.

'Not yet. The mocked-up photo isn't ideal, but even so . . .'

'Early days,' Mariner said.

'Yeah.' Griffith tucked the funeral brochure back into his pocket. 'Although strange that no one should have come forward.'

'Well, if you get stuck there's always the locket.'

'Locket?'

'I found it in the foot well of my car the morning after I gave Bryce a lift. It's a gold locket, like a woman or girl might wear around their neck. I didn't get round to giving it back to him, so it's still in my rucksack. You must have it. It contains a lock of his daughter's hair. Something happened to her, but again, he didn't get the chance to explain what exactly.'

'You mean he was hiding something?'

'No, it was just late at night when we had the conversation. The timing was wrong. It's a long shot, but if hers was some kind of unnatural death there might be something on record, and it would be a start.'

'It would. I'll get someone on to it.' Griffith looked momentarily sheepish. 'We should be able to let you have the rest of your stuff back soon.'

'Whenever you're ready,' said Mariner. 'And let's hope that in the meantime Joe Hennessey decides to show his face again.'

## Chapter Thirty

Tony Knox had learned that wherever Kat might be she was still accessing her bank account. At least he hoped it was her. When he finished work on Wednesday he returned to her apartment building. As he was inserting the key in the door he noticed that the lock had been patched up, as if it had broken, or smashed. He tried not to worry too much about that, but, opening the door, he walked into an odd scene, as if a burglar with a conscience had been at work. Drawers and their contents had been pulled out, but haphazardly replaced again. There was no sign of a handbag or phone or any of the personal items that women were in the habit of carrying round with them, nor was there much evidence from the kitchen that anyone had cooked or even eaten there for some time. The place had a strange feel to it and Knox's intuition told him that something here was very wrong. Having gleaned nothing from it, Knox let himself out again and as he stepped into the hall he heard the clunk of a door being closed, very carefully. He walked along the passage to Saira's apartment and rang the doorbell. There was no response.

'Saira,' he called impatiently. 'It's DS Knox. I know you're there, I heard you close the door.' He was rewarded by the door opening just a crack.

'Sorry,' she said. 'I knew it was someone in Katarina's flat, but I didn't know who.'

'Can I come in?' Knox asked.

'All right,' she said, eventually, though she didn't sound too keen.

They sat across from each other on Ikea reclining chairs.

'How long ago was Kat's flat broken into?' Knox asked.

It hit the spot and she blushed. 'About a couple of weeks ago.'

'And given what's been happening, you didn't think that was worth telling me?'

'Kat made me swear not to tell anyone . . .'

'Even someone who's trying to help her?'

'I . . .'

'It's all right,' said a voice from behind where Knox sat. He spun round to see Katarina standing in the doorway. 'Is my problem, so I must explain.'

Katarina looked a very different young woman from the one Knox had first met. Today her hair was healthy and strong, growing down to her shoulders. Her face had filled out a little and she had a hint of a tan. But the haunted look that Knox remembered so well had returned to her eyes.

'That would be a good start,' he said, unsure whether to feel relieved that she was here in front of him, clearly safe and well, or annoyed that he had been led a dance. 'So, what's going on? Where have you been?'

Katarina came to sit beside Saira, who immediately took her hand in a gesture of support.

'I went to see my friends in London, just for a short time,' Katarina said. Maybe it was having been among fellow Albanians but Knox noticed that her accent was more pronounced today. 'I had to get away from Giles and mostly from his friend Hugo.'

Knox shook his head in disgust. 'I've come across him, although we weren't exactly introduced. He seems like bad news all round. You were worried about the drug-taking?'

She nodded. 'When Giles first brought him to our house I thought he was an okay guy. Right after he came Giles said he has to tell me something, and Hugo says that he has been addicted to heroin but he is trying real hard to get clean. Giles says he needs somewhere to stay away from that shit, so he is going to live with us. From the start I didn't trust him. He was living with Giles and eating his food, watching his TV, but he didn't offer any money and soon I know he's taking drugs again. Giles is out at work all day, but sometimes I came back in the afternoon and I would see what Hugo has been doing. Money and things start to disappear from the flat and sometimes he stays out all night. I tried to talk to Giles but he says he must help his friend. One day I came home and Hugo is rushing round the flat in a panic. He says I have to help him. There are some men after him but he doesn't know why. He thinks it might be his dealer made a bad deal. I try to find out what men, but he says I won't understand. They are from Tirana. Is a big shock. Now I think maybe they are not after him, but they are after me. The next day I came home to get some things and my door is broken down and my flat is wrecked. I was afraid. I had to go away.'

'Why didn't you call Tom?' Knox asked. 'He could have helped you; we both could.'

She stared down at her hand, twisting a ring around her middle finger. 'Tom has already been too good to me. I didn't want to get you involved again. I don't want him to think I can't take care of myself.'

'I think Hugo took your key to Tom's house and has been hiding out there,' Knox said. 'I went back a couple of days ago and it was trashed too.'

‘Oh God, is my fault.’ She looked up at him, distraught.

‘It might not be,’ said Knox. ‘Tom has been caught up in some stuff out in Wales. There’s a possibility that someone is after him and they may be after you too.’

‘I don’t want to go back to my flat. Hugo has been there and he might have made a new key.’ She shuddered. ‘He knows some bad people.’

Knox was thinking on his feet. Partly he was imagining what Mariner would do. ‘You can come and stay at my place for a couple of days, at least until you can get the locks changed on your flat,’ he said. ‘It’s right away from here and I can keep an eye on you.’

‘Thank you.’ Both girls looked relieved and Knox realized at that point the risk that Saira had been taking in helping her friend. Knox waited while Kat collected together her things then, as quickly as possible, they left.

* * *

Mariner had just seen Griffith on his way and was considering where he might go for the afternoon, when the door of the bar swung open and Suzy came in. For a moment he thought she was going to avoid him, but then she came directly across to where he was sitting. ‘Can I get you a drink?’ Mariner asked.

‘No, you’re fine.’ She sat down beside him on the edge of the bench but made no effort to take off her coat. ‘I’m not staying, I just came to apologize.’

‘For what?’

‘Last night.’

‘No apology needed,’ Mariner protested mildly, wondering with some apprehension where this might be going. ‘It was a great stir-fry and the wine was my fault.’

‘That’s not what I meant.’ She was finding it hard to look at him. ‘I shouldn’t have come on to you like that. I realized afterwards that I made some big assumptions about you, and I shouldn’t have.’

'What kind of assumptions?' Mariner was intrigued.

'Oh God, you're not going to make this easy for me, are you?'

'I just don't understand,' Mariner said, genuinely baffled. 'What assumptions?'

She took a deep breath. 'Well, firstly that you're straight, and secondly that you would have any interest in me. I'm really quite embarrassed now. I made a fool of myself.'

'No, you really didn't,' said Mariner gently, but with a growing awareness that he was going to have to somehow explain his way out of this. 'You were right on both counts. I am very straight and I am also very attracted to you. But . . . there's a complication.'

'You're married,' she smiled, suddenly understanding, 'or at least in a relationship. See, I've thought through all the possibilities.'

'No, it's not that either. It's an even worse cliché.'

She read his hesitation. 'Oh look, I'm sorry. If this is something you don't want to talk about . . .'

'No, I owe you some kind of explanation at least,' said Mariner.

'Is it to do with that "some other time"?'

'Sort of,' said Mariner, relieved that she was helping him towards the obvious escape route. 'I *was* in a serious relationship. But it ended suddenly, and not because I wanted it to,' he said. So far so true. 'I'm still coming to terms with it. It just doesn't seem like a good idea to get involved . . .'

'No, of course,' she said. 'I get it.' She got to her feet. 'I'll let you finish your lunch in peace. I hope we can still be friends?' she said hopefully.

'Of course,' Mariner said. 'When's your next day off?'

She shrugged. 'I could probably sneak some time off on Friday.'

'Well how about a walk then?'

'Okay, I'll see you Friday at ten. You can call for me.'

'Great.'

She headed towards the door. 'For the record,' she said, hesitating in the doorway. 'It was only sex. I wasn't expecting any long-term commitment.' Mariner stared after her as she walked out of the bar, leaving him with a smile and the sudden sense that an opportunity had been missed.

* * *

Knox must have picked up Mariner's message, because when he got upstairs that afternoon he found a text to say that Kat had been found, safe and well. Mariner rang him from his room.

'Kat is fine, but her flat's been turned over too. She's come to stay with me for a couple of days.'

'Good,' said Mariner. 'So where has she been?'

Knox told him about Giles' unwanted guest. 'I think she just heard "Tirana" and panicked. It may have nothing to do with Zjalic at all. Her flat has been turned over in the same way as your house, but it sounds as if this Hugo has been behind all that.'

'Any progress on the drugs thing with Charlie?'

'I haven't heard about any new developments,' said Knox. 'But I have had a message from Rick Fraser about your soil samples. It sounds complicated, so you may want to give him a call yourself, get it from the horse's mouth.'

It was a good idea, and when he'd finished speaking to Knox, Mariner rang the lab. Rick Fraser was typically laid back, something that belied his thoroughness and the speed of his thinking. 'How's it going?' he asked, as if this was a social call.

Mariner wondered if Fraser knew anything about the situation he was in. 'Fine,' he said. 'What have you got for me?'

'Two bags of soil, right?' Fraser confirmed. 'On the parsnips; on its own.'

'That's it,' said Mariner.

'Right. The soil on its own is just about chemical-free,' Fraser said. 'A bit of homemade compost but that's about it.' The soil was from Elena's garden, so no surprises there. 'The soil on the parsnips is a different story,' Fraser continued.

'Oh yes?' said Mariner in anticipation.

'There are compounds present there that are consistent with most of the commercially available pesticides — the same stuff that's used all over the place.'

'Pesticides?' Mariner echoed. 'That doesn't sound very organic.'

'Depends on your definition of organic, I suppose,' said Fraser. 'But no, I wouldn't class them as particularly natural or wholesome.'

'So what about this supposed magic formula that this guy is meant to be developing?'

'I didn't find anything magic or even unusual. There was one *weird* thing though,' said Fraser, typically saving the best till last. 'The two soil types are totally different.'

'How do you mean?' asked Mariner.

'The soil on its own is a heavy, clay-based soil, of the type you would expect in that part of Wales,' Fraser told him. 'But the soil stuck to the parsnips is a much lighter, sandy soil. I'm not an expert and I wasn't sure what that meant so I talked to someone who is. She said that the parsnip soil is characteristic of what you'd find in the east of the country, Norfolk or Kent; those kinds of areas.'

'So what are you saying?' Mariner asked, wanting to be clear.

'I'm saying that those parsnips were not grown where you found them, nor anywhere near it.'

* * *

Letting Katarina into his house, Tony Knox was suddenly ashamed of the way he'd let things slide. Housework had never been his forte. But Kat was so delighted to meet Nelson that she seemed not to notice.

He showed her where everything was and told her to make herself at home.

'I hope it won't be for long that I get in the way,' Kat said, her English suffering under the stress of it all.

'You're not in the way,' Knox reassured her. 'Me and Nelson are glad of the company.'

'And Tom, he's coming back soon?' She seemed anxious about it and Knox wondered if she realized herself how much she missed his presence.

'I hope so,' he said. There was no option but to explain to her what had been happening in Wales.

'But he is innocent!' she insisted, without knowing any of the details.

'He is,' said Knox, mirroring her confidence. 'But he needs to stay around there for now, in case they have to speak to him again.'

'And he is safe?' She seemed almost afraid to say it.

'Yes, I'm sure he is,' Knox said, with more certainty than he felt.

There was no reason to believe that anyone other than Knox, Saira and Kat herself, was aware of where she had moved to, but when the doorbell rang it startled them both. 'Wait here,' Knox said. Opening the door, he found Michael on the doorstep.

'Wondered if Nelson wanted a walk,' the boy said awkwardly.

'That'd be great,' said Knox, keen to re-establish communication. 'Come through, he's in here.' Michael followed him into the kitchen where Knox introduced him to Katarina.

'Can I come with you?' she asked, seeing what Michael's plans were, 'Then I will know where I can take him too.'

She took Michael's indifferent shrug as encouragement and they both set off with Nelson trotting along beside them. Before they left Knox gave Katarina a spare key. 'I need to go into work for a couple of hours to catch up with a few things. Don't answer the door to anyone you don't know, and if you're worried about anything, you call me straight away.' Unnecessary precautions, he felt sure, but it made him feel marginally better about leaving her.

* * *

When Mariner went downstairs, he found the pub uncharacteristically empty. Ron Symonds was on his own behind the bar replacing clean glasses, replenishing the chiller cabinets and preparing for the evening's business. 'Police have put people off probably,' he speculated, casting around the empty room.

'Any sign of Joe Hennessey?' Mariner asked, knowing the answer.

'Not yet, but I hope for his sake he turns up soon,' said Symonds. 'He's not a bad young man to have around. What'll you have?'

Mariner indicated one of the pumps and Symonds drew him a pint. Perhaps because it was quiet, for once the landlord had his own drink on the go, and passing Mariner his pint, he lifted it in a toast. 'Joe Hennessey,' he said.

'Joe Hennessy,' said Mariner, reciprocating. 'How's Megan coping?' he asked.

'Not well, if I'm honest,' said Symonds. 'I don't know why but Joe seemed to have taken a real shine to her and she'd got very fond of him too. If he's done a runner she'll be gutted.'

'You get your veg from Abbey Farm, don't you?' Mariner said conversationally, handing over the payment for his drink.

'We do,' said Symonds. 'We like to do our bit to support the local economy.'

'So Willow sells direct to you, or is it part of the mail order service?'

'Mail order? That must be something new. I didn't know he was into that too.'

The door swung open to admit a group of customers, and Mariner hoped that the sudden rush might include the returning Joe Hennessey, but when he retired to his room and the rather hard bed, the Irishman still hadn't put in an appearance.

# Chapter Thirty-One

Day Ten

After breakfast on Thursday morning Mariner went up to his room and had a look at his maps to try and decide on a walk for the day. He squinted out of the window trying to ascertain how likely it was that the rain would hold off, and at the same time noticed the Abbey Farm van parked outside. Ron Symonds must have been taking delivery of his vegetables. The legend on the side read: 'Abbey Farm Organic Vegetables; all products locally grown.' Not quite accurate after all, if what Rick Fraser had learned was true. Something else Mariner noticed: there was no email or website address given.

Today Mariner took the local bus a few miles up the valley, with a view to walking back along the footpaths. He returned to the Hart in the middle of the afternoon to find a police squad car parked outside and officers loading evidence bags into the boot. Mariner walked inside with a sickly, sinking feeling, knowing that whatever had happened here, it wasn't going to be good. Eventually

Ryan Griffith appeared. He took Mariner to one side. 'We've found Hennessey,' he said. 'Something about his disappearance was bothering me, so I took your advice and had a trace put on his mobile phone signal. His car was parked at a picnic site off the road a couple of miles up the valley. There was blood on the ground immediately behind the car, so we opened up the boot. He'd been stabbed, cleanly and fatally, in the chest.'

'Jesus,' said Mariner. 'Any idea when?'

'Not until the PM, but rigor's been and gone so I'd say he's been there at least twenty-four hours. I've come to talk to Megan again so that we can try to establish more precisely his last known movements. As far as we know she was the last one to see him leave here on Monday afternoon but we're hoping there might have been further sightings after that.' Griffith walked over to the boot of the car and retrieved something from inside. 'We're doing a more thorough search of his room now, but we've already come across this.' The evidence bag he held up for Mariner's inspection contained a small business card: *Joseph Hennessey, Private Investigator.*

'We've also found a small stash of dope. It's not enough to worry us too much, but one of my officers thinks it might be the strong stuff: skunk. Not that I know the difference.'

'Skunk is more powerful,' Mariner said. 'Usually the plants have been genetically modified. So Joe Hennessey definitely wasn't here just for the wildlife,' he concluded.

'We still don't know exactly what drew him here, though,' said Griffith. 'We found his wallet at the scene but no mobile. My guess would be that the killer took it, possibly because there were incriminating calls or texts on it.'

'Like an arrangement to meet. Megan told me he went out quite suddenly.'

'The big question is, who was Hennessey working for?' said Griffith. Taking a packet of cigarettes out of his pocket, he offered one to Mariner, who declined, then lit one up for himself.

Mariner agreed. 'If we can get to the bottom of that we can understand why he was killed.'

'Either way this is shaping up like a professional job,' said Griffith. 'And that puts you in danger.'

'How do you work that out?'

'The implication is that someone has been tracking you from the point of Anna Barham's funeral, employing Hennessey to report back on your movements,' said Griffith. 'The two men killed first — Theo Ashton and Jeremy Bryce — were killed in error.'

'So why kill Hennessey?'

'Because you're still alive. Hennessey's intel wasn't accurate enough. The killer, or more likely the man the killer is working for, has blamed Hennessey and punished him for that, or has decided that he knew too much to be allowed to live.'

'There is another factor that might more easily explain Theo Ashton's death,' said Mariner. 'I've been puzzling over Abbey Farm since I first got here. Given the size of the plot and the fact that Willow's magic formula is still, according to him, in its experimental phase, I've never understood how it could possibly produce enough to sustain weekly market sales and a mail order business, and make the profit it does.'

'Go on,' Griffith encouraged.

'I had Tony Knox take some of the veg to a lab for analysis.' Mariner told Griffith about the test results. 'That got me wondering about what it was I'd really seen on the farm the night after Theo Ashton was killed. I assumed I'd seen crates of produce being loaded into a transit. It made sense because the following day you told me about Willow's request to get out a delivery.'

'It adds up,' said Griffith, puzzled.

'Except I'm pretty sure there is no mail order operation,' said Mariner. 'I checked with Ron Symonds first of all, and he knew nothing about one.'

'He might not know everything.'

'But mail order these days is all done online,' Mariner persisted. 'If you look at the contact details for Abbey Farm on the side of the van, there's no email or website address.'

'What are you getting at?' asked Griffith.

'That the whole organic veg thing is a scam,' said Mariner. 'Those crates that I saw being loaded into the transit were in fact being *unloaded*. They were the crates of vegetables we saw the next day in the new aluminium shed. Parsnips, like the ones Tony Knox got analysed. Remember the logo on those crates? It was Dutch. Willow made some crack about having "acquired" the crates illegally, but that was to cover the fact that the veg itself is imported. You should contact that company and find out what relationship they have with Nigel Weller, because I think they're selling him cheap, non-organic vegetables in bulk, which he's then been passing off as home-grown organic veg and making a tidy profit from them. There is no magic formula, or even fertilizer.'

'The sly bastard,' said Griffith. 'I've never trusted that stuff.'

'That in itself is fraudulent, but what if Theo Ashton was about to expose what was going on?'

'It would bring Willow's business and credibility crashing down around him and may well be enough to provide a motive for murder.'

'And if Willow thinks that both Hennessey and I saw something, then Hennessy's murder is self-evident,' said Mariner.

'And Jeremy Bryce's?

'That could, as we first thought, be a case of mistaken identity; him instead of me,' Mariner pointed out. 'I have been sniffing around the farm. Mainly innocently, as it turns out, but Willow isn't to know that.'

'Joe Hennessey could have been directly involved,' said Bryce. 'Seems as though he was pretty versatile. He *was* a photographer of sorts; he syndicated photos to the national press. If he had media connections then he might have been helping Theo Ashton to put together a story.'

'It would explain the pictures of the farm on his laptop,' Mariner agreed. 'Where was he based?'

'Looks like north London somewhere, which doesn't really help us yet.' Griffith had smoked his cigarette down and stubbed it out on the wall beside him before flicking the dog end into the gutter. 'Either way, it's about time we went and had another chat with Mr Weller.'

Much as he'd have liked to be, Mariner realized that he wasn't included in that 'we.' 'Well, if there's anything I can do . . .' he said instead.

'Sure. Just talking to people, keeping your eyes peeled, would be good. If there's anything you find out before we do, I'd be grateful.' In the circumstances it was the most that Griffith could realistically offer.

As he was walking away, Griffith's phone rang and he pulled it out to answer it. The call stopped him in his tracks. 'What? Are you sure about that?' Mariner heard him say. Turning back, he caught Mariner's eye, though he continued talking into his phone. 'I'll need confirmation, and if it is true, then there needs to be a search of all places west of here. The CCTV will need to be looked at again too.' Griffith paused, frowning, as he listened to the speaker at the other end. 'Well, if that's the case we've got somewhere to start. See if you can get hold of the footage there too.' Ending the call, he pocketed his phone and walked back towards Mariner. 'The search of this holiday cottage has turned up an empty prescription medication bottle. It belonged to Glenn McGinley.'

'Christ, are they sure?' But as he said it Mariner knew it wasn't the kind of thing that anyone could mistake. 'So they've been wrong all along in thinking he escaped to Ireland.'

'He must have set up that car as a decoy,' Griffith said. 'I've just been told too that a member of the public phoned in a sighting of him at Aberystwyth station last Friday. They saw a man fitting McGinley's description who looked in a bad way. But because Caernarfon police were certain that he'd already boarded the ferry by then, it wasn't taken seriously. Even with what you've just told me about Abbey Farm I don't think we can entirely rule out McGinley any longer.'

Mariner didn't contradict him. He was having exactly the same thought. Suddenly it turned everything on its head again. 'One of my constables, Millie Khatoon, has been convinced all along that McGinley was headed down here,' he told Griffith. 'I don't know what it might be, and I certainly don't have any recollection of Glenn McGinley, but Tony Knox told me that Millie has been working on trying to identify some connection between McGinley and me.'

'It would be good to find out if there is one,' said Griffith. He seemed to be considering something. 'I'll get one of my men to drive you in to the town. We'll see if we can set up a conference call.'

* * *

Tony Knox arrived in CID that morning to find a uniformed PC waiting for him. 'I understand you've been looking for a Hugo Westerby?' she said.

'That's right.'

She handed Knox a slip of paper with a number written on it. 'That's the ward he's on at present, but you'll need to be quick.'

'They're getting ready to ship him out?'

She gave the briefest shake of the head. 'Only on a mortuary trolley. A bunch of girls on a night out fell over him in an alleyway off Broad Street a couple of nights ago.

He's had the living crap beaten out of him by someone; he's got a fractured skull and cerebral haemorrhaging among other things. If you're planning to talk to him I wouldn't get your hopes up.'

Knox went straight to the ward at City Hospital where Hugo was being intensively cared for. One of Knox's counterparts from Handsworth CID, Sue Jericho, was also there for the same purpose — to talk to Westerby as soon as he regained consciousness. 'Bit of a mystery really why he was attacked,' she said. 'It could have been robbery, though the state he was in it's hard to imagine he was carrying anything of much value, or that muggers would have been in any way attracted to him.'

'You might be looking at something drugs-related,' said Knox. 'He was a user and it's possible he'd got himself into trouble with someone further up the food chain.'

'That would explain why they weren't interested in the phone in his pocket,' she said. 'We managed to use that to trace the next of kin.'

'Who's that?' Knox asked. He nodded towards the room where Hugo lay, bandaged and wired up to several complex looking machines, watched over by a young woman.

'His sister, Annabel,' said Jericho. 'The mother is around somewhere too. Gone off to make a phone call I think. They've travelled up from Gloucestershire. The mother admits that Hugo's dabbled in drugs in the past, but insists that he'd cleaned up his act, had got a respectable job working in a bar, and was back on the straight and narrow. Some of it might be true — he had a security ID in his pocket — but the physical state of him tells a different story.'

'Have you been in touch with his flatmate?'

'Didn't know there was one,' said Jericho.

'Giles Ridley-Coburn,' Knox said. He recited the details while she wrote them down. 'I think he'll give you a more realistic picture. He may even know something about what happened here, and if he doesn't, at the very least he'll be wondering where Hugo's got to. Either way I think you'll find out that our friend Hugo was well and truly back on the hard stuff. I'm pretty sure I caught him at it.' Describing the encounter at Mariner's house, Knox peered in through the window again. 'Hard to tell under all that machinery, but I'm pretty sure that it was him.'

'I won't break it to his mum or sister just yet,' she said.

Knox was inclined to agree. 'No point in making it any worse for them.' He turned to his colleague. 'When he does come round though, can you let me know? I'd like to talk to him.'

In the meantime, Knox did step in to take a closer look at Hugo Westerby. The young woman looked up as he entered and he raised his warrant card to identify himself. For a couple of minutes Knox stood silently watching, before Annabel said: 'This is my fault.' Her voice came out as little more than a whisper. 'He called me and told me he was in trouble. He wanted money; a lot of it.'

'Did he say what he wanted it for?' Knox asked, carefully.

'He owed it to someone. I know Mum thinks Hugo's clean, but that's because he *was*. He had treatment and had kicked loose from it. Then he came to Birmingham and got a job working in a bar.' Across the hospital bed, she caught Knox's expression. 'I know, not the ideal place for a recovering junkie to work, but the job offers weren't exactly flooding in. To begin with it was fine; Huey was doing well, making a lot of money on tips and things. But it didn't take him long to find out that the staff had a sideline in distributing what they called "optional extras." He was invited to join in, except he decided to set up his own informal distribution network.'

'Selling what?' asked Knox.

'Weed mainly, I think, but the strong stuff.'

'Skunk?'

'Yes. It was all done very discreetly and only for certain customers. Then they started trusting Huey with the stash. I don't know where it was kept, but he had access to it. And Huey, being Huey, saw an opportunity.'

'To start his own business,' Knox guessed.

'That's about it, yes. It was so stupid. He took a large chunk to sell himself and planned to use the profit to buy cheaper stuff and replace what he'd taken.'

'That sounds like a dangerous game.'

'He got found out almost straight away, the idiot. They came after him, wrecked his place. He managed to avoid them at first but clearly they caught up with him.'

'Have you any idea who these people were?'

'I'm not sure that Huey even knew exactly.'

'And the name of the club?'

'Sorry, I only know it's some place in the middle of Birmingham. Huey didn't tell me.'

Leaving Annabel to return to her brother's bedside, Knox went out to Sue Jericho. 'What happened to Hugo Westerby's possessions?'

'There wasn't much. Just the phone, security pass and some other worthless crap.'

'That security pass. Do you remember which bar it was?'

'Yes, it was RedZone, on Broad Street. Good club, I go there sometimes . . .'

'Thanks,' said Knox.

Outside the hospital Knox checked his mobile and found a message from DCI Sharp asking him to return to Granville Lane as soon as possible, but no later than two p.m. He managed to make it with eight minutes to spare.

## Chapter Thirty-Two

Knox went up to CID to tell Sharp about what he'd learned. 'I think we can discount Goran Zjalic,' he said. 'This is just some dispute between Hugo Westerby and whoever these guys are. I think we'll find that the prints at Tom's house match those at Katarina's flat. Any Albanian connection is purely coincidental.'

'I think you're right,' said Sharp, surprisingly. 'And from what I've heard about these killings in Wales, we're looking at an assailant who feels comfortable in the outdoors,' pointed out Sharp. 'There's every reason to think that McGinley is at home in that kind of environment.'

'McGinley?' Knox thought he must have misheard.

'Yes — you haven't heard, have you? McGinley didn't make his escape to Ireland after all. He's in mid-Wales, and there's strong evidence to suggest that he's been in the vicinity of Caranwy in the last few days. I needed you back here because we've scheduled a conference call with DI Griffith and Tom for two p.m. We need to share our information.' Getting up, Sharp went to the door. 'Have you talked to Millie since you got back?'

'Not yet, no.'

'Well, I know you think she's been going off on one, but she has turned up something interesting. I'll get her in here now.'

Millie seemed reluctant to come in and Knox regretted having been so dismissive before. She asked after Mariner and he updated her. It was the appointed time for the conference call so they went into the meeting room where the big screen showed Ryan Griffith and Mariner. They all exchanged greetings.

'And congratulations, Millie,' Mariner added.

She blushed in response. 'Sorry, boss, there never seemed a good time . . .'

'I know,' said Mariner. 'Just make sure you take care of yourself. You on light duties?'

'I will be soon, sir.'

'DCI Sharp said you've come up with something,' said Griffith.

'I looked up Glenn McGinley's history,' said Millie. 'I started on the premise that DI Mariner and he had crossed paths, but there was no obvious overlap from the DI's arrest record and McGinley's convictions. So then I spoke to DI Glenda Scott on Merseyside. Turns out that McGinley spent quite a lot of time sounding off to an old guy undergoing medical treatment at the same time he was. The old guy didn't take much notice at the time, but of course he then sees in the news that McGinley was more than just talk. He says McGinley was hell bent on what he perceived as revenge. Some of it was for himself, but some of it was also what he called "a favour" for someone else, so I started looking at who he might have spent time with when he was inside. Again, nothing really stood out until I remembered the riots we had two years ago at Birmingham Prison. Because of them, some prisoners had to be temporarily moved and McGinley ended up at Long Lartin for a month. And guess who was also residing there at the time?'

'Goran Zjalic?' offered Knox.

'No, Frank Crosby.'

'Jesus Christ,' said Mariner.

'No, really, Frank Crosby,' Millie insisted.

'Crosby.' Knox had only met the man once and at that time he hadn't been their suspect, but he knew that he and Mariner had considerable history.

'But if this is true, how would McGinley, or for that matter, this Crosby, know where DI Mariner is?' asked Griffith.

'Crosby's got plenty of contacts,' Mariner said. 'And he knew Anna Barham's brother, Eddie. He could easily have put McGinley up to all this and provided the backup. But what I don't get is why? I didn't realize things had got that personal.'

'Maybe they hadn't. This could all be in McGinley's head.'

'But even if it is, why the hell would McGinley agree to do it for someone he barely knows?'

'I found out some other stuff about him,' Millie said. 'McGinley's father died after a scuffle years ago at a football match. The other people involved were police officers. McGinley has a pathological hatred of the police.' She paused. 'Oh, and he's dying from liver cancer,' she added. 'He's got nothing to lose.'

Everything went quiet as those facts were digested.

'It certainly explains a few things,' said Griffith eventually, blowing out air. 'If McGinley's doing this as a favour, it means he doesn't know you and is working on a description, or at best some kind of photograph. It would explain why we might have some cases of mistaken identity.'

'That's entirely possible,' Mariner agreed. 'If McGinley was looking for a man walking, say, in Plackett's Wood, he could feasibly have mistaken Theo Ashton for me, especially from the back. There's a big age difference, I know, but we're of a similar height, same sort of hair colour.'

'Could that investigator — what was his name, Hennessey? — have been working for McGinley?' asked Sharp. 'How long had he been in Caranwy?'

'He was already established by the time I got here.'

'He'd been here since the Saturday,' said Griffith. 'And then a day after you arrived, Theo Ashton was killed, right in the area where you were walking.'

'When I came across him, Hennessey looked pretty shocked. I assumed it was because of the discovery of the body, but maybe it was seeing me alive and well.'

'He would have found out that afternoon that you were staying at the hostel—'

'—and a couple of days later Bryce is murdered there.'

'We found a shortwave radio at the byre,' said Griffith. 'If it belonged to McGinley he'll have realized pretty quickly that he'd fucked up.'

'Or Hennessey communicated that to him,' said Sharp.

'So then he will have found out where I'm staying and tried to do the job properly.'

'How does this fit with the SUV though?' Griffith queried.

'Crosby's contacts are many and varied,' said Mariner. 'It would be like him to not just rely on one person.'

'There's a big difference in the MOs of all these attacks,' Griffith pointed out.

'They're all knife attacks though,' Mariner countered. 'McGinley's first victims, the ones personal to him, were shot, which would indicate he's more comfortable with firearms. Maybe when he killed Theo Ashton it was the first time he'd used a knife. The attack smacks of desperation because he was unsure of his weapon and working out in the open, so needed to get it done quickly and thoroughly. He does it over and over to make sure of it. With Bryce he thinks he's alone in the hostel and has got all night to allow Bryce to slowly bleed to death.'

'It's more of an assassination,' Griffith seemed to agree, although the frown on his face seemed to belie his words.

Even though he barely knew the man, the expression was a familiar one to Mariner. Something wasn't adding up. 'What?' he asked.

'It's just that, from what little is known about McGinley, it all sounds too organized, too resourceful. McGinley is small time; an inadequate petty criminal. Would he go to these lengths simply to earn the respect of someone like Frank Crosby?'

'Going out in a blaze of glory?' suggested Sharp. 'If he wanted the notoriety, he's certainly achieved that, if only in the short term.'

The discussion had come to its natural conclusion and DCI Sharp ended the conference call, on the undertaking from those in each locality that information would continue to be shared at intervals, or whenever fresh intelligence came to light.

In Wales, Mariner was considering spending some time exploring Llanerch, prior to returning to Caranwy, when Griffith unexpectedly said: 'We're just about to interview Willow about his organic produce business. Since you're here, you might want to stop by the observation room?' Mariner didn't need to be asked twice.

In the interview suite, Nigel Weller was looking decidedly uncomfortable. Griffith didn't pull any punches. He disclosed what had been learned through the soil analysis, keeping Mariner's role out of it, then he asked a simple question: 'If you are a vegetable grower, why do you import in bulk from the continent?'

Nigel Weller was a sensible man and knew when he had been rumbled. He sighed heavily. 'I didn't set out to con anyone,' he said. 'When I first moved out to Caranwy it was with every intention of growing and selling organically produced vegetables. On paper the fertilizer looked promising, but it just didn't work. Oh, it altered the soil temperature a little but not enough, so then I invested in the poly tunnels, and finally the turbines to try heating them, but it was impossible to ensure that they were adequately insulated. And the plants needed warmth but they also needed more hours of sunlight than they were ever going to get realistically out here. I thought infra-red lamps might do the trick but they didn't. After a couple of years it started to become clear that I was never going to be able to create the right conditions, least of all naturally. There had been some commercial interest in the product and I'd even attracted a couple of sponsors, but they started to become impatient, and what savings I had were dwindling. But somehow I couldn't quite let go. I still had some ideas about the fertilizer, so I just needed to make some money to be able to continue the development a little longer. And by this time I'd become used to the life out here. It suited me and I didn't want to lose it and that was quite apart from all the investment I'd made in the farm.

'Then one day, by chance, I got chatting to a guy running a successful stall at one of the markets and he let me into a secret — that he supplemented his organic produce with non-organic. He said that if you were careful about how you did it, nobody could tell the difference. I hadn't ever intended it to be long term; it was just to generate some extra income to keep us going until the fertilizer was perfected. He gave me his contact in Holland, and that was when I set up the scam.'

'And was Theo Ashton planning to shop you?'

'Theo?' Weller seemed genuinely taken aback by the suggestion. 'Of course not. He was like a son to me. He and Amber have been happy at the farm. Why would he have wanted to destroy what we've got?'

'Perhaps he'd been offered something more enticing by Joe Hennessey,' Griffith suggested.

'The wildlife photographer? What's he got to do with anything?'

'Hennessey was a jack of all trades; part-photographer, but he was also a private investigator and a journalist,' said Griffith. 'Maybe this was a story he was going to sell to the papers.'

Weller leaned back in his chair. 'I don't believe it,' he said. 'Theo would not have sold us out under any circumstances. He and Amber have — had — too much to lose. I hold my hands up to deception, but if you think I had anything to do with the death of Theo Ashton, you are insane.'

Afterwards Griffith joined Mariner in the observation room. 'So what now?' asked Mariner.

'We'll turn him over to Trading Standards. It's all we've got.'

'And Theo Ashton?'

Griffith looked through the glass at Weller. 'I don't think he would have killed the lad. And the bottom line is that we have no evidence for it anyway.'

For Mariner the whole afternoon's experience had been very like being back at work, so it felt strange when a squad car deposited him at the White Hart, returning him to the middle of his so-called holiday. He felt drained by the experience, but tomorrow he had the walk with Suzy to look forward to. He went to bed and slept soundly.

## Chapter Thirty-Three

Day Eleven

On Friday morning Mariner got his stuff together and walked up to Gwennol at the appointed time. It was bitterly cold again, with squalls of rain blowing in from angry clouds. The door to the MIU was open but there was much less activity going on up here now. It was always the same when the heat began to go out of an investigation, and Mariner didn't envy Griffith the task that lay ahead. They'd gone from having no suspects to several, but none of them was straightforward and they all lacked any sound evidence. Climbing the wooden steps to Suzy's flat he found the door open and her waiting for him, all ready in boots and walking gear.

They set off this time across the Gwennol estate, round the back of the Hall and away from the village, crossing a stone bridge on the far side of the valley that took them up on to the hillside, branching off along a narrow track that began to climb steeply. They kept up a steady pace and soon, aside from the wind rustling the trees, the only sound was that of their own breathing and the occasional rook cawing overhead. After walking for more than an hour, they crested the rocky outcrop of the hill and stopped to catch their breath for a moment.

'Did your "some other time" girl like walking?' Suzy asked suddenly.

Despite a sudden stitch of pain, the mere thought made Mariner smile. 'Absolutely not,' he said. 'She could never get her head round the attraction of it. Her idea of a walk involved her credit cards — or, even better, *my* credit cards — and armfuls of designer shopping bags. I took her up Clent once, one of the little hills just outside Birmingham, on a beautiful, warm, sunny day, and she asked me what was the point, if all we were going to do was climb down again.'

'So the two of you didn't do any of this — walking holidays?'

'No. We were only together a couple of years and holidays were one of the few things we ever argued about. To be honest it would probably always have been like that. Anna was always wanting to *go somewhere* and *do things*, which as far as I'm concerned, means visiting places that other people consider worth going to — by definition, those are the places I'd do anything to avoid.' They'd done it once, he remembered; a long weekend in Florence in July, when among other things, Mariner was subjected to the torture of queuing for four hours in the baking sun, along with hundreds of other tourists, for the privilege of shuffling past Michelangelo's David. When they finally got there, the statue didn't look any more impressive to him in the flesh than the photographs he'd already seen in books. He made the mistake of saying so. It hadn't been the most successful of weekends — apart from the sex, he thought ruefully.

Setting off again they began a descent into the valley running in parallel to the Vale of Caranwy, joining the course of a stream that cut a groove through the hillside.

As the path flattened out, the sound of trickling water increased and they came into a hollow, alongside a twenty-foot limestone cliff, with a deep tarn at its base. 'What do you think? Perfect, isn't it?' Suzy cried, scrambling over to the water's edge.

'Perfect for what?' Mariner asked naively, noticing that she had already dumped her rucksack on the rocks and was fiddling with her watch.

'A swim.'

'*What?*' Mariner thought he must have misheard her, even though as he watched, she was starting to remove her outer clothes.

'A swim,' she repeated. 'Haven't you ever done wild swimming?'

'Not in bloody April,' said Mariner. Walking over to the water's edge, he squatted down and dipped his fingers into the green water. 'It's arctic.' His voice came out as a squeak.

She sat down on a rock to take off her boots and gazed up at him, rolling her eyes. 'Don't be so pathetic. It'll just be a quick dip. I thought you liked the outdoors.'

'I do,' said Mariner defensively. 'But I also have an aversion to bronchial pneumonia. I haven't brought a towel or anything.'

This time she openly laughed. 'My God, you're a wuss after all. Who'd have thought?'

Ordinarily Mariner never felt a need to prove himself to anyone, but for some reason that remark stung, so he put down his pack and started removing his clothes with the same enthusiasm he'd have had for a particularly invasive medical exam. 'This is complete madness,' he muttered, half to himself. 'We'll die of exposure.'

'Rubbish,' she shot back, stepping out of her very skimpy underwear. 'It's great for your circulation and your heart. The Scandinavians do it all the time.'

'But they have the sense to follow it up with a hot tub,' he grumbled. Her olive skin contrasted ridiculously with his own pasty white flesh; not that she'd have noticed. She was already wading into the icy water, shrieking with the cold, and as Mariner dropped his boxer shorts on to the pile he'd created, he saw her plunge into the water and swim strongly across the pond. Stepping gingerly into the water, his feet sliding on the slimy rocks, Mariner suppressed an anguished cry and the desperate urge to run back out again. No chance of that. She was paddling about underneath the cliff, where the rock shelved away. 'Look, there's a cave under here!' she called, and disappeared momentarily.

Mariner watched, his limbs starting to throb with the cold, but she didn't reappear. 'Suzy?' he called uncertainly. 'Suzy!' He started to thrash out across the pond, then suddenly she was there again, grinning broadly. 'It's a tunnel,' she said. 'It goes right into the mountain.'

'There's a whole network of them underneath these hills,' Mariner said, his teeth chattering. 'Can we get out now?'

They were in the water for no more than five minutes, which was about four minutes fifty-nine seconds more than was comfortable for Mariner, and as soon as he could, he was out again and pulling on his clothes.

'There, wasn't that exhilarating?' Suzy said, her head popping through her thick sweater.

Now that it was over, Mariner had to admit that it had been. 'Probably caught my death though,' he complained.

'Come here then, I'll warm you up.' Stepping over to him, she put her arms around him, rubbing them up and down his body. Mariner couldn't resist. He leaned forward and kissed her, briefly on the lips, or at least that's what he'd intended, but it was so good that he carried on, and then his arm was around her, drawing her in to him.

'Well,' Suzy said, when he finally broke the kiss. 'That was unexpected.' She looked at him. 'How far is it back to Gwennol?'

'Not far, if we take the shortest route,' said Mariner.

'All right then.'

Scrambling back down the path, they were making their way across to the estate, when they came across a small stone cottage set back behind a neat garden. 'It must be the Reverend Aubrey's,' Mariner said, lowering his voice. 'He used to be the local pastor but left the ministry in disgrace some years ago.'

'What kind of disgrace?'

'The kind of disgrace the clergy is renowned for lately.'

'Looks like he's still unpopular,' Suzy observed. 'Someone's chucked wood stain all over his windows.'

She was right; although Elena had given Mariner the impression that things had died down, there was a transparent brown liquid splattered over the window panes, standing out against what were rather grimy net curtains. 'Could have been there years,' said Mariner. 'An old guy living on his own, maybe he doesn't clean his windows very often.' He didn't want to pry, but he walked the few feet into the garden and ran a finger down the glass to try and ascertain what the substance was. And that was when he realized it wasn't on the outer window but on the inside, and that it was the staining of the curtains themselves that made it that odd translucent brown colour. 'Wait here,' he told Suzy firmly. Walking round to the back of the cottage he found the back door of the property an inch or so ajar. He pushed it gently and called out a cautious, 'Hello?' But as the door swung open, wafting out a cloying, metallic smell, Mariner knew that there would be no response.

'What is it?' Suzy had followed him around the side of the cottage.

'It's ugly,' said Mariner. 'Have you got your phone with you?'

'Yes.'

'Carry on down to the estate and keep going until you can get a signal or to a landline, and call the police,' he said. 'Ask for Ryan Griffith if possible. That unfortunate habit of mine? It hasn't gone away.'

Mariner didn't enter the cottage but sat and waited on the grassy bank to one side. It was a long, cold wait and he was relieved to finally see a mud-spattered Land Rover bumping along the grassy track towards him. He let Griffith and Blaine put on their forensic suits and go into the cottage.

Griffith emerged a few minutes later and immediately lit up a cigarette, before coming came over to join Mariner. 'It is the Reverend Aubrey,' he said. 'He's been shot multiple times, including in the head. What you can see all over the windows, well, you can guess. Either he was sitting in his armchair when the killer got in, or he was made to sit there.'

'How long ago?' asked Mariner.

'Hard to say exactly, of course, but a matter of days I'd say. It's pretty gruesome. Scenes of crime are on their way.'

The two men sat in silence while Griffith smoked his cigarette. 'We've had news about Joe Hennessey too,' he said, at last. 'The post-mortem has given us a ToD somewhere on Monday afternoon.'

'Monday? So that's before Bryce was killed,' Mariner remarked.

'May or may not be significant,' said Griffith. 'But it does start to undermine our idea about Hennessy being killed for incompetence. The other result we've had is from the waterproofs found at the byre. The blood all over them is definitely Theo Ashton's, so it's likely they were worn by his killer, but we're pretty certain it wasn't Glenn McGinley who's been sleeping rough there.'

'How can you be so sure?' asked Mariner.

Griffith raised his cigarette. 'McGinley's a chain smoker, and there were no dog ends. I'm not sure that he'd have bothered to go round clearing up after himself.'

'Probably not,' conceded Mariner. 'But someone has been hiding out there?'

'Oh yes,' said Griffith. 'Just a question of working out who.'

* * *

When Tony Knox arrived home from work on Friday afternoon it was to find his house transformed. Kat was in the kitchen, in rubber gloves, attacking his grimy stove. 'I hope you don't mind,' she said, removing iPod earphones. 'Is good for me to do some cleaning and keep busy. Is therapeutic.'

There was a further surprise when the doorbell rang and Knox opened the door to Michael, scrubbed, smart, bright-eyed and looking — as kids sometimes did — like an extra from the *Magic Roundabout*, all pipe cleaner legs in skinny jeans and oversized converse trainers. 'Is Kat here?' he asked hopefully, peering past Knox and into the hall. 'I thought we could take Nelson for a walk?'

Knox smiled to himself. He recognized a crush when he saw one. Perhaps Kat did too, because she happily went off with Michael, returning more than an hour later at the point when Knox was starting to wonder if something had happened to them. And maybe it had, because, when they came into the kitchen to give Nelson his post-walk treat, the air between the two of them seemed heavy with expectation. It was Kat who finally broke the tension. 'You should tell him now, Michael,' she said. 'It's okay.'

'Tell me what?' Knox asked.

Michael was staring at the floor.

'He knows,' said Kat. 'Someone told him who gave Kirsty the pill.'

Michael looked up at her accusingly. 'I told you that in confidence,' he said, his eyes shining.

'Kirsty *died*,' Kat reminded him. 'And she was your friend. These are bad people and believe me, I know about bad. He might do it again to another girl.'

'But they'll know it was me who grassed him up,' Michael whined miserably. 'I'll get into so much trouble. My mum . . .'

'Your mum?' said Knox. 'What's she got to do with this?'

'Nothing. You don't understand.' Finally, Michael dragged his eyes up so that they met with Knox's. 'It was his mate,' he spat with disgust. 'The man who gave the pill to Kirsty is a mate of Mr Lennox.'

'Your teacher?' Knox checked that he'd understood correctly.

'Lennox brought him to the party,' said Michael. 'He was meant to be there helping out, but all he did all night was hit on the girls, especially Kirsty. Georgia told me, he kept trying to get Kirsty to have a drink and when she wouldn't he offered her a pill. He told her it wasn't like alcohol; it wouldn't do her any harm. It would make her feel relaxed. When he saw what it did to her, he legged it. He'd gone way before you got there.'

'Does Mr Lennox know about this?' demanded Knox.

Michael shrugged. 'What if he did? Where does that leave Mum?'

'Your mum can make her own choices,' said Kat. Stepping over, she put an arm around Michael's shoulders. 'Well done,' she said. 'It was the right thing to do.'

Leaving Kat and Michael watching TV, Knox went across to Jean's house.

'Was there another teacher at Michael's party?' he asked.

Jean looked momentarily puzzled. 'Not a teacher, but Pete brought a friend of his; a gym-buddy. He was extra help in case anything got out of hand.'

*There's an irony*, thought Knox. 'Which gym?' he asked.

'I don't know the name. One of those fancy ones on Broad Street.'

From his own house, Knox rang Charlie Glover. 'You need to go and talk to Peter Lennox again,' he said. 'And ask him about his mate.'

* * *

When Griffith had finished with him, Mariner chose to walk back to Caranwy and stopped off at Gwennol to check that Suzy was all right. She seemed now to have grasped the enormity of what it was they'd found and was visibly upset.

'Would you like me to stay with you for a while?' Mariner asked.

She smiled weakly. 'That would be nice. I know it's completely irrational, but I keep thinking about what happened to the pastor — that something or someone may still be out there. Do you mind?'

'Of course not.'

'I'll make us something to eat.' But as it turned out, neither of them had much of an appetite. So instead they just curled up together on the sofa, watching the fire. After a while Mariner couldn't resist putting out an arm to her and she leaned in to him. 'I don't understand what's going on with you,' she said. 'You need to give me more of a clue.'

Mariner shifted uncomfortably. 'I haven't been entirely honest with you.' He broke off. He'd never in his life discussed anything like this openly with anyone and now didn't seem like a particularly good place to do so for the first time.

He took a deep breath. 'My feelings about Anna only make up half of the story.'

'So what's the other half?'

'When I said the other night that I might disappoint you, that's exactly what I meant. I've had a couple of . . . unfortunate experiences in the past, when I haven't been able to . . . deliver, as it were. I never know if . . . I really am afraid I'll let you down.'

Suzy was mortified. 'Oh God, and now here I am, making you talk about it. That's even worse, isn't it? But isn't there something I can do to help?' Instinctively she put her hand on his thigh, but immediately snatched it away again. 'Oh God, I'm sorry. That's probably not a good idea.'

That made Mariner laugh. 'It's all right, it won't fall off.'

'And this Anna. Are you certain it's over?'

'It's definitely over,' said Mariner. And though he hadn't planned to, he found himself telling Suzy about Anna's last hours. 'I wasn't there, of course, but there are certain advantages to being in the job and the Hereford police have been incredibly co-operative in terms of allowing me access to witness statements. I think the other woman involved was relieved to be able to offload to me too, in the mistaken belief that doing so might help to ease some of her own pain. She gave me enough detail to be able to reconstruct the chain of events reasonably accurately. Sometimes it just plays inside my head like a silent movie on a loop.'

'Poor you,' she said. 'I can't imagine what it must be like to lose someone so suddenly.'

Mariner finished up staying the night at Gwennol. This time when Suzy moved over to his side of the bed he didn't make any excuses, and Anna stayed away.

## Chapter Thirty-Four

Day Twelve

Still warmed from the pleasure of the night before, Mariner strode out across the fields and back towards the pub. He was feeling rather pleased with himself and with the day, and decided to extend his route back via the footpath that took him close to Abbey Farm. As he did so, he heard the sound of a vehicle starting up, and craning his neck, he watched over the hedge as Willow's van drove out along the track and up to the farm gate. It stopped for Amber to get out and open the gate, before moving off again. They were still apparently going to market, to sell their fake organic produce. Mariner watched the truck bounce along to the end of the drive and make a left towards Llanerch. He thought about how calm Willow had been, in the interview room at the police station, despite having learned that his business was about to become discredited and go down the pan. The only reason he could have been that relaxed was because it didn't matter. He must be seriously wealthy to get by. Even with the mark-up on the vegetable prices, the profit margins couldn't be that great. Turning away, Mariner's gaze swept over the rows of poly tunnels. He wondered if they would be retained to keep up the illusion that the farm was still a working one, and that Willow's product was a going concern.

For a millisecond, he thought he saw what looked like a faint plume of smoke rising from one of the structures. That couldn't be right. It couldn't be smoke, it must be steam. On a warm day that might be explained by the sun heating off the moisture of the dew, but not on a chill, cloudy day like today. In a sudden rush, Mariner recognized a possibility that both he and Griffith had overlooked.

The new barn may be there for refrigerating produce but what about those poly tunnels? Willow had said that they couldn't be insulated, but what if he'd been lying about that? Climbing the flimsy fence Mariner went first to investigate the source of that vapour. Unfastening the flaps on the tunnel, he hoped and expected to see the rows of green plants that had eluded them in the barn, but he was to be disappointed for a second time. What confronted him instead was a vast expanse of brown, putrid vegetables showing little sign of growth, very like the parsnips Willow had shown him on that first day he came here. The air inside the tunnel was warm and humid, which explained the steam he had seen, but it didn't account for why there seemed to be nothing of value growing in such a carefully manufactured atmosphere. Kneeling down Mariner examined the growth more closely. Was this simply some kind of plant matter he'd never come across before? As he stooped he felt a blast of warm air on his face — as if he were leaning over a kettle spout — and, lifting the vegetation, he saw underneath the steel grille of some kind of ventilation pipe coming up from under the ground. Standing upright, he emerged from the tunnel and looked over at the farm buildings, about two hundred yards away.

He thought back to the time when he had worked on the farm, and suddenly Mariner knew exactly where that steam was being vented from, and why. This was the moment he should contact Griffith to report his suspicion, but the principle of evidence-based claims was deeply ingrained in his psyche, and having come unstuck before, this time he wanted to be absolutely sure of what he thought he knew. It wouldn't do any harm to just take a quick look first. Given the circumstances, he would be in and out of the farm without anyone even knowing.

Walking back up the track Mariner found, as expected, that all was quiet. He went round to the back door of the farm house which, with extraordinary vigilance for this neighbourhood, he found locked via both mortise and Yale. Mariner rattled it but could see that it wasn't going to budge. He stepped back to survey the rest of the building. A small frosted-glass window on the ground floor to his left was slightly ajar. A pantry, if Mariner remembered rightly. Reaching up he was able to unhook the inside bar and open the window to its full extent, which gave him a rectangular opening of about two square feet; perfectly manageable if it hadn't been eight feet or more off the ground. This was where he wished he had Tony Knox's agility. Pulling up on the crossbar, he managed to scramble up and get a toe-hold on the window ledge, then, hoping that the frame would take his weight, he thrust the upper half of his body in through the window. Not a pantry but a WC, the cistern and lidless bowl immediately below him.

Leaning in as far as he could, Mariner reached down, taking his weight on his arms, so that in effect he was doing a handstand on the cistern. Then he tried easing the lower half of his body in through the window. But he was six feet tall and, unsurprisingly, ran out of space. The only way to get his legs through would be to 'step' down with his arms on to the rim of the toilet bowl, but that was a two-foot drop, and if he missed, he ran the risk of crashing face first into the toilet or onto the stone flags of the floor. Meanwhile the balance of his weight had shifted and trying to heave himself back out through the window again would place a huge strain on the wooden frame. He eased forward a little, yelping in pain as the spike of the window fastening drove into his groin. In an effort to alleviate the agony, Mariner did the only thing open to him, which was to shift even more of his weight forward. His arms were beginning to shake with the effort of supporting himself and suddenly the decision was taken out of his hands. Lurching forward with his right hand, Mariner managed to grab on to the toilet seat but, as the full weight of his body followed, his elbow buckled under the force and he fell, collapsing in a heap on the stone floor to the side of the toilet, his shoulder hitting the ground with an excruciating crunch. There was a noise outside the door. He listened, the only sound the rasp of his laboured breathing. A clock somewhere in the house finished chiming eleven, and Mariner relaxed. He lay there for a couple of seconds assessing the damage and found that, despite the indignity of it, he seemed to have remained intact. His shoulder and bollocks would be sore for a couple of days, but he was otherwise unscathed.

Inside the house Mariner made his way to the kitchen, trying to get his bearings and recall where the entrance to the cellar had been. After prowling all the ground-floor rooms, he finally identified the door leading off a small utility room at the back of the house. It was bolted on the outside and swung open easily to reveal a dark, cavernous void. It was here that Mariner realized what the biggest obstacle in all this was going to be: his own fear. As a young man, Mariner had been down to these cellars a couple of times with Bob Sewell. He'd never enjoyed the experience and had always been glad to get out again, and that was before his ordeal of a couple of years ago, when he'd spent days incarcerated in his own cellar, waiting to die. He took a deep breath to try and calm his racing heart and ran his tongue around his mouth in an effort to moisten it, before taking the first faltering steps down the steep wooden staircase.

Almost immediately he was hit by an overpowering wall of hot, moist air, like stepping into a sauna, and he instantly felt the damp prickling of sweat gathering on his face and neck. The wooden stairs were greasy and he had to concentrate hard on keeping his footing, all the time fighting the urge to turn back and slam the door shut. All he needed to do was go down there, take a few photographs on his phone and get out again. Ryan Griffith would do the rest. Mariner passed a light switch on the wall, but as he neared the bottom of the stairs, it became apparent that he wouldn't need it, for his way was lit instead by an eerie bluish glow emanating from the depths of the cellar. From the bottom step he finally looked up and gaped at the spectacle. The glow cast a light over thousands and thousands of spidery plants whose leaves, trembling in the moving air, gave the illusion that they were alive and about to crawl all over him like a thousand scurrying creatures. The main cellar was as Mariner remembered it, a natural limestone cavern that extended backward into a further series of smaller caves. What he could see here were hundreds of plants at varying stages of growth, some as high as four and a half feet tall, and the air was thick with a powerful herbal smell. If the other caves were similarly full this was a massive operation.

Mariner made his way gingerly along the stone floor, past a couple of workbenches holding trays, plant pots and fertilizer, and what was evidently the processing and packaging section. He saw what he recognized as a trimming machine — a rotating blade with a mesh above it and a bowl below. The largest leaves would be harvested by hand and fed through this machine, whilst smaller leaves would be gathered using handheld garden shears, cutting them carefully from around the flowering buds. Somewhere in the operation, perhaps in one of the cellars at the back, or up in the main farm house, there would be an air-cooled room where the leaves would be placed on silk screens to dry. The plants themselves were lined up on long trestle tables that raised them up close to the high-powered lights that heated the air, and the cellar roof was lined with reflective foil for further insulation and to maximize the heat. Here Mariner took more photographs; he'd just get some shots to illustrate the scale of production, and then he could be gone. But at the far end of one of the benches something caught his eye that looked out of place. It was a black leather wallet, sitting alongside a mobile phone. He opened the wallet and a photograph of two little girls looked out at him.

Then a voice said, quietly, from a few feet away. 'I don't think that concerns you, does it?'

Mariner looked up towards the steps and into the twin barrels of a twelve-bore shotgun, behind which stood Amber, her hair illuminated to a golden haze, like some ethereal, ancient goddess. Mariner's head was beginning to pound, from both the heat and now from fear. He could feel the sweat running off his forehead and down his face.

Amber's voice, when she spoke again, was stronger and much more resolute than he was expecting. 'I'm really sorry, but I won't be able to let you leave here alive. You know that, don't you?'

'You can't keep me here,' Mariner said unconvincingly. 'Sooner or later DI Griffith will start looking for me. Suzy Yin will tell him where I disappeared and it won't take them long to track me down.'

'Oh, I'll probably let them find you,' Amber said. 'But by then you won't be in any condition to tell them very much. They'll see that you met with an unfortunate accident.'

Mariner eyed the gun. 'The kind of accident that involves a twelve-bore?'

'I'm of a very nervous disposition, Mr Mariner — or can I call you Tom? After what happened to Theo, and the possibility of Glenn McGinley being at large, it would be only natural that I should be afraid for my safety. It gives me every reason to protect myself, and I'm not terribly experienced with guns. Who'd be to say the whole thing wasn't just a dreadful accident? After all, you are trespassing on private property. And we've never really met before, have we? As far as I'm concerned, you could be anyone.'

Mariner was still holding the wallet, trying to grasp its significance. 'But I don't understand. Why have you got . . .?'

'Haven't you worked it out yet?' She was smiling. 'I'm surprised. Elena says you're very smart. Look at the photograph.'

Mariner did as she said and looked back at the two smiling little girls. Then he looked back at Amber. 'Jeremy Bryce was your father,' he said, understanding at last.

'Not fully accurate on either count,' she said. 'His name wasn't Jeremy Bryce; it was Jonathan Bruce — Jonny to his friends. Not that he actually had many of those. It's one of the reasons the police haven't been able to identify him yet. I expect he planned it that way. The beard and the hair helped too; not really his style at all. He was always clean shaven; hair cut with military precision.'

'The other count?' Mariner said.

'I suppose biologically he fathered me, but I stopped thinking of him in that way long ago,' Amber said bitterly. 'I reviled him. The man was a monster. Even if someone has recognized him, it doesn't surprise me that they haven't come forward to claim him. I can't think of anyone who'd want to. He destroyed my whole family.'

'He abused you?' Mariner guessed.

She blinked, and for an instant the shotgun slipped in her grasp, but she quickly recovered. 'He started on me when I was about five,' she said. 'Funny, isn't it, how child abuse is so rife, so commonplace these days that we are almost inured to it. The idea of it ceases to be shocking. I remember the occasion, of course, in vivid detail, though not exactly how old I was at the time. Mum was a nurse and did shift work, so it was easy for him. He took such *special* care of me when she was on nights. And he was such a pleasant, likeable man that no one ever suspected a thing. Even I didn't at first. For such a long time I thought that all little girls shared those special secrets with their daddies. By the time I was old enough to have figured out how wrong it was, I was too ashamed to do anything about it. And as he reminded me on frequent occasions, by then I was making a choice. I'd been colluding with him for years.'

'Did your mother know what was going on?' Mariner asked.

'I honestly don't know. I prefer to think that she didn't; it's easier that way, although I still feel angry at her.'

'You didn't tell her?'

'The first person I ever told was a total stranger. Theo.'

'A stranger?'

'I was about to kill myself, but Theo found me and stopped me. It was a complete fluke. He was delivering leaflets to the houses in our street. Our letterbox used to stick sometimes and he had to push it open. He saw me trying to tie one of Dad's climbing ropes to the banister. He broke down the door and I ended up telling him everything. The fact that he was a stranger made it easier.'

'So the baby wasn't his?'

She laughed, a bitter, staccato laugh. 'How could it have been? Theo and I never had sex. Ours was a chaste relationship. *He* hadn't fathered my baby.' It didn't take much for Mariner to work out who had. 'Theo rescued me. He brought me here, to Caranwy. He'd planned to come here anyway, so he brought me with him. Theo was a romantic; he was certain that fate had intervened, that we would live here happily ever after.'

'But Theo is dead,' Mariner pointed out.

'The shame of what happened to me is unbearable sometimes and I've always been petrified that one day my father would find me and it would start all over again. Theo said he was going to end it once and for all. I didn't know what he meant. He wrote to my father anonymously, hinting that I wanted reconciliation. When Joe Hennessey turned up in the village we knew Jonny had taken the bait and was scouting the way ahead. Theo told me he was going to meet my father, to tell him what he knew and threaten him with exposure if he didn't stay away for good. Then I realized he was planning something more final.' Tears began to stream down her cheeks.

'He was going to kill your father.'

'When Theo didn't come back that morning I knew something terrible must have happened.'

Mariner couldn't believe how naive their plan had been. 'But when you found out Theo was dead, why didn't you tell the police?'

'Because we didn't know for sure what had happened. Willow and Elena said it would be better to wait. They didn't want me to have to tell my story if it was all for nothing.'

'Elena?'

'She's been such a good friend since I came here; a better mother than mine ever was.'

A noise at the top of the steps made them both look up, to see one of Shapasnikov's sharp-suited henchmen descending the staircase and holding a handgun out in front of him. Sighing, Amber lowered the shotgun. 'Dmitri, thank God. My arms were about to drop off.'

'You know each other?' Mariner wasn't sure why that should be such a surprise.

'Of course. You don't think Willow, Theo and I could have run this place on our own, do you?'

'Shapasnikov's behind it?'

'No,' said Amber, affronted. 'It's our project. After the vegetables failed, Willow was dismantling the infra-red lamps and it occurred to him that they could have another purpose. It started small, genuinely our own personal supply, and grew from there. Once it began to take over we had the problem of distribution. Cannabis isn't the kind of thing we could openly sell at the markets. But then Nikolai moved into the Hall. Willow knew about his nightclubs and how they operated, so there it was, our distribution network.'

'So Shapasnikov contributes his manual labour and takes a cut,' said Mariner, seeing how it all worked.

'Exactly,' said Amber. 'We couldn't manage without him, especially in situations like this one.'

'And the land dispute?'

'Oh, Mr Shapasnikov's historian really did turn up some contestable paperwork. But, in truth, no one could care less about who owns Plackett's Wood.'

'Behaving like arch rivals with an outward display of animosity was a good cover for the operation,' said Mariner.

'We've got quite good at subterfuge,' Amber admitted. 'And now Dmitri will be able to make you disappear.'

'Oh, he's a magician too, is he?' said Mariner.

'Not exactly, but we still have the lime pit, left over from when this farm was hit by foot and mouth. Perhaps your friends won't find you after all.' She turned to Dmitri. 'We should get this over with, before Willow gets back.'

Dmitri started down the stairs past Amber. If Mariner was going to get out of this he needed to do it now. Backing away slowly to begin with, he chose his moment, then suddenly ducked down behind one of the long trestle tables of trailing plants. Dmitri fired a deafening shot, but it was a split-second too late, allowing Mariner to scramble along the ground, putting as much distance as possible between himself and the gunman.

'You're wasting your time,' Amber called out, her voice echoing around the chamber. 'You won't be able to get out of here.'

Rationally Mariner knew she was right. With Amber standing guard at the only escape route, it was just a matter of time before Dmitri caught up with him. But his survival instinct wouldn't let him give up just yet. In the unbearable heat, Mariner could feel his shirt sticking to him like a second skin. Crouching uncomfortably, he strained to maintain his concentration, though he was beginning to feel faint and light-headed, the blood roaring in his ears. He stuck his fingers in to try and clear them, and the roaring temporarily stopped. The roaring wasn't in his head, after all — it was in the cellar and getting louder. The floor trembled and, from somewhere deep at the back of the cellar, came a gust of blissfully cool air followed by a foaming, solid wall of water that blasted into the main chamber. Mariner caught a last glimpse of Amber part way up the staircase, and then there was a bang. The electricity shorted out and everything went black, and Mariner was hit by a slab of icy water so powerful that it slammed him against the wall, before dragging him back into the swirling maelstrom. Submerged in choking blackness and pummelled on all sides by rocks and debris, Mariner thrashed his arms in a blind panic. For what seemed like an eternity he was churned around in a muddy, freezing washing machine. Some years ago his life had almost ended in an underground tomb, and now it seemed that it was about to happen for real.

## Chapter Thirty-Five

Kicking against the powerful current, Mariner realized abruptly that the rush of water was slowing down and he was able to force himself upwards. Surfacing, he choked out a mouthful of gritty water and simultaneously cracked his head on the solid rock of the cellar ceiling. He'd found an air lock, the surface of the water only inches from the ceiling. In the pitch darkness Mariner could feel the water swirling and settling, lapping over his chin. Flotsam and jetsam bobbed by and he cried out as what felt like felt human hair fluttered across his face, before he realized it was only plant matter. With the immediate danger over, cold was starting to numb his limbs, and he had to work his arms hard to prevent the weight of the water in his clothes from dragging him under. Somehow, working in short bursts, he managed to discard his heavy fleece and shirt, and at once his buoyancy increased. By turning his head to one side and banging it along the ceiling of the cellar, he could manage to gulp in enough air to sustain himself — but for how long?

His first thought was to try to swim back to the cellar entrance, but he had no idea which direction that might be.

He began to propel himself blindly in what he thought must be the right direction, but suddenly the ceiling that he was pressing against disappeared, and he felt cool air moving around his head. The cave had opened out. Working his arms and legs to stay afloat, he strained his ears to listen; running water was trickling in from somewhere to his right. Turning his head towards it, Mariner struck out in that direction, encouraged by the faintest movement of air, before he came up against a solid wall. Reaching out his hands, he felt an opening in the rock directly above his face that sloped away from him upwards at an angle. Wedging his numbed fingers into a crack in the surface, he heaved himself upward and his head struck solid stone. For a few seconds, dazed, he managed to cling, shivering, to the ledge he had found, conscious that at any time another deluge could wash him back down to the cellar or worse.

Groping his way around the opening he identified it as some kind of narrow tunnel, through which a strong draught blew. Inch by inch he dragged himself up the slippery rocks, his progress agonizingly slow, his deadened fingertips bruised and starting to bleed. The icy water combined now with the chill breeze, causing him to shake uncontrollably and, overwhelmed with exhaustion, it suddenly all felt like too much effort. Laying his head down on the cold stone, he closed his eyes for a moment. So much easier to just stay here . . .

A splash of water in his ear made Mariner open his eyes, and he noticed then a subtle change in the light. He could now see the faintly defined shapes of the rocks around him and a clear contrast of black and grey. Lifting his head he saw high above him the tiniest sliver of daylight. It looked impossibly small. Energized nonetheless, Mariner stiffly resumed his crawl, breathing deeply to try and control the violent shivering. Bit by bit the tunnel began to widen until he found himself at the bottom of a sloping scree-covered cave. He scrambled on his hands and knees towards the chink of light, sliding on the loose boulders and knowing, after all this, that if the gap at the end was too narrow, he was finished. But as he got nearer, the area of light expanded, turning into an opening that was wide enough for him, bent double, to step through. The water continued to lap over the rim into the passageway but with profound relief Mariner scrambled out into the dazzling daylight, emerging at the foot of a rocky crag that rose up from the river. It was a pool very like the one he and Suzy had swum in.

In any decent movie Mariner would have been greeted by a welcoming committee of armed bandits, guns trained in his direction, but in this case his escape was noticed only by a noisy mallard, indignant at being disturbed. He waded across to the far side of the pool to climb out of the icy water and onto the rocks, where he sat for a moment trying to summon up some energy. Bruised and battered, his body ached and he was frozen to the marrow. He wondered if Dmitri and Amber had survived. Although there was no way of knowing how long he had been in the cellar, or how long it had taken him to find his way out, he estimated that at most it could only have only been a matter of an hour or so, meaning that if they had escaped they couldn't yet have got far. He was frozen and exhausted, and needed to do what he could to avoid setting off in the wrong direction. The valley closest to him must be the one adjacent to Caranwy. Mariner followed the course of the river in that direction, through the gorge, until it began to level out. The river emerged sooner than he could have hoped and he rounded a bend into a meadow, flooded by the high water — and there, ahead of him, were farm buildings.

His clothes were sodden and filthy, and he could see the cuts and bruises on his bare arms. And so, fully aware of how bad he must be looking, Mariner approached the buildings with caution. As he got nearer, dogs started barking, then he became aware of human voices and next saw a small group of men standing in the farmyard, talking. As Mariner limped towards them they turned as one and stared. 'There's been an accident,' was all he could manage before collapsing on to the ground. He felt himself being helped into the farmhouse. 'I need to use a phone and then get back to the White Hart at Caranwy as soon as I can,' he said, as soon as he could make himself coherent. Revived with brandy and swathed in blankets, Mariner dialled 999 and insisted he be put through to Ryan Griffith. He summed up what had happened as best he could. 'You need to get over there. It's a mess, but all the evidence you need is there. I don't know what happened to Amber or Dmitri.'

Mariner would have been content to wait for a taxi, but one of the farmers was heading home in the direction of Caranwy, and took him in his battered old Land Rover. The twenty-minute journey did little to soothe Mariner's sore and aching limbs, and he felt obliged to offer the farmer, Jim, at least some manner of explanation. He kept it simple; he'd been down in the cellar with two others when it had flooded.

'You had a lucky escape,' observed Jim, with some understatement.

DC Debra Farthing was waiting for Mariner at the Hart. 'My God,' she said, gaping at him. 'You took a beating. Are you sure you don't need a doctor?'

Mariner shook his head, regretting it instantly. 'It's superficial,' he said. 'Mostly I just need to lie down.'

'You need some food inside you too,' fussed Josie Symonds.

Farthing waited while Mariner showered and changed into dry clothes, then as he ate she took notes on what had happened at Abbey Farm. 'DI Griffith is over there now?' Mariner asked.

'Yes, like you said, the cellar is still awash. There's no sign of Dmitri or Amber, but we don't know yet if that's because they've drowned or bolted. They're waiting for

Willow to get back from the market so they can re-arrest him.'

'What about Shapasnikov?'

'Not there. We'll bring him in for questioning, of course, but without Dmitri there's nothing to link him directly with Abbey Farm so my guess is that he'll deny any involvement.'

## Chapter Thirty-Six

That evening Ryan Griffith came down to the White Hart. Mariner stood him a pint and the two men settled into one of the snugs. Mariner talked him through what had happened in the cellar.

'And it didn't occur to you to call for some support before you went in there?' said Griffith mildly.

'What would you have done?' asked Mariner. Griffith's slight dip of the head was answer enough. 'So we know now who killed Theo Ashton,' Mariner went on. 'But we can't say the same for Jeremy Bryce.'

'Not yet, no,' Griffith agreed. 'But we have a powerful motive, along with a limited group of likely suspects.'

'Is there any news on Amber or Dmitri?'

'The water in the cellar subsided pretty quickly to a couple of feet deep. We're dredging the rest, but a man's body was recovered an hour or so ago.'

'Suit and tie?'

Griffith nodded. 'We're assuming Dmitri. But there's no sign of Amber.'

'She was halfway up the steps when it flooded. She could easily have got out.'

'There's a car missing from the farm,' said Griffith. 'We've put out an alert for it.'

'Do you think she could have killed her father?' Mariner asked.

'I don't know,' said Griffith. 'You spoke to her.'

'There's a lot of hatred there, just underneath the surface,' Mariner said. 'But to cut a man's throat? I honestly don't know.'

'I think there are people around who would have been ready to help her,' said Griffith, carefully.

'Willow treats her like his daughter,' Mariner agreed.

'And she's close to Elena Hughes.'

Mariner stared at him. 'You think Elena would . . .?'

'Approaching it from a purely pragmatic perspective, aside from you, Elena was the one with the perfect opportunity. The post-mortem on Bryce found traces of a sedative in his bloodstream.'

'He had a cold,' Mariner said. 'Elena gave him some Night Nurse to help him sleep.'

Griffith shook his head slowly. 'Doc says it's more than that.'

'Maybe he was taking some other medication,' Mariner frowned, 'though I didn't notice anything.'

'It was in your bloodstream too,' Griffith added.

'What?'

'When we took the sample of your blood for elimination purposes, the same sedative was found. Were you taking anything?'

'No.'

'But you drank something at the hostel that evening.'

'Elena offered me a night cap.' They both paused to let that sink in and Mariner thought back to the sluggishness and blinding headache he'd had the following day. Another random thought swam into his head. 'The washing machine was running,' he said. 'When I went over to Elena's kitchen after finding Bryce, she was doing a load of washing. Why would she have been doing it at that time in the morning?'

'At the very least it's likely that Elena aided and abetted a criminal offence, and I wouldn't confidently rule her out from committing it. She's pretty skilled with a butcher's knife, and she doesn't have a very high opinion of some men. Did she tell you much about her ex?'

'Only that he was a git,' said Mariner.

'That's an interesting way of putting it,' Griffith said, with a humourless smile. 'I got to know Elena when I first joined the police; we were called out to her place on a regular basis. Her old man was a psychopathic, manipulative control freak with anger management issues. Quite a respectable one, mind — good job, nice manners and all that — but underneath the veneer was an aggressive bully, who routinely took out his frustrations on his wife.'

'Is that how she got into counselling?'

'Yes, and that, in turn, was where she built her relationship with Amber. Incidentally, Amber isn't her real name either. The lab ran DNA tests on blood samples from Bryce and that hair from the locket. We didn't get anything on Bryce, or Bruce, but the hair sample hit on a fifteen-year-old girl on the missing persons database, who disappeared from Bristol eight years ago — Ruby Bruce, reported missing by her family.'

'The ruby on the locket,' said Mariner. 'She just changed her name from one precious stone to another. Do you know what Bryce said to me? He said: "you do what you can to keep your children safe." He had a pretty warped idea of what that was. He got his own daughter pregnant.' Mariner took a sip of his pint. 'Nearly thirty years in the job and you think you have a reasonable grasp of humankind. You'd think it would get easier to spot the deviants.'

Griffith snorted. 'They're the most difficult; the ones who are sly enough to conceal it. He wasn't quite the incompetent orienteer that he led you to believe either. Turns out he was twenty years in the Territorials.'

'Played me like a Stradivarius,' said Mariner. 'I can't get over how easily I fell for it. He seemed such an ordinary man.'

'Which, in many ways, he was,' agreed Griffith. 'But the family has history. Shortly after Ruby eloped with Theo Ashton, Bryce's wife left him and moved away along with the older daughter, who herself suffers from mental health problems.'

'Chances are she was abused too,' said Mariner.

'Bryce hasn't worked at a university for years, and even then he didn't teach. He was a glorified lab assistant. He quit his job after Amber ran away to devote all his time to looking for her.'

'So how do you think it went?' Mariner asked.

'Well,' said Griffith. 'I think that when Bryce got Theo's letter he hired Hennessey to check it out, perhaps with a view to reconciliation, but I think it's more likely that he had a more specific outcome in mind. Having confirmed Amber's presence at Abbey Farm he set off on his across-Wales walk, choosing the Black Mountain Way quite deliberately. If then it later emerges that he's been in the area, he has a valid explanation for visiting and has put down a series of alibis nearby — including, conveniently, you. Bryce arranged, through Hennessey, to meet Theo in Plackett's Wood. We still have no murder weapon, nor can we guess its origins, so we don't know if Theo's intention was to kill Bryce, or if Bryce had the same aim. In any event, for one of them, something went wrong. Perhaps Theo wasn't strong enough to overpower Bryce, who turned on him and killed him before escaping back to the abandoned byre.' Griffith looked at Mariner. 'I think it's safe to assume that it was Bryce who was hiding out there, and had been since shortly after you got to Caranwy. Telling you about it at the time when McGinley was back on the radar just confused the issue. What we've got from here on in is pure speculation, but it seems to me that Hennessey, when he found Theo Ashton, guessed what had happened, and arranged to meet Bryce. Having killed Ashton, Bryce had no choice but to kill Hennessey too, leaving him in his abandoned car. We have a witness who recalls having seen Bryce setting off in the direction of where the vehicle was found on Monday afternoon.

'Knowing he'd got to get away, Bryce was probably hoping to pass back through the village unnoticed, when you spotted him and persuaded him to stay at the hostel. He probably felt relatively safe; he could be fairly sure that no one except Theo and Hennessey had known he was there, and to refuse your invitation would have been to blow his cover as a bumbling incompetent. But Amber must have found out, perhaps from Elena, what was going on, and when Bryce turned up as an extra guest at the hostel, the chance to end it once and for all would have been too great a temptation. What we have no way of knowing, of course, is whether Amber carried out the execution herself or had someone do it for her, which brings us back to those suspects. Incidentally, given the relationship with Gwennol Hall, we can perhaps also add Dmitri or one of his buddies to that list. Forensically, we've turned up nothing that places anyone other than Elena, Bryce and you in the hostel, but that doesn't mean that Willow, Amber or Dmitri couldn't have entered and been very careful. We haven't enough evidence yet to make any fresh arrests.'

'So we may never know,' said Mariner.

'If we keep questioning them, sooner or later someone might let something slip.' Glancing up, Griffith emptied his glass. 'Looks like you've got another visitor,' he said, as if Mariner was in hospital. 'I'll leave you to it.'

Mariner looked across to see Suzy Yin loitering in the doorway. As Griffith was leaving, she came over. 'My God,' she said, staring in horror. 'What happened to you?'

Mariner gave her the abridged version.

'And Glenn McGinley?' Suzy asked. 'He wasn't after you?'

'Not me, no. But a patch of blood and mucous was found by the side of Aubrey's cottage, which is quite likely to be McGinley's. Elena told me that the Reverend had interfered with some of the kids round here. I think his reach extended far beyond Caranwy.'

'So you're going back to Birmingham tomorrow?' she asked.

'First thing in the morning.' Mariner looked at her. 'It's worth a visit,' he said. 'Contrary to popular belief we do have some interesting historic and cultural features.'

'I know,' she smiled. 'I looked it up.'

'And it's not a million miles from here.'

'Even closer to Cambridge,' she said. 'I'll be heading back there in a couple of weeks. Ever been to Cambridge?'

'Only for work.'

'Well, we must rectify that.'

'Yes,' said Mariner. 'Very soon.'

## Chapter Thirty-Seven

Day Thirteen

On his way back to Birmingham, Mariner drove the eight or so miles north-west to the Towyn Farm Community. The sudden deaths of the Barhams' parents had left Jamie well provided for financially, so his care had never been in question. Mariner could remember how Anna had enthused about Towyn when Jamie first came here, though Mariner had rather cynically believed her eagerness to be driven mainly by her attraction to a certain GP and her desire to move out to this area anyway. Now he would see for himself. He drove along the track to what looked to have originally been an old, fairly modest manor house. Both house and gardens looked reasonably well tended. Mariner tried to work out how long it was since he'd last seen Jamie. It must be a couple of years, which made him wonder if Jamie would even remember him, especially beyond the context of Anna's house in Birmingham.

The set up seemed very informal. Mariner parked up and walked unimpeded into what looked like the main entrance to the house, but there was no one around to talk to and there seemed to be no means of attracting attention. A table with a visitor's book stood to one side and Mariner was about to sign himself in when a door opened and a young man hurried out carrying a pile of folded clothing. 'You all right?' he asked, though it didn't appear that he cared one way or the other. A badge identified him simply as 'Dave.'

'I've come to see Jamie Barham,' Mariner said.

'Oh, right-oh. Do you want to wait in there?' He indicated a door off to the left. There seemed no question of challenging Mariner's identity or the purpose of his visit. 'I'll go and get him.'

Mariner went into the room, which like the rest of the ground floor, was painted a nondescript beige colour and had no decoration, not even a pair of curtains at the small window that overlooked a large garden. There were a dozen or so easy chairs, some stained and torn, and a solid wooden cupboard to one side was closed. The only other accoutrement was a small flat-screen TV on a bracket high on the wall. The place had a dusty unused smell and there were marks on the walls, one of them looking disconcertingly like a smear of blood. Mariner heard yelling somewhere far away in the house that stopped abruptly. Several minutes later the door opened and Jamie was ushered into the room, shoulders hunched and shuffling along in a pair of shapeless corduroy slippers. He looked older, some streaks of grey starting to appear at his temples, but then he'd be — what, thirty-six or thirty-seven by now? He was clutching the waistband of his tracksuit trousers in his fist, as if holding them up, and Mariner noticed the sharp rectangular creases on his sweatshirt, perhaps freshly laundered, or recently removed from its packaging. Mariner wasn't expecting eye contact or any acknowledgement, but Jamie's eyes flickered briefly towards him, registering his presence.

'Jamie, sit there,' the man said loudly, as if addressing a deaf person, and gesturing to one of the chairs. Jamie meekly complied. There was a faded bruise on the side of his forehead.

'He bangs his head sometimes,' Dave said, seeing Mariner take that in. An explanation was unnecessary. Mariner had witnessed that the first time he met Jamie, trying to interview him for a crime he could never have committed.

'Give us a shout when you've finished,' Dave said. 'He should be all right.' And he left the room.

'Hello, Jamie,' said Mariner, keeping his distance. 'How are you doing?'

Jamie continued to stare at the floor.

Mariner was stumped already. 'Thought I'd come to see you, see where you live. It's just you and me now, mate.'

Jamie had started to rock gently back and forth. It was something Anna had always hated and instinctively Mariner walked across to him. 'Jamie, sit still,' he said and went to put a hand on his shoulder, but Jamie flinched away, as if he was about to be struck.

'Hey,' said Mariner, backing off again. 'It's all right.' At close quarters he caught a whiff of body odour and could see the unevenness of the stubble on Jamie's chin. He couldn't help wondering what Anna would think of her brother's appearance. She'd always insisted that Jamie be well groomed and dressed like the adult he was, and often in designer clothes. But perhaps they'd be out of place here. For the first time Jamie looked directly at him. 'Spectre man,' he said.

Mariner was disproportionately pleased to hear that inaccurate reproduction of his title 'Inspector Mariner.' When they'd first met it was the best Jamie could do and before long Anna had started using it and the name had stuck. It was an indication of some recognition at least. He'd stopped off at a village shop on his way here and bought a couple of packs of the Hula Hoops that Jamie used to like. Now seemed like a good time to offer them, and pleasingly they were obviously still a favourite. Mariner sat down on one of the chairs and the two men remained in a sort of companionable silence, save for Jamie munching his way through the crisps. When he'd finished he carefully passed Mariner the empty packet, before standing up and moving to the door. It seemed like a signal for him to leave. Before leaving, Mariner wanted to introduce himself to whoever was in charge, though that proved less straightforward than it should have been. Eventually he managed to find his way to a main office and a man called John this time, whose badge also declared him the manager.

'Jamie used to have a friend here; Julie, I think her name is,' Mariner said. 'Is she still about?'

'I'm sure we haven't got a Julie,' John said. 'Let me just check.'

He came back a few minutes later. 'Julie Apney left us about three months ago,' he said.

'Oh, do you know why?'

John shrugged, neither knowing nor, it seemed, caring. 'Sorry.'

'Would it be possible to get contact details for parents? I wouldn't ask but my partner lent them a number of books,' said Mariner, improvising. 'I'd like to get them back.'

Even though Mariner was sure that it might contravene various data protection regulations, John had no hesitation in obliging him and Mariner left with the name and address in his pocket.

Leaving Towyn, he stopped for a beer and a sandwich at a pub a couple of miles down the road, where he sat and assessed what he had seen. Staff who seemed largely indifferent, Jamie dressed in old and ill-fitting clothes that were possibly not even his, and that distant yelling and possible blood stain on the wall. Something about the whole set up made Mariner uneasy. Finishing his pint, he made a snap decision and outside, he climbed into his car and headed back towards Towyn. This time he asked to go up to Jamie's room. Jamie shared the small cell-like space with someone who, from the prevailing smell, seemed to have incontinence issues. Mariner had taken his small day sack in with him and collected up the few personal possessions from Jamie's locker, including a photograph of Anna. Then, with promises of McDonalds, he persuaded Jamie down to the entrance hall and went to find Dave who was back on his own in the office. Adopting his casual approach, Mariner said: 'I'd like to take Jamie out for a bit — that okay?' Apparently it was.

Mariner had half expected at any point that Jamie would vocally and physically resist, which was his normal reaction to most disturbances to his routine. But as Mariner strapped him into the passenger seat of his car Jamie co-operated fully — in fact, Mariner was pretty certain he saw a faint smile pass across his face. They drove out of the Towyn grounds unchallenged. Though utterly convinced that this was the right course of action, it wasn't until they were well on their way up the motorway heading back to Birmingham that Mariner started to consider the enormity of what he was taking on. He was trying with limited success to avert the sudden onset of panic, when a news item on the radio caught his attention and he turned up the volume. 'There has been a breakthrough in the M5 road-rage stabbing earlier this year. A key witness has come forward with new evidence which has led to the arrest today of two men.'

## Epilogue

After a cold start to the year, the months of May and June were unseasonably warm. On a caravan park near Aberystwyth, residents began to complain about an unpleasant smell in one area of the park. The manager was baffled; he'd had all the sewerage pipes in the vicinity thoroughly checked. Eventually, at the suggestion of a couple of holidaymakers, he forced entry into unit 71 and found the decaying body of Glenn McGinley, thought to have been there for some weeks. Among the possessions spread out on the dining-room table was a photograph of McGinley as a boy along with his handsome younger brother, Spencer, amid a group of other children, taken at the youth hostel in Caranwy in 1974. Standing smiling in the centre of the picture, with a fatherly hand on Spencer's shoulder, was the Reverend William Aubrey.

THE END

Thank you for reading this book. If you enjoyed it please leave feedback on Amazon, and if there is anything we missed or you have a question about then please get in touch. The author and publishing team appreciate your feedback and time reading this book.

Our email is office@joffebooks.com

www.joffebooks.com

**DI TOM MARINER SERIES**

DEADLY LIES

DEADLY INNOCENT

KILLER LIES

BABY LIES

MARRIED LIES

BURIED LIES

More coming soon!

43880908R00194

Made in the USA
Middletown, DE
30 April 2019